"F. Paul Wilson is a hot writer, and his hottest, and my favorite creation is Repairman Jack. No one does this kind of weird-meets-crime better than Wilson. Gripping, fascinating, one of a kind. That's F. Paul Wilson and Repairman Jack."
—Joe R. Lansdale

"Jack is righteous!"
—Andrew Vachss

Praise for *Conspiracies*

"Repairman Jack, willing to fix almost any trouble for a price, is on the prowl again. . . . Wilson's paranormal thriller gains speed and tension with every page as it surges toward an ending that screeches 'to be continued.'"
—*Publishers Weekly*

"The third Repairman Jack novel is by far the best. . . . This is a funnier novel than the first two Repairman Jacks; those who look at conspiracy theories with a skeptical eye will have a great time, as will anyone who likes a well-plotted, spooky thriller. Wilson tells a great story."
—*Booklist*

"In his long career F. Paul Wilson has created many a memorable character, but none quite so memorable as his secretive hero known only as Repairman Jack. . . . This is one of the most entertaining novels the always-reliable Wilson has yet produced. He mixes elements of horror, mystery, science fiction, and fantasy together with a master's panache. The book is packed full of fascinating characters. . . . The spectacular finale satisfactorily ties up all the loose ends, but makes it clear that only a battle has been won, not the war. Jack will be back yet again. I, for one, cannot wait."

Also by F. Paul Wilson

Healer (1976)*
Wheels Within Wheels (1978)*
An Enemy of the State (1980)*
Black Wind (1988)
Soft & Others (1989)
Dydeetown World (1989)
The Tery (1990)
Sibs (1991)
The Select (1993)
Implant (1995)
Deep as the Marrow (1997)
Legacies (1998)**
The Barrens & Others (1998)

THE ADVERSARY CYCLE:
The Keep (1981)
The Tomb (1984)**
The Touch (1986)
Reborn (1990)
Reprisal (1991)
Nightworld (1992)

Mirage (1996) (with Matthew J. Costello)
Nightkill (1997) (with Steven Spruill)
Masque (1998) (with Matthew J. Costello)

EDITOR:
Freak Show (1992)
Diagnosis: Terminal (1996)

*Anthologized in *The LaNague Chronicles* (1992)
**A Repairman Jack Novel

F. PAUL WILSON

CONSPIRACIES

A Repairman Jack Novel

TOR®

A TOM DOHERTY ASSOCIATES BOOK
NEW YORK

This is a work of fiction. All the characters and events portrayed in this book are either products of the author's imagination or are used fictitiously.

CONSPIRACIES

Edited by David G. Hartwell

A Tor Book
Published by Tom Doherty Associates, LLC
175 Fifth Avenue
New York, NY 10010

www.tor.com
www.repairmanjack.com

Tor® is a registered trademark of Tom Doherty Associates, LLC.

ISBN: 0-812-56699-8

First edition: February 2000
First mass market edition: October 2000

Printed in the United States of America

0 9 8 7 6 5 4 3 2 1

for
Ethan Paul Bateman
(E-Man!)

Special thanks to
Tom Valesky (again) and
Gerald Molnar for their
marksmen's eyes for
weapons errors.

TUESDAY

Jack looked around the front room of his apartment and figured he was either going to have to move to a bigger place, or stop buying stuff. He had nowhere to put his new Daddy Warbucks lamp.

Well, not new exactly. It had been made sometime in the 1940s, but it was in great shape. The base was a glazed plaster cast of Daddy from the waist up, his hand gripping a lapel of his tuxedo, a tiny rhinestone in place of his diamond stick pin. He was grinning, and his pupilless eyes showed not the slightest trace of concern about the lamp stem and socket shell emerging from his bald pate.

Jack had found it in a Soho nostalgia shop, and talked the owner down to eighty-five dollars for it. He would have paid twice that. The apartment didn't need another lamp, but Jack needed this one. Warbucks was such a stand-up guy. No way Jack could pass it up. No bulb or lampshade, but that was easily remedied. Problem was, where to put it?

He did a slow turn. His home was the third floor of a brownstone in the West Eighties, and smelled of old wood. Not surprising since the place was crammed with Victorian golden oak furniture. The walls and shelves were cluttered with memorabilia and tchotchkes from the thirties and forties. Everything in sight except for the computer monitor existed before he was born. Even the Cartoon Network—he could see the large-screen TV in the extra bedroom— was playing a toon from the thirties with a big-eyed owlet crooning how he loved "to sing-a, about the moon-a anna June-a anna spring-a. . . ." And here in the front room, not a single empty horizontal surface left . . .

Except for the computer monitor.

Jack placed the Daddy Warbucks lamp on top of the monitor, which sat atop Jack's antique oak rolltop desk. The processor sat on the floor in the kneehole, and the keyboard hid under the rolltop. The monitor didn't look comfortable perched up there, but then, the computer didn't really fit anywhere in the room—a plastic iceberg adrift in a sea of wavy-grained oak.

But you couldn't be in business these days without one. Jack didn't understand all that much about computers, but he loved the anonymity they afforded in communications.

He hadn't checked his email since this morning, so he lit up the monitor and rolled up the tambour top to reveal his keyboard. He logged on through one of his ISPs—Jack had multiple accounts under various names with a number of Internet service providers, and maintained a Web site through one of them. Everything he'd read said that people were increasingly looking to the Internet to solve all sorts of problems, so Jack figured he might as well make himself available to folks searching there for his kind of solution.

Half a dozen emails from the Web site waited, but only one seemed worth answering, and that barely:

Jack—

I need your help. It's about my wife. Please call me or email me back, but =please= get back to me.

It was signed "Lewis Ehler" and he'd left two numbers, one in Brooklyn, the other on Long Island.

It's about my wife . . . not some guy who wanted to

know if she was cheating, he hoped. Marital problems weren't in Jack's line.

He had another job just starting up, but that promised to be mostly night work. Which meant his days would be free.

He wrote down the numbers, then headed out to make the call.

2

Jack walked east toward Central Park, looking for a phone he hadn't used recently, while the little toon owl's song echoed in his head.

I love to sing-a, about the moon-a anna June-a anna spring-a . . .

Spring had sprung and NYC was lurching out of hibernation. The air smelled fresh and clean, bright flowers peeked from window boxes on the upper floors of the brownstone regiments, and tiny leaf buds bedizened the branches of the widely spaced trees set in the sidewalks. The late morning sun sat high and bright, keeping Jack comfortable in a work shirt and jeans. Winter coats were gone, leaving short skirts and long legs on display again. A good day to be alive and heterosexual.

Not that the women paid much attention to him. They barely seemed to notice the guy with the so-so build, average-length brown hair, and mild brown eyes. Which was just fine with Jack. He'd be disappointed if they did, considering the effort he put into being a walking *trompe l'oeil*.

Jack cultivated anti-presence. The anonymous look took effort—not too trendy, not too retro. He kept an eye on what the average guy on the street was wearing. Jeans and flannel shirts never went out of style, even here on the Upper West Side; neither did sneakers and work boots—*real* work boots. Twill work pants were another safe bet—never stylish, but they never attracted attention either.

He found a pay phone on Central Park West. The apartment buildings stopped dead here, as if sliced off with a knife for dozens of blocks in either direction to leave room for the park across the street. Through the still-naked trees he could see the Lake, a blue lozenge in the greening grass. No boats on it yet, but it wouldn't be long.

He tapped in the access number on his prepaid calling card. He loved these things. As anonymous as cash and a hell of a lot lighter than the pocketful of change he used to have to carry.

Everybody seemed so frightened of the potential threat new electronics posed to security. And maybe it was a genuine peril for citizens. But from Jack's perspective, electronics offered an anonymity bonanza. He used to keep an answering machine in an empty office on Tenth Avenue, but a few months ago he unplugged it and had all calls to that number forwarded to a voicemail service.

Email, voice mail, calling cards . . . he could almost hear Louis Armstrong singing, "What a wonderful world."

Jack punched in the Brooklyn number Ehler had left. He found himself talking to the Keystone Paper Cylinder Company and asked to speak to Lewis Ehler.

"Whom shall I say is calling?" said the receptionist.

"Just tell him it's Jack, calling about his email."

Ehler came on right away. He spoke in a wheezy,

high-pitched voice accelerating steadily in an urgent whisper.

"Thank you so much for calling. I've been half out of my mind not knowing what to do. I mean, since Mel's been gone I've—"

"Whoa, whoa," Jack said. "Gone? Your wife's missing?"

"Yes! Three days now and—"

"Wait. Stop right there. We can save me time and you a lot of breath: I don't do missing wives."

His voice rose in pitch and volume. "But you must!"

"That's a police thing. They've got the manpower and resources to do missing persons a lot better than I ever will."

"No-no! She said no police! Absolutely no police."

"She *told* you? When did she tell you?"

"Just last night. I . . . I heard from her last night."

"Then she's not really missing."

"She is. Please believe me, she is. And she told me to call you, only you. 'Repairman Jack is the only one who will understand' is what she said."

"Yeah? How does she know about me?"

"I don't know. I'd never heard of you until Mel told me."

"Mel?"

"Melanie."

"Okay, but if Melanie can call you, why can't she tell you where she is?"

"It's very complicated—too complicated to get into over the phone. Can't we just meet? It'll be so much easier to explain this in person."

Jack thought about that. He stared at the hulking mass of the Museum of Natural History a few blocks away and watched a yellow caravan of school buses pull into the parking lot. This gig sounded a little wacky. Hell, it sounded way wacky. A missing wife who calls and tells her husband don't go to the police, call Repairman Jack instead. Kidnapped, maybe? But then . . .

"No ranson demand?"

"No. I doubt whoever's behind Mel's disappearance is interested in money."

"Everybody's interested in money."

"Not in this case. If we could just meet . . ."

Wackier and wackier, but Jack had nothing doing the rest of the day. . . and Ehler *had* said no cops involved. . . .

"Okay. Let's meet."

Ehler's relief flooded through the receiver. "Oh, thank you, thank you—"

"But I'm not going to Brooklyn."

"Anywhere you say, just as long as it's soon."

Julio's was close. Jack gave Ehler the address and told him to be there in an hour. After Ehler hung up, Jack pressed the # key and an electronic voice told him how much credit he had left on his calling card.

God, he loved these things.

He hung up and walked away from the park, thinking about what Ehler's wife had said.

Repairman Jack is the only one who will understand. . . .

Really.

3

Jack sat at his table near Julio's rear door. He was halfway through his second Rolling Rock when Lewis Ehler showed up. Jack tagged him as soon as he saw the gangly, brown-suited frame step through the door. Julio's crowd didn't wear suits, except for occasional adventuresome yupsters looking for something different, and yuppie suits were never wrinkled like this guy's.

Julio spotted him too, and ducked out from behind the bar. Julio had a brief conversation with the guy, acted real friendly, standing close, clapping him on the back in welcome. Finally satisfied the stranger wasn't carrying, Julio pointed Jack's way.

Jack watched Ehler stumble toward him—the darkness at the rear here took some adjusting to after stepping in from daylight—but he seemed to be having extra trouble because of a pronounced limp.

Jack waved. "Over here."

Ehler veered his way but remained standing when he reached the table. He looked fortyish, starvation lean, with a big jutting nose and a droopy lower lip. Close up, Jack saw that the brown suit was shiny and worn as well as wrinkled. He noticed how the sole of his right shoe was built up two inches. That explained the limp.

"You're him?" Ehler said in that high-pitched voice from the phone. His prominent Adam's apple bounced with each word. "Repairman Jack?"

"Just Jack'll do," Jack said, offering his hand.

"Lew." His shake was squishy and moist. "You don't look like what I expected."

Jack used to ask the next question, the obvious one, but had stopped long ago after hearing the same answer time after time: they always expected a glowering Charles Bronson type, someone bigger, meaner, tougher-looking than this ordinary Joe before them who could step up to the bar in front and virtually vanish into the regulars hanging there.

Jack took the You-don't-look-like-what-I-expected remark as a compliment.

"Want a beer?" he asked.

Lew shook his head. "I don't drink much."

"Coffee, then?"

"I'm too nervous for coffee." He rubbed his palms on the front of his jacket, then pulled out a chair and folded his Ichabod Crane body into it. "Maybe decaf."

Jack waved to Julio and mimed pouring a coffee pot.

"I thought we'd meet in a more private place," Lew said.

"This is private." Jack glanced at the empty booths and tables around them. The faint murmur of conversation drifted over from the bar area on the far side of the six-foot divider topped with dead plants. "Long as we don't shout."

Julio came strutting around the partition carrying a coffee pot and a white mug. His short, forty-year-old frame was grotesquely muscled under his tight, sleeveless shirt. He was freshly shaven, his mustache trimmed to a line, drafting-pencil thin, his wavy hair slicked back. This was the closest Jack had got to him this afternoon, and he coughed as he caught a whiff of a new cologne, more cloying than usual.

"God, Julio. What *is* that?"

"Like it?" he said as he filled Lew's mug. "It's brand-new. Called *Midnight*."

"Maybe that's the only time you're supposed to wear it."

He grinned. "Naw. Chicks love it, man."

Only if they've spent the day in a chicken coop, Jack thought but kept it to himself.

"Say," Lew said, pointing to all the dead vegetation around the room, "did you ever think of watering your plants?"

"Wha' for?" Julio said. "They're all dead."

Lew's eyes widened. "Oh. Right. Of course." He looked at the mug Julio was pouring. "Is that decaf? I only drink decaf."

"Don't serve that shit," Julio said tersely as he turned and strutted back to the bar.

"I can see why the place is half deserted," Lew said, glancing at Julio's retreating form. "That fellow is downright rude."

"It doesn't come naturally to him. He's been practicing lately."

"Yeah? Well somebody ought to see that the owner gets wise to him."

"He is the owner."

"Really?" Lew leaned over the table and spoke in a low voice. "Is there some religious significance to all these dead plants?"

"Nah. It's just that Julio isn't happy with the caliber of his clientele lately."

"Well he's not going to raise it with these dead plants."

"No. You don't understand. He wants to lower it. The yuppies have discovered this place and they've started showing up here. He's been trying to get rid of them. This has always been a working man's bar and eatery.

The Beamer crowd is scaring off the old regulars. Julio and his help are rude as hell to them but they just lap it up. They *like* being insulted. He let all the window plants die, and the yups think it's great. It's driving the poor guy nuts."

Lew seemed to be only half listening. He stood and stared toward the grimy front window for a few seconds, then sat again.

"Looking for someone?"

"I think I was followed here," Lew said, looking uncomfortable. "I know that sounds crazy but—"

"Who'd want to follow you?"

"I don't know. It might have something to do with Melanie."

"Your wife? Why would—?"

"I wish I knew." Lew suddenly became fidgety. "I'm not so sure about this anymore."

"It's okay. You can change your mind. No hard feelings." A certain small percentage of customers who got this far developed cold feet when the moment came to tell Jack exactly what they wanted him to fix for them. "But don't back out because you're being followed."

"I'm not even sure I am." He sighed. "The thing is, I don't know why I'm here, or what I'm supposed to do. I'm so upset I can't think straight."

"Easy, Lew," Jack said. "This is just a conversation."

"Okay, fine. But who are you? Why did my wife say to call you and only you? I don't understand any of this."

Jack had to feel sorry for the guy. Lewis Ehler was no doubt a one-hundred-percent solid, taxpaying citizen; he had a problem and felt he should be dealing with one of the institutions his sweat-procured taxes paid for, instead of this stranger in a bar. This wasn't the way his world was supposed to be.

"And why do you call yourself Repairman Jack?" Ehler added.

"I don't, really. It's a name that sort of became attached to me." Abe Grossman had started calling him that years ago. Jack had used it for awhile as a lark, but it had stuck. "Because I'm in a sort of fix-it business. But we'll get to me later. First tell me about you. What do you do for the Keystone Paper Cylinder Company?"

"Do? I own it."

"Really." This guy barely looked middle management. "Just what does a Keystone Paper Cylinder Company make?"

And don't tell me paper cylinders.

"Cardboard mailing tubes. The 'paper cylinder' bit was my father's idea. Thought it sounded classier than cardboard mailing tubes. He retired, left the place to me. And yeah, I know I don't look it, but I own it, run it, and make a decent living at it. But I'm not here to talk about me. I want to find my wife. She's been gone three days and I don't know how to get her back."

His features screwed up and for a moment Jack was afraid he was going to cry. But Lew held on, sniffed twice, then got control.

"You okay?" Jack said.

Ehler nodded. "Yeah."

"Okay. Let's start at the beginning. When did you last see your wife—Melanie, right?"

Another nod. "Yes. Melanie. She left Sunday morning for some last-minute research and—"

"Research on what?"

"I'll get to that in a minute. The thing is, she said something that didn't sound so strange then, but sounds kind of creepy in retrospect. She told me if I didn't hear from her for a few days, not to get worried, not to report her missing or anything. She'd be all right, just out of touch for a while. 'Give me a few days to get back,' she said."

"Get back from where?"

"She didn't say."

"Don't know about you," Jack said, "but that sounds pretty strange from the git-go."

"Not if you knew Mel."

"Got a picture?"

Lew Ehler fished out his wallet. His long bony fingers were surprisingly agile as he whipped a creased photo from one of the slots and handed it across the table.

Jack saw a slim, serious-looking brunette in her mid-thirties wearing a red turtleneck sweater and tan slacks, pictured from the hips up. Her hands were behind her back and her expression said she wasn't crazy about having her picture taken. She had pale skin, thick black hair and eyebrows, and dark penetrating eyes. Not a raving beauty, but not bad looking.

"How recent is this?"

"Just last year."

Jack suddenly had a bad feeling where this was going: younger pretty wife leaves older, limping scarecrow husband to run off with younger man . . . and maybe tries to run a game on him in the process.

"No," Lew said, smiling thinly. "She's not having an affair. Mel's probably the most direct person you'll ever meet. If she were leaving me, she'd simply say so and go." He shook his head and looked again like he was going to cry. "Something's happened to her."

"But you know she's alive, right?" Jack said quickly. "I mean, you heard from her last night."

He bit his upper lip and shrugged.

Jack said, "What did she say?"

"She told me she was okay, but needed help, and that

she wasn't where I could find her. 'Only Repairman Jack can find me,' she said. 'Only he will understand.'"

But Jack did *not* understand. He was baffled. "She gave no hint where she was calling from?"

Lew licked his lips. He seemed uncomfortable. "Let me explain a few things about Melanie first."

Jack leaned back with the beer bottle between his fingertips. "Be my guest."

"All right," Lew ran his fingers through his thinning hair. "I met her through my accountant. He had a heart attack and his firm sent her over to do Keystone's quarterly tax estimate. Melanie Rubin . . ." Lew's lips curved into a smile as he said the name. "I've never met anyone before or since so full of energy, so determined, so *focused*. And yet so pretty. It was love at first sight for me. And best of all, she liked me. We went out for a while, and five and a half years ago we were married."

"Any kids?"

He shook his head. "No. Mel doesn't want any."

"Ever?"

"Never."

Sounded like Melanie Ehler ruled the roost. Jack hesitated, mulling his phrasing . . . the next question was a bit delicate.

"I couldn't help but notice that you said it was love at first sight on your part, but she 'liked' you. Is that . . . ?"

Lew's smile was shy, his shrug a little embarrassed. "We have a good relationship. We live a quiet life, with very few close friends. Melanie loves me as much as she can love anyone. But she's too driven to really, truly love anyone."

"Driven by what?"

A deep sigh. "Let's see . . . how do I put this? Okay . . . Melanie might be considered a kook by some standards. She's been involved in fringe groups since she was a teenager."

"Fringe groups? How fringey? Objectivism, the Church of the Sub-Genius, Scientology?"

"More like SITPRCA, MCF, CAUS, ICAAR, LIU-FON, ORTK, the New York Fortean Society, and others."

"Wow." Jack hadn't heard of any of those. "Alphabet city."

Lew smiled. "Yeah, they love their acronyms almost as much as the government. But they're all concerned with one sort of conspiracy or another."

"You mean like who *really* killed JFK and RFK and MLK, and who's covering it up and why?"

"Yeah, some of them are like that. Others are really far out."

Swell, Jack thought. A missing conspiracy nut. He could feel the rear exit door beckoning from behind him. If he jumped up and ran now, he could be out before Lew Ehler could say another word about his lost wife.

But the missing Melanie had said that only Repairman Jack would understand, hadn't she. He wondered what she'd meant.

Something must have showed on his face because Lew started waving his hands in front of him.

"Don't get me wrong. She wasn't really into all that stuff—she was more of an interested observer than a serious participant in those groups. She was looking for something—she's been looking for something most of her life—and didn't know what it was. She once told me she wasn't looking for answers from these groups, just enough information to know what questions to ask."

Could have been a Bob Dylan lyric.

"And did she find it?"

"No. And she was very frustrated until last year when SESOUP was formed."

"Sea soup?" Sounded like an appetizer.

"The Society for the Exposure of Secret Organizations and Unacknowledged Phenomena."

"SESOUP . . ." Jack had heard that name, but couldn't remember where. "For some reason, that sounds familiar."

"It's an exclusive organization, started by—" Lew froze as he glanced toward the front. "There!" he said, pointing at the window. "Tell me that guy isn't watching us!"

Jack looked—and damn if Lew wasn't right. A figure was silhouetted against Julio's front window, nose pressed against the glass, hands cupped on either side of his face. He sure as hell seemed to be staring their way.

Jack jumped up and headed for the door. "Come on. Let's go see."

The figure ducked away to the left, and by the time Jack reached the door, he'd vanished into the rest of the foot traffic on the sidewalk.

"See anybody who looks familiar?" Jack said as Lew joined him in the doorway.

Lew eyed the stream of shoppers and workers and mothers with strollers, then shook his head.

"Could have been a thirsty guy just checking the place out," Jack said as they returned to the table.

Of course that didn't explain why he'd hurried off when Jack started moving.

"Could have been," Lew said, but no way he believed it.

"All right. You were telling me about this soup society or something."

"SESOUP." Lew looked spooked, and kept glancing at the window as he spoke. "It was put together by a fellow named Salvatore Roma. Membership is by invitation only, which has caused a lot of bad feeling in the conspiracy subculture—some well-known names were excluded. It's designed as a clearing house for most of the major conspiracy theories. Roma's idea is to sort through them all for the purpose of finding common elements among them. Melanie loved the idea. She's sure that's the path to the truth."

"The truth? About what?"

"About what's *really* going on in the world. Something that would help identify the powers, the planners, the string-pullers behind the mysteries and mayhem and secret organizations that plague the world." He held up his hands again. "Not my words—Roma's."

That rear door was calling like a siren.

"And who's this Roma?"

"Salvatore Roma came out of nowhere—actually he's a professor at some university in Kentucky—and got everybody fired up. He's been very helpful to Melanie in her research."

"I take it then that you're not into that stuff."

"Not like Melanie. I got involved out of pure curiosity—plus, attending the various gatherings and conventions around the country gave us an excuse to travel—but I've got to tell you, mister, after spending time with these people, I'm not so sure they're half as crazy as they're painted. And in some regards, I don't think they're crazy at all."

"It's called brainwashing," Jack said.

"Maybe. I don't say I'm immune to that. But Mel . . . Mel is so tough minded, it's hard to imagine her being brainwashed by anything or anybody."

"Does any of this have anything to do with Mel's disappearance?"

"I'm sure of it. You see, over the years Mel became convinced that none of the conflicting theories about secret societies and UFOs and the Antichrist and world domination conspiracies was completely right."

"I'm glad for that," Jack said.

"But she also thought that none of them was completely wrong. She figured each formed around a kernel of truth, a tiny piece of the big picture. She spent years analyzing them all, trying to come up with what she called her Grand Unification Theory."

"And?"

"And a couple of months ago she told me she believed she'd found it."

"And you're going to share it, right?"

"I wish I could. All she told me was that she'd identified a single heretofore unsuspected power behind all the world's mysteries and unexplained phenomena, something totally unrelated to current theories. She refused to say any more until she had absolute proof. That was the 'research' I mentioned before. She thought she'd found a way to prove her Grand Unification Theory."

"Let me guess: You think that she maybe *did* find this proof, and whoever's behind it all has abducted her."

More like a job for Mulder and Scully, Jack thought.

"That's a possibility, of course," Lew said, "but I'm afraid it might be something more mundane. And part of it might be Mel's fault. You see, she's been so excited about finally pulling her Grand Unification Theory together, that she's been sort of bragging."

"To whom?"

"To anyone who'll listen."

"But didn't you tell me you two have very few friends?"

"She's been bragging in the Usenet groups she participates in."

"Isn't that part of the Internet?"

Lew looked at him strangely. "You have a Web site and you don't know about Usenet groups?"

Jack shrugged. "I had a guy at my ISP throw it together. You didn't see many bells and whistles, right?" Christ, the designer had wanted to festoon the site with animated tools—bouncing screwdrivers, pirouetting pliers, slithering tool belts. Remembering the demo still made Jack shudder. "It's not there to impress anyone. It's just another way for customers to get in touch with me. And as for the rest of the Internet, I don't do much surfing. It's a black hole for time, and I've got other things to do. So ... what's a Usenet group?"

"It's a kind of bulletin board divided into interest topics where people post messages, news, facts, theories, opinions. The Internet is loaded with conspiracy topics, and Mel visited them all regularly, mostly lurking. But recently she began posting and, uncharacteristically, bragging, saying how her Grand Unification Theory was going to 'blow all other theories out of the water.' She said she was going to reveal her findings at the first annual SESOUP conference."

"And that's bad?"

"Well, yes. I think someone in one of those Usenet groups is trying to silence her."

"That doesn't make sense. I thought these conspiracy nuts—sorry, no offense—were supposed to be looking for the truth that's presumably been hidden from them."

"That's what you'd think, of course. But once you've gotten to know these folks ... well, you can see how some of them would feel threatened by a theory that proved theirs wrong, or worse yet, made theirs look foolish. You've got many people out there who've blamed all the problems in their lives on a certain conspiracy; some of them have built reputations in the conspiracy community by becoming experts on their section of the conspiracy landscape. Jack, these people *live* in that landscape, and the conspiracy community is all the social contact they've got. Someone like that wouldn't want to be proved wrong."

"Badly enough to move against your wife?"

"Loss of face, belief, support structure, status—think about it. That could be utterly devastating."

Jack nodded. Damn right. Take a guy who's not too tightly wrapped to start with, and a threat like that could completely unravel him.

Now we're getting somewhere, he thought.

If Lew had started insisting that his wife had been abducted by aliens, or fallen victim to a faceless bogeyman or agents of some all-powerful shadow government, Jack would be waving bye-bye now. He wasn't into chasing phantoms. But a bad guy who was a fellow conspiracy nut, maybe working alone or with one or two of his brother kooks—that sounded real. Jack could handle real.

"This Roma you mentioned—could he be a player in this?"

Lew shook his head. "I can't see how. He's been very supportive of Mel's research, and she's often credited him publicly for his help."

That still doesn't rule him out, Jack thought.

"Okay, then," Jack said. "If someone's got her, how did she call you?"

Lew looked away. "She didn't exactly call."

The guy looked positively embarrassed.

"Well then, how did she 'exactly' contact you?"

"Through the TV."

"Oh, hell."

"Listen to me," Lew said hurriedly, looking at Jack now. "Please, I'm not crazy. She spoke to me from my TV—I swear!"

"Right. And what were you watching—*The X-Files*?"

"No. The Weather Channel."

Jack laughed. "Okay, who put you up to this? Abe? Julio? Whoever it is, you're good. You're very good."

"No, listen to me," he said, sounding frantic now. "I know how it sounds, but this is no joke and I am completely sane. I was sitting there with The Weather Channel on, not paying it much attention—when I'm alone I use it like Muzak, you know? Just to have something on. And I'm sitting there having my after-dinner coffee when suddenly I hear Melanie's voice. I jump up and look around but she's not there. Then I realize it's coming from the TV. The weather maps are running but the sound is gone and Melanie is talking to me, but she's talking like she's on a one-way line and only has a short time to speak."

"What did she say? *Exactly.*"

Lew put his head back and squeezed his eyes shut. "Let me see if I can get this right. She said, *'Lew? Lew? Can you hear me? Listen carefully. I'm okay now, but I need help. I'm not where you can find me. Only Repairman Jack can find me. Only he will understand. You can find him on the Internet. Remember: only Repairman Jack and no one else. Hurry, Lew. Please hurry.'* And then the weatherman's voice came back on and Mel was gone."

Jack hesitated. Every so often he ran into a potential customer who was missing a few buttons on his remote. The best thing was to let them down easy and not return any future calls.

"Well, Lew, I wish I could help you but—"

"Look, I'm *not* crazy. For a while I had my doubts, and I'm sure I was staring at that TV screen just the way you're staring at me now. I waited for the voice to return but it never came. So I did what she'd told me: I looked for you on the Internet. I've never heard of you, yet when I did a search for your name in Yahoo, 'repairmanjack.com' popped right up. That got me thinking that maybe I didn't imagine her voice."

"Well, you could have——" Jack began, but suddenly Lew was leaning over the table, reaching across it with pleading hands, his Adam's apple bobbing like a piston.

"Please—she says you're the only one who can do it. Don't turn me away. If you want to think I'm crazy, fine, but humor me, okay? Something has happened to Melanie and I'll pay you anything you want to get her back."

Tears rimmed Lew's eyes as he finished.

Jack didn't know what to say. The guy didn't seem crazy, and didn't strike him as a put-on artist, and he did appear to be genuinely hurting. And if his wife was truly missing, whether through her own doing or taken against her will . . . well, maybe Jack could fix it for him.

And beyond that was the nagging question: If Lew's wife had indeed contacted him—though Jack would never buy the through-the-TV story—why had she stipulated Repairman Jack and no one else?

Jack knew the question would go on biting at his ankles indefinitely if he didn't look into this.

"Okay, Lew," he said. "I'll probably regret this, but I'll see what I can do for you. I'll——"

"Oh, thank you! Thank you!"

"Just hear me out first. I'll give it a week, max. Five thousand cash up front, non-negotiable, non-returnable. If I find her, it's another five thou, cash, on the spot."

Jack was hoping the price might put him off, but Lew didn't bat an eye.

"Okay," he said without an instant's hesitation. "Fine. Done. When do you want it?"

Must be good money in the paper cylinder business.

"Today. And I also want to go through any papers

Melanie might have left around your place. Where do you live?"

"Out on the Island. Shoreham."

Jeez, that was a haul—almost out to the fork—but Jack didn't have much else on the slate for the day, so . . .

"All right. Give me the address and I'll see you out there in a couple of hours. Have the down payment with you."

Lew glanced at his watch. "Okay. I've got to move if I'm going to make it to the bank." He pulled out a card and wrote on the back. "There's my home address. Take the LIE—"

"I'll find it. Let's make it five o'clock. I want to beat the rush."

"Fine. Five o'clock." He reached across the table and grabbed Jack's right hand in both of his. "And thank you—thanks a million. You don't know what this means to me."

I'm sure I don't, Jack thought. But I got a feeling I'm going to find out.

Only Repairman Jack can find me. Only he will understand.

Why me?

4

"So why should you call them nuts?" Abe said. "We are surrounded by conspiracies."

Jack had swung by the Isher Sports Shop to say hello to Abe Grossman, a graying Humpty Dumpty of a man in his late fifties with a forehead that went on almost forever, and Jack's oldest friend in the city. In the world. They sat in their usual positions: Jack leaning on the customer side of the scarred wooden counter, Abe perched on his stool behind it, and around them, a gallimaufry of sporting goods tossed carelessly onto sagging shelves lining narrow aisles or hung from ceiling hooks, all in perpetual, undusted disarray. A Sports Authority outlet designed and maintained by Oscar Madison. One of the reasons Jack liked coming here was that it made his apartment look neat and roomy.

"You know the root of the word?" Abe said. "Conspire: it means to breathe together. The world is rife with all sorts of people and institutions breathing together. Just take a look—" He broke off and cocked his head toward the pale blue parakeet perched on his stained left shoulder. "What's that, Parabellum? No, we can't do that. Jack is a friend."

Parabellum tilted his beak toward Abe's ear and looked as if he were whispering into it.

"Well, most of the time he is," Abe said, then straightened his head and looked at Jack. "See? Conspiracies everywhere. Just now, right in front of you, Parabellum tried to engage me in a conspiracy against you for not bringing him a snack. I should be worried if I were you."

Usually Jack brought something edible, but he'd neglected to this time.

"You mean I can't drop in without bringing an offering?" Jack said. "This was a spur of the moment thing."

Abe looked offended. "For me—*feh!*—I shouldn't care. It's for Parabellum. He gets hungry this time of the day."

Jack pointed to the Technicolor droppings that festooned the shoulders of Abe's half-sleeve white shirt.

"Looks like Parabellum's had plenty to eat already. You sure he doesn't have colitis or something?"

"He's a fine healthy bird. It's just that he gets upset by strangers—and by so-called friends who don't bring him an afternoon snack."

Jack glanced pointedly at Abe's bulging shirt front. "I've seen where the bird's snacks usually end up."

"If you're going to start on my weight again, you should save your breath."

"Wasn't going to say a word."

But he wanted to. Jack was getting worried about Abe. An overweight, sedentary, Type-A personality, he was a heart attack waiting to happen. Jack couldn't bear the thought of anything happening to Abe. He loved this man. The decades that separated their birthdays hadn't kept them from becoming the closest of friends. Abe was the only human being besides Gia Jack could talk to—really talk to. Together they had solved the world's problems many times over. He could not imagine day-to-day life without Abe Grossman.

So Jack had cut back on the goodies he traditionally brought whenever he stopped by, or now if he did bring something, he'd sworn it would be low cal or low fat—preferably both.

"Anyway, I should be worried about weight? If I want to lose some, I can do it anytime. When I'm ready, I'll go to Egypt and eat from street carts for two weeks. You'll see. Dysentery does wonders for the waistline. Richard Simmons should be so effective."

"Im-Ho-Tep's revenge, ay?" Jack said, keeping it light. He didn't want to be a complete pain in the ass. "When do you leave?"

"I have a call in to my travel agent now. I'm not sure when she'll get back to me. Maybe next year. But what about you? Why are you so careful with your foods? A guy in your line of work should worry about choles-terol?"

"I'm an optimist."

"You're too healthy is what's wrong with you. If you don't get shot or stabbed or clubbed to death by one of the many people you've royally pissed off in your life, what can you die from?"

"I'm doing research. I'll find something interesting, I hope."

"Nothing you'll die of! And how will that look on your death certificate? 'Cause of death: *Nothing.*' Won't you feel foolish? Such an embarrassment. It will have to be a closed-coffin service to hide your red face. And really, how could I come to your funeral knowing you died of nothing?"

"Maybe I'll just die of shame."

"At least it's something. But before you pass on, let me tell you a little something about conspiracies."

"Figured you have something to say on the subject."

"Indeed I do. Remember that global economic holo-caust I used to warn you about?"

For years Abe had gone on and on about the impend-ing collapse of the global economy. He still maintained a mountain retreat upstate, stocked with gold coins and freeze-dried food.

"The one that didn't happen?"

"The reason it didn't happen is that they didn't want it to happen."

"Who's 'they'?"

"The cabal of international bankers that manipulates the global currency markets, of course."

"Of course."

Here we go, Jack thought. This ought to be good.

"'Of course,' he says," Abe said, speaking to Parabel-lum. "Skepticalman Jack thinks his old friend is *meshugge.*" He turned back to Jack. "Remember when the Asian and Russian markets went into free fall awhile back?"

"Vaguely."

"'Vaguely,' he says."

"You know I don't follow the markets." Since he didn't own stocks, Jack pretty much ignored Wall Street.

"Then I'll refresh your memory. The fall of 1997: the bottoms fell out of all the Asian markets. Less than a year later, the same thing in Russia, making rubles good only for toilet paper. People were losing their shirts *and* their pants, banks and brokerage houses were failing, Asian brokers were hanging themselves or jumping out windows. Do you think that just *happened?* No. It was planned, it was orchestrated, and certain people made money that should be measured in cosmological terms."

"What people?"

"The members of the cabal. They're drawn from the old royal families and international banking families of Europe along with descendants of our own robber barons. Most of their influence is concentrated in the West, and they were probably miffed at being left out of all the emerging economies booming in Asia. So they invited themselves in. They manipulated Asian currencies, inflated the markets, then pulled the plug."

Jack had to ask: "How does that help them?"

"Simple: They sell short before the crash. When prices have bottomed out—and they know when that is because they and their buddies are pulling the strings—they cover their short positions. But that's only half of the equation. They don't stop there. They use their stupendous short profits to buy up damaged properties and companies at fire sale prices."

"So now they've got a piece of the action."

"And no small piece. After the crash, enormous amounts of Thai and Indonesian stock and property were bought up at five cents on the dollar by shadow corporations. And since the lion's share of profits from those upstart countries will now be flowing into the cabal's coffers, those economies will be allowed to improve."

"Okay," Jack said. "But *who* are they? What are their names? Where do they live?"

"Names? You want I should give you names? How about their addresses too? What's Repairman Jack going to do? Pay them a little visit?"

"Well, no. I just—"

"If I knew their names, I'd probably be dead. I don't *want* to know their names. Someone else should know their names and stop them. They've been pulling the world's economic strings for centuries but no one ever does anything. No one hunts them down and calls them to account. Why is that, Jack? Tell me: Is it ignorance or apathy?"

"I don't know and couldn't care less," Jack said with a shrug.

Abe opened his mouth, then closed it and stared at him.

Jack fought the grin that threatened to break free. Goading Abe was precious fun.

Finally Abe turned to Parabellum. "You see what I put up with from this man? I try to enlighten him as to the true nature of things, and what does he do? Wise he cracks."

"As if you really believe all that," Jack said, grinning.

Abe stared at him, saying nothing.

Jack felt his smile fading. "You don't *really* believe in an international financial cabal, do you?"

"I should tell you? But one thing you should know is

that a good conspiracy theory is a *mechaieh*. And also great fun. But this group you mentioned, this Bouillabaisse—"

"SESOUP."

"Whatever. I'll bet it's not fun for them. I'll bet it's very serious business for them: UFOs and other stuff far from the mainstream."

"UFOs are mainstream?"

"They've been mainstreamed. That's why sightings are up: believing is seeing, if you should get my drift. But when you start talking with members of Zuppa De Peche—"

"SESOUP."

"Whatever—I bet you'll run into *meshuggeners* so far from the mainstream they're not even wet."

"I can hardly wait." Jack glanced at his watch. "Look, I've got to be heading out to the Island. Can I borrow your truck?"

"What's the matter with Ralph?"

"Sold him."

"No!" Abe seemed genuinely shocked. "But you loved that car."

"I know." Jack had hated parting with his 1963 white Corvair convertible. "But I didn't have much choice. Ralph's become a real collector's item. Everywhere I took him people stopped and asked me about him, wanted to buy him. Don't need that kind of attention."

"Too bad. All right, since you're in mourning, take the truck, but remember: she only likes high test."

"That old V6?"

Abe shrugged. "I shouldn't spoil my women?" He extracted the truck keys from his pocket and handed them to Jack as the bell on the shop's front jangled. A customer entered: a tanned, muscular guy with short blond hair.

"Looks like a weekend warrior," Jack said.

Abe returned Parabellum to his cage. "I'll get rid of him."

"Don't bother. I've got to go."

With obvious reluctance, Abe slid off the stool and left his sanctum behind the counter. He sounded bored as he approached the customer.

"What overpriced recreational nonsense can I sell you today?"

Jack headed for the door, holding up the truck keys as he passed Abe.

Abe waved, then turned back to his customer. "Water skis? You want to spend your free time sliding on top of water? What on earth for? It's dangerous. And besides, you could hit a fish. Imagine the headache you'd cause the poor thing. A migraine should be half so bad. . . ."

5

The Incorporated Village of Shoreham sits on the north shore of Long Island a bit west of Rocky Point. All Jack knew about Shoreham was that it was the home of a multibillion-dollar nuclear power plant that had never ignited its reactor—one of the greatest boondoggles in the state's long history of boondoggles.

And no doubt the subject of a number of conspiracy theories, Jack figured.

After asking at a 7-Eleven along 25A, he found Lewis Ehler's street. Briarwood Road led north, twisting and turning into the hills bordering the Long Island Sound. Poorly paved and bouncy, but he guessed the residents liked it that way because the houses were big and well kept. All the lots were wooded, and the homes to his right perched on a rise overlooking the water. Between the houses and through the trees, Jack caught glimpses of the Sound. Connecticut was a darker line atop the horizon.

He found the Ehler place and pulled into the gravel drive of an oversized ranch. The dark cedar shake siding and white trim and shutters blended with the budding oaks, maples, and birches surrounding the house. The landscaper had gone for a low-maintenance yard, substituting mulch and wood chips for grass. Perfectly trimmed rhodos and azaleas hugged the foundation; nothing ostentatious, but Jack knew from his teenage days as a landscaper's helper that everything here was first quality. A lot of money had been invested into this yard's "natural" look.

Lew met him at the door and scanned the road running past the house.

"Did you see anyone following you?"

"No." Jack hadn't been looking, but he hadn't noticed anyone. "How about you?"

"I thought I saw a black sedan a few times but . . ." He shrugged and ushered Jack inside where he gave him an envelope stuffed with cash. Jack didn't count it.

The interior had a lot of nautical touches—hurricane lamps, a big brass compass, fishnets and floats on the walls, all looking very staged.

"I didn't particularly want to live way out here," Lew said as he showed Jack through the house. "It means a longer commute for me, but Mel said this was the place she really wanted to live, so . . . this is where we live."

The only non-decorator touches about the house were the paintings—dark, brooding abstractions on all the walls.

"Really something, aren't they," Lew said.

Jack nodded. "Who's the artist?"

"Mel. She did them when she was a teenager."

She must have been a real fun date, he thought, but said: "Impressive."

"Aren't they? She's been getting back into it again, when she can steal time from her research."

"And where does she do that?"

"In her study. I'll show you," he said, leading Jack toward a spiral staircase. "She used the second bedroom for a while but all her reference materials pretty quickly outgrew that, so we converted the attic for her."

Lew's short leg made for slow progress on the narrow treads, but finally they reached the top. Jack found himself in a long, low-ceilinged room running the length of the house; a beige computer desk near the staircase, a window at each end—an easel by the far window—four filing cabinets clustered in the center, and all the rest an enormous collection of paper—a Strandesque array of books, magazines, pamphlets, article excerpts and reprints, tear sheets, and flyers. The shelves lining every spare inch of wall space were crammed full; the tops of the filing cabinets were stacked at least a foot deep, and the rest was scattered in piles on the carpeted floor.

"Her reference materials," Jack said softly, awed.

He sniffed the air, heavy with the scent of aging paper. He loved that smell.

"Yeah." Lew walked past one of the shelves, running a finger along the book spines. "Everything you could ever want to know about UFOs, alien abductions, the Bermuda Triangle, Satanism, telepathy, remote viewing, mind control, the CIA, the NSA, HAARP, the Illuminati, astral projection, channeling, levitation, clairvoyance, seances, tarot, reincarnation, astrology, the Loch Ness monster, the Bible, Kaballah, Velikovsky, crop circles, Tunguska—"

"I get the picture," Jack said when Lew stopped for a breath. "All for her Grand Unification Theory."

"Yes. You might say she's obsessed."

Jack noted Lew's use of the present tense when he referred to his wife. A good sign.

"I guess so. I was going to ask you what else she did with her time, but I guess we can skip that."

"She was also into real estate for a while. Not that we needed the money, but she got her license and did a few deals."

"I doubt that has anything to do with her disappearance."

"Well, it might. She didn't do real estate the way most people do. She never gave me the details, but she did tell me her activities were related to her research."

"Such as?"

"Well, she'd buy a place herself—always in the developments along Randall Road on the south side of the highway. Then she'd hire some men to dig here and there around the yard, then resell it."

"Did she tell you what she was looking for?"

"She just said it was part of her research. And I couldn't complain much, because she usually resold the properties at a profit."

One weird lady, Jack thought, looking around. And part pack rat, to boot. I'm supposed to find a clue to her whereabouts in this Library of Congress of the weird? Fat chance.

Jack wandered down toward the far window. The Sound was visible through the bare branches of the trees. As he turned he caught a glimpse of the canvas on the easel, and it stopped him cold. This one made the grim paintings downstairs seem bright and cheery. He couldn't say why the seemingly random swirls of black and deep purple bothered him. The longer he stared at it, the more heightened the feeling that *things* were watching him from within the turbulent shadows. He gave into a sudden urge to touch its glistening surface. Cold and . . .

He pulled back. "It feels wet."

"Yes," Lew said. "Some new paint Mel started using. Supposedly it never dries."

"Never?" He checked his fingertips—no pigment on them, even though they still felt wet. "Never's an awful long time."

He touched the surface again, in a different spot. Yes . . . cold, wet, and—

"Damn!" he said, jerking his hand away.

"What's wrong?"

"Must be something sharp in there," Jack said as he stared at the tips of his index and middle fingers.

He didn't want to say that he'd felt sharp little points digging into them, like tiny teeth snapping at his flesh. But the skin was unbroken. Still felt wet, though.

"Let me show you something on her computer," Lew said, heading for the desk.

With a final glance into the hungry depths of the painting, Jack shook off a chill and followed Lew, still rubbing his moist fingertips.

At the deck, Jack noticed a green and blue image of the earth spinning on the monitor screen; and as it spun, chunks began disappearing from its surface, as if some invisible being were gnawing at it. After the globe was completely devoured, the sequence looped back to the beginning.

"Cheerful screen saver," Jack said.

Mel programmed that herself."

"Imagine that."

"But here's what I wanted to show you," Lew said, fiddling with the mouse. The apple-core shaped remnant of the earth disappeared, replaced by a word processor directory. Lew opened a directory labeled GUT.

"Gut?" Jack said.

"G-U-T. That's how Mel refers to her Grand Unification Theory. And look," he said, pointing to the blank white screen. "It's empty. She had years of notes and analysis stored in that folder, and someone's erased it."

"The same people who have her, you think?"

"Who else?"

"Maybe the lady herself. She knew she was going away; maybe she copied the contents onto floppies and"—he resisted saying *gutted*— "cleared the contents herself to keep them secret. Is she the type to do something like that?"

"Possibly," he said, nodding slowly. "It never occurred to me but, yes, that's definitely something she might do. She was pretty jealous about her research— never gave anybody but Salvatore Roma so much as a peek at what she was up to."

Roma . . . that name again. "Why him?"

"As I said, he was helping her. They were in almost daily contact before Mel . . . left."

Mr. Roma was looking better and better as the possible bad guy here.

"Did you contact him?"

"No. Actually, he contacted me, looking for Mel. She was supposed to call him but hadn't. He was worried about her."

"And he had no idea where she might be."

"Not a clue."

Why don't I believe that?

Jack looked around the cluttered study and the missing Mel's words came back to him: *Only Repairman Jack can find me. Only he will understand.*

Sorry to disappoint you, lady, he thought, but Jack doesn't have a clue.

"How about friends? Who'd she hang with?"

"Me, mostly. We're both pretty much homebodies, but Mel has acquaintances all over the world via the Internet. Spent a lot of time on her computer."

"How about her car? What does she drive?"

"An Audi. But I haven't gotten a call that it's been found anywhere."

"No other contacts?" Jack said. He felt his frustration mounting. "What about family?"

"Both her folks are dead. Her father died before we met, her mother died just last year. Mel was an only child so she inherited the house and everything in it. I keep telling her to sell it but—"

"She has another house? Why didn't you tell me?"

"I didn't think it was important. Besides, I searched the place just yesterday. She wasn't there. I've been there before, but never actually searched through it. I found something odd in the cellar, but—"

"Odd? Odd how?"

"In the cellar floor." He shrugged. "Nothing that would relate to Mel's disappearance."

We're talking a very odd woman here, Jack thought. Two odds sometimes attract.

"Can't hurt to look," he said, desperate for something to give him direction. "Where is it?"

"It's a ways from here. A little town named Monroe."

"Never heard of it."

"It's near Glen Cove."

"Great," Jack said. "Let's take a look."

Not that he had much hope of finding anything useful, but this Monroe was back toward the city, and he had to head in that direction anyway.

But if the Monroe house yielded as much as this place, he'd have to return Lew's down payment. This was going nowhere.

Jack cast a final look at the painting at the far end of

the study as he followed Lew down the stairway. His fingertips didn't hurt any longer—must have been something sharp within the paint; it simply had *felt* like a bite—but damn if they didn't still feel wet.

Weird.

6

Monroe turned out to be a Gold Coast town, smaller and prettier than Shoreham. It had a picturesque harbor, for one thing, and no room for a nuclear plant. Jack guessed from the faux whaling-village facades on the harbor area shops and buildings that the town must do a fair amount of tourist trade in the summer. A little early for that now. Traffic was minimal as he followed Lew's Lexus through the downtown area, then uphill past the brick-fronted town hall and library, the white steepled church—a real postcard of a town. He trailed him past rows of neat colonials, then came to a development of mostly two- and three-bedroom postwar ranch houses.

Lew pulled into the driveway of a house that wasn't so well-kept. Its clapboard siding needed a fresh coat of paint; last fall's leaves clogged the gutters; dark green onion grass sprouted in the weedy, anemic, threadbare lawn. A detached garage sat to the right. A huge oak dominated a front yard that was unusually large for the neighborhood—looked like half an acre or better.

Jack parked Abe's truck at the curb and met Lew at the front door.

"Why does she keep this place?" Jack asked.

"Sentimental reasons, I guess," Lew said, searching

through his key ring. "I've wanted her to sell it, or maybe even subdivide the lot. Be worth a pretty penny, but she keeps putting it off. She grew up here. Spent most of her life in this house."

Jack felt a chill as they paused on the front stoop. He looked around uneasily. They were standing in the deep shadow cast by the massive oak's trunk as it hid the late afternoon sun. That had to be it.

Lew opened the door and they stepped into the dark, slightly mildewy interior. He turned on a light and together they wandered through the two-bedroom ranch.

Jack noted that the place was filled with pictures of Melanie at various ages—birthdays and graduations, mostly; no sports or dancing school shots—and always that *Must*-you-take-my-picture? expression. The walls of her old bedroom were still hung with framed academic achievement certificates. A bright child, and obviously cherished by her folks.

"Where's this 'odd' something you mentioned?" Jack said.

"Down in the basement. This way."

Through the tiny kitchen, down a narrow set of stairs to an unfinished basement. Lew stopped at the bottom of the steps and pointed at the floor.

"There. Don't you think that's odd?"

All Jack saw was a rope ladder lying on the floor. A typical fire safety type with nylon rope and cylindrical wooden treads, sold in any hardware store. Other than the fact that it was kind of short and in the basement of a ranch house, he couldn't see anything odd about—

Wait. Were his eyes playing tricks on him, or did the end of the ladder disappear into the floor?

Jack stepped closer for a better look.

"I'll be damned."

The bottom end of the rope ladder was imbedded in

the concrete of the floor slab. Jack squatted and tugged on the last visible tread—no give at all. He looked back along the ladder and saw that the top end was tied to a steel support column.

"What's this all about?"

"Beats me," Lew said, stepping closer and standing beside him. "I've never been down here before yesterday, so I can't say how long that's been there."

Jack scratched the front of his shirt. He chest had begun to itch.

"Can't be long," he said, touching the nylon cord. "This ladder is new."

"But the concrete isn't," Lew said. "These houses were built shortly after World War Two. This slab's got to be at least fifty years old."

"Can't be. Look at this. It's obvious the concrete was poured around the ladder."

"Look at the concrete, Jack. This is *old*."

Jack had to admit he was right. The concrete was cracked, chipped, obviously old. And Jack could find no telltale seam that would indicate a recent patch.

"What we have here," Jack said, "is what you call a mystery."

As he was straightening, Jack noticed a small dark splotch on the concrete. He leaned closer. Half-dollar sized, black, irregular, flared on its edges, it looked like some sort of scorch mark. He scanned the rest of the nearby floor and found seven more, evenly spaced in a three-foot area around where the ladder disappeared into the concrete.

"Any idea what might have made these?"

"Not the slightest," Lew said.

Jack rose and looked around. Two steel columns supported the central beam; the foot of the staircase was attached to one of them. Not much else: a washer and dryer, a sump pump in the corner, a sagging couch against the rear wall, a rickety old desk, a folded card table and some chairs. Jack went to the desk. An electric screwdriver, a wrench, a dozen or so nuts and bolts sat on the top, along with three large, oblong, amber quartz crystals. The drawers were empty.

Still scratching at his chest, he turned and stared at the rope ladder. Something about this really bothered him, but did it have anything to do with Melanie Ehler's disappearance? Jack couldn't see how.

"All right," he said. "Let's go back upstairs."

"I told you there was nothing here," Lew said, once they reached the kitchen.

"That you did."

Lew's cell phone rang. While he spoke to someone in California about a late shipment, Jack wandered back to Melanie's bedroom, looking at the photos, trying to get a feel for her. No pics with other kids, only adults, undoubtedly family members. Not a lot of smiles in those pictures. A serious child.

He opened a closet and pulled a box off the shelf. A bunch of old dolls, Barbie and the like, some dressed, some not. He was about to put it back when he noticed that one of the dolls was missing its left hand. Not broken off or cut off . . . more like whittled off, ending in a point.

Odd . . .

He pulled out another and found its left hand whittled away as well. And the others—each missing its left hand. Some forearms had concentric grooves near the end, as if they'd been stuck in a pencil sharpener.

Beyond odd into very weird.

Jack returned the box and stared at the ten- or twelve-year-old girl in one of the larger photos. Dark hair and dark, piercing eyes, and somewhat pretty. Why

aren't you happy, kid? Can someone make you smile?
Where are you now? And why do you want only me to
look for you?

Jack was hooked now. He was going to have to find
this strange lady and ask her face to face.

He wandered back to the kitchen as Lew was finish-
ing his call.

"Sorry," Lew said. "That call couldn't wait."

"Speaking of calls," Jack said, "is there anybody we
can call that Melanie might have called? A friend? A
relative?"

"No relatives, but she did have one childhood friend
in Monroe she kept in touch with. His name's Frayne
Canfield. He's in SESOUP too."

"All right. Let's get in touch with him."

Lew shrugged and called information on his cell
phone, punched in a number, listened for a moment,
then broke the connection.

"His answering machine says he'll be out of town for
a few days but he'll be checking his messages."

Interesting, Jack thought. Mel's away . . . her old
friend's away. . . .

"What are you thinking?" Lew said.

As he spoke, Jack stared out the kitchen window at
the backyard where an old swing set rusted under
another big oak. The itching on his chest seemed to have
eased.

"I'm thinking that people disappear for two reasons:
they run away or are abducted. Either way, in almost
every case, someone they know is involved. Yet all the
people Melanie 'knows' except for you and this Frayne
Canfield are spread all over the globe."

"Not this week, they're not. Most of them, including
Frayne Canfield, I'm sure, will be in Manhattan for the
first annual SESOUP conference."

Lew started toward the front door. Jack followed.

"Is that where she promised to 'blow all other theories out of the water' with her Grand Unification Theory?"

"The very same."

"And Roma will be there too, I assume?"

"Of course. He put it all together."

Jack felt as if a weight suddenly had been lifted from his shoulders. All the possible suspects in one place—perfect.

"When's it start and how do I get into this conference?"

"Day after tomorrow, but you can't get in. Members only—and only one guest each."

"Then I'll be yours."

"I'm not a member. I'm Mel's guest."

"Why so restrictive?"

"I told you—it's very exclusive. This is serious business for them."

"I want you to get me in."

"Why? Mel won't be there."

"Yeah, but I bet the person who knows where she is will be."

"Yes," Lew said, his Adam's apple moving in and out as he nodded. "I can see that. I'll see what I can work out. But you'll need a cover story."

As they stepped out the front door, movement on the street caught Jack's eye. At the far corner of the property to his right, a black sedan began pulling away from the curb. He watched its rear end coast away.

He wondered about that. Had they been followed? He didn't remember seeing any cars parked on the street when he arrived.

"Why do I need a cover story?" he asked Lew.

"I assume you're not planning to go up to people and ask them if they've seen Melanie Ehler lately."

"Well, no. I figure you'll introduce me around—"

"But you need a reason to be there and a connection

to Mel. I'll think on it. The conference is in the Clinton Regent—you know the place?"

"Vaguely. Not exactly the Waldorf."

Far from it. If Jack remembered correctly, the Clinton Regent was in Hell's Kitchen.

"Well, SESOUP's membership isn't exactly poor, but the typical midtown room rate is over two hundred dollars a night, plus twenty-five percent additional in taxes. That would strain a lot of budgets. Roma got the Regent to give us a more affordable rate if we could fill the whole hotel, which we will."

"Okay. I'll see you there Thursday morning. What time?"

"Registration opens at noon. Meet me in the lobby around eleven-thirty. I'll have something cooked up for you by then."

They parted—Lew heading back to Shoreham, Jack to Manhattan.

He rubbed his fingers against his pants leg. Why couldn't he get them to feel dry?

7

He awakens feeling wet. He turns on the light and sees that his sheets are red. He leaps from the bed with a cry of alarm. The sheets, top and bottom, are *soaked* with red, so are his shorts and T-shirt.

Blood. But whose?

Then he notices that his right palm is full of thick red liquid . . . trickling from his index and middle fingertips—the ones that touched Melanie Ehler's painting earlier. Squeezing the fingers to stanch the flow, he hurries to the bathroom, but stops halfway when he spots the easel and canvas set up in the center of his front room.

He stares in cold shock. Where the hell did that come from? This is his home, his fortress. Who could have—?

As Jack steps warily into the front room, he recognizes the painting. He saw it earlier at Lew Ehler's house, the disturbing one in Melanie's study, only now the glistening impasto swirls are alive on the canvas, twisting and contorting into Gordian tangles of black and purple pigment, and from deep within the kinetic madness of those tortured coils, meteoric crescents of yellow glare briefly, then disappear.

Jack rotates slowly, searching for the intruder, and when he completes the turn, he sees that the canvas has changed—no, is *changing* as he watches. The color is leaking away, draining like a tainted transfusion from a befouled IV bottle into a pool on the rug before the easel. The stain spreads quickly, too quickly for Jack to step back and avoid it. But instead of feeling pigment ooze against his bare toes, he feels nothing—nothing against his skin, nothing but air beneath his soles.

Jack windmills his arms wildly, reaching for something, anything to stop his fall. Somehow the paint has eaten through his floor and he's plunging into the apartment below. He twists, clutches at the edge of the hole, but his fingers slip on the slick pigment and he plummets into the waiting darkness.

He lands catlike, in a crouch, and knows immediately that he's not in the second floor apartment. Neil the anarchist may not be a personal hygiene poster boy, but he's never smelled *this* bad. Jeez, what is it? Choice strips of three-day-old roadkill folded into rotten eggs and left out in the sun to warm might come close.

And worse . . . Jack recognizes it.

But it can't be.

And then he realizes that he's not crouching on wood flooring or carpet, but metal grating—cold, and slick with a sheen of engine oil. Some sort of catwalk. He looks up—a tangle of ducts and wiring, but no sign of the hole that dropped him here. And from far below . . . light—faint, flickering off the steel plates of the inner walls of a ship's hull. . . .

"Shit!" Jack whispers.

He knows where he is—the *Ajit-Ruprobati*. But it can't be. *Not* possible. He sank this rustbucket and everyone aboard it—human and non-human—last summer. This old freighter rests and rusts now in the silt of lower New York Harbor. No way he can be aboard it. . . .

Which means this must be a dream. But it sure as hell doesn't feel like one. He had nightmares about this place and the creatures it harbored for months after he damn near died sinking it, but never this real.

The creatures . . . the rakoshi . . . Jack feels every muscle in his body recoil at the thought of them. If the ship is back and awash with their stink, then they too must have returned from the Land of the Dead.

Movement below catches his eye. Jack freezes as a massively muscled, shark-snouted creature glides along another catwalk directly below his. It stands six or seven feet tall and the flickering light plays over its glistening cobalt skin as it moves with sinuous grace.

A rakosh.

Jack wants to scream. This isn't happening. He killed these creatures, incinerated every damn one of them in this very hold last summer. But Jack doesn't dare even to breathe. Hold statue-still until it passes, then find a way out—fast.

But as the creature moves beneath him, it slows, then stops. In a strobe-flash of motion it whirls into a hissing crouch, its head darting back and forth as it sniffs the fetid air.

Does it sense *me*? Jack wonders as his heart races even faster. Or does it simply sense something different?

The rakosh tips back its shark-like head and looks up. As Jack gazes into the glowing yellow slits of its eyes, he fights a primal urge to jump up and run screaming from this abomination.

I'm in the dark up here, he tells himself, forcing calm. I'm on the far side of this steel mesh. If I don't breathe, don't blink, it won't see me. It'll move on.

Finally, it happens, just as he hoped. The creature lowers its head and looks around, indecisive. It turns, but as it starts to move away, Jack sees something falling through the mesh of his perch. Something small . . . globular . . . red.

A drop of his blood.

He watches in horror as the ruby bead drifts like a snowflake toward the rakosh's head, splatters against its snout. He cannot move as a dark tongue snakes from a lipless mouth and licks the smear, leaving no trace.

What happens next is blurred: a hiss, the flash of bared teeth, a three-taloned hand thrusting up, bursting through the steel mesh as if it were window screen, grabbing Jack's bloody hand and yanking it down through the opening. Jack cries out in terror and pain as his right shoulder slams against the mesh. He tries to wrench his hand free but the rakosh's grip is like a steel band.

And then he feels something writhe against his hand, something cool and wet, with the texture of raw liver.

Jack looks down and sees the rakosh licking the blood off his hand. Flooded with revulsion, he tries to grab the slimy tongue, to rip the damn thing out of the creature's head, but it's too slippery.

And then he sees other forms emerging from the

shadows, converging from both ends of the catwalk below. More rakoshi. They begin to fight over his hand, baring their fangs and snapping at each other. The tugging on his arm grows increasingly fierce until Jack begins to fear they'll rip his arm out of its socket.

Then one of the creatures rears up and bites into Jack's forearm. He screams with the blinding agony of razor teeth slicing through skin and muscle, crunching through bone, and then it's gone—the lower half of his forearm, his hand, his wrist, all gone—and the rakoshi are lifting their heads and opening their cavernous maws to lap the crimson rain spewing from the stump.

Helpless, his consciousness fading, Jack watches his life draining away. . . .

"No!"

Jack sat up in bed, gripping his right arm. He fumbled for the switch on the bedside lamp and turned it. Relief washed through him as he checked his hand— still there, with all five fingers.

And the fingertips—no bleeding. Same with the sheets—no bloodstains.

He flopped back, gasping. God, what a nightmare. So real. He hadn't dreamed about those demons since . . . must have been sometime late last year that he'd stopped having rakoshi-mares. What had brought one on tonight? Melanie's painting had been in the dream. Had that triggered it? Why? How? He didn't remember seeing anything in it to remind him of those creatures.

He rolled out of bed and padded to the front room. Everything was as he'd left it. He took some comfort from the familiarity of the crowded shelves, but he knew he wasn't going to have an easy time getting back to sleep.

He held up his hand and wiggled the fingers, just to

be sure. He could almost feel a phantom ache in the bones above the wrist where they'd been bitten off in the dream. That shouldn't be. And then he remembered other mangled limbs, plastic limbs—the left arms of little Melanie's Ehler's dolls. Had seeing them been the trigger for losing his hand in the dream?

Sure. Jack could buy that. But why the rakoshi? Why should they return to haunt him now?

He headed for the kitchen. He needed a beer.

WEDNESDAY

I

Still frazzled from last night's dream and his fragmented sleep, Jack struggled out of bed late and checked his voice mail while he nuked a pint of water for coffee. He found two messages waiting: the first was from his father. He groaned when he heard it:

"Jack? Jack? Are you there? You're never home. This is Dad. Please give me a call back. I want to discuss some travel plans."

Travel plans . . . he knew what that was about. Last fall Jack had promised to visit his father in Florida. Here it was spring and he still hadn't made the trip. Not that he had anything against seeing Dad, it was just that he knew his father's ultimate goal was to set up Jack in business down there, "something more stable" than the appliance repair trade he thought his younger son was involved in now.

The second message was also from his father.

"Jack, this is Dad. I don't know if you got my last message—I mean, you never called back—so let me tell you about the trip I'm planning."

Jack listened with a steadily sinking feeling as Dad described his itinerary: He had his reservations all set to leave his retirement development in Florida to visit Jack's sister and her two kids in Philadelphia next week, then hop over and visit Jack's brother in Trenton. Then he dropped the bomb, the dreaded words that struck pure terror into Jack's heart.

". . . and since I'll be back in the Northeast, I

thought I'd swing by New York and spend a couple of days with you."

Stay *here*? He's got to be kidding.

Jack saved the message as a reminder. He'd call back later. Much later. Right now he had to get himself together in time to meet Gia and Vicky for lunch.

He shaved, showered, and left early, figuring a good brisk walk would clear the fuzzies from his head.

Rakoshi-mares . . . he hoped this wasn't the start of a trend.

On the way out he grabbed the book he'd picked up for Vicky. In the downstairs foyer he checked his mailbox and found the annual circular from the local Little League, asking for donations. That time already? He always gave them a generous anonymous donation. Which meant he'd have to start his Little League collection drive soon—the Annual Repairman Jack Park-a-thon.

Jack cut through Central Park, heading for Midtown. He ambled past a pond where two mallards and a drake were nuzzling around a floating "I ♥ NY" bag and a latex surgical glove in search of a snack.

Cooler today; not too many people parking it. A guy sitting on one of the pond bridges breaking up a hot dog roll and splitting it between the ducks on the water below and the sparrows and pigeons on the pavement; a woman walking four tiny Italian greyhounds with fleece-lined collars; a couple of hand-holding Rollerbladers flashing by. The path wound between a procession of giant granite domes, weeds sprouting anew from their cracked surfaces; a young woman sat on her raincoat atop one of them, eyes closed, feet tucked into the lotus position, meditating.

In a few weeks the park would be fully awake and people would be sunning themselves on those rocks. The willows, oaks, and maples, along with the ubiquitous tree-sized urban weed, the ailanthus, would be in full leaf. Lovers would be walking hand in hand, guys would be tossing Frisbees, parents would be pushing baby carriages; there'd be jugglers and ice cream carts along the paths, couples making out on the benches next to old folks enjoying the shade.

Jack spotted a knot of people near the Shakespeare statue. At first he thought it might be one of the hawkers who specialized in thirty-five-dollar Louis Vuitton bags and twenty-buck Rolexes; they'd been pretty much chased off Fifth Avenue in the past few years, but they hadn't gone away. Then he spotted the two sliders on the cub, grimly eyeing the paths.

Jack smiled. A monte game. He loved to watch these.

He was still fifty feet away but one of the sliders had locked onto him as a possible incoming "d." The guy and his partner a dozen feet further down looked barely eighteen and sported the big-puffy-jacket, los-ing-my-pants, and I-forgot-how-to-tie-my-sneakers look. The nearer slide's hair was faded and his Yankee cap was facing the wrong way; his black face gave away nothing, but Jack knew his quick dark eyes were doing a laser-sharp read of his clothes, gait, his entire demeanor.

I'll be highly insulted if you think I'm a plainclothes dick, Jack thought.

He slowed his pace and put on a curious expression. If this was a typical monte set up, there'd be five guys in the team. Two "slides," or lookouts; a pair of "sticks" acting as shills, and a "shaker" working the caps and ball at the cardboard table.

If the slide thought Jack was trouble, that was the word he'd shout: "Slide!" And then the team would fold up its boxes and melt away.

But Jack must have passed muster because no alarm was raised as he approached. He slowed to a crawl as he passed, craning his neck for a peek at the action. Then he stopped but hung back as if uncertain about whether he'd be welcome.

A tall thin black guy in a dark blue knit cap glanced at him, then started yelling at the shaker.

"Hey, I wanna turn. You lettin' this guy have all the fun. Gimme my turn now. You got forty dollah mine. Lemme get it back." He turned to Jack. "Hey, bro. C'mere and watch this. Gonna break the bank, yo."

Jack glanced around with a he-isn't-talking-to-me-is-he? expression, then turned back to Knitcap. He pointed his finger at his own chest.

"Yeah, you," Knitcap said. A large gold bulldog hung on a heavy braided gold chain around his neck. "I want you to watch and make sure this guy ain't cheatin' me."

Jack took a hesitant step forward, then stopped.

Another tall black, bareheaded and grinning, moved aside to make room for Jack. "Right here, man."

Okay. Jack knew the sticks now. And from the size and number of the gold rings on their hands, business must be good lately.

"Winnin' ain't sinnin'," said the shaker at the center of the semicircle, a black ferret in a dark blue hoodie, hunched behind the makeshift cardboard table. In his mid-twenties, he was the old man of the crew, and its leader. "I repeat, I never cheat, I'm just the one you gotta beat."

Jack shrugged. Might as well join the crowd. This would be a good dose of reality to help banish the rakoshi remnants from last night.

He moved into the opening, bringing the number of marks up to three. To his right stood a Hispanic couple looking about thirty; the guy had a mullet haircut and wore a diamond earring; the woman had a round face and shiny black hair pulled back into a tight bun.

"Awright!" said Knitcap with a welcoming grin. "Keep your eyes open now, yo."

Jack smiled, accepting the welcome. Sure, they were glad to see him: fresh meat. Knitcap didn't want him as an extra pair of eyes watching the shaker; he wanted another sucker at the table. Jack slipped Vicky's book inside his shirt and watched the action.

He figured monte had to be five thousand years old, much older than its more common cousin, three-card monte. Somebody using three walnut shells and a dried pea probably had ripped off the pharaoh's workers during breaks between hauling stone blocks to the pyramids. The modern day version substituted white plastic Evian caps and a little handmade ball of rouge, but the object was the same: find a sucker and fleece him.

The shaker leaned over a piece of cardboard supported on two cardboard boxes. He clutched a thin stack of tens and twenties in his left hand, secured by his middle, ring, and little fingers, leaving his thumb and index finger free to manipulate the caps and ball. His hands flew back and forth, crisscrossing over and under as his nimble fingers lifted and dropped the caps, skedaddling the little ball back and forth, a flash of red appearing and vanishing, but not so quickly you couldn't see where it came to rest.

That was the whole point, of course. Let the marks think they had a lock on the ball's location.

Jack ignored the ball and listened to the shaker's patter. That was where the real action was. That was how he communicated with his sticks.

"Watch till you're blind, no tricks will you find. I pay forty if you put down twenny. Forty down earns a hunnert, and believe me that's plenty. The ball goes around, it hides and it shows. It goes in, it goes out, till nobody knows. Forty's come to play, now cop me the money. You cry when I win, I laugh 'cause it's funny."

Hidden in the chatter was a set of precise instructions to Knitcap.

Jack never played monte, but out of curiosity he'd made a practice of eavesdropping on shaker patter whenever he had the chance. They all used a similar code, and by careful watching and listening he'd managed to break it.

"Cop" told the stick to win, "blow" to lose. "Money" signaled the cap near his left hand where the shaker held his money, although Jack had heard other shakers call it "rich." "See" was the middle cap, "switch" was the one on the other end from the money hand.

By loading his riff with "forty's come to play, now cop me the money," the shaker was telling Knitcap to bet forty bucks and win by picking the cap near the shaker's left hand.

Sure enough, Knitcap bet forty bucks, found the rouge ball under the cap next to the money hand, and collected a hundred dollars.

"I'm no sinner," the shaker announced. "We have a winner!"

Knitcap was all smiles. "I'm up!" He pointed his money at Jack. "You my good luck, yo. You wanna play, I'll watch for you."

Before Jack could decline, the Hispanic guy jumped in. "Hey, no. It's me this time. I'm down."

"Santo, you've lost enough," said his wife. At least Jack assumed it was his wife. Both wore wedding rings.

"Hey, how about me?" said Nocap, close on Jack's left.

"Let's not fight, I'll make things right," said the shaker as he started the skedaddle again. "Everybody gets a turn, I'm a man with time to burn."

Santo dropped two twenties onto the cardboard. The shaker kept up his chatter but no instructions now since neither stick was in the game. He shuffled the caps, skittering the ball between them, demonstrating absolute control. But just before he stopped he let the rouge ball slow so that everyone could see it come to rest under the middle cap.

"Didja see it?" whispered Nocap.

"Yep," Jack said.

Doing your damnedest to lure me in, aren't you.

Jack watched closely as the shaker slid the three caps forward and arranged them along the front of the cardboard. Jack knew that was when the ball would be moved from under the cap to the web between the shaker's thumb and forefinger. He was expecting the transfer, looking for it, but still didn't spot it. This guy was slick.

The shaker said, "There they are, lined up tight. Forty pay a hunnert if you pick it right."

Santo didn't hesitate. He pointed to the center cap.

The shaker lifted it—nothing. He lifted the other two and . . . out rolled the little red ball from under the one in his right hand.

Santo pounded his fist against his thigh and cursed in Spanish.

"Okay," said his wife, tugging on his arm. "That's it. That's a hundred twenty dollars you lost now."

Knitcap stepped around, blocking their retreat, and started yelling at the shaker. "Hey, yo, you gotta give this guy another chance!"

Nocap chimed in. "Yeah, man. Give him a double or nothing so he can get even at least!"

Knitcap added. "What he said. Help this guy out or I'm walking!"

Let the sucker go, Jack thought. You've soaked him enough.

Apparently they didn't think so.

The shaker shrugged. "Awright, awright. He puts down fifty he can win back his one-twenty."

What, no rhymes? Jack thought.

"No, Santo," said the wife.

But Santo had the fever. He popped his diamond earring into his hand and held it out.

"I got no more cash. How 'bout this?"

"No!" his wife gasped. "I bought you that!"

The shaker took the earring, held the tiny diamond up, twisting it this way and that in the light.

Say no, Jack thought, sending the shaker a mental message. Let him go.

The shaker shrugged. "Awright," he said with almost believable reluctance. "I'll make an exception this once."

"Mah man!" Knitcap said, slapping Santo on the back. "You gonna win! I can smell winnin' in the air!"

Jack ground his teeth. Sons of bitches.

The woman wailed. "Santo!"

"Don't worry," Santo told her. "I won't lose it."

Oh, yes you will, Jack thought, but could say nothing.

He fumed as he watched the shaker put the earring on the cardboard and begin the skedaddle. One thing to fleece a sucker. Rules of the street were, someone stupid enough to bet on a game like this deserved to lose, and Jack had no quarrel with that. Sort of a tax on the street impaired. But there were limits. You collected the tax and moved the guy along. It was stone cold to suck him dry, especially in front of his woman.

Jack usually ran his Annual Park-a-thon for the Little League at night, but he was incensed enough now to make an exception for this monte crew.

He studied the sticks, then turned and checked out the slides. Most likely they were all carrying knives;

none of them looked to be packing heat, but damn near impossible to tell under those bulky coats.

He made a decision as he turned back to the game: He would accept a donation from these generous fellows, allowing them the honor of being the first contributors to this year's Little League fund.

He felt his pulse quicken a little. He hadn't come prepared for this. Usually he avoided spur-of-the-moment gigs, but the opportunity was here, so why not grab it?

Jack watched the shaker and his flying hands. Same routine as before, then the caps were pushed forward.

"Didja see it?" Nocap whispered again.

"Sure did," Jack said, nodding and smiling, looking like a guy taking the bait and waiting to be reeled in.

Santo picked the money cap, but the ball rolled out from under the center cap.

"Shit!"

His wife wailed again as the earring disappeared into the shaker's pocket.

"Hang on a sec," Jack said, grabbing the stricken Santo's arm as he turned to go.

"No!" the wife shouted, her voice rising in pitch. "No more!"

"Please," Jack said. "I think I've got this figured and I want witnesses. I'll make it worth your while when I win."

Jack was telling the truth. He didn't want to be alone at the table when he played.

The possibility of salvaging *something* from their disaster changed their minds, and Santo and his wife nodded. He looked sullen, chastened; she stood teary eyed with her arms folded across her chest.

"Great," Jack said. He turned to Nocap and said, "You were next, I believe."

"Hey, no, that's okay," Nocap said, grinning. "Be my

guest. Wanna see if you really do got this thing scoped, yo. 'Cause then you can tell me."

"Thanks." Jack pulled two fifties from his wallet. "What does this get me?"

"Two-fifty," the shaker said.

"Come on," Jack said. "A hundred bucks on one play—that should get me at least three hundred."

"Sorry, man. Two-fifty's the limit."

"Hey, yo, c'mon," said Knitcap, playing his advocate's role to the hilt. "Pay the guy three!"

Jack said, "How about two-fifty and the earring?"

"Yeah!" said Nocap. "That's fair!"

"Awright," said the shaker with another of his put-upon shrugs, making a show of reluctantly bowing to pressure.

Truth was, Jack could have been asking for five hundred and it wouldn't have mattered—no way, no how was the sucker going to win—but he didn't want to push it too far.

"But I need to know if you've got two-fifty," Jack said.

"I got it," the shaker said, holding up the stack in his left hand.

Jack shook his head. "If my money's on the table, so's yours. And the earring with it."

Another shrug, but wary this time. "Awright. If that's the way you wants to play, what else is there for me to say?"

Jack laid his money down. The shaker counted out two-fifty in tens and twenties next to Jack's bills, then dropped the earring on top.

"If everything's okay with you, now I got my work to do."

"Just one more thing," Jack said. He turned to Santo and his wife. "I want you two on either side of me, watching, okay?"

He centered himself on the makeshift table, then positioned Santo on his right and the wife on his left.

"All right," he told the couple. "Don't let that ball out of your sight."

"Now are we ready?" the shaker said.

Jack nodded. "Okay. Do it."

Jack felt his muscles coil as the shaker started his yammer and went into the skedaddle. Finally he stopped, pushed the caps forward.

"The ball is hidden in its groove. Time for you to make your move."

Jack took a deep, tension-easing breath, then squared himself in front of the table. He pointed at the caps with both index fingers, moving them in circles as if they were fleshy divining rods.

"I choose . . . I choose . . . "

He moved his hands closer to the caps.

". . . I choose . . . "

Closer . . . quick glances at the positions of the sticks . . .

Then he struck.

". . . the middle!"

With one lightning move he overturned the two end caps, shouted, "I win!" when no ball showed, then snatched up the two piles of bills and the earring.

"What the fuck?" said Nocap.

Jack was already moving as he shoved the earring into Santo's hand.

"Bye."

"Hey!" yelled the shaker.

"That's okay," Jack said, backpedaling away down the path. "I don't need to see the ball. I trust you."

He turned and broke into a jog. Behind him he heard Santo laugh. He glanced back and saw his wife hugging him. He also saw Knitcap and one of the slides starting after him.

He quickened his pace. He knew he wasn't going to lose them. Fifth Avenue was less than a hundred yards away, but even if he got there ahead of them, that wouldn't stop them. They'd jump him on the sidewalk and take back the money. Or try to. Jack didn't want to deal with them in public; witnesses could describe him, a camera-toting tourist might even snap a photo. Or worst case—a cop might come to his rescue.

No, he'd have to deal with both of them here. He needed a spot where they'd think they had him all to themselves. And up ahead he saw just the place.

He hopped over a low fence onto the grass and half ran, half slid down a steep slope to a lower walkway that ran into a short tunnel beneath the path he'd been on. He stopped midway in the brick-lined underpass and ducked into one of the shallow arched recesses that lined the walls. He pulled his Semmerling LM-4 from its ankle holster and stuck it in the side pocket of his jeans for easier access.

He was hoping he wouldn't have to use it—that simply showing it would be enough. Trouble with the world's smallest .45 automatic was its size. People saw it and thought it was a toy. But it packed a wallop, especially loaded as it was the MagSafe Defenders.

The frangible loads gave Jack the option of inflicting a disabling wound—say, to the thigh—or an almost guaranteed kill with a shot anywhere into the chest. And he didn't have to worry about the bullet coming out the other side and hitting an innocent passerby—frangibles did devastating damage to their target, but stayed put.

He was making a show of counting his money when they found him.

"Awright, mothahfuckah," Knitcap said. He held a six-inch blade point down by his right thigh.

Jack slid his hand toward the Semmerling pocket but

stopped it halfway there. He'd been expecting knives; he hadn't expected the pearl-handled .38 revolver in the young slide's hand.

"Yeah," said the slide, pointing the pistol at Jack's head. "Yeah!"

For one frozen, heart-stopping, bladder-squeezing second as the barrel lined up with his face, Jack thought he was going to die. He saw murder in the slide's face. The kid was all of seventeen, but his cold dark eyes said he hadn't been a real kid for a long time.

But Jack calmed somewhat when he saw how the kid was holding it. Maybe he'd been watching too many gangsta videos, or bad shoot-'em-up flicks. Whatever the reason, the slide was holding his pistol sideways . . . *beyond* sideways—he'd rotated it a good 150 degrees so that the heel of the grip was higher than the barrel. And he had his ring and pinky fingers sticking up in the air like he was having afternoon tea.

When he was ready to pull the trigger he'd need to get a firmer grip or risk having the pistol jump out of his hand.

So Jack figured he was safe for the moment—the kid was stylin' now, showing off for the older stick—but as soon as those waving fingers wrapped themselves around the grip . . .

What now? Look scared, then attack? The one thing he could not afford to do was the expected.

"You lunched?" the kid said. "That what wrong with you? That what make you think you get away with this shit?"

Jack's mind raced as his eyes fixed on the snub-nose revolver—looked like a custom job, nickel plated with curlicue engravings all over it. A pretty piece, despite the fact that its muzzle was pointed at Jack's face.

"Hey-hey-hey," Jack said in a frantic voice that

wasn't completely put on. He thrust his hands out in front of him, money and all, as if to hold them off. "No need for violence!"

"Yeah?" said Knitcap through his teeth. He stepped closer and Jack raised his hands over his head. "You think I *like* chasin' you 'bama ass around?"

"I won fair and square!"

"That ain't the way we play." He stuck the point of his knife against Jack's throat. "Maybe we just cut your thumbs off so this never be a problem again."

"Or maybe I just one-eighty-seven you," the slide said, pushing the pistol closer to Jack's face. "Bust one in you face so you don't even *think* about trying this shit again!"

The revolver was so close now that Jack could see the tips of the bullets in its cylinder. His stomach gave a twist when he recognized the little posts in the center of the jacketed hollow points: Hydra-Shoks. He had a nightmare flash of what would happen if he took one of those in the face as threatened—he watched the rim of the hollow nose peel back from that central post into a wide-winged lead butterfly, saw it flutter though his brain, bouncing off the inner walls of his skull, pureeing the contents.

Think-think-think! Where's the hammer? Down. Good. If and when the kid fired, the trigger would need a double-action pull . . . just a teeny bit more pressure to get off the shot. Wasn't much, but every little bit helped.

A little closer . . . Jack had to bring that pistol just a little closer . . .

Very aware of the blade point just to the left of his voice box, he nodded carefully at the sideways pistol. "Uh, I assume you know that's not the recommended way to hold a pistol."

"What?" the slide said, his eyes widening. *"What?"*

"I said—"

"I know what you said. And now I *know* you fuckin' lunched! I hold a gun in you face and you tell me I'm holding it *wrong?*" He glanced at Knitcap. "Ay yo trip—he miss his medication today or somethin'?"

"No," Jack said. "It's just that it's not a secure grip."

The slide stepped closer, rage lighting in his eyes as he yanked back the hammer. But he didn't change his grip—he wasn't going to let anyone tell him how to hold *his* gun. Stylin' to the end.

"Don't you be tellin' me—"

"Here!" Jack cried in a high, terrified voice, releasing the bills he held over his head and scattering them into the air. "Take the money!"

In the instant their attention shifted to the money, Jack batted Knitcap's knife away with his left hand while whipping his right hand down at the slide's pistol. He caught the stubby barrel and the trigger guard, ramming the pistol back and down as he twisted. The weapon tore free and Jack switched it to his left hand.

And pointed it—right side up—at Knitcap just in time to abort a backhand slash at Jack's face with the knife.

"Uh-uh."

Knitcap froze. The slide looked down at his empty hand, then back at his pistol in Jack's, his expression a study in shock and confusion.

"Oh, fuck!" said Knitcap and turned to run.

"Don't want to shoot you in the back," Jack said, flipping the pistol to his right hand, "but I will." He touched a wet, stinging spot on his throat. His fingers came away bloody. "Especially after you cut me. Dammit!"

Knitcap mustered a sick sounding, "Shit!" as he dropped his knife. He looked at Jack's throat. "It's only a scratch, man."

Jack stepped out of the recess to where he could better cover both men.

Out of the corner of his eye he saw a jogger approach the underpass, realize what was going down, make a quick U-turn, and sprint away.

Knitcap glanced angrily at the slide. "How the *fuck* you let that happen?"

The slide said nothing.

"You fuckin' b-g!" Knitcap went on. "You had the gun in his face and let it go?"

"As I was saying," Jack told the former gun owner, "that's a stupid way to hold a pistol. Not secure at all." He gestured to the ground. "Okay, guys. Have a seat."

The slide finally spoke. "Fuck you!"

Jack lowered the pistol and shot him in the foot. The report echoed like a cannon blast in the tunnel as the slide cried out and fell to the ground, moaning, rolling, and clutching his abruptly four-toed foot.

Knitcap was down in a sitting position before the sound of the shot had completely faded away. He held his hands in the air.

"I'm down! I'm sittin'!"

Jack knew the appearance of the jogger had set a timer in motion, and the sound of the shot would only accelerate that. The underpass would funnel the report right toward Fifth Avenue. He had to figure someone in that direction had heard it, and was probably dialing 911 right now. Times like this, Jack hated cell phones.

Had to move fast.

"All right. Both of you—empty your pockets. I want to see everything you've got, even the lint. Put it all in Mr. Smith and Wesson's Yankee hat."

Slowly, grudgingly, Knitcap complied, but the slide wouldn't let go of his bloody foot.

"I can't, man!" he moaned. "My foot!"

"Weren't you the tough guy gonna bust one in my face a minute ago?" Jack said. "You can get along fine with nine toes, but let's see how far you'll get with one knee, because that's where I bust the next one if you don't start emptying pockets now!"

The slide got to it. Another knife appeared, extra rounds for the pistol, some change, and about a hundred in small bills between them.

"Don't forget the rings and necklaces," Jack said.

"Aw, not my dog, man," said Knitcap.

"You're obviously a betting man," Jack said, pointing the pistol at his neck. "How much you wanna bet I can shoot that big fat chain holding the dog without hitting your neck?"

With a sullen look he tugged off the rings and tossed them into the cap. Then with a look of utter misery, he grabbed the gold bulldog, broke the chain, and dropped it into the cap with the rest. He punched the back of the slide's shoulder—hard.

"Told you to let me handle it, but no, you gotta bring out the fuckin' chrome."

The slide just clutched his bloody sneaker and said nothing.

Jack bent, retrieved the cash he'd dropped, then picked up the hat.

"Nice doing business with you guys," he said, then trotted off, leaving them sitting in the shadows.

He didn't expect them to come after him again. After all, they were unarmed now and one of them wasn't walking too well. And at the moment they were probably lots more interested in getting out of the park before the cops came, then coming up with a good story for the shaker as to why they were returning bloody footed and empty handed.

Jack shoved the take into his pockets, then pressed

the cap against his bleeding throat as he slowed to an energetic walk. Not a lot of blood there, but enough to attract attention.

He felt a little shaky from the adrenaline aftereffects. Too close back there. He'd been lucky. It could have come out a lot worse—the slide could have simply shot him on sight and Jack would have been done.

Why had he given in to a spur-of-the-moment gig? It went against all his rules. These things had to be planned. Stupid, stupid, stupid.

He passed the statue of Balto the sled dog, then angled past the zoo. By the time he'd climbed the steps to Fifth at Sixty-fourth Street, he'd calculated that his little haul probably would add up to over a thousand after he hocked the gun, knives, and jewelry. The Little Leaguers ought to be able to buy lots of uniforms and equipment with that.

He doubted they'd want the bloodstained Yankee cap, though.

2

"A couple of days and then he'll be on his way back to Florida," Gia said. "You survived this food . . . you can survive your father."

She glanced up at him with her azure eyes, then returned to flipping through the *Little Orphan Annie* book. Jack had picked up the Fantagraphics collection of all the strips from 1935 along with the Daddy War-bucks lamp. He'd bought it for Vicky but Gia immedi-ately had taken possession of it.

Blond and beautiful, she sat across from him at a tiny table far from the big street-front windows. The remains of three lunches lay scattered and mostly eaten before them. Vicky, Gia's daughter, had had a hamburger; Gia, complaining that all the salads had meat, had finally settled for some vegetarian chili. Jack had ordered the Harley Hog Special—a mass of pulled pork stuffed into a roll.

"What *is* pulled pork, anyway?" Gia said, looking askance at the scraps left on his plate.

"It's the other white meat."

"Cooking a pig sounds nasty enough, but why *pull* it?"

"I think they cook it on the bone, then grab handfuls and—"

"Stop right there. Please. Oh, and look," she said, folding her paper napkin and reaching across the table, "your Band-Aid is oozing a little."

He let her dab at his throat.

"That must have been some shaving cut. What were you using—a machete?"

"Just careless."

Jack was still unsettled and annoyed at himself for getting hurt. He'd picked up some Band-Aids at a drug-store on Seventh Avenue, and cleaned the wound in the bathroom of a McDonald's. It wasn't deep, but it had needed two Band-Aids to cover it.

He hadn't actually said it was a shaving cut—he hated lying to Gia—but he hadn't corrected her when she arrived at that conclusion. She tended to overreact when he got hurt, going on about how easily it could have been so much worse, how he could have been killed. Sometimes that led to an argument.

A shaving cut was good.

"There!" she said, balling up the napkin. "All cleaned up."

"I had a rakoshi dream last night," he told her.

They usually avoided talking about the horrific episode last summer that had ended in the deaths of Vicky's two aunts and damn near Vicky herself. But he needed to share this, and Gia was one of the four other people who knew about the creatures.

She looked up at him. "Did you? I'm sorry. I think I've finally stopped having them. But every once in a while Vicky wakes up with the horrors. Was I in it?"

"No."

"Good." She shuddered. "I don't ever want to see one of those things again, not even in someone else's dream."

"Don't worry. You won't. That I can promise you."

Gia smiled and went back to flipping through the *Annie* book; Jack looked around for Vicky. The pigtailed eight-year-old reason they were in this particular place was over by the window, gyrating on a coin-fueled motorcycle ride. A delicate warmth suffused Jack as he watched her pretend she was racing it down some imaginary road. Vicky was the closest he might ever come to having a daughter, and he loved her like his own. Eight years old and no secrets to keep from her mom, just the moment and learning something new every day. That was the life.

"Think she'll grow up to be a biker chick?"

"That's always been my dream for her," Gia said without looking up from the book.

Jack had promised Vicky a lunch out during her grammar school's spring vacation week, and she'd chosen the Harley Davidson Café. Vicky liked all the wheels and chrome; Jack loved the fact that only tourists came here, reducing to near zip his chances of running into someone he knew. Gia had come along as chaperone, to make sure the two of them didn't get into trouble. None of them was here for the food, which was mostly suitable for staving off hunger until the next meal. But as far as Jack was concerned, having the two ladies in his life along transformed any place into Cirque 2000.

"These are really good," Gia said, spending about two seconds per page on the *Little Orphan Annie* book.

"You can't be reading that fast," Jack said.

"No, I mean the art."

"The art? They're drawings."

"Yes, but what he does with just black ink in those little white boxes." She was nodding admiringly. "His composition is superb." She closed the book and looked at its cover. "Who is this guy?"

"Name's Harold Gray. He created her."

"Really? I know *Annie* from the play and the movie, but why haven't I ever heard of him, or seen his strips before?"

"Because your Iowa paper probably didn't carry *Annie* when you were growing up. She'd become passé by the late sixties, and hardly worth reading after Gray died."

"How many strips are there?"

"Well, let's see . . . *Annie* started in the twenties. . . . "

"Wow. He kept this up for forty years?"

"The thirties and forties contain his best stuff. Punjab gets introduced in that book you've got there."

"Punjab?"

"Yeah. The big Indian guy. Geoffrey Holder played him in the film. I've always loved *Little Orphan Annie,* mostly for characters like Punjab and the Asp—you didn't mess with the Asp. This guy Gray is the American Dickens."

"I didn't know you were into Dickens."

"Well . . . I liked him in high school."

"But I can see what you mean," Gia said, flipping again. "He seems to deal with all classes."

"Never thought much of his art, though."

"Think again. This guy is good."

Jack would take her word for it. Gia was an artist, doing commercial stuff like paperback covers and magazine illustrations to pay the bills, but she kept working on paintings on the side, always trying to interest a gallery in showing them.

"I can see Thomas Nast in him," she said. "And I know I've seen some of him in Crumb."

"The underground guy?"

"Definitely."

"You know underground comics?" Jack said.

Gia looked up at him. "If it involves any kind of drawing, I want to know about it. And as for you, I've got to start dragging you to some art shows again."

Jack groaned. She was always after him to go to openings and museums. He gave in now and then, but usually hated most of what he saw.

"If you think it'll help," he said. "But no urinals stuck to the wall or piles of bricks on the floor, okay?"

She smiled. "Okay."

Jack gazed into the wild blue yonder of Gia's eyes. The very sight of her gave him a buzz. She shone like a jewel here. A couple of guys seated near the windows kept looking at her. Jack didn't blame them. He could stare at her all day. She wore little make-up—didn't need any, really—so what he was seeing was really her. Humidity tended to make her blond hair wavy. Because she wore it short, the waves created feathery little wings along the sides around her ears. Gia hated those wings. Jack loved them, and she had a whole bunch of them today. He reached out and stroked a few of the feathers.

"Why did you do that?" she said.

"Just wanted to touch you. Have to keep reassuring myself that you're real."

She smiled that smile, took his hand, and gently bit his index finger.

"Convinced?"

"For now." He held up his tooth-marked finger and wiggled it at her. "Meat, you know. And you a brand-new vegetarian."

He snatched his finger back before she could bite it again.

"I am *not* a vegetarian," she said. "I'm just off meat."

"Not some sort of religious thing? Or a plot against plants?"

"No . . . it's just that lately I've found myself with less of an appetite for things that were walking around under their own power not too long before they landed on my plate. Especially if they resemble what they looked like alive."

"Like a turkey?"

She made a face. "Stop."

"Or better yet, a squab."

"Must you? And by the way, anybody who eats squab in this city should know that they're eating Manhattan pigeon."

"Come on."

"Oh, yes." She dropped her voice to a conspiratorial whisper. "You order squab, they send some guy up to the roof with a net. A few minutes later . . . 'squab.'"

Jack laughed. "Is this sort of like the fur coat thing?"

"Please—let's not discuss fur coats today. Spring is here at last and their vacuous owners will be stuffing them into vaults for the rest of the year."

"Jeez. Can't talk about fur, squab, pulled pork—none of the fun subjects."

"I can think of a fun subject," she said. "How about your father?"

"My turn to say 'Stop.'"

"Come on, now. I've never met him, but he can't be as bad as you make him out."

"He's not bad, he's just relentless. And he can*not* stay with me. You know what my place is like."

Gia nodded. "Like the 168th Street Armory."

"Right. I can't move all that stuff out. No place to stash it. And if he finds any of it—"

"You mean like I did?"

Jack nodded. "Yeah. And you know what happened."

Gia and Jack hadn't been together that long then. He'd told her he was a security consultant. She'd been doing him a favor, a little spring cleaning, when she stumbled onto one of his caches—the one in the false rear of the antique secretary. It almost had broken them up. Even though they were back together now, tighter than ever, Jack still shuddered at how close he had come to losing Gia and Vicky. They were his anchors, his reality checks, the two most important people in the world.

"He's an uptight middle class guy who already thinks his younger son is something of a loser; don't want him thinking he's a gun nut too. Or worse yet, figure out he's been lying to him all these years about being in the appliance repair business."

Gia shook her head and smiled. "You're unbelievable, Jack. Here you've spent your whole adult life cutting yourself free from just about every string society attaches, and yet you still crave your father's approval."

"I don't *crave* it," he said, perhaps a tad too defensively, he realized. "It's just that he's a good man, a genuinely concerned parent, and it bugs me that he thinks I'm some sort of loser. Anybody else—present company excepted, of course—I wouldn't care. But dammit, he's my father. And I can't have him crashing with me."

"Then you should simply say your place is too small and offer to put him up in a hotel for his stay."

"I don't know if that's going to fly." Frustrated, he

groaned and stared at the ceiling. "I'll think of something. I've got to."

"Speaking of thinking," Gia said softly, "you might want to think about making some time in your busy schedule to stop by sometime late Friday morning."

"I don't know, Gi. No telling what's going to be happening. What's up?"

A tiny shrug. "Nothing much. It's just that Vicky's got a play date and she's being picked up at eleven—"

"And we'll have the place to ourselves?"

Those blue eyes locked onto his. "Completely."

Jack grinned. Ooh, yes. "Something just opened up. See you one minute after eleven."

He glanced over to the motorcycle and realized with a start that Vicky was no longer on it. He stiffened and scanned the dining area.

"Relax," Gia said. "She's over there talking to those kids."

Jack looked to where she was pointing and saw Vicky talking to a crowd of children about her age. They all had backpacks and were under the wings of a couple of matronly chaperones. As Jack watched, Vicky led one of the boys over.

"Hey, Jack," she said, grinning. "His name's Jack too!"

"Jacques," the boy said.

"That's what I said. He's from France." She gestured to the group behind her. "They're all from France. They're visiting."

"And where else would they come for fine American cuisine," Jack said. He extended his hand to the little boy and repeated his entire French vocabulary. "*Bonjour,* Jacques."

The kid beamed. "*Bonjour,* Monsieur!" and then went into overdrive Français, incomprehensible to Jack.

Gia answered him in kind and the two of them babbled back and forth for a couple of minutes until his chaperone called him back.

Jack was amazed. "I didn't know you spoke French."

"President of the French club in college."

"It's so . . . sexy. Will you speak French to me on Friday?"

She smiled and patted his hand. "Easy, Gomez."

"I had no idea."

"Well, it's not like I have much chance to use it. French isn't a very useful language in Manhattan."

"Jack," Vicky said, "will you teach me to play baseball?"

"Sure," Jack said. "But I've got to tell you, I wasn't a great player."

"I just want to hit a home run."

"That I can probably help you with."

"Swell!" she said and kissed him on the cheek. Then she ran back to the motorcycle.

"Why the sudden interest in baseball?" Jack said to Gia.

"Not exactly baseball—T-ball. Some of her friends are going out for the local team and she wants to be part of it." She looked at him. "Not a great player? I'd have guessed you for an ace player."

"Nah. Too boring. I could hit it a mile, and that's the only reason I ever made a team. I was a disaster on defense. Coaches moved me all over, infield and out-field, didn't matter—a minute out there and my eyes would glaze over and I'd be daydreaming, asleep on my feet. Or watching the bees and wasps in the clover—I was terrified of being stung."

He smiled at the memory of being literally and figu-ratively out in left field and hearing the crack of a bat against the ball, waking up to see everybody staring at him, the pure terror of realizing the ball was coming his way and not having the faintest clue as to where it was. Stomach-clenching panic as he looked up, searching the bright summer sky for a dark round speck, praying he'd see it, praying even harder he'd catch it, praying hardest it wouldn't land on his head and leave him in a coma.

Ah, the joy of being one of the boys of summer.

"Which reminds me," Gia said, "I hope you're not going out collecting for the West Side Little League again this year."

Uh-oh. "Well . . . it's for a good cause."

She made a face. "Do they know *how* you collect for them?"

"Of course not. They just know I'm their top fundraiser."

"Can't you just go door to door like most people? You could get hurt your way."

He loved the concern in her eyes. "Tell you what. I'll give them whatever I already have put aside for them, and that'll be it for this year. How's that sound?"

"Great," she said. "And what other kind of trouble have you got planned for yourself?"

"Well, there's that guy I told you about."

"With the missing wife?"

"Right. Shouldn't be any rough stuff with that. More like a Sherlock Holmes thing."

"But you're not a detective. Why did she specify you rather than a private eye?"

"She thinks I'm the only one who will 'understand.'"

Gia raised her shoulders. "Don't ask me why, but that gives me the creeps."

Jack reached across and squeezed her hand. "Hey, don't worry. This has all the makings of a Gandhi job— strictly non-violent."

"I've heard that before—and you almost wound up dead."

"Not this time. This one's going to be smooth as glass."

He didn't mention the other customer he'd be meeting with late tonight, however. That might be a different story.

3

"A beauty," Abe said, examining the gleaming Smith and Wesson 649. "Checkered rosewood stocks, even. Very nice. But as you know, my clientele tends to prefer functional over flashy."

Jack had brought the pistol he'd confiscated from the slide to Abe for an appraisal.

"Get the most you can for it," Jack said. "It's for the Little League."

"Will do, but no promises. You should keep it, maybe."

"And what?" Jack slapped a hand over his heart in shock. "Replace my Semmerling?"

"I should suggest you abandon your favorite little baby gun? Never. But maybe consider replacing that Glock 19 you're using lately. After all, the Smitty's a revolver."

Jack rolled his eyes. "Not this again."

"It's a thought."

Abe never had trusted automatics. And he never stopped trying to convert Jack, who leaned toward them.

Jack said, "That thing's heavy and holds only six rounds—five if you keep it down on empty like I tend to do with revolvers. My Glock's small, about as light as they come, and gives me a helluva lot more shots."

"With the kind of close situations you get yourself into, even a lousy shot like you shouldn't need more than three or four rounds. And a revolver will never jam."

"Call it a security blanket. And I've never had a cycling problem. Mainly because you sell me only the best ammo."

"Well, yes," Abe said, thrown off by the compliment. "Quality makes a difference. Speaking of which, how are you fixed for ammo?"

"Pretty good. Why?"

"Just got in some new stock." He pulled a box from under the counter. "Look. Those Magsafe Defenders you're using."

"Great. I'm running low on the .45s."

Jack had been using frangibles like Glaser Silvers and MagSafe Defenders for a while now—hollow point rounds packed with birdshot that released after impact.

"Forty-fives and nines, ready to go."

Jack shook his head, remembering how naïve he'd been when he'd first started in the fix-it business. He'd thought all you had to do was buy a gun and some bullets and that was it.

Not by a long shot. Accuracy, chambering, weight, concealability, number of rounds in the magazine or cylinder, the safety mechanism, the weight of the single-action pull, the weight of the double-action pull, ease of maintenance—all had to be weighed and considered. Then came the ammunition: different situations required different loads. Did he want full metal jackets, jacketed hollowpoints, or frangibles? What size load? Choose from ninety-five to 230 grains. Medium compression or high compression? And don't forget, recoil is directly proportional to the compression of the load and inversely proportional to the weight of the pistol. A lightweight model with +P+ loads will want to fly out of your hand every time you fire.

Jack was still feeling his way.

"Frangibles are nice," Abe said. "But you should be carrying something with more penetration maybe?"

Jack shook his head. He felt safer with the frangibles. "Penetration doesn't equal stopping power in my book."

"Stopping power," Abe said, holding up one of the Defender rounds. "That they've got."

"I'll pick some up tomorrow. I don't want to be carrying them around with me the rest of the day."

"Big wounds," Abe said, speaking to the gleaming bullet in his hand. "Deep as a well and wide as a church door."

"They're good," Jack said, "but I think that's overstating it a little, don't you?"

"That was Shakespeare, sort of."

"Shakespeare? No kidding. I didn't know he used frangibles."

Jack backed toward the door as Abe cocked his arm to throw the bullet at him. "Got to go. By the way—Ernie's still in business, isn't he?"

"Sure. You need new ID?"

"I'm feeling the need for a new SSN."

"*Another* Social Security number?" Abe said. "You're trying to corner the market, maybe?"

"Just being careful."

"Always with the careful. I've used the same phony number forever. Do you see me getting a new one every couple of years?"

"I need a wider comfort zone than you," Jack said. "Besides, you've got a real one you can use. I don't."

"You're crazy, you know. What's it for?"

"A new credit card."

"Another card!" He slapped his hands to the sides of his face and rocked dramatically. "Oy! I never should have got you started. You've become an addict!"

Jack laughed. "And can I borrow the truck again? I've got to meet a customer in Elmhurst tonight."

"No one's going to be shooting at you, I hope. I don't want holes in my lady."

"No. This is just a reconnoiter. I'll rent something for the rest of the gig."

He wouldn't want Abe's plate reported near the scene of a felony.

4

"That him?" Jack said.

He crouched in the bushes behind a two-story, center-hall colonial in a middle-class neighborhood in Elmhurst. A guy named Oscar Schaffer hunkered next to him. This was their second meeting. They'd agreed to pre-liminary terms earlier in the week; now they were iron-ing out details.

"Yeah," said Schaffer, glaring through the French doors into the house's family room. The man of the house was a big guy, easily six-four, two-fifty; crew-cut red hair, round face, and narrow blue eyes. A bulging gut rode side-saddle on his belt buckle. "That's Gus Castleman, the no-good slimy rotten bastard who's beating up on my sister."

"Seems like there's a lot of that going around."

This wouldn't be the first wife-beater Jack had been asked to handle. He thought of Julio's sister. Her husband had been pounding on her. That was how Jack had met Julio. They'd been friends ever since.

"Yeah? Well it never went around in my family. At least until now."

A thin, mousy, brittle-looking woman whose hair was a few shades too blonde to be a natural human color entered the family room.

"And that, I take it, is your sister."

"That's Ceil, poor kid."

"Okay," Jack said. "Now that I know what they look like, let's get out of here."

They crept along the six-foot stockade cedar fence that separated the Castlemans' yard from their neighbors—one of the good things about this set-up. Also on the plus side: they had no kids, no dog, and their yard was rimmed with trees and high shrubs. Perfect for surveillance.

After checking to make sure the street was empty, Jack and Schaffer stepped back onto the sidewalk and walked the two blocks to the darkened gas station lot where they'd left their respective rides. They chose the front seat of Schaffer's dark green Jaguar XJS convertible.

"Not a great venue for a meeting, but it'll do."

The Jag smelled new inside. The leather upholstery was buttery soft. Bright, bleaching light from a nearby mercury vapor street lamp poured through the windshield and illuminated their laps.

Oscar Schaffer was some sort of big-time developer, but he didn't look like Donald Trump. He was older, for one thing—late fifties, at least—and fat. A round face with dark thinning hair above, and a second chin under construction below. One of the biggest land developers on Long Island, as he was overly fond of saying. Rich, but not Trump-rich.

And he was sweating. Jack wondered if Donald

Trump sweated. The Donald might perspire, but Jack couldn't imagine him sweating.

Jack watched Schaffer pull a white handkerchief from his pocket and blot the moisture. Supposedly he'd started out as a construction worker who'd got into contracting and then had gone on to make a mint in custom homes. His speech still carried echoes of the streets, despite occasional words like "venue." And he carried a handkerchief. Jack couldn't think of anyone he knew who carried a handkerchief—who *owned* a handkerchief.

"I never thought it would happen to Ceilia. She's so . . ."

His voice trailed off.

Jack said nothing. This was the time to keep quiet and listen. This was when he tended to learn the real deal about the customer. He still didn't have a handle on Schaffer. He did know he didn't particularly care for the guy. Maybe it was the Mr. Bigtime Success Story attitude.

"I just don't understand it. Gus seemed like such a good guy when they were dating and engaged. I liked him. An accountant, white collar, good job, clean hands, everything I wanted for Ceil. I helped him get his job. He's done well. But he beats her." Schaffer's lips thinned as they drew back over his teeth. "Dammit, he beats the shit out of her. And you know what's worse? She takes it! She's put up with it for ten years! I'm to the point where I'm thinking the best thing that could happen to Ceil was Gus meeting with some sort of fatal accident."

Jack knew all this. They'd covered this ground during their first meeting.

"You're probably right," he said before Schaffer could go on.

Schaffer stared at him. "You mean you'll . . . ?"

"Kill him?" Jack shook his head. "Forget it."

"But I thought—"

"Forget it. Sometimes I make a mistake. If that happens, I like to be able to go back and fix it."

Schaffer's expression flickered between disappointment and relief, finally settling on relief.

"You know," he said with a small smile, "as much as I'd like Gus dead, I'm glad you said that. I mean, if you'd said okay, I think I'd have set you to it." He shook his head and looked away. "Kind of scary what you can come to."

"She's your sister. Someone's hurting her. You want him stopped but you can't do it yourself. Not hard to understand how you feel. Anyway, why do you need me? Lots of laws against this stuff, you know."

"Right. Sure there are. But you've got to sign a complaint. Ceil won't do that."

"She's probably afraid."

"Afraid, hell! She defends him, says he's under a lot of pressure and sometimes he just loses control. She says most of the time it's her fault because she gets him mad, and she shouldn't get him mad. Can you *believe* that shit? She came over to my place one night, two black eyes, a swollen jaw, red marks around her throat from where he was choking her. I lost it. I charged over to their place ready to kill him with my bare hands. He's a big guy, but I'm tough. And I'm sure he's never been in a fight with someone who punches back. When I arrived screaming like a madman, he was ready for me. He had a couple of neighbors there and he was standing inside his front door with a baseball bat. Told me if I tried anything he'd defend himself, then call the cops and press charges for assault and battery. I told him if he came anywhere near my sister again, he wouldn't have an unbroken bone left in his body to dial the phone with!"

"Sounds like he knew you were coming."

"He did! That's the really crazy part! He knew because Ceil had called from my place to *warn* him! And the next day he sends her roses, says how much he loves her, swears it'll never happen again, and she rushes back to him like he's done her a big favor. Can you beat that?"

Jack had felt himself going through a slow burn as Schaffer was speaking. Now he turned in his seat to face him.

"*Now* you decide to tell me this?" He wasn't quite shouting, but Schaffer could have no doubt he was pissed.

"What? What's wrong?"

"Don't give me that! You knew nobody'd get involved in this once they learned your sister's some sort of masochist!"

"She's not! She—"

"Tell you what," Jack said, reaching for the door handle, "you go get a bat of your own and wait for this guy in an alley or a parking lot. Take care of it yourself."

"Wait! Please! Don't think I haven't thought of it. But I've already threatened him—in front of witnesses. Anything happens to him, I'll be number one suspect. And I can't get involved in anything like that, in a felony. I mean I've got my own family to consider, my business. I want to leave something for my kids. I do Gus, I'll end up in jail, Gus'll sue me for everything I'm worth, my wife and kids will wind up in a shelter somewhere while Gus moves into my house. Some legal system!"

Jack waited through a long pause. Here was the familiar Catch-22 that kept him in business.

Schaffer finally said, "I guess I figured if I got you out here and you saw how big he is and how small and frail Ceil is, you'd . . ."

"I'd what? Go all mushy? Forget it. Busting up this slug isn't going to change things. Sounds like your sister's got as big a problem as he does."

"She does. I've talked to a couple of doctors about it. It's called co-dependency or something like that. I don't pretend to understand it." He looked at Jack. "Can you help?"

"I don't see how. Domestic stuff is complicated to begin with, and this situation sounds like it's gone way past complicated. Not the sort of thing my kind of services can help."

"I know what you're saying. I know they need shrinks—at least Ceil does. Gus . . . I don't know. I think he's beyond therapy. I got the feeling Gus *likes* beating up on Ceil. Likes it too much to quit, no matter what. But I want to give it a try."

"If that's true, I can't see him getting chummy with a shrink just because you or anyone else says he should."

"Yeah. But if he was hospitalized . . ." Schaffer raised his eyebrows, inviting Jack to finish the thought.

"You really think if your brother-in-law was laid up in a hospital bed for a while, a victim of violence himself, he'd have some kind of burst of insight and ask for help?"

"It's worth a try."

"No, it isn't. Save your money."

"Well, then, if he doesn't see the light, I could clue his doctor in and maybe arrange to have one of the hospital shrinks see him while he's in traction."

"You really think that'll change anything?"

"I don't know. I've got to try something short of killing him."

"And what if those somethings don't work?"

His eyes took on a bleak look. "Then I'll have find a way to take him out of the picture. Permanently. Even if I have to do it myself."

"I thought you were worried about your family and your business."

"She's my sister, dammit!"

Jack thought about his own sister, the pediatrician. He couldn't imagine anyone beating up on her. At least not more than once. She'd had a brown belt in karate at seventeen and had never taken guff from anyone. She'd either kick the crap out of you herself or call big brother, the judge, and submerge you to your lower lip in an endless stream of legal hot water. Or both.

But if she were a different sort, and somebody was beating up on her, repeatedly . . .

"All right," Jack said. "I'll look into it. I'm not promising anything, but I'll see if there's anything I can do."

"Hey, thanks. Thanks a—"

"That's half down just for looking into it—no refund. Even if I decide not to do anything. The rest is due when I've done the job."

Schaffer's eyes narrowed. "Wait a sec. Lemme get this straight. You get five large with no commitment?"

"Might take me weeks to learn what I need to know just to make that decision."

"What do you need to know? How about—?"

"We're not practicing 'the Art of the Deal' here. You've already held out on me about this co-dependency thing; how do I know you're not hiding something else?"

"I'm not. I swear!"

"Those are the terms. Take it or leave it."

For a moment it looked as if Schaffer might leave it. Then he shook his head.

"You're asking me to bet on a crap shoot—blindfolded. You hold all the aces."

"You're mixing metaphors, but you've got the picture."

"Aw, what the hell." Schaffer sighed and reached into

his breast pocket. He handed an envelope across to Jack. "It's only money. Here. Take it."

Without hiding his reluctance, Jack tucked the envelope inside his shirt.

"When do you start?" Schaffer said.

Jack opened the door and stepped out of the Jag.

"Tomorrow night."

5

Jack started back to Manhattan, then remembered he was due to pick up his mail. And since he was already in Queens, why not?

He rented boxes in five mail drops—two in Manhattan, one in Hoboken, one in Brooklyn, and a large box in Astoria on Steinway Street. But he used that drop as a collection point only. Every two weeks his other drops bundled up his mail and sent it to Astoria. Every two weeks Jack hopped the R train and collected all his mail. An easy trip—the drop was only a couple of blocks from the subway stop.

He double-parked in front of the big, brightly-lit window of Carsman's Mail and Packaging Services and trotted inside. He'd chosen Carsman's because it was open twenty-four hours a day. The clerk behind the barred window at the rear barely looked up as he entered, but Jack kept his head turned anyway. He unlocked the box, scooped out the four manila envelopes inside, and was out the door and tooling down Steinway Street in Abe's truck in less than a minute.

In and out, showing up at all odd hours of the night, seeing no one, speaking to no one—the only way to fly.

As he drove he emptied the envelopes onto the seat beside him. At successive stop lights he sifted through the letters. Most were bills for the credit cards he carried under various identities. But one envelope addressed to John L. Tyleski caught his eye. Tyleski was one of his more recent *noms de guerre*. Jack didn't remember any mail for him before. He tore open the envelope.

Jack smiled. Because of John L. Tyleski's excellent credit record, a Maryland bank had preapproved him for a Visa card.

Damn nice of you people.

Credit cards . . . Jack hated them. Plastic money left a trail of electronic footprints, a detailed record of every purchase—books, theater tickets, clothing, plane tickets—a diagram of your lifestyle, a map of your existence. The very things he wanted most to avoid.

He'd held out as long as he could, but with each passing year it had become increasingly difficult to get by without them. A man with no credit cards raised eyebrows, and the last thing Jack wanted to attract was a second look. He'd found himself in an odd position: in order to remain invisible, he'd have to become a part of the national credit databases.

So he jumped into Plastic Moneyland with both feet. He now kept four credit card accounts running at once, each under a different name, each attached to a different mail drop. He paid his monthly bills promptly with USPS money orders. He could have used another money order service with equal anonymity, but the idea of using a wing of the very government he was hiding from appealed to him.

Early last year he'd added John L. Tyleski as an additional cardholder to the Amex account of John J. O'Mara.

Tyleski's record of payment since then had been so sterling that a competitor was offering him his own account.

"On behalf of Mr. Tyleski," Jack said, "I wish to thank you very much. We will sign him up first thing tomorrow."

Something deeply satisfying in the predictability of large financial organizations.

And in a few months, John J. O'Mara would request that John L. Tyleski's name be removed from his Amex account, leaving Tyleski as a free and independent entity in the Visa databank.

The timing was perfect. He'd been planning to visit Ernie tomorrow and start legitimizing a new identity anyway. He'd eventually attach that to the Tyleski Visa account.

He smiled as he paid the toll at the Midtown Tunnel. This was shaping up to be a busy week.

6

Salvatore Roma stood at the window of his suite on the top floor of the Clinton Regent Hotel and gazed at the blazing skyline.

He had been staying at the hotel since Monday, preparing for the SESOUP conference. A few of the attendees had arrived today to get in some sightseeing before the conference began. Tomorrow the rest would arrive, filling the hotel. Every room was booked by an attendee, just as he'd planned.

Anticipation bubbled through him, making him

almost giddy. All the pieces were falling together perfectly. By this time tomorrow night, the building would be packed with those special, chosen people.

And then it would begin.

After endless waiting, after repeated reverses at the hands of lesser beings, his time had come at last. He'd earned his reward, paid for it with blood and lives—his own—and now he was due to collect. *Past* due.

All he needed were the proper tools. The people packing this building over the next few days would help provide those. After that, nothing could stop him. And he would grind to pulp anyone who got in his way.

Mine, he thought, gazing at the city and beyond. Mine at last.

THURSDAY

THE 1ST ANNUAL CONFERENCE OF
THE SOCIETY FOR THE EXPOSURE OF
SECRET ORGANIZATIONS AND
UNACKNOWLEDGED PHENOMENA

SCHEDULE OF EVENTS
THURSDAY

Registration Desk Open:	Noon–8:00 P.M.
Exhibits Open:	Noon–8:00 P.M.
3:00–5:00 P.M.:	**Special Screening** of the new independent film, *We Are Not Alone*
5:00–5:30 P.M.:	**Welcome Address**—Prof. Salvatore Roma, founder of SESOUP
5:30–7:00 P.M.:	**Cocktail Reception**—meet the panelists
9:00 P.M.–???	**Films:** *The Late Great Planet Earth, Seven Days in May, The Day the Earth Stood Still*

I

Jack had time, so he walked down to Midtown. It had rained last night as a front pushed through, and the temperature had dropped a good ten or twelve degrees below yesterday's. The breeze had a raw edge to it. Coats were back on, legs were hidden again. Spring seemed an empty dream—

He'd decided to dress like a Midtown tourist today, so he was wearing Nikes and a black-and-purple nylon warm-up over a Planet Hollywood T-shirt. The indispensable fanny pack completed the look. The nylon made an annoying rhythmic swishing sound as he quick-walked down Columbus, which magically became Ninth Avenue once he crossed Fifty-ninth Street. He paused to check out the trays of used paperbacks in the concrete plaza on the southeast corner of Fifty-seventh, then moved on. From there the avenue began its downward slope toward Hell's Kitchen.

At least that was what they used to call it. The presence of the Intrepid Museum and the Javits Convention Center had somewhat revitalized the area, but even so, real estate folks had found a neighborhood called Hell's Kitchen a tough sell. So they'd started calling it "Clinton"—not after the president, but the former governor whose carriage house was still around here somewhere, a leftover from the old, old days when the area was a summer retreat for Manhattan's wealthier folk.

Then the Irish moved in. When the tenements rose,

people started calling it Hell's Kitchen. Italians and Greeks and Puerto Ricans followed, successive immigrant waves moving through the same apartments.

The buildings tended to average about five stories in height with brick fronts, some decorative, most just plain red clay, thinly veiled with a steel lace of fire escapes clinging to their faces. Most of the streets, sloping upward on his left and down to the Hudson on his right, were lined with budding trees—Jack had forgotten how many trees grew in Hell's Kitchen. Reminded him in some ways of his own neighborhood before the great gentrification of the eighties.

Many of the doorways he passed were occupied, either by sleeping men or smoking women.

Ahead of Jack a guy was peeking in the windows of all the parked cars he passed. He was trying to be coy about it, but no question: an hour from now, one of those cars would be missing.

Jack remembered the Clinton Regent as being somewhere in the lower Fifties or upper Forties. He should have looked up the address before starting out. No matter. He'd find it.

He thought about swinging down by the docks and grabbing a cup of coffee at the Highwater Diner. He'd done a job for the owner, George Kuropolis, a while ago, and had been impressed with how clean he kept the place. He glanced at his watch. No time. Maybe later.

No shortage of restaurants in the area, and just about every ethnic group that had passed through the neighborhood was represented—lots of bodegas, a Greek bakery, Italian delis, Irish pubs, an Afghan kabob place, Caribbean, Thai, Chinese, Senegalese, even an Ethiopian restaurant.

What do they serve in an Ethiopian restaurant?

He'd have to check it out. If nothing else, meals would not be boring on this gig.

The overcast sky threatened rain, but that didn't seem to faze the tourists. The West Side was full of foreigners. He was stopped by a group of Japanese women who seemed to know only one word.

"Gucci? Gucci?" they said.

He pointed them toward Fifth Avenue. "Gucci."

Then a dapper elderly gent with a British accent stopped him at a corner and wanted to know which way to Grand Central. Jack pointed him toward Forty-second and told him to walk left—couldn't miss it.

"But now let me ask *you* something," Jack said as the man thanked him and began to walk away.

He was bothered by the fact that, despite his best efforts to dress like an out-of-towner, two foreigners had chosen him to ask directions.

"How did you know I wasn't a tourist myself?"

"That nylon thingie you're wearing, for one," the Brit said, smoothing his neat little white mustache. "Whenever we see one in London, we know there's an American inside. The same goes for that miniature rucksack on your hip."

"Okay, but how did you know I wasn't from Des Moines or someplace?"

"By the way you crossed the street. If you'll notice, native New Yorkers completely ignore the DON'T WALK signals, and rarely break stride as they cross the street."

Have to remember that, Jack thought.

He moved on, stopping at all the DON'T WALKs, and found the Clinton Regent Hotel in the upper Forties between Ninth and Tenth. A whopping eight stories tall, it towered over its neighbors.

A low marquee overhung a small paved plaza shaded by half a dozen slim elms in planters. Through the windows to the left of the revolving doors he could see a half-filled coffee shop; to the right, the crowded lobby. He stepped inside and stuttered to a stop as a deep uneasiness wrapped around him like a tentacle.

He looked around the low-ceilinged lobby, wondering what it was about this place that made him so uncomfortable. Just people, standing, sitting, wandering about. No one particularly sinister looking or threatening. They were all so ordinary he wondered if he was in the right place. Then he spotted a backpacking girl wearing a T-shirt decorated with the familiar black-eyed ET-ish alien and he knew this had to be the place.

As he stood there the sensation eased away, but did not leave entirely.

Jack spotted a tall, lanky figure waving from an alcove: Lew Ehler, and he was motioning to Jack to join him.

"Good," Lew said as they shook hands. He wore gray slacks and a green plaid shirt under a blue V-neck sweater; he looked more relaxed out of a suit. "You're right on time." He was staring at Jack's throat. "What—?"

"Cut myself shaving."

"Oh. We should go over your cover story before we try to register you."

"Try?"

"Yes. I think I have a way to get you in, and if we pass that hurdle, you'll need a cover story."

"Maybe we should see about registering first."

"No. Trust me, you should have the story set in your mind before you get involved here."

"Okay. Who am I?"

He glanced around. "Too crowded in here. Let's step outside."

They stood near an elm in a concrete planter. Lew gave the street and sidewalk a careful once-over before turning to Jack.

"I've given this a lot of thought and I think you should be an experiencer."

"What's an experiencer?"

"Someone who's had a UFO experience."

"You mean abducted?" Jack didn't know if he could pull that off without laughing.

"No. Too many phony abductees around—either delusional crazies or publicity hounds. You've got to be more subtle. You'll simply say you experienced an incident that left you with unaccounted-for hours in your life. Where are you from?"

Jack didn't want to answer that. "Why?"

"Because you should be familiar with where this event supposedly happened. It should be a fairly unpopulated area."

Jack knew Jersey—he grew up there—and the pine woods that filled the belly of the state were about as deserted as you could get.

"How about the Jersey pine barrens?"

"Perfect! Mel always talked about a 'nexus point' out there."

"What's that?"

"I'm not sure. It was part of her research. We drove through last year, looking for one of these nexus points but got lost. Okay, so that's where you were . . . driving through the pine barrens, when you saw a light moving along the tree tops."

"I've heard of lights like that—the Pineys call them 'pine lights'—but I never saw one."

"Yes, you did: you saw this light . . . and as you slowed to watch it, you spotted this glowing figure off to the side. You stopped for a closer look . . . and the next thing you knew, it was dawn. You'd lost five-six hours."

"That's it?"

Lew nodded. "That's all you need. It's perfect because it's so vague. No one can trip you up on details because there aren't any. Anybody starts questioning you too closely, you just act confused . . . you wish like crazy you could remember . . . you'd give *anything* to remember."

"What about reporting it? That can be checked, so I'll have to say I didn't report it. Why not?"

"No problem. You never told anybody because you were too embarrassed—you don't want people to think you're some sort of nut. It's a common story. Most people who are into this stuff believe that only a small fraction of sightings and contacts are on record; the rest remain unreported due to the very real fear of being labeled a kook."

"Okay. I can handle that. But what's my connection to Melanie?"

Lew grinned. "Here's the beauty part: you never reported the incident to anyone, not even your own family, but then, out of the blue, Melanie Ehler called you and asked him to come to New York to talk to her about it."

"But how did she know?"

Lew's grin broadened. "That's what *everyone* will be asking. That will make you a *very* interesting experiencer. Everyone will want to talk to you about it. And the thing is, you've never met Mel, never even *heard* of her, so you're free to ask all sorts of questions about her."

Jack looked around. "But here I am, sitting with you for all to see. How come I know you?"

"You showed up at the house, looking for Mel. But she's gone. So I brought you along to help me look for her." He beamed with pride. "Isn't that great? All bases covered." His smile faltered and his Adam's apple made a single convulsive bob. "Mel would be so proud."

It *was* great. Brilliant, in fact. But Jack saw a way to improve it.

"I'm sure she would. And I'm impressed too. But let's ratchet it up one more notch. Let's say that I heard from Melanie Tuesday."

"Tuesday? But that was after . . ."

"Right. She called me *after* she was abducted." *If* she was abducted, he mentally added. "That ought to shake up the guilty party and bring them sniffing around, don't you think?"

"I guess it would."

"And as for you—play it straight."

"What do you mean?"

"I want you to pretty much tell it like it is: Melanie took off Sunday on some last minute research and you haven't seen her since. Despite the fact that she told you she'd be gone for a while, you're worried about her—you even suspect foul play. The only thing you hold back on is who I really am and the, er, TV message you got from her Monday night. Got that?"

"Yeah, sure. I guess so. But what—?"

"Lew?" said a woman's voice.

Jack turned and saw a matronly woman, maybe fifty or so, approaching them from the hotel entrance.

"Oh, hi, Olive," Lew called, then spoke hurriedly in a low voice from the corner of his mouth. "Olive Farina, one of the cornerstones of SESOUP. A born-again everything."

"Lew, it's so good to see you again!" she said, smiling warmly and opening her arms.

Lew stooped for a brief embrace. "Good to see you too, Olive." He turned to Jack. "I'd like you to meet . . ."

Jack saw Lew's face go blank, no doubt mirroring his mind. They hadn't settled on a name.

"Jack Shelby," Jack said, extending his hand. "Lew and I met only Tuesday. Nice to meet you."

Olive Farina had a sweet face and short graying hair. She wore a white turtleneck with flower-embroidered collar, a brocade vest that looked like it had been cut from a wall hanging, maroon polyester slacks and matching stockings with flat black shoes. Jack figured this was how nuns must dress when they resign from their convent. Her jewelry reinforced the ex-nun image: silver crosses as earrings, a gold crucifix as a ring, and a big silver crucifix suspended on a long chain necklace.

"Bless you, and nice to meet you as well." She turned to Lew. "Where's Melanie? I'm so anxious to speak to her." She grinned and lowered her voice to a stage whisper. "I'm hoping she'll give me a preview of her address on Sunday."

"I'm sorry, Olive," Lew said, "but Mel's not here. Frankly, I don't know where she is, and I'm getting worried."

He launched into his story, then worked Jack's "experience" into it. Jack watched Olive's expression carefully during the whole exchange, but saw nothing suspicious.

"I'm sure Mel's just fine," Olive said. "You know how she is. She's like a bird dog once she gets on the trail of something. She's probably lost all track of time. Don't worry, Lew. Melanie will be here as scheduled on Sunday to tell us what she's discovered, and I know in my heart she'll prove that Satan is the master manipulator. He has to be—the devil is the source of all evil. Why just last night as I was praying I—"

Her voice cut off as two long-haired heavy metal

types strolled by on the sidewalk. Her head almost managed an *Exorcist* swivel as she fixed on the one with the Black Sabbath T-shirt. Her expression grew furious.

"Excuse me," she said and hurried after them.

Jack watched as she grabbed the Black Sabbath guy by the arm and got into his face.

"Are you a Satanist?"

"Sod off," the guy said in a British accent and kept walking.

"Even if you're not a follower, you're doing the devil's work!" she said, following him. "You're spreading the Evil One's message with that shirt!"

The voices faded as the trio moved off.

"As you can see, Olive is a bit, um, intense," Lew said. "She represents the thinking of a fairly large segment of the membership—fundamentalist Christian types who believe the End Days are near and that Satan is preparing the way for the Antichrist."

"Keep thinking those happy thoughts."

"She's a nice lady, really," Lew said. "Just don't push any of her hot buttons. The one you really have to be careful with is Jim Zaleski—a real hot-head, and a diehard ufologist."

"You-follow what?"

"Ufologist—an expert on UFOs. He's a spokesman for the alien contact faction of SESOUP."

"So SESOUP's not a united group."

"About as united as the United Nations. Each subgroup pushes its own theory as the Real Truth. The other bigwig is Miles Kenway. He's ex-military and . . . well, a little scary. He speaks for those who believe in the New World Order conspiracy. If I had to pick one of them as most likely to be behind Mel's disappearance, I'd pick Kenway."

I love this, Jack thought. It's like an alternate reality.

"Have you seen either of those two around?" he said, wanting a look at them.

"No. But I'm sure they'll be at the cocktail reception later. And Roma's giving the welcoming address. You can meet them all tonight—*if* we can get you in." Lew glanced at his watch. "Registration should be opening soon. Let's get up there early. Let me do the talking."

Back inside, they took the escalator up one level to the meeting floors and found the registration desks in a corridor. Lew was pre-registered so he simply had to sign in. Jack stood back while the thin, middle-aged brunette behind the desk assembled Lew's badge and program. Movement to his right startled him—something small and brown with a long curved tail scurried along the floor. It disappeared behind the registration table.

Jack was bending into a squat to check it out when the thing jumped up onto the table.

A monkey. One of those cute little organ-grinder types with the pale face and the dark fur on the head—a capuchin, or something like that. It sat on the far end of the table and stared at him.

Jack heard Lew say, "I'm also going to pick up my wife's registration packet."

"Sure, Lew," the woman said, digging into an accordion file folder. Her badge read *Barbara*.

Still staring at Jack, the monkey moved closer. Barbara glanced at it but said nothing. Jack didn't understand why it was staring at him like that. Didn't much like it, either.

What's your problem, little guy?

He pointed to the monkey. "Is he a member too?"

Barbara smiled. "No. He belongs to Sal. Isn't he cute?"

"Sal?" Lew said.

"Professor Roma. He tells everyone to call him Sal."

She handed Lew an envelope. "Ask Melanie to stop by and say hello later."

"I'm not sure when Mel's arriving," Lew said. "In the meantime, I'm going to let Mr. Shelby use her badge and pass."

Jack noticed that the monkey shot upright onto its hind legs, almost as if it were alarmed at something.

"Are you a member?" she said to Jack.

"Nope. But I'd sure like to be."

"Oh, dear," Barbara said. "I don't think we can allow that."

"I don't see why not. Melanie's going to be delayed so she wants Mr. Shelby to take her place until she arrives."

"But Lew," Barbara was saying, "he's not a member—"

"But Melanie is, and I'm her husband, and this is what she told me: Jack is to take her place until she arrives."

"But you can't just give him—"

"Yes, he can," Jack said, noticing other registrants backing up behind them. Enough jawing. "Watch." He took Melanie's registration from Lew and held it before him. "There. It's done."

Before Barbara could reply, the monkey screeched and leaped at Jack. It grabbed the envelope and tried to tear it from his grasp. Startled, Jack stumbled back a step. A few of the people behind him cried out in alarm.

"What the—!"

He snatched the envelope from the monkey's paws, grabbed the creature around its chest, and gently dropped it back onto the registration desk. As if bounding off a trampoline, the monkey sprang at him again, screeching shrilly all the while. This time Jack was ready. He caught it around the chest again and held it up at arms length. He stared at it.

"Hey, pal, what's with you? Cool it."

The monkey stopped its screeching and glared at him. Then it tried to bite his wrist.

"Damn!" Jack said and tossed it—none too gently this time—back onto the table. He looked at his wrist. The skin was scraped but unbroken.

Undaunted, the creature looked ready to spring again when a voice rang out.

"Mauricio!"

The monkey froze. It and everyone else turned to look at the man approaching from the far end of the corridor.

"Oh, Professor Roma!" Barbara said. "I'm so glad you're here. I don't know what got into him."

Jack took in Professor Salvatore Roma, founder of SESOUP: a lot younger than Jack had expected, with close-cropped black hair, just this side of a buzz cut, slim nose, dark eyes, and full lips; maybe five-ten with a lean body. He wore a white shirt—one of those collarless jobs—and dark gray pleated slacks. Looked like he'd just come from a *GQ* shoot.

For some reason he couldn't explain, Jack hated him on sight.

Roma snapped his fingers at the monkey and, after a heartbeat of hesitation, it scampered along the table and hopped up on his shoulder. Roma approached Lew and Jack.

"Hello," he said, extending his hand to Lew. "I'm Sal Roma."

"Lew Ehler. We've spoken on the phone."

Roma smiled brightly. "Melanie's husband! So good

to finally meet you in person! I've been looking forward to meeting her in the flesh as well. Where is she?"

Roma was handsome and graceful, warm and friendly—why did Jack have such an urge to punch him in the face?

Lew said, "She's not here at the moment."

Roma turned to Barbara. "What was all the commotion?"

"Lew wants this non-member"—she nodded toward Jack—"to use his wife's conference pass."

Lew launched into their cover story, and did a great job—Jack detected a few murmured *oohs* and *aahs* from the people around them. Roma listened patiently while the monkey on his shoulder continued to glare at Jack. In the end, Roma wasn't moved.

"I'm sorry," he said, smiling sympathetically at Jack and Lew. "As much as I'd like to include you, Mr. Shelby, the conference is for members only." He extended his hand toward Jack. "Please return the envelope."

Jack shook his head. "I don't think so. I'm here. I'm staying."

"I must insist, Mr. Shelby," Roma said. Sudden fury darkened his smooth features.

Surprisingly, Jack heard support from the other SESOUPers—people saying, "Let him stay" . . . "Give him a break" . . . "One more person isn't going to hurt" . . . and the like.

Roma glanced around, opened his mouth, apparently thought better of it, and closed it again. The monkey looked ready to hurl itself at Jack's throat.

"Very well," Roma said finally, with a tiny shrug as he looked around at the SESOUPers. "If you wish him to stay, so be it."

Roma's quick about-face surprised Jack; something

about it bothered him. The monkey seemed to agree: It began jumping up and down and screeching as if protesting Roma's capitulation.

"Easy, Mauricio," Roma purred, stroking its fur. His lips smiled as his eyes bored into Jack's. "I could have security eject you, but it is not worth the disruption. Enjoy your stay at the conference, Mr. Shelby. But if you interfere at all with these proceedings, I shall remove you. Is that clear?"

Jack grinned into the combined glares of Roma and his monkey. "Does this mean I don't get to call you Sal?"

Roma turned away, but the monkey kept watching Jack from his shoulder, hissing at him as they walked off. Finally the monkey jumped to the floor and ran the other way, as if disgusted with all of them.

"What happened between you and that monkey?" Lew said.

"Don't know. I get along pretty well with dogs and cats. Maybe monkeys don't like me. His master wasn't exactly crazy about me either."

And vice versa, Jack thought. He couldn't remember experiencing such instant unprovoked animosity toward another human being.

"But you're in," Lew said, slapping him on the back. "That's the important thing."

"Yeah." Jack shuffled through his—Melanie's—registration envelope, and pulled out the program. He thumbed the pages. "What now?"

"Not much doing yet. It's too early for me to check into my room. We could have lunch."

"I'll have to take a rain check. I've got some errands. And I need to see about a room of my own."

"That might be a problem. The place is booked solid. If necessary, you could stay with me."

"Thanks," Jack said, but hoped it wouldn't come to that. He wanted to stay here because this was where the action—such as it was—would be. But being a roommate went against his nature, unless of course the other occupant was Gia.

"Maybe I can go on a wait list, in case there's a cancel or a no-show." He checked today's schedule in his program. "How about we meet at this Welcome Address at five?"

That was fine with Lew. They split, and Jack headed back uptown to see a guy named Ernie.

2

Roma watched the stranger leave and fought and urge to follow him and wring his neck. It wouldn't do to have him turn up dead. That might upset the attendees, might even send some of them scurrying back home—the last thing he wanted.

But who was he? And why had Melanie Ehler's husband lied about him, saying that Melanie wanted this newcomer to use her conference pass until she arrived? Nothing could be further from the truth.

He calmed himself. It didn't matter, really, who he was. The hotel was full, so Mr. Jack Shelby would have to find himself some other place to stay. That was the important matter—that he not replace one of the attendees. If he did that, something would have to be done about him. Roma needed them *all* here tonight.

Yes. He closed his eyes. Tonight.

3

The sign in the dirty window read:

ERNIE'S I-D
ALL KINDS
PASSPORT
TAXI
DRIVERS LICENSE

Jack pulled open the door and stepped inside.

"Hey, Jack," said the skinny, basset-faced man behind the counter. "How y'doin'. How y'doin'." Not a question, just Ernie's habitual rapid-fire greeting. "Lock the door and flip the sign to 'closed' there, will ya?"

Jack did just that, then approached the counter, passing racks of sunglasses, customizable T-shirts, sports caps, and bootleg videos. Ernie developed film and made legitimate photo IDs, and generally sold anything that had a fat mark-up, but his main income came from people who wanted to be someone else, or at least be known as someone else.

Over the years Ernie had made dozens of driver's licenses and photo IDs for Jack.

"You said you need another high school ID, right?" Ernie said, lifting an accordion file from the floor and removing the elastic band that encircled it. "Here in the city?"

"No. Hoboken."

Ernie flipped through the pockets in the file, an extensive collection of ID cards and badges for most of the schools, factories, and offices within a ten-mile radius.

"Hoboken . . . Hoboken . . . what's the kid's name?"

Jack unfolded a photocopy of a certified birth certificate and placed it on the counter.

"Here he is. And I'll need you to notarize this copy for me, too."

Ernie had a Notary Public seal, the duplicate of a legitimate Notary down in the financial district.

"Sure thing." He squinted at the birth certificate. "D'Attilio, huh? D'Attilio the Hun, maybe?" He flashed Jack a quick, Charlie Callas grin. "For a D'Attilio we should probably enroll him in St. Aloysius." More searching. "Here it is."

He removed a high school ID from the file and clipped it to a yellow legal pad.

"Okay," he said, scribbling on the pad. "We've got John D'Attilio. D-O-B?"

Jack pointed to the birth date on the certificate. "Right there."

"Got it. Address?"

Jack gave him the address of his Hoboken mail drop.

Ernie nodded. "Yog?"

"What's that?"

Ernie raised his eyebrows and gave Jack a Do-I-have-to-spell-it-out? look. "Y-O-G?"

Of course—year of graduation. It was on all school IDs.

"Let see . . . he's just turning sixteen, so he'll graduate two years from now."

"Got it. And I've got a nice photo to go with that name. Okay. When do you need it?"

"No hurry. Next week's okay."

"Good. Cause I'm a little backed up."

"Usual price?"

"Yeah."

"See you Monday."

Jack turned the sign, unlocked the door, and stepped back onto Tenth Avenue. He glanced at his watch. Time to check back with the hotel. He hoped the reservation desk had scrounged up a room for him. He found himself looking forward to mingling with the Society for the Exposure of Secret Organizations and Unexplained Phenomena. He'd never been an "experiencer" before.

4

Jack lucked out with a room: One of the SESOUPers had to cancel because of some family emergency, and Jack took her place.

He wound up in a fifth floor room overlooking the street. The decor was typical hotel blah: stucco ceiling, heavy duty beige wall paper, TV, dresser, and a pair of double beds, double drapes on the window, and framed nondescript prints of ponds and tree branches on the walls. But the bland surroundings didn't allay the strange uneasiness he felt every time he stepped into this building, as if the air were charged with some sort of cold energy.

He was unpacking the gym bag that held the change of clothes he'd brought from home, when he heard a knock on his door. He eyeballed the peephole, expecting to see Lew. Instead he found Olive Farina standing in the hall.

"I hope I'm not disturbing you, Mr. Shelby?" she said

as Jack pulled open the door. "May I come in? I have a question or two I'd like to ask you."

Jack hesitated, puzzled. What did she want here?

But she looked harmless enough, and he was curious to hear her question or two.

"Sure."

He stepped aside and Olive entered uncertainly, peering into the bathroom as she passed, as if expecting someone to be hiding in there.

"You're alone?"

"Last time I looked."

When she reached the center of the room, she stopped in front of the TV cabinet and turned to him. "Before we speak, will you do something for me?"

"Depends on what it is."

She lifted the silver crucifix that hung from her neck. "Will you hold this for me?"

"Hold it?"

"That's right. Just wrap your fingers around it for the count of ten."

Uh-oh, Jack thought. *Loony Tunes* times.

But he said okay and gripped the crucifix in his fist, firmly resisting the manic urge to scream in agony and fall writhing to the floor. Very doubtful this audience would find much humor in that.

"Good," she said after a few heartbeats. "You can let go now." She inspected Jack's open palm.

"Looking for scorch marks?" he said.

She gave him a tolerant smile. "Laugh if you will, but at least now I feel I can trust you."

Jack shrugged, thinking, if that's all it takes, you're already way too trusting. He gestured to one of the upholstered chairs by the big plate glass window.

"Have a seat." Jack turned the chair from the writing desk to face her and dropped into it. "What did you want to ask me?"

"Well," she said, adjusting her wide frame into the narrow seat, "if I understand correctly, you were the last one to speak to Melanie Ehler."

"I don't know that for sure. She could have called lots of other people."

"Yes, of course. But I want to know . . . when she spoke to you, did she mention anything else . . . did she mention the End Times?"

"No," Jack said. "I'm not familiar—"

"That must be what Melanie learned," Olive said, her voice revving up. "Because everything that's going wrong in the world is evidence of the End Times." She pointed to the night stand between the beds. "There's a *Holy Bible* in that drawer, and it's all recorded right there in the Book of Revelations."

"Really."

"That glowing figure you saw in the woods? That could have been an angel—the Book of Revelations mentions angels appearing to the Righteous near the End Times. Are you righteous?"

"I sure hope so."

"And that light you saw? Some will claim it was a UFO peopled with aliens. Don't believe them. UFOs are not from outer space—they're the chariots of Satan."

She was working herself up. It was almost as if she were talking to herself. Jack could only watch and listen, fascinated.

"Yes! Satan! For isn't the Dark One, after all, referred to as 'Prince of the Air?' The lights in the skies are proof that Satan is here. He and his forces are at this very moment working to hurl America into anarchy by destroying religious freedoms. That's why there's been so many church burnings recently—and don't forget Waco! But he'll also try to undermine from within by striking at us through our children! Even now his minions are teaching those innocent minds about evolution and life on other planets, trying to convince them that science proves the Bible wrong! And it's working, trust me, it's working. And what is Satan's purpose? Just before the End Times, he is going to join the USA and Canada into a single government and install the Antichrist as overall leader."

Jack listened raptly. He loved this stuff.

"Any idea who this Antichrist is?" he said when she took a breath. He could think of a few politicians who fit the description.

"No. Not yet. We'll know soon enough, though. But not all of us are going to sit around and just let this happen. The Righteous Faithful will resist to the end. The Devil is going to mark his billions of followers with a special microchip. It will run at six hundred and sixty-six megahertz—six-six-six is the Number of the Beast, you know. His followers, those who have the chip, will be able to buy food and roam free; the Righteous who refuse the chip and stay faithful to God will starve or be rounded up and put into camps."

Got to make sure I get me one of those chips, Jack thought.

"It will be a terrible time," she said, shaking her head as she wound down and her voice softened. "A terrible, terrible time."

"How did you learn all this?" Jack said.

"I told you: it's right here in the Bible, and in the papers every day!"

"Right. Of course." He knew she hadn't been born like this. He wondered when she'd gone off the deep end. And he wanted to know if she was far enough gone to make a move against Melanie Ehler. "But when did you first begin putting it all together?"

Olive leaned forward. "I can tell you the exact date I became aware of Satan's evil hand in world affairs. Up till that time I was just like everybody else, blithely going about my business, thinking everything was fine—well, I had a bad weight problem and couldn't seem to do anything about it. But I had no idea my obesity was related to Satan."

Jack couldn't resist. "The Devil made you eat?"

"Are you mocking me, Mr. Shelby? Because if—"

"Call me Jack, and no, I wasn't mocking you." Had to tread softly here. "Go on."

"All right. As I was saying, I was getting nowhere with my weight until I went to this wonderful therapist. She took one look at me and said, 'You were abused as a child—that's why you're overweight. Your mind has forced you to build up that layer of fat as symbolic insulation against further abuse.'"

"She made the diagnosis first, before she started interviewing you? Isn't it usually the other way around?"

"She's an exceptional woman. At first, of course, I thought she was crazy, but she convinced me to go through memory recovery therapy. And, to my everlasting horror, I found she was right. I recovered memories of Satanic ritual abuse when I was a child."

Jack said nothing. He'd read an article in the *Times* about memory recovery therapy and how it tended to create more memories than it supposedly recovered.

Olive pulled a tissue from the pocket of her flowered vest and dabbed at her eyes. "My parents denied it all till their dying days, so I couldn't find out if they'd implanted one of those 666 chips in me."

"What makes you think—?"

"Because they *hurt* me!" she said, her eyes puddling up again. "I remember that! I can see those black robed figures standing over me—you hear about men in black, and there was that so-called comedy movie about them, but these were the *real* men in black, and believe me, there was *nothing* funny about them!"

"Easy, Olive," Jack said, fearing she was about to lose it. "It's all right."

"It's *not* all right! These Satanic cults sacrifice most of their victims, and so for a while I thought I was lucky because I'd survived. And then I started thinking maybe I was allowed to live for a reason. Maybe I'd been implanted with the 666 chip. If that's true, it will control me during the End Times. I'll be marked as unfaithful. I'll miss the Rapture and suffer the Tribulation."

"A simple X ray ought to—"

"They don't show up on X rays! I've had countless pelvic exams, plus CAT scans and ultrasounds and MRIs, but they all supposedly come back negative."

"Supposedly?"

"I'm beginning to suspect that the medical profession is in league with the CIA and Satan, implanting these chips in everyone they can. That's why I've got to know when the End Times are coming . . . so I can prepare myself . . . purify myself. If you hear from Melanie again, ask her about the End Times, will you? Please? I've got to know."

Jack's sense of derisive amusement with Olive melted away in the face of her genuine anguish. Her fears were whacked out, but the deeply troubled woman before him was real, and she was hurting. He would have liked a few minutes with the so-called therapist who got her started down this road.

"Sure, Olive," he said softly. "If I hear from her again, that's the first thing I'll ask her."

"Thank you," she said, brightening. "Oh, thank you. And tell her I've still got the disks." Her eyes widened and her hand darted to her mouth.

"What disks?" Jack asked.

"Nothing," she said quickly. "It was nothing. Forget I said that."

Jack remembered the empty "GUT" folder in Melanie's computer.

"Computer disks, Olive?" he said, improvising. "Melanie told me she had large computer files on her Grand Unification Theory. She said she made copies for safekeeping and that she was giving them to someone she trusted." He was stabbing in the dark here. "Was that someone you?"

"Her theory? All her work?" Olive sat frozen, staring at Jack. "She told you?"

Jack nodded. "You've got them in a safe place, I hope."

"Yes, but I don't know anything about computers, so I have no idea what's on them. And I was wondering why she didn't give them to Lew. Do you think she doesn't trust him?"

Good question. Why *hadn't* she given them to her husband?

"I can't say, Olive. I never met her, and I've only known Lew since Tuesday."

"Melanie and I are very close. She's such a good, warm person. She'll always listen to me, always comfort me. She never has a bad word to say about anyone. She's been like a sister to me."

That didn't jibe with Lew's description of a woman with few friends or social contacts.

"If something's happened to her . . ." Olive sniffed and blinked back tears.

"You know," Jack said slowly, cautiously, "I know a little about computers. Maybe I could help you get into those disks and—"

Olive was shaking her head. "No." Here eyes narrowed. "Why should you care about what's on those disks?"

"Well," Jack said, improvising again—this was one suspicious lady. "Melanie seemed to know about my, um, experience. I want to know how. Those disks might give us a clue as to—"

"No-no!" she said, her voice rising. "No one can see them! I promised!"

"Okay," Jack said, raising his hands in a conciliatory gesture. He didn't want her getting worked up again. "Good for you. You have to honor Melanie's trust. Does anyone else know about the disks?"

She shook her head. "Not another soul . . . until now."

"Good. We'll keep it that way. I won't mention it to anyone, not even Lew."

She wiped her eyes and composed herself, then rose to her feet.

"Thank you. You're a good man. And I'm sorry I made such a scene. I didn't mean for this to happen. It's just that I seem to cry so easily lately. Maybe it's because something inside me senses the End Times coming. Do you think that could be it?"

"I couldn't say, Olive. But I'll bet they're still a long ways off."

"Let's hope so—for both our sakes."

"What do you mean?"

She stepped closer and lowered her voice. "Get yourself a check-up, Mr. Shelby."

"Me? Why?"

"Those missing hours after you saw the light and the figure—they might have planted one of the 666 chips in you. Get a thorough examination by a doctor you trust. Soon."

Jack led her toward the door. "Yeah. That's probably a good idea. Thanks for the advice."

"And watch out for Jim Zaleski."

"Who?"

"One of our more prominent members."

Jack remembered the name now—Lew had called him a "ufologist."

"I don't know why he was ever allowed in this organization. He's so foul mouthed. He cannot seem to speak a single sentence without blaspheming or taking the name of the Lord in vain."

"I don't see how—"

"And he has a temper nearly as terrible as his tongue. I'm just hoping that Melanie didn't come to him with some information that upset him, because there's no telling what he might do."

"I'll keep that in mind."

"And the other one to watch out for is Professor Roma himself."

"I've already had a run-in with him."

"I heard. That's why I thought I could trust you . . . because I *don't* trust him. At least not yet. He could be an ally, or he could be in league with the devil."

"Why do you say that?" Jack remembered his instant dislike of the man.

"That monkey . . . I've seen him talking to it."

"Well, everybody talks to their pets now and again."

"Yes, but I've seen it answering him, whispering in his ear. I even overheard it once."

A chill shot through Jack. The way that monkey had glared at him earlier, with almost human hatred. . . .

"What did it say?"

"I don't know . . . it was speaking a language unlike any I've ever heard, almost like . . ." She glanced at him. "Have you ever heard anyone speaking in tongues?"

"Can't say I've had the pleasure."

"Well, I have. And many times the Spirit has taken me over and I've spoken myself. That's what it sounded like to me—Speaking in Tongues."

"You could be mistaken."

She nodded slowly. "Yes, I could be. But what if that monkey is some sort of familiar? That would tell us which side he's on, wouldn't it." Her eyes narrowed again. "That's why I'm watching him . . . watching him whenever I can. I'll find out the truth about Professor Salvatore Roma."

Jack opened the door and ushered her into the hall. Movement to his left caught his eye and he turned in time to see a man in a hat and a dark suit moving quickly down the hall and ducking out of sight into the elevator alcove. He had a sense that he'd been standing outside the door a few seconds ago.

Listening? he wondered. Somebody watching me? Or watching Olive? Or just somebody heading for the elevator?

He considered heading down to the alcove to get a better look at the guy, but dropped the idea when he heard the elevator bell ring. He'd never make it in time.

He turned back to Olive. "If you learn anything about You-know-who, be sure to let me know."

"I will. And remember," she said, a fearful need growing in her eyes. "If Melanie calls again—"

"I'll ask her. I promise I'll ask her."

"Bless you. I'm in 812. Call me as soon as you have any news, no matter how late the hour."

Jack closed the door and sighed with a mixture of relief and pity. One very disturbed woman. At least he hoped she was. None of that could possibly be true, could it?

Nah. Jack figured he didn't know much about the End Times, but he did know a lady who should probably be on some heavy-duty medication while she was waiting for them.

5

Jack sat with Lew during Professor Roma's welcoming address. He was less interested in the words—some mishmash about "confluence of ideas" and "spreading the Truth" and "ripping the cover off" and so on—than in the man.

Roma—sans monkey—wore a very dapper light gray Armani suit with a black collarless shirt buttoned to the top, giving him the appearance of a very rich and hip minister. Much as Jack hated to admit it, the guy was a mesmerizing speaker. He prowled the little stage with a cordless mike, gesturing dramatically, speaking without notes. Sincerity and dedication fired his every word. Here was a man with a mission.

The biographical sketch in the rear of the program book said he was a native of South Carolina and now a professor of anthropology at Northern Kentucky University.

Jack wondered how a college professor afforded Armani suits. Maybe he did a lot of public speaking, because he seemed to have a gift. He'd seized this audience of about three hundred. They listened in rapt attention, breaking into applause every time he paused. The crowd itself surprised Jack. The SESOUPers were older than he'd expected. The average age had to be forty-plus. Lots of gray heads in the audience, which was pretty evenly divided between the sexes, but almost exclusively white—he'd seen only one black face since he'd entered.

He'd been anticipating more picturesque types, and indeed he'd spotted a few ethereal, long-haired New Agers, and the inevitable bearded fat guy doing the Michelin Man thing in a stretched-to-the-limit "Abductees Do It In Space" T-shirt, but mostly he saw lots of old guys wearing white shoes and string ties with a flying saucer cinch, matrons in warm-ups and polyester pants suits, nerdy engineer types with pocket protectors and suspenders. The home towns on their badges were in states like Colorado and Missouri and Indiana.

On the whole, what was so striking about SESOUP's members was their very ordinariness. Middle America seemed to be heavily into conspiracies.

Jack didn't know whether to be heartened or dismayed.

After the standing ovation for Roma's address, everyone streamed into a large adjoining room for the cocktail reception. Jack watched singles, couples, groups greeting each other with smiles and hugs.

"Looks like a pretty friendly group," he said.

Lew nodded. "They're good people. A lot of us know each other from other similar organizations. Most are like Melanie and me—no close living relatives, not much in common with their neighbors. For many of us, these conferences are almost like family gatherings." He held up a couple of drink tickets. "Thirsty? I'm buying."

"I thought you didn't drink."

"I'm making an exception tonight."

"Okay. I'll take a beer. Anything as long as it's not made by Anheuser-Busch."

As Lew threaded his way through the crowd toward the bar, two middle-aged women stopped before Jack.

The taller of the pair introduced herself as Evelyn Something-or-other, a big, chunky blonde wearing a bright red dress, little white socks, and shiny Mary Janes on her tiny feet—all Jack could think of was an old comic book character . . . Little Dot's voracious friend. . . .

Little Lotta.

"I'm the program chairwoman?" Evelyn said. It sounded like a question. In fact, just about everything out of her mouth sounded like a question. "Lew told me about your experience? We're planning on holding panels? You know, with experiencers? Would you care to participate?"

"No, thanks," Jack said. "I'd rather not."

Evelyn smiled sympathetically. "I know there's some controversy? I mean, about your being here? But that shouldn't put you off? It's good to share? And the audience? It will be totally nonjudgmental?"

"I really don't have all that much to tell," Jack said. "I hardly remember a thing about it." How true, how true.

"I can fix that," said the other, a hawk-faced, anorectic-looking woman.

"Oh, I'm sorry," said Evelyn. "This is Selma Jones? A memory-recovery therapist?"

Selma fixed him with an intent share. "I've helped many, many experiencers regain 'lost' hours. I can help you."

And maybe turn me into an Olive Farina? Jack thought.

"Maybe some other time."

"Well, if you, you know, change your mind?" Evelyn said, laying a gentle hand on his arm. "About the panel? You'll let me know?"

"Sure. Thanks for asking. You're very kind to care."

He meant that. She seemed sincere. And it couldn't hurt to have an ally or two among the membership.

The pair moved off, and Jack looked around for Lew.

He spotted him limping toward him with a Bass Ale in each hand. He had a trim, middle-aged man in tow.

"Jack," Lew said, handing him a bottle. "I want you to meet one of SESOUP's more prominent members, Jim Zaleski."

Jack had read about Zaleski in the program book which described him as "the world's foremost ufologist who has devoted his entire life to unexplained aerial phenomena and alien manifestations." In person he appeared to be in his late forties with thin lips, horn-rimmed glasses, and longish dark hair that he repeatedly brushed off his forehead.

"Lew says you're the last one to hear from Mel," Zaleski said, giving Jack a quick handshake while his voice did light speed. "Want to talk to you about that. Got plans for breakfast tomorrow?"

"Nothing firm: a couple eggs, maybe bacon, but I could go the pancake route."

Zaleski didn't even blink. "Great. Meet me down in the coffee shop about eight. We'll talk." He clapped Lew on the shoulder. "Gotta run, Lew. Gotta work the goddamn room."

As Zaleski melted into the throng, Jack told him about turning down Evelyn's offer to be on the experiencers panel.

"Did I do the right thing?"

Lew nodded. "I'd say so. Keep things as vague as you can. The more you tell, the less interesting you'll be."

"Well, thank you very much."

Just then Lew reached out and grabbed the shoulder of someone passing by, a stocky older man with short gray hair.

"Miles! Miles, I want you to meet someone." The man stopped and turned their way. "Miles," Lew said. "This is Jack Shelby. I told you about him earlier. Jack, this is Miles Kenway."

Kenway's handshake was firm and lingering. He had a lined face and a military bearing. He wore a snug herringbone sport jacket, and appeared to be in good shape.

His icy blue eyes bored into Jack. "Good to meet you, Shelby. We must talk in depth of your experience sometime, but first let me ask you: Do you remember seeing any black helicopters at the time?"

"Uh, no," Jack said slowly, hesitating. Was this a trick question? "It was night."

Kenway's brow furrowed. "Yes. Yes, of course. Well, carry on then," he said and marched off.

"Warm fellow," Jack said to Lew as he watched Kenway work his way into the crowd.

"And now you've met all the SESOUP big shots—except Melanie, of course. Miles is the one that worries me. He's a former Army Intelligence staff sergeant who was attached to NATO where he says he came across secret UN plans to take over the country. He now heads a militia unit outside Billings, Montana."

"You mean one of those white supremacist groups?"

"He's not a racist as far as I can tell. Just staying prepared for when the shock troops of the New World Order invade the United States." Lew raised an eyebrow.

"Whatever gets you through the night," Jack said.

He watched Kenway's broad retreating back and thought he noticed a slight bulge in his sport coat at the small of his back. Was he carrying?

Both military and intelligence training, most likely armed, and probably a few Fruit Loops shy of a full bowl. Dangerous combination. This was a guy to watch.

He glanced at Lew and found him staring at the carpet, a million miles away, and lost there.

"Thinking of Melanie?" Jack said.

He nodding, blinking and biting his upper lip.

"We'll find her."

"But will she be okay when we do?" Lew said.

Jack couldn't answer that with any authority, so he said nothing.

"I really miss her," Lew said. "Especially now. This kind of gathering was always the best time for us." He took a deep shuddering breath. "I think I'll go back to my room and leave the TV on . . . maybe Melanie will contact me again. You'll be okay?"

"Sure," Jack said. The poor guy looked truly miserable . . . like a hound dog who'd lost his master. Jack felt for him. "Go ahead. I'll just hang out and . . . mingle."

Mingle? Jack thought as Lew moved off. I haven't the faintest idea how to mingle.

He never went to cocktail parties and had no skills at small talk. He felt like a stranger at a family reunion. But at least it seemed like a friendly, open family. He started weaving among the small groups clustered throughout the crowded room—

And came face to face with Professor Salvatore Roma. Jack swallowed another surge of distaste and forced a smile. He'd have to build bridges here if he was going to learn anything about Melanie Ehler's whereabouts.

"Good speech, professor," he said.

Roma blinked in surprise; his expression remained guarded, as if waiting for a zinger. When it didn't come, he smiled cautiously. "Why . . . thank you, Mr. Shelby. Very kind of you to say so. It seems we got off on the wrong foot earlier."

"Just a misunderstanding." Jack imagined himself extracting a few of Roma's too-white teeth. "I've forgotten it already."

"So have I." But Roma's eyes said otherwise.

"By the way, where's your better half?"

"My better—?"

Jack tapped his own shoulder. "Your affectionate little pet."

"Oh, you mean Mauricio." He chuckled mirthlessly. "'My better half,' indeed. Mauricio is back in my room. He doesn't do well in crowds."

"Not too cool in the one-on-one department, either. He tried to bite me before you showed up earlier."

Roma's grin broadened. "Over the years I've found Mauricio to be an excellent judge of character."

As much as he hated to, Jack had to smile. Score one for you, Sal.

"Later," Jack said, and began to turn away.

"Oh, one more thing," Roma said.

As Jack faced him again, Roma raised his right hand with his three middle fingers raised and curved. He moved it slowly downward on a diagonal in front of Jack's body.

"What's that?" Jack said. "The secret SESOUP salute?"

Roma sighed. "Hardly," he said softly. He shook his head. "How easily we forget."

Jack stared at him, baffled. "Forget what?"

But Roma only smiled and moved off into the crowd.

6

Miles Kenway swirled his scotch on the rocks and watched Roma and the newcomer talking. Something not right between those two. Everybody knew about the showdown between them this morning—almost came to blows from what Miles had heard—and now they were smiling at each other. How do you figure that?

Maybe I'm just cranky, he thought.

Not without good reason: When he'd checked into his room today he'd found that it faced east. No way he was staying in a room that faced toward the UN. No telling what kind of devices those NWO types over there would be aiming at him during the night. He'd gone back to registration and got in their faces until they put him in a west-facing room.

He took a sip of his scotch and watched Roma and the newcomer go their separate ways. Roma was okay. Miles had him checked out—a professor just like he said; a family man with a wife and two kids, no criminal record, no ties to shady organizations. But the newcomer . . .

Jack Shelby . . . I'll just bet.

Miles couldn't say exactly what it was, but something about this fellow didn't sit well. Maybe it was the way he looked at people. Those eyes . . . just sucking in everything. But sneakily: watch him raise his beer to his lips and scan the room while he takes a long, slow sip.

Wouldn't surprise me a bit if he's already spotted my .45, he thought.

Or maybe it was the way the newcomer moved. Like a cat. No, not just a cat—a jaguar. A just plain nobody who just happened to lose a few hours after seeing a light in the Jersey Pines shouldn't move like a predator cat.

Miles had seen men like that. He had a couple of them in his unit back in Montana. Always looked ready to spring into action. Both were ex-Navy SEALs.

Was this fellow special forces too? Had the One Worlders brainwashed him, changing him from someone sworn to protect his country into someone dedicated to bringing it down?

He wouldn't be the first.

Another thing that bothered Miles about Shelby was the way he'd appeared out of nowhere and insinuated himself into a supposedly exclusive group.

But why should that surprise me? he thought with a mental shake of his head. The SESOUP folks aren't the most alert bunch.

Lew was too gullible, pure and simple. He took far too many things at face value. And unless Shelby was wearing a pentagram or inverted cross tattooed on his forehead, Olive would think he was okay. And Zaleski . . . he was only on the lookout for aliens.

Miles knew that the threat to the world as he knew it would arrive as a perfectly normal human being. Melanie probably knew it too. Were she here, she'd keep this Shelby character at arm's length. Miles and Melanie were the only sensible ones among the members . . . and sometimes he wasn't so sure about her. She'd been getting some weird ideas lately.

As usual, Miles would have to rely on himself. And his contacts.

He still had a few trusted moles in the intelligence community. His best was in the FBI—a good man, recently converted to the cause, who'd agreed to stay with the Bureau in order to keep an eye on things from the inside. It might be wise to ask him to do a background check on this Jack Shelby, just like he'd done on Sal Roma.

Miles would keep a close watch on Shelby tonight and see where he left his beer bottle. He'd use that as a fingerprint source. An excellent starting point.

7

Jack wandered the room, focusing here and there on the various conversations in progress around him. He heard "JFK" mentioned to his right and saw half a dozen middle-aged men and women standing in a loose circle. He sidled their way.

"Look," said a silver-haired fellow with a neatly trimmed beard, "all the evidence shows that Kennedy was killed because he was going to reveal MJ-12's deal with the grays."

Jack blinked. MJ-12? Grays? Was this some sort of code?

"Haven't you seen the latest?" said a round-faced woman with long straight brown hair. "His driver was the second gun, and he administered the *coup de grâce* because Kennedy was going to pull us out of Vietnam!"

"Going to take us out of Vietnam?" said another guy. "Like hell! He'd just committed more troops to Vietnam. No, you two are looking for way-out solutions when the truth is much more mundane. Kennedy was whacked by the mob for screwing with Giancana's babe!"

They all began talking at once. Just for the hell of it, Jack added to the babble: "Um, how about Oswald?"

That stopped them cold. They all turned to stare at him. He suddenly felt like a caterer who'd just brought a platter of glazed ham to a Moslem banquet.

Finally the bearded man spoke. "Oswald? You some kind of nut?"

They all started babbling at once again, but this time at him. Jack backed away and escaped before they could encircle him, and in the process he bumped into someone.

"Sorry," he said, turning and offering an apologetic smile to a guy holding an eight-by-ten photo.

"It's okay," said the guy, who looked to be about eighty. He thrust the photo toward Jack. "Here. Take a look at this." He turned to the younger fellow with him who sported a Fu Manchu mustache. "Here's a completely neutral observer. Let's see what he says." Then to Jack: "Go ahead. Tell us what you see."

Jack looked at the photo and shrugged. "It's the Earth—looks like a picture of the northern hemisphere of the Earth from orbit."

"Right—a satellite shot of the North Pole. I had this part of it blown up. See that dark spot? That's the hole that leads to the inside."

"Inside where?"

"Inside the earth. It's hollow, you know. There's a whole other civilization inside, and that's the entrance."

"Looks like a shadow."

"No, you're not looking closely enough." He snatched the photo from Jack and jabbed his finger at the dark splotch. "That's a huge opening. That's where the saucers come from."

"Saucers?" Jack said.

Over the guy's shoulder Jack saw his Fu Manchu'd companion rolling his eyes and rotating his finger by his right temple.

"Yes!" said the old guy, brandishing the photo. "People have been brainwashed into thinking that UFOs are from outer space. They're not! UFOs are from inside the earth!"

He stomped off with his photo.

"UFOs from inside the hollow earth," the guy with the Fu Manchu said derisively, watching him go. "Some people will believe almost anything."

Jack nodded enthusiastically. At last—someone with an ounce of common sense. "A bit of a nut, ay?" he said from the corner of his mouth.

"I'll say. Everybody knows they're based on the dark side of the moon."

Jack said nothing, just kept nodding and smiling as he backed away. He heard "Princess Di" as he passed another group, and paused.

"It was the Royal Family, I tell you. Queen Liz offed Di with the help of the Masons. It was the minefield thing."

"The minefields? Oh, don't be silly!"

"Those mines are where they are for a *reason*. You don't really believe they're all just *normal* land mines, do you? If the poor girl had just kept her mouth shut, she'd still be with us."

"She *is* still with us! Nobody offed Di. That whole thing was faked. She's in hiding from the Royal Family."

"With whom?" Jack said. "Elvis?"

"Hey, now there's a thought!"

And there's my cue to move on.

He glanced at his watch. He had to get out to Elmhurst to set up watch in the Castlemans' backyard, to keep an eye on Gus and the purportedly abused Ceil.

On his way to the escalators, he saw a squat, red-haired man with a full beard in a wheelchair exiting the elevator. The man began rolling along but after a dozen feet or so he suddenly braked and stared at Jack. He looked almost startled to see him.

Do I know you? he thought as he passed.

No. He'd remember a guy like that.

Jack kept moving. He checked the front of his shirt and pants, but no, his fly was closed and he hadn't spilled anything. As he stepped on the escalator, he glanced back and found the red-haired guy still staring after him.

First the monkey, then Roma, now this guy. What is it about me that's so damn interesting?

8

Jack rubbed his grainy eyes as he crouched in the rhododendrons by the Castlemans' fence. Had to love rhodos—they provided the same cover year round.

His back ached and his butt was cold from sitting on the ground. He pulled his gym bag under him for insulation. The hard irregular lumps of the tools inside were almost as uncomfortable as the ground. Had to remember to bring a cushion tomorrow night.

He'd spent hours observing the Castlemans' home life and so far hadn't seen a hint of anything even remotely violent. Or remotely interesting. These were not exciting people.

Skinny little Ceil apparently had got home shortly before Jack arrived. Schaffer had said his sister worked for a small publishing house in Manhattan. The little kitchen TV was on—Jack recognized *Eyewitness News*—and she was pouring herself a stiff vodka. She watched the news as she started slicing and dicing for dinner; she'd smoked three cigarettes and downed another vodka by the time big Gus Castleman came in from a hard day of accounting at Gorland Industries. He peeled off his suit coat and went straight to the fridge. Maybe he grunted hello to Ceil; Jack couldn't be sure. Sure as hell no hello kiss. Gus pulled out two Bud Lights and sat down before the family room TV—Jack couldn't see what he was watching.

When dinner was ready Gus came to the kitchen table and they ate watching the TV. After dinner, more TV. Gus fell asleep around ten. Ceil woke him up after the 11:00 news and they both went to bed.

Such was life at the Castlemans'—boring to live, excruciating to watch. But Jack had a rule about being sure of a situation before he did a fix. After all, people lied. Jack lied to most people every day. Schaffer could be lying about Gus, might want him laid up for something that had nothing to do with his sister. Or Ceil might be lying to her brother, might be telling him it was Gus who gave her those bruises when all along it was some guy she was seeing on the side. Or Schaffer and Ceil could be conspiring against Gus. . . .

Jack smiled and shook his head. Less than one day with the SESOUP folk and already he was hunting up conspiracies.

Whatever, Jack needed to be sure Gus was doing what his brother-in-law said he was before he made a move on him.

But so far Gus was just boring and inattentive. That didn't rate hospital-league injuries.

If something was going to break here, Jack wanted it to happen before Sunday. Clocks were due to get pushed ahead then and the extended daylight would make surveillance a lot tougher.

Calling it a night, he crept back to the street. As he headed for his rented sedan, he heard the hum of a car engine growing behind him. He tensed. Cops, maybe? He continued strolling along with his gym bag over his shoulder, doing his best to look like a local on his way back from a late night work-out. Trouble was, the bag wouldn't withstand even a cursory inspection: under the sneakers and sweatsuit lay a full set of burglar tools and a special .45 ACP automatic.

Jack didn't turn, didn't give a hint he'd even heard the car until it came even with him. Then he glanced over, real casual like, preparing to nod and give a friendly little neighborly wave.

The car was passing under a streetlight—a black Lincoln Town Car, a later model than the one he'd seen in Monroe. And the two guys in the front seat weren't cops. Jack wasn't sure what the hell they were: Ditko characters with pale faces, black suits, white shirts, black ties, and black hats with the brims pulled low over dark glasses.

Dark glasses? It was edging toward midnight.

The driver was closer, staring straight ahead, but the passenger was leaning forward, studying Jack. Without changing speed, it glided past and cruised on down the street.

Just two guys dressed like the Blues Brothers.

So how come they left him with a case of the creeps?

IN THE WEE HOURS

Roma . . .

Salvatore Roma paced the narrow, ill-lit space between the antique boilers in the hotel basement.

It's beginning, he thought.

He could feel it, but it was building so *slowly*.

Patience, he reminded himself. Patience. You've waited so long already, you can wait a little longer now.

Mauricio had made room for himself on a low shelf. He rummaged in the white plastic shopping bag he'd brought along and removed a human finger. He held up the severed digit for Roma to see.

"Look at that fingernail," he said in the Old Tongue, his tone dripping contempt. The nail was very long, perfectly shaped, and painted a bright fuchsia with a diagonal turquoise stripe. "Where do they get the idea that this is attractive?" He bit into the nail with his sharp teeth and wrenched it free, exposing the raw nail bed. He spat it back into the bag. "I'm glad their time is up. I hate them."

Roma watched with amusement as Mauricio began to gnaw on the bloody stump of the finger, tearing off bits of flesh with quick, jerky movements. He could tell that his old companion was in a foul mood. Roma said nothing. He knew more was coming.

"As I am sure you can tell," Mauricio said finally, "I'm very upset with this recent turn of events."

"Really?" Roma hid a smile. He was fond of Mauricio but wished he had a sense of humor. "You hide it *so* well."

"I'll thank you not to mock me. You should not have

admitted that stranger. The instant I laid eyes on him I knew he was trouble."

"And how, pray tell, did you know that?"

"I *felt* it. He is a wild card, an unexpected, unquantified element who spoke not a word of truth. You should have ejected him and not allowed him to set foot through the door for the rest of the weekend."

"That was my first impulse as well, but I had a change of heart."

"The hotel was supposed to be filled with sensitives—at least one in every room. He now has one of those rooms."

"True, and I believe he may be a sensitive himself."

Mauricio had gnawed the finger's proximal phalanx clean. He cracked the bone in half and began sucking out the marrow.

"Oh? And on what did you base that decision?"

"The fact that he is marked. You noticed that, I assume."

"Of course. Immediately. But he is not merely 'marked,' he is *scarred,* and that means he has fought the Otherness—fought and survived."

"'Fought' is a loaded term, Mauricio. He was most likely just an innocent bystander, a wounded civilian."

"Perhaps, but the very fact that he survived bothers me—bothers me very much. He could be working for the enemy."

Roma laughed. "Do not be such an old woman, Mauricio. We know the enemy's agents and he is not one of them."

"We know only of the Twins. How do we know there are not more? I say we should call this off."

Roma felt his amusement fade, replaced by irritation. "I wish to hear none of that. You have been against this plan from the start and you will latch onto any excuse to abort it."

Mauricio had finished with the first phalanx. He tossed the bone fragments back into the sack, then went to work on the rest of the finger.

"I've tried to discourage you for good reason. I was put here to advise you, remember?"

"To *serve* me, Mauricio."

The monkey glared at him. "I serve the Otherness, as do you."

"But I am The One. I decide, you facilitate. Do not forget that."

They'd had this argument before—many times. Mauricio had been sent to aid him, but over the years he had come to see himself as a mentor. Roma resented that. No one on this plane had worked longer in service of the Otherness than he. He had learned the hard way, through pain, imprisonment, even death, and the last thing he needed was someone offering half-baked advice, especially at this late date.

Mauricio said, "Why won't you listen to me when I tell you this whole plan is premature? You are too impatient."

"Impatient? I have waited ages—*literally* ages—for this. Do not dare call me impatient!"

"Very well then: You are not impatient. But you have not dealt with The Lady, and the signs are not quite right yet."

They *are* right, Roma thought, because I *say* they are right.

"The Lady does not matter."

"And why here?" Mauricio went on. "New York is too crowded. Too many variables, too many ways for something to go wrong. Why not somewhere in the desert? A hotel in, say, Nevada, or New Mexico?"

"No. I want it here."

"Why?"

"I have my reasons."

Mauricio hurled the partially eaten finger across the room and leaped to the floor. He shot upright to stand on his hind legs. His usually high-pitched voice dropped two octaves as he abandoned his capuchin monkey guise and expanded to his true self—a powerful, bull chested, midnight-furred creature with blood-red eyes, standing four feet tall,

"You're not *allowed* reasons! You are The One. You are here to open the way. It is your duty and your destiny. Personal vendettas have no place in your life!"

"Then someone else should have been chosen," Roma said calmly, coldly. "Not someone with a past—a *long* past. Not someone with scores to settle. But there is no one else on this plane with the capacity to make the choice. So if I say it begins here, then here is where it will begin."

"I see I have no say in the matter," Mauricio said sullenly. He shrank into the capuchin guise again. "But mark my words well: I still think this is premature—the wrong time as well as the wrong place—and that it will end badly. I also think allowing that stranger in was a mistake. He's an enemy. And a terrible dresser."

Roma laughed, glad to ease the tension between them. Mauricio needed to be put in his place every so often, but he was too valuable an ally to alienate. "Admit it, Mauricio. That is what really bothers you about him, isn't it."

"Well, after all, did you see that hideous warm-up he wore? Absolutely dreadful." He looked Roma up and down. "How about your new suit? Any compliments on it?"

"Many." Not that he cared in the least.

"See? I told you—"

Roma held up his hand. "Wait!" A tingle began running over his skin. "Feel it? It's happening . . . the power is growing, building. Any moment now."

A portal would be opening soon. And as it did, he could only imagine what was going on with the sleeping sensitives racked on the floors above him. The last place he'd want to be right now was in their dreams. He almost felt sorry for them.

Almost.

Olive . . .

. . . awakens to the sound of chanting. She forces her eyes open and gasps.

Hooded forms, thirteen of them, crowd around her bed, each holding a thick black candle. She screams but only a muffled squeak struggles past the cloth gag bunched in her mouth. She tries to move but her hands are tied behind her and she's bound to the bed.

Panic detonates within as she realizes her rings are gone, and the crucifix has been taken from around her neck.

"Did you think you could be saved, Olive?" says a voice.

It echoes from one of the forms but she can't tell which because their faces are lost in the inky shadows within their cowls. It sounds like her father's voice, but that can't be . . . he's dead—he died ten years ago.

She begins to pray. *Our Father, Who art in Heaven . . .*

"Yes," says the voice, "I really do believe she thinks she's saved. Pathetic, isn't it."

Laughter from the other forms, male and female voices, mocking her.

"Let us remind you why you can never be saved," says the voice. "Let us take you back and show you why the face of God will be forever turned from you."

Olive screams through her gag. *Not that! Oh, please, not that again!*

She feels herself shrinking, the gag popping out of her mouth, the cords on her hands and feet falling away, to be replaced by bands of duct tape winding around her body, pinning her arms to her sides and her legs together. She tries to scream again but she has no voice here. The hotel room melts away, leaving her in a dank subcellar lit by smoky torches.

And she knows this place, oh, dear God, she remembers every detail of the horrors that were perpetrated here. For years, decades, she had no memory of these events, but gradually, through many sessions with her memory recovery therapist, she unlocked doors that had been sealed shut by her protective brain. One after another they opened and she learned what had happened to her.

And her father was the villain. After the divorce, her Bible-toting mother had filled her ears with maledictions about his drunken, no-account ways, yet still Olive had to spend every other weekend with him. And on one of those weekends, he and some of his friends dragged her along to one of their "services.". . .

And now she sees the subcellar more clearly than ever before . . . almost as if she's there. . . .

Suddenly she realizes that she *is* here. They're not going to make her remember . . . she's five again and she's going to *relive* the horror.

No-no-no-no-no! PLEASE NO!

But she cannot turn away, cannot even close her eyes. It's all here—the pentagrams and inverted crosses painted in blood on the walls. Straight ahead lies a huge marble block, dripping red. In the high, deep fireplace to the right, something that looks like a monkey is turning on a spit.

A goblet is pressed to her lips.

"Drink!" says her father's voice.

When Olive sees the thick red fluid within, and sniffs the coppery odor, she turns her head away in revulsion.

"Drink!" the voice commands.

Her head is grabbed and tilted back, her jaws forced open; thick, warm, salty liquid pours into her mouth. She coughs, gags, but they keep pouring. She feels it running over her face, clogging her nostrils, she must swallow or drown, swallow or drown. . . .

Olive swallows, gasps, tries to vomit it back up, but they squeeze her throat and keep it down.

Then she's dragged to a table—a rough wooden bench, really—and watches as one of the hooded figures slices flesh from the monkey turning on the spit . . . a chubby little thing with an unusually large head for a monkey. The flesh is laid before Olive. They don't even give her a chance to refuse it. The greasy meat is thrust into her mouth, then her jaws are forced shut and her nostrils pinched.

Again—swallow or suffocate.

She swallows.

Still gagging, she is carried to another corner of the room where a huge sow lies spread-eagled on a stone block. Its throat has been slit; its many-nippled abdomen has been opened and all the organs removed. Olive is folded into the red stinking cavity, her head in the pelvis, her feet against the diaphragm. She kicks and screams and twists as they sew the skin flaps closed, but to no avail. Soon she is entombed in the wet, suffocating darkness.

Never in her life, before or since, has Olive been so terrified, so mortally sick with fear and loathing. She is sure she is going to die. Past her sobs and whimpers she hears muffled chanting around her. The rotten air clogs in her throat. She can't breathe.

As a roaring grows in her ears and bright spots flare before her eyes, she feels a pair of hands gripping her head, the fingers curving under her jaw and pulling. Darkness still engulfs her. Where did the hands come from?

The hands pull, harder and harder, until she is sure her head will come off. She kicks toward the pressure and suddenly she's moving, squeezing through a tight, tight passage, and then there's air! Who'd have thought this dank subterranean air could smell so sweet? She sucks deep drafts as the rest of her body is pulled free of the sow through the space between its legs.

The chanters cheer and tear off their robes. They are naked beneath, and now they dance and drink and go into a rutting frenzy—men with women, women with women, men with men.

Child Olive squeezes her eyes shut while adult Olive thinks about all that followed after she regained these memories. She remembers confronting her father as he lay dying of cirrhosis—despite his toxic state, he gave a great performance of wounded incredulity. And even his mother, who hated the man and never had a good word to say about him, declared that he never could have been a part of such horrendous doings.

Lies, all lies.

Olive went to the local police. They investigated but could find no evidence of such a cult. Of course not. How could they? The evidence was three decades old.

Then she heard that the FBI was investigating the wave of reports of Satanic ritual abuse sweeping the country. Olive told them her story. The agents were properly sympathetic, and dutifully took down her information, but their investigation also yielded nothing.

How could that be? she wondered in all her naïveté. How could one of the finest crime fighting organizations in the world find no evidence of such a widespread cult?

When she went back to the federal office and insisted that they keep looking, one of the investigators took her aside. He told her that they'd investigated hundreds of these claims and had yet to find any corroborating evidence. They'd combed through houses where others with recovered memories claimed that dozens of children had been ritually abused and sacrificed, and had found not a trace of blood. He even went so far as to suggest to Olive that what she remembered most likely never happened, that it was something called false memory syndrome, instilled by suggestions from her memory recovery therapist.

Olive thanked him very much . . . and fled the building.

Because then she knew . . . the very people she was turning to for help were part of the problem. This was bigger than she ever had imagined. Higher-ups in the government were linked to a powerful worldwide network of murderous satanic pedophiles and pornographers who destroyed all evidence when they could, and planted disinformation when they could not. And when that didn't work, the Lord of Evil protected them— Satan himself implanted distortions in the brains of survivors, to make them seem like poor delusional fools.

A filigree of deceit encasing the world, concealing the truth . . .

Abruptly Olive is no longer lying on the floor. She feels sheets around her, a mattress against her back. And she is no longer a child.

She opens her eyes. She is back in her hotel room, and the Satanists are gathered again around her bed.

"So you plainly see, Olive," says her father's mocking voice, "why you can never be saved. You have drunk human blood and eaten human flesh. In God's eyes you are a blight on His creation, you are anathema. You will be cast into hell where we can all be together—for eternity!"

"No!" she cries. "I'm saved! I've been born again!"

Vicious laughter all around as her father says, "Born again? Olive, dear, you cannot be born again into the Spirit, because you have *already* been born again—of a sow!" The laughter grows louder. "And when did you last hear of a *pig* entering heaven?"

Olive sobs. She squeezes her eyes shut and claps her hands over her ears—for some reason, her hands are free now—to shut out the laughter. Soon the laughter fades. Hesitantly, she opens her eyes. . . .

She was alone.

Olive sat up in her bed and rubbed her eyes. She looked around in the darkness. Across the room, next to the square shadow of the TV, the red glowing numerals on the alarm clock read 4:28.

Relief flooded through her. A dream . . . an appalling, horrifying dream, but only a dream. Her father was dead. He couldn't hurt her anymore. He—

Olive froze. The glowing numerals had disappeared . . . as if someone had stepped between her and the clock. She sensed movement on both sides of her.

Oh, no! Please, God, NO!

She couldn't bear to relive that again. She opened her mouth to scream but a leather-clad hand slithered across her face and sealed her lips . . .

Jack . . .

. . . awakens to a sound . . . a scratching noise. . . .

He sits up and focuses on it. Coming from the door. He reaches under the pillow and finds the Glock; he works the slide to chamber a round, then pads to the door.

As he reaches it, he notices the odor.

Rakoshi stink.

Not again. But that was a dream. This is real.

He puts his eye to the peephole and peers into the hall. Something wrong out there. All the lights are out. It's like peeking into a coffin . . . but it smells worse.

Then he sees the eyes, pairs of glowing yellow almond-shaped slits floating in the darkness, and he knows.

Rakoshi!

No time to wonder how as a huge weight slams against the other side of the door. Jack jumps back. The weight hits the door again, and again, until the wood shatters, sending splinter missiles hurtling toward him.

Jack backpedals across the room, firing all the way. He jumps onto the bed. With his back to the wall he blasts wildly, down and around, everywhere he sees the eyes.

When the clip is empty, he stands there panting, sweating. The eyes are gone and he can't hear anything past the ringing in his ears. Slowly, cautiously, he bends, gropes, finds the switch on the bedside lamp, and turns it.

Blinking in the sudden glare, he gasps at the sight of a dozen or more hulking, cobalt-skinned creatures milling about the room, unharmed by the fusillade he's just loosed at them. They turn their shark-snouted heads his way, bare their teeth, and rake the air with their talons, but they do not approach. They merely watch him with their yellow basilisk eyes, as if waiting for him to fall over dead. No hurry. He's not going anywhere.

How? How did they get to his room without causing a panic and leaving a trail of bloody carnage in their wake?

And what the hell are they waiting for?

He should be glad they're waiting. His extra clips are in his gym bag over by the door. Not that they would do much good—bullets never seemed to have much effect on these things. But fire . . . yeah, fire works.

He glances at the lamp. If he broke the bulb, could he spark a flame with the exposed innards?

He's reaching for it when he hears a voice.

"Do not be afraid, Jack."

He jerks around. Who—?

One of the rakoshi, larger than the rest, has moved closer, gesturing to him.

"We are your brothers."

The voice seems to be coming from the rakosh. But that's impossible.

"What?" he says aloud, feeling like an idiot.

The rakoshi he knew had the brains of pit bulls and the deadly homing instincts of Tomahawk missiles— and were about as explosively destructive. The ones he killed could say a word or two, but were far behind the dumbest parrot in the vocabulary department.

And yet the voice is there, calling him by name.

"You are half rakosh, Jack. You have denied your true nature long enough. It is time at last to come out of the closet."

What the hell is it talking about?

"Purge your human side, Jack, and come the rest of the way over. It is just a step. Just one easy step."

"You're crazy," he says, and it sounds so lame.

"Still in denial, then? We feared that. We know what is keeping you from embracing your true nature, and because you are our brother, we will help you cross over."

Jack notices a commotion over by the shattered door—the rakoshi there seem suddenly agitated. Jack pauses, then feels his blood crystallize as Gia and Vicky are dragged into view. All the air seems to rush from the room, leaving him gasping.

"Jack!" they scream in unison as they see him.

He moves toward them but the big rakosh slams him back against the wall and pins him there.

"Wait," it says.

Jack watches in horror as Gia is driven to the floor. Half a dozen rakoshi surround her, blocking her from view. He struggles frantically to get free, clubbing at the big rakosh with his empty pistol, but he's pinned like a moth to a board. He shouts in rage and anguish as he sees their talons rise and fall, going down clean, coming up red. He hears Gia's wails of pain, Vicky's cries of horror. Gia's blood spatters the wall and Jack goes mad—black closes in around the edges of his crimson vision. With a joint-popping lunge he breaks free of the rakosh's grasp and makes a diving leap toward the melee.

In the air he has a glimpse of Gia's torn body, her wide blue eyes beseeching him as the life fades from them. He shouts in horror, but is batted away—powerful arms grip him and hurl him toward the window. He crashes through the glass but manages to twist and catch the sill. He's hanging by his fingertips, kicking for purchase on the brick wall, unable to see into the room but hearing Vicky's wails of terror turn to screams of pain, and then end with a gurgle and he knows she's gone and it's too late to save her, too late for both of them, and without them, what's the point of going on? Because if he can't save them, if of all people he can't protect Gia and Vicky, then his whole life is a sham and he might as well end it here.

He looks down and sees a gaping hole in the street below, growing larger, swallowing the asphalt pavement, then the sidewalk.

A hiss above him—the big rakosh, hanging over the sill. It raises its three-taloned hands, dripping red.

"They are gone. Nothing stands in your way now, brother. Join your true family."

"No!" Jack shouts.

"You must!" The rakosh hops up onto the sill, poised like a diver. *"Come! We are going home."*

The creature leaps over Jack and plummets toward the ever-widening maw of the hole. With a chorus of shrill cries, the rest of the rakoshi do the same, arcing over Jack in a dark hellish cataract, cascading toward the bottomless pit yawning below.

And finally they're gone, and all is still. But Jack can't bring himself to crawl back into that room and see the torn bloody ruins of the two most important people in his life.

In complete despair, he lets go and begins to fall, crying out not with fear but with the pain of incalculable loss as he tumbles through space, eager for the dark embrace that will blot out the horror of his failure—

But he lands softly . . .

. . . on a mattress. . . .

Jack twisted violently and almost fell out of bed.

"Wha—?"

Dark. He was in his hotel room. No scratching at the

door, no odor. He turned on the light—the room was empty. He checked the pistol under the pillow—full clip; a sniff of the muzzle showed it hadn't been fired recently. He looked around the room: everything in its place, the drapes still drawn as he'd left them.

He sagged and moaned, "Oh, Christ!" A dream—it had been a dream. He was so filled with relief he almost sobbed.

He glanced at the clock. 4:32 A.M.

Another rakoshi-mare. And this time Gia and Vicky were in it—torn to pieces in it. The dream had had a premonitory feel. Jack's stomach roiled at the thought. But it couldn't be. The rakoshi were gone. What the hell was going on then?

He shook himself and, pistol still in hand, left the bed. Thirsty. He flipped the bathroom light switch. As the fluorescents flickered to life he jumped back.

A crate, dark, dark green, five feet long and a foot high and wide, floated in the center of the bathroom, maybe three feet off the floor. Smoky wisps trailed off its surface like steam, white tendrils drifting toward the floor like dry ice fumes. Cold air seeped around his ankles . . . flowing from the crate.

Jack's first instinct was to point his pistol at it. Then he realized . . .

"I'm still dreaming. Got to be."

A glance left showed that the room door was still locked, the sturdy swing latch still in the closed position. But that didn't mean a whole hell of a lot. Jack knew those could be bypassed—he'd done it a few times himself. The gym bag was the clincher—it was still snug against the door, right where he'd left it.

He didn't feel as if he was dreaming. He slapped his face. It stung.

And then with a crash that sent him diving for cover, the box dropped to the floor.

Bomb was the first thought to flash though his head. But who'd leave a bomb in a big green crate in a bathroom? And it hadn't exploded when it dropped.

He peeked around the corner. The box sat cold and quiet on the tiles. Looked completely harmless. But Jack was in no hurry to see what was inside.

He checked the door again. No way it had been opened. So how—?

He stopped himself.

Wait. What am I thinking? This isn't happening. It's no more real than those rakoshi of a few minutes ago. I keep forgetting I'm still asleep.

This felt pretty damn real for a dream, but what else could it be? Which meant he shouldn't be wasting his time trying to answer unanswerable questions when all this would be gone when the dream ended.

He headed back to the bed, closed his eyes, and waited to wake up.

Roma . . .

"Where is it?"

Roma stood in the center of the basement and turned in a slow circle, arms spread in bafflement. The portal had opened and closed—he knew it, he'd *felt* it—but he had nothing to show for it.

Anger mixed with new, unfamiliar emotions: confusion and, strangest of all, uncertainty.

"Where is the device? Why was it not sent?"

"It *was* sent," Mauricio said, tying up his plastic bag. "I sense it somewhere in this building. But not here."

"But it was supposed to be delivered *here*. To me."

"Obviously it wasn't."

The creature's serene tone rankled Roma. "Mauricio . . ."

"Something has gone wrong—as I predicted."

Roma felt his anger flare to incandescence. "I want no more talk of your predictions! I want that device. You say it is somewhere in this building—find it! *Now!*"

Mauricio stared at Roma a moment, then hopped down to the floor.

"It's that stranger," he said. "I'm sure of it."

"Then find him. Let him be a stranger no more. Learn about him—where he lives, who he knows, who he loves—*especially* who he loves. A man who loves is vulnerable. Love is an excellent lever, one we should not hesitate to use should we need to."

Mauricio nodded and, without another word, trotted off, dragging his plastic bag behind him.

Disquiet nibbled at the base of Roma's spine as he watched him go. Could Mauricio be right? Was it not yet his time?

No. That was not in question. Then what had gone wrong? Was he right that the stranger—the insect who called himself Jack Shelby—was the problem?

He would have to learn more about him. And if he proved to be the source of interference, Roma would see to it that he sorely regretted the day he had dared to insinuate his insignificant presence into something so momentous.

FRIDAY

THE 1ST ANNUAL CONFERENCE OF THE SOCIETY FOR THE EXPOSURE OF SECRET ORGANIZATIONS AND UNACKNOWLEDGED PHENOMENA

SCHEDULE OF EVENTS
FRIDAY

Registration Desk Open:	8:00 A.M.–8:00 P.M.
Exhibits Open:	8:00 A.M.–8:00 P.M.

8:00–9:20 A.M.:	**Experiencers' Panel**
9:30–10:20 A.M.:	**The Nephilim of the Bible:** Fallen angels—or the first alien visitors?
10:30–NOON:	**Blue Helmet Warning:** An ex-NATO official tells of the actual plans he saw for a UN-led takeover of America
NOON–1:30 P.M.:	Lunch Break
1:30–2:50 P.M.:	**El Niño:** The unnatural "natural" phenomenon—evidence that heat from CIA solar mirrors are creating El Niño conditions in the Pacific waters off the west coast of South America.
3:00–5:00 P.M.:	**UFOs Over Tokyo:** Eyewitness accounts with photos!
5:00–7:00 P.M.:	**Cocktail Reception**—meet the panelists
9:00 PM–???:	**Films:** *Invasion USA, The Devil's Bride, Earth vs. the Flying Saucers*

1

Jack tried but couldn't sleep. And when dawn came, he returned to the bathroom and found the dark green crate still there.

Impossible.

No, he didn't want to say impossible. Because obviously it was possible. Once you started believing the impossible, the next step was maybe hearing someone speaking to you through your TV.

He pulled the curtains and looked outside. The city was awakening. Garbage trucks rumbling and clanking, people walking their dogs before heading for work. . . .

Just another day in Hell's Kitchen.

But not just another day in this particular hotel room. That crate wasn't a dream. The part about it floating in mid-air—*that* had been a dream—but the damn crate was real.

Back to the bathroom.

All right, let's think about this, he told himself, staring at the box. If the crate's real and it didn't come through the door, how did it get here? How did someone sneak it into the room without me hearing anything?

Cautiously he stepped into the bathroom. The crate wasn't steaming anymore, the air against his feet no longer cold. He reached his hand toward its surface but didn't touch it: seemed to be room temperature now. Close up like this, he could make out fine traces of black within its dark green surface.

Avoiding contact, Jack knelt and checked the floor

around the crate, inspected under the sink counter, opened all the drawers . . . no sign of an opening or hidden door.

Baffled, he sat on the edge of the tub and stared at the crate. How had the damn thing got here?

Gingerly, he nudged it with his toe. The wood didn't feel like any wood he'd ever known. The cover moved under light pressure from his toe and he jerked his foot back.

It wasn't sealed.

Giving the crate wide clearance, Jack retrieved the desk chair from the next room. He felt like a jerk, leaning around the edge of the bathroom doorway and poking at the crate with the chair leg, but he freely admitted that this thing had him spooked and he wasn't taking any chances.

Finally the lid slid off. No explosion, no snakes or giant spiders came crawling out. The overhead lights gleamed off . . . metal bars.

He stepped in for a closer look. The crate held a jumble of miniature girders. Looked like an oversized erector set, with nuts and bolts and braces, but no plans.

Was he supposed to know what this was? Hell, was it even meant for him?

And then he saw part of the underside of the lid. Looked like a diagram. He flipped it the rest of the way over. Yeah. Plans that looked like an old blueprint for assembling whatever it was, not printed on the material, more like engraved in white into its dark green surface. Some sort of an oil rig, or something that resembled one. But the plans looked incomplete. The top of the structure appeared to be cut off at the upper end of the lid, as if they'd run out of room.

Didn't matter. He wasn't about to start assembling it. He had better things to do. He searched the crate inside and out for an address. He'd take an invoice, or a "To" or a "From"—he wasn't picky—but found nothing.

He replaced the lid—*weird* texture to that material—and slid the crate under the sink counter.

Is somebody gaslighting me? he wondered.

After all, he was surrounded by loons.

Probably best to sit on it—figuratively—for now and see if anyone asked about it, or came looking for it.

He wasn't too crazy about showering with that crate in the bathroom, but he managed it—warily. He stood under the hot geyser and wondered what he'd got himself into here. That nightmare with the rakoshi and that voracious hole gobbling up the city . . . how could a dream leave him so unsettled? Maybe because he couldn't shake the feeling that it was more than a dream . . . that it was some sort of premonition. But of what?

And then the crate . . .

He pulled back the curtain to see if it was still there. Yeah, right where he'd left it under the counter. A woman disappears, a strange box appears. Any connection? And if so, how?

The hot water relaxed his tight muscles, but did little to ease his mind.

Feeling as if the walls were closing in, he quickly dried off, threw on a flannel shirt and jeans, and called Lew.

2

Jack met Lew outside the coffee shop where they found James Zaleski waiting with a guy in a cowboy shirt and boots he introduced as Tony Carmack. Tony had a more-than-generous nose and wore his hair in a long-banged Caesar cut. He looked like the old Sonny Bono from the '60s, but when he opened his mouth he was pure Dallas-Fort Worth. Zaleski had shed his suit for a long-sleeved red shirt and a dark blue down vest.

The receptionist led them to a rear booth. Jack got stuck on the inside, which he never liked, but decided not to make an issue of it. Lew was next to him on the end. Carmack had the other end; Zaleski was directly across from Jack.

The young, dark-haired waitress with an Eastern European accent left them with menus and a carafe of coffee. Jack jumped on it. Caffeine . . . he needed caffeine.

So did Zaleski and Carmack, apparently.

"What a fucking night," Zaleski said, brushing his hair off his forehead. "Worst dream of my life."

"You too?" Carmack said. "I dreamed I was in a cornfield being crushed by a landing UFO."

What is this place? Jack wondered. Nightmare city? He didn't mention his own.

"Are you a ufologist too?" he asked Carmack. He couldn't resist using the term.

The Texan shrugged. "Of sorts. Actually I'm what they call a 'cereologist.'"

"An expert on crop circles," Lew offered.

"Crop circles?" Jack said as he added sugar.

"Yep. Never thought too much of this UFO stuff," Tony said. "Then one day I woke up and found the corn in one of the back fields of my farm crushed flat in three big ol' circles—*concentric* circles, all of 'em perfect. That made me a believer. I just—"

"Yeah, yeah," Zaleski said, jumping in and waving Carmack off. "You and Shelby can trade sheep-humping farm stories later." He stared at Jack through his thick horn rims. "The reason I wanted to talk to you was to find out if Melanie mentioned anything else when she called you."

Carmack grimaced and sighed. Looked like he was used to being cut off by Zaleski.

"Like what?" Jack said as innocently as he could.

"Like about what else she might be working on."

Jack shook his head. "She just asked me to come out to her place to discuss my 'experience.' I was pretty shocked, seeing as I hadn't mentioned it to a soul, and I asked her how she knew. She said, 'I just do.' And that was pretty much it."

This didn't seem to be at all to Zaleski's liking. "Come on, Shelby—"

"Jack."

"Okay, Jack. There had to be more to it than that. Hell, she talked everybody's fucking ears off"—a glance at Lew—"no offense, man." Lew shrugged and Zaleski went right back to Jack. "You're *sure* she didn't say anything else?"

"That's what I told you, isn't it?" Jack said. This guy had the personality of a piranha. "I can make something up if you like. . . ."

As Zaleski frowned, Jack noticed Carmack grinning and giving him a secret thumbs up.

What's the score between these two? he wondered.

Jack added, "I'd really like to find her so I can ask her how she knew."

"Just what *did* happen to you?" Carmack said.

Jack told his story.

"Typical alien abduction," Zaleski said when he was through.

"I wasn't abducted."

"Hell you weren't. That's what happened during those missing hours. The Jersey pine barrens are notorious for big-time alien activity. You notice any pain up your ass afterwards?"

"Any *what?*"

"Let me rephrase," he said with faux delicacy. "*Rectal* pain. The grays like to use anal probes on their abductees." He made a twisting motion with his hand. "Right up the old wazoo."

"Not to me, they didn't," Jack said, squirming at the thought. "And who are the grays?"

Zaleski rolled his eyes. "The gray aliens, man—you know, with the oval-shaped heads and the black almond-shaped eyes, like you see on T-shirts and bumper stickers? They're known as grays."

"Oh, like in *Close Encounters*."

Zaleski's expression at the mention of the film would have been right at home on someone who'd just bitten into a wormy apple.

"I think I'd remember *them*," Jack said.

"Not if they wiped your memory, dude. And if you start to remember anything, keep mum, otherwise the Men in Black will come calling."

Jack smiled. "Yeah? You mean like Tommy Lee Jones and Will Smith?"

Zaleski's face darkened. "Trust me, you won't be visited by some wisecracking clowns like in the movie. That travesty was produced for the sole purpose of making the real Men in Black look benign, to hide the fact that they're ruthless agents of MJ-12."

"What's MJ-12?" Jack remembered hearing mention of that at the reception last night.

Zaleski stared at him. "Christ, you really are a virgin, aren't you."

"Easy, Jim," Carmack said, leaning forward. "Not everyone knows what we know."

"I just can't believe how *ignorant* people are."

As Jack was debating whether to laugh or break Zaleski's nose, the waitress reappeared.

She took their orders, and hurried off. Jack poured himself more coffee and glanced at Lew where he sat on the end of the booth cushion. He was staring off into space, his gaze fixed somewhere out near the grays' home planet maybe. He had to have heard all this a zillion times before. Probably bored out of his skull. Or maybe just missing Melanie.

"Okay," Carmack said. "Here's how it is: I've got to assume you've heard about the Roswell crash and Area 51 and all that."

"Sure," Jack said. He'd figured how he could get Zaleski's goat. "I learned all about that in *Independence Day*. Saw it twice."

Zaleski slapped a hand over his face. "Oh, Christ!"

"Cool it, Jim," Carmack said. To Jack: "Then you know that a saucer crashed and members of an alien race were found in the wreckage. But the real skinny is that we've been in ongoing contact with that alien race since Truman was president. All the rapid technological advancements since the fifties didn't come from the billions of dollars spent on the arms and space race: it was donated. By the gray aliens."

"How generous of them," Jack said.

"It doesn't come without a price," Zaleski said, "but nobody's reading the small print."

"Just let me finish," Carmack said, showing a little annoyance. "We're going to need all that help—all the help we can get. When the grays arrived in their saucers in the 1940s, they warned us of a flesh-eating reptilian race called the Reptoids that's been roaming the galaxy in a spacecraft that looks like an asteroid. When they find us—not if, *when*—they'll turn Earth into a giant cattle ranch, and we'll be the cattle."

Zaleski was shaking his head in disagreement. He said nothing but looked as if he were about to explode.

"The grays made us a deal," Carmack continued. "They'd supply us with some of their advanced technology in return for allowing them to experiment on animals and abduct people now and again."

"They abduct animals too?"

"You've heard about cattle mutilations, right?"

"Sure, but—"

Carmack nodded sagely. "The grays."

"But why?"

"They're an ancient race, and apparently they need to borrow some human DNA—just a little—to rejuvenate their own damaged genes. That's where MJ-12 comes in. Back in 1952 an ultra-secret government within the U.S. government called Majestic-12 was set up to deal with the aliens. MJ-12 has been keeping all evidence of the aliens under wraps. Thus the ongoing cover-up of the Roswell crash."

They paused as the waitress delivered their platters. Eggs for Zaleski and Lew, waffles for Carmack, a stack of buttermilk pancakes for Jack.

"I'd think contact with another race would be the biggest, greatest story of all time," Jack said as he drowned his cakes in syrup.

"It would be . . . except for the part about the approaching Reptoids. Think of the panic that would cause. And then if news of government-sanctioned alien abductions ever got out . . . we'd have riots in the streets."

Jack shook his head in disbelief. "You mean this has been going on for over half a century and *nobody's* blown the whistle?"

Zaleski jumped in. "*Very* few people know—even presidents are kept in the dark. JFK found out, however, and he was going to go public with what he knew. That's why he was offed. Unfortunately he told his brother, who then told Marilyn Monroe while he was boffing her, so the two of them had to go as well."

"But *you* guys know," Jack said. Or at least think you know. "How come you're still walking around?"

"Because we're nobodies," Carmack said. "And nobody's listening to us . . . at least nobody that really matters."

Zaleski pounded his fist on the table. "The Freedom of fucking Information Act revealed that every government agency—from the NSA to the Department of Education—has files on UFOs. Thousands of pages on something that officially doesn't exist. But people *still* don't believe." His voice rose as he pounded his fist again. "When are they going to wise up? We're a country of Pollyannas! Dickhead Nation!"

People at surrounding tables were craning their necks to see what was going on. He overheard someone mutter, "Uh-oh, Jimmy Z's at it again."

"Easy, Jim," Carmack said. "You don't want to have one of your hissy fits."

"The hell I don't." He turned to Jack. "Tony's only telling you part of the story. He—"

"Shoot," Carmack said. "You ain't gonna lay that Grand Deception cowflop on him are you?"

"Damn right. You had your turn, now I'll have mine. Okay?"

Carmack leaned back with a disgusted expression and nibbled a piece of toast.

"In my opinion, and I'm not alone in this," Zaleski said, "there are no Reptoids coming to Earth. That's all a big lie cooked up by the grays to gain our confidence and pursue their real agenda: crossbreeding with us and taking over the Earth."

"Now hold on a sec," Jack said. "I'm no biologist, but I've never heard of a goat crossbreeding with a cow, and I know cats don't crossbreed with dogs, so how can aliens from light years away crossbreed with us?"

"I don't pretend to know how, but they're doing it. You wouldn't believe some of the aborted fetuses I've seen: big heads, grayish skin, big black eyes. It's happening. Maybe it's advanced science, maybe there's a common human-gray ancestor somewhere. Maybe that's what Melanie's Grand Unification was about. Maybe her Grand Unification Theory will prove my Grand Deception Theory."

Lew seemed to perk up at the mention of Melanie's name, but then lapsed into Neverland again. His barely touched eggs were congealing on his plate.

"But the grays have got something else up their sleeves," Zaleski said. "They're inserting tiny probes into the brains of abductees for—"

Carmack threw down his fork with a clatter. "Hogwash!"

"No, Tony," Zaleski said with forced patience. "It's fucking true. You just won't see it. You think they're these goody-goody Munchkin allies. Sorry, bro, they're not. They've been controlling MJ-12 since 1984 and the rate of abductions has skyrocketed. And they've started implanting probes to monitor and program abductees after they're released."

"They're not, dammit. They're on our side!"

Zaleski put a finger up his nose and leaned toward

Carmack. "Probes, Tony." He wiggled the finger. "Right up the nose and into the fucking brain."

"That's it," Carmack said, rising. He pulled ten bucks from a pocket and tossed it onto the table. "I'm outta here." He pointed to Jack. "And you'll leave too, if you're smart."

He turned and stomped toward the exit.

Zaleski called after him: "You just don't want to believe about the probes because your honker's so big you've probably got a couple dozen up there already!"

Carmack never looked back.

Zaleski grinned. Not a nice sight—his already thin upper lip disappeared completely. "I love that fucker."

"I can tell," Jack said.

"No, really. We're good friends, it's just that he strays too far from mainstream ufology."

Now *there,* Jack thought, is an oxymoron to conjure with.

"But in all seriousness," Zaleski said, tapping his forehead, "you oughta think about getting a skull X ray to see if you've got a fucking alien probe in the ol' noggin."

"You really think so?" Jack said, putting on a concerned expression.

Which should I check for first? he wondered. The 666 chip or the alien brain probe?

"Definitely. The aliens have been using the probes to program abductees about some momentous event that will occur in the next few years."

"Like what?"

"Don't know. They've got a secret plan. That's another reason I'm anxious to hear Melanie's Grand Unification Theory. Maybe she'll shed some light on what the grays are up to." He stretched. "In the meantime, I gotta go take a dump. Don't wander off. We ain't finished yet."

He slid out and headed for the men's room.

"Classy guy," Jack said.

Lew didn't answer. His gaze was focused on a toddler who'd wandered over from a neighboring table. Jack watched Lew as he crossed his eyes and made goofy faces; the little girl loved it, grinning and squealing with delight. They went on and on, Lew never seeming to tire of performing for her.

Finally the mother came over and pulled her away. "Let the man eat in peace," she said.

"No bother," Lew said softly. "No bother at all."

Jack saw a look a desperate longing in his eyes as the child was reinstalled in her highchair.

"You really should have kids, Lew. You're good with them."

Lew shook his head. "Mel never wanted any. She had her reasons . . . good ones, I suppose."

"Like what?"

"She was terrified they'd be deformed. Still, I wished we'd tried."

Deformed? Jack thought. Was he referring to his short leg? Was that a birth defect?

He was debating whether to press for details when he spotted Evelyn heading their way. The program chairwoman was dressed in yellow today and still a dead ringer for Little Lotta.

"I'm looking for Olive?" she said. "Have either of you seen her?"

Jack and Lew shook their heads.

"I saw her at the reception last night," Lew said.

Evelyn nodded. "So did I? But she didn't show up for her panel? The one she was supposed to moderate this morning? And she's not in her room?"

Lew frowned. "That's not like her."

Jack checked his pocket program: a panel about angels. From his one encounter with Olive he didn't see how she'd miss something like that . . . unless something was big-time wrong.

"Well, if you see her?" Evelyn said. "Tell her to get in touch with me right away?"

As she moved off, Zaleski reappeared, and Evelyn stopped him.

"Here comes Mr. Personality again," Jack said. "What's he do for a living—euthanize stray dogs and cats?"

Lew said. "He used to work for one of the Baby Bells, but now he runs a hardware store with his brother . . . and I understand he's got a contract from a major publisher to write a UFO book."

The waitress brought the check. Lew grabbed it. As he signed it and charged it to his room, Jack watched Zaleski.

The guy was crass, abrasive, dogmatic, obviously frustrated, and seemed to have a short fuse. He'd implied that he expected vindication from Melanie's Grand Unification Theory, but what if he'd learned the theory would counter his "mainstream ufology?" Something like that could threaten not only his reputation and standing in the UFO community, but his book contract as well. He seemed hot-headed and unstable enough to do something rash.

Finally Zaleski finished with Evelyn and returned to the booth.

"Yes sir," he said, slapping his belly as he slid behind the table. "Nothing like a healthy shit to get the day off to a good start." He craned his neck and looked around the restaurant. "You've heard about the missing Olive?"

"Evelyn just told us," Lew said. He rose from the seat. "I think I'll wander around and see if I can find her. See you later," he said to Jack, then walked off.

"Come on outside," Zaleski said. "I need a smoke."

Jack debated the offer. He had a bad feeling about Olive. Had she joined Melanie on the missing persons list? But it was too early yet to call her missing.

He checked his watch—still too early to head over to Gia's too. He hungered to be alone with her, and the clock was limping toward eleven.

"All right," Jack said. "As long as you sit downwind."

3

Outside they found a concrete planter to the left of the front entrance and settled on its rim. Even in the mid-morning sun, the air still held a chill. Some of the hotel workers lounged around them, taking a tobacco break.

"Here we are," Zaleski said, gesturing to his fellow smokers as he lit up. "The latest persecuted minority."

Jack made the same gesture toward the clouds of smoke wafting through the air, and at the confetti of fil-tered butts on the surrounding pavement and in the dirt around the flowers in the planter.

"Gosh-a-rootie, I can't imagine why."

Zaleski smiled thinly and sucked greedily on his Camel.

"You think Olive might be with Melanie?" Jack said, watching him carefully.

Zaleski made a sour face. "I doubt it. Melanie couldn't stand that nut."

"Really? That's not the impression I got."

"Yeah?" he said, eyes narrowing. "When did you get this impression?"

Jack had no idea what Zaleski knew, so he figured the best course would be to play this straight.

"Olive stopped by my room yesterday and—"

"Did she make you hold her silver cross?" Zaleski said with a smirk.

Jack nodded. "And she asked me the same thing you did: What else did Melanie say when she contacted me? She gave the impression they were close friends."

"Melanie's not into religion, and if you ain't got religion, you can't be close friends with Olive. I mean, she's got no fucking sense of humor, and a real set of hot buttons. I get such a boost out of pissing her off. You should see her face when I say something like, 'Jesus paid for our sins, so let's get our money's worth.' Goes so purple she looks like Goofy Grape. Or when I tell her the pillars of cloud and fire that led the Israelites through the desert weren't from God, that they were UFO-generated instead—which they very likely were—she almost goes postal on me." He laughed. "But what can you expect from someone who blames Satan for everything that goes wrong in the world?"

When you really should be blaming the gray aliens, right? Jack thought.

"It's like her brain's gone five hundred years back in time," Zaleski said, shaking his head. "You should hear her go on about computers—666 chips and other eschatological bullshit. Thinks they're tools of the Devil."

He grimaced as a guy in an "Area 51" cap and a blue jumpsuit studded with UFO badges strolled by. The front was open to reveal his T-shirt. It read: *Abduct me now! I wanna go home!*

"Asshole," Zaleski said under his breath. "Why the fuck did Roma invite jerks like him into SESOUP?

Can't figure it. They make me crazy. Trend-humping dilettantes. UFO fans—*fans,* can you believe it? This is serious shit and they make a fucking *hobby* out of it." He growled. "Guess I can't blame them. They've got the government, Madison Avenue, and Hollywood messing with their heads."

"Hollywood?"

"Christ, yes. Those bastards were bought off a long time ago. Spielberg's the worst. I wonder what MJ-12 paid him to do *Close Encounters of the Third Kind* and *ET.* Those two films started the whole aliens-are-cute, aliens-are-our-friends bullshit. *Men in Black* was another, probably the most blatant example, and unquestionably financed by MJ-12 to make the MIBs look ridiculous. But that's their tactic: Take a fucking serious problem and defang it by making a joke out of it." He ground out his cigarette. "And where Hollywood leaves off, Madison Avenue takes up."

"The advertising industry's in on it too, huh?"

"From Day One. Just watch the fucking tube for an hour and you'll see flying saucers delivering Maytags or families of gray aliens driving around in Buicks. None of that's accidental. They've trivialized the grays. When the aliens finally reveal themselves, they'll be welcomed with open arms and given the keys to the whole fucking planet."

Jack spotted a pair of orthodox rabbis walking by.

"Look," he said, shrinking back. "Men in black."

"Oh, you're a comedian," Zaleski said sourly, but Jack sensed him battling a smile. "You're no Jan Murray of course, but you're a real fucking comedian."

"Sorry," Jack said, not sorry at all. "Couldn't resist."

And then he remembered the two men in the black sedan on the Castelemans' street last night. He hadn't got a good look at them, but they'd appeared to be dressed in black.

"Seriously, though," Jack said. "Have you ever actually seen one of these men in black?"

"No, and I'd like to keep it that way, thank you very much. They're supposed to mean SOBs."

"What do they look like?"

"Like men in black suits, ties, and hats, with white shirts, and black sunglasses. They wear their sunglasses *all* the time."

"Even at night?"

"Word is they're human-alien hybrids, supposedly with very pale skin, and eyes that are very sensitive to light. Usually tool around in black sedans . . . with the headlights off."

Jack felt a prickle at the base of his spine. Zaleski was describing last night's car and its passengers to a T. And what about that black sedan out in Monroe? He didn't believe for a moment in human-alien hybrids, but he couldn't discount the very real possibility that he was being watched . . . and followed. How else would they cross paths in Monroe and Elmhurst? No one but Oscar Schaffer knew about the Queens job. Could Schaffer be involved in—?

Wait. Stop. I'm beginning to think like a SESOUPer.

But the idea that someone—anyone—was dogging him changed the prickle in his back to a crawly sensation in his gut. Who? And why?

"You all right?" Zaleski said.

"Yeah, why?"

"You looked like you went away for a while."

"Just thinking."

"Thinking's good." He rose and flipped his cigarette toward the curb. "And right now I'm thinking I'm freezing my ass off out here. Let's go inside. I think I'll check out Miles's panel. Wanna come along?"

"Maybe I'll sneak in later. I want to check out the exhibit room."

"Yeah, well, don't expect to find any fucking exhibits," he said with sudden heat. "It should be called the huckster room. Nothing but piles of worthless shit for sale in there."

"I think I'll check it out anyway," Jack said. Still a ways to go before he was due at Gia's, and he wondered where Zaleski's resentment was coming from.

"Go ahead," Zaleski tossed over his shoulder as he walked away. "You'll see what I mean."

4

Jim Zaleski fled the New World Order panel after about ten minutes. What a load of paranoid horseshit. Miles and his crew were totally clueless. They'd taken every lousy crumb of disinformation MJ-12 had tossed their way and swallowed it whole.

But even if Jim had found the panel vaguely interesting, he doubted he would have been able to focus on what was being discussed. He had Jack Shelby on his mind.

Something strange about that dude. Nothing Jim could put his finger on, but something was not fucking right.

For one thing, he didn't talk enough. He made a comment here and there, but mostly he listened. That could be because he was a newbie—he did seem genuinely ignorant of even the basics of ufology—but it might also mean he was a spy of some sort. And not necessarily from MJ-12 or the grays. Last year a writer had come to a UFO convention and pretended to be an experiencer. He'd hung around, talking, listening, and secretly recording everything on a hidden mike. A few months later an article about SESOUP appeared in *The Skeptical Inquirer.* None of the quotes had been directly attributed beyond "a man said" this and "a woman said" that, but Jim had recognized a couple of his own comments, and had been furious.

You couldn't be too careful about whom you spoke to these days.

Maybe that was what it was about Jack Shelby—his vague air of amusement. Nothing overt, but a sense that he found SESOUP and its members . . . ridiculous.

Was he another *Skeptical Inquirer* type playing games? They didn't believe in *anything*. Probably even had doubts about gravity. But they'd be true believers soon enough. They were like the guy who's falling from the top of a skyscraper, and when people at the windows he's plummeting past ask him how he's doing, he says, "So far, so good!"

But it won't be so good when the grays reveal themselves, Jim thought. I'll have the last laugh, but BFD: nothing funny about Earth being turned into a cattle ranch.

Might not be a bad idea to check Shelby out while he wasn't looking. He'd said he was going to the huckster room. Jim hated the place, but supposed he could handle a quick fly-by without blowing his stack.

He headed for the room marked "Exhibit Area." Jim had lobbied Professor Roma against a huckster room, saying it put SESOUP in the same league as a Star Trek or comic book convention, but Roma had said he found the dealers' wares amusing. "Wares"—the pompous ass had actually use the word "wares."

He stepped inside and paused at the door. The "Exhibit Area" room always looked the same: long tables lining the perimeter and squared off in the center, each displaying the hucksters' junk. Always the same dealers, who all knew each other. Like gypsies—more like camp followers, really—they followed a circuit of conspiracy conventions.

Keeping an eye out for Shelby, Jim wandered past rows of books and pamphlets on astral projection, the secrets of interdimensional travel, even something called the Cholesterol Conspiracy (*"People with the highest cholesterol live the longest!!!"*).

I might have to come back and check that one out, he thought.

He strolled past the *real* truth about Vince Foster, the *real* truth about the Oklahoma City bombing, all written by "foremost experts," many calling themselves "doctor." Doctor of what? Jim always wanted to know.

Next came a whole array of exposés on the CIA, ranging from a hardcover by Bob Woodward, to pamphlets by the ever-popular Anonymous.

In the services section he passed a guy offering to take pictures of your aura for $20, a woman reading palms for $10 ("Quick! Fast! FUN!"), "Divine Astro-Tarot Readings" for an undisclosed price, then a travel service offering tours to "Places of Power" (Stonehenge and Macchu Picchu, and various Mayan temples).

"Oh, Christ," he muttered as he saw the UFO section. It was biggest of them all, easily claiming the most tables in the room.

God, I can't take this shit, he thought, readying to turn around.

But then he spotted Shelby in the thick of it.

He'd have to go in there.

Jim fought a wave of futility. Sometimes it seemed as if his whole life was a lost cause. He kept fighting to get the truth out, but every time he thought he was making headway, he found himself batted back to square one.

He's begun reading about UFOs in his early twenties. He'd become obsessed with them, and the more he'd read, the more he'd become convinced that a massive cover-up was blocking the truth from the world. He'd committed himself to uncovering that truth.

His commitment had cost him his job with the telephone company—something he was sure had been arranged as a warning, although he could never prove it. But he hadn't let that silence him. His wife left him, but he hadn't let that stop him either. He went into business with his brother, and their hardware store was doing well, although Tom was getting annoyed with all the time he was spending away from the business. Tom didn't understand that *this* was his life, not hardware.

Maybe if he could finish that book and make it a bestseller, he could leave the store and be on his own, devote every waking hour to making people see. This was when he felt most alive: when he was with fellow believers or preaching to the unconverted. This was what he lived for.

But even this had its dark side—people taking the truth, warping it to commercial ends, and making a quick buck on it. That was what the bastards in here were up to. And Jim hated them for it.

Taking a deep, calming breath, he forced himself forward past racks of glossy photos of crop circles, many of which looked to be more the result of Adobe Photoshop than alien space craft.

Then came rows of videos about UFOs and close encounters ("Actual footage!!!") and videos of recent Ecuadoran sightings, all narrated by the ubiquitous "foremost experts." Books about UFOs and close encounters ("True accounts!!!") followed.

Lost amid the bright covers and hokey posters were serious pamphlets and broadsides that told the plain unvarnished truth, but nobody was pushing those. The fast-buck artists and second-handers and recyclers had moved in and were making a killing while the real truth languished unnoticed, unread.

He found Shelby amid the flying saucer refrigerator magnets, green alien glo-pops, action figures of Men In Black and gray aliens, and miniature flying saucers of all shapes and sizes, labeled as either "scouts" or "motherships."

"See?" Zaleski said through clenched teeth as he came up behind Shelby.

He hadn't meant to speak but this shit never failed to put him over the edge. Every time he stepped into one of these places he felt like doing a Jesus-and-the-moneychangers number.

Shelby turned. "Oh, hey, Jim. I thought you were going to the—"

"See what I was talking about?" Jim said, hearing his voice rise. "This is what I meant by trivialization. These creeps are selling the human race down the river with this cutesy shit. Anything to make a lousy fucking buck. Lemme outta here before I strangle one of these assholes!"

To hell with Shelby. Who cared who he was. The worst enemies of the truth were right here in this room!

Without saying anything more, he pushed his way through the crowd and found the door.

5

Definitely a loose cannon, Jack thought, watching Zaleski go. Ready to blow somebody away at the slightest provocation—if he hasn't already.

Jack hung around a little longer, checking out the goodies. He found a wristwatch in the shape of a gray alien's head, with flying saucers on the hour and minute hands. He bought it for Vicky. She was going to love it.

He sighed as he stuffed the watch in his pocket, fighting the feeling of futility that was slowly enveloping him. At least he'd come out of the morning with something. He sure as hell hadn't got any closer to finding Melanie Ehler.

Jack had been giving some thought to this gig while browsing the exhibit area. The nightmare last night, the weird crate in his bathroom . . . something very wrong here . . . and a damn certain feeling that things were going to become much more wrong before the conference was over. His gut urged him to cut and run now.

At least the tension he'd sensed coiling in the hotel all yesterday seemed to have eased this morning, as if a pent-up charge had been released.

He spotted Lew in the common area outside the exhibit room, and ducked toward the escalator, hoping to get away without being seen. He was itching to get over to Gia's.

But no such luck.

"Jack!" Lew called, hurrying toward him. "Have you found any leads?" he asked when he reached him.

Jack shook his head. "Nothing useful. Look," he said slowly, not sure exactly how to phrase this, "I don't know if I'm the right guy for this job."

Lew stared at him with a stricken look. "You can't be serious."

Yeah, he could be . . . pretty much.

"I'll give you the money back, Lew."

"I don't care about the money. It's Mel I want!" His face screwed up. He looked like he was about to cry.

"Easy, Lew."

"Don't say that when you don't know what she means to me. I was nothing before I met her."

"I thought you said you owned that plant over in—"

"Yeah, sure, I owned it, but I was letting it go to hell. I thought it was too much for me, that I wasn't up to running a business by myself. I was trying to sell it when I met her. She turned me around. She told me I could do it. She said I was perfectly capable of handling it, and she helped me. She showed me how. And you know what? She was right. I damn well *could* do it. I just never believed it. With this gimpy leg, I was never able to keep up with the other kids while I was growing up—couldn't run worth a damn, couldn't climb worth a damn—and that's how I began to think of myself: not worth a damn."

"Yeah, but—" Jack said, trying to sneak a word in. He didn't need to hear Lew's life story.

"But Mel changed all that. In my whole life I've never felt so good about myself. And it's all because of Mel. That's why you've got to find her, Jack. Without her, life means nothing to me. And you're the only one. 'Only Repairman Jack can find me. Only he will understand.' Remember?"

"Yeah," Jack said glumly, feeling trapped. "I remember."

"So please, I'm begging you—"

"All right. I'll keep plugging, but—"

"Oh, thank you! Thank you!"

Lew tried to wrap him in a bear hug but Jack dodged clear.

"Hey, hey. None of that. We haven't even known each other two days. But I've got to tell you, it's not looking great."

"You're the one," Lew said with a burst of confidence. "Mel said you're the one and Melanie's never wrong."

"Let's hope so," Jack said.

6

Roma stood with a group of SESOUP members, trying to appear interested in their vacuous blather as he kept an eye on the stranger. The man who called himself Jack Shelby was in animated conversation with Lew Ehler at the far end of the common area. He wished he knew the connection between those two.

He heard a sudden burst of high-pitched screeching and turned to see Mauricio scampering toward him across the floor. Something in the creature's voice sounded almost like . . . terror.

Roma stooped and extended his hand toward Mauricio, to allow him to scamper up to his shoulder, but Mauricio, eyes wide with apprehension, was having none of it. He grabbed Roma's fingers and began tugging him toward the elevators.

A prickle of apprehension urged Roma to follow him. Had he found the device? Had something gone wrong with it?

He put on a wry smile and turned to the knot of attendees. "Excuse me, but apparently Mauricio wants lunch. We'll finish this discussion later."

They laughed as he moved off. At least he was free of those dullards, but what could have put Mauricio in this state? He saw the elevator doors open and half a dozen attendees step out, leaving the car empty. He hurried inside and pressed the "8" button.

"The Twins!" Mauricio said breathlessly as soon as the doors slid shut. "I saw one of the Twins!"

A chill rippled down Roma's back. "Impossible!"

"Don't say it's impossible when I saw him with these two eyes!"

"Where?"

"On the eighth floor—*your* floor."

The chill became a frozen hand against his spine. "Lots of other people on that floor as well. Just one Twin? What was he doing?"

"Sneaking along."

"Near my room?"

"No. He was at the other end of the hall. I didn't stay around to see any more. I was afraid I'd be recognized."

Roma glanced up and saw a red "6" on the floor indicator. Quickly he jabbed the "7" button.

"Good idea," Mauricio said. "You wouldn't want to step out of the elevator and come face to face with the Twins."

"They cannot possibly know who I am. But your true nature is not so well insulated. They might spot you. As for me, I'm sure I could walk right past them without their guessing."

"Why else would they be here? It's obvious the Enemy knows—"

"Hush," Roma said as the car stopped. "Let me think."

The doors opened onto the seventh floor elevator alcove. Roma stepped out, pressed the DOWN button, and checked the hallway. Empty. As the elevator doors closed, he paced the alcove, trying to order his thoughts.

The Twins—ruthless, relentless agents of the opposition. Created sometime during World War Two as watchmen, after the first guardian was released from his duties, they had proved to be a nettlesome pair, barging into areas where the Otherness was making inroads. But their ham-handed methods often proved effective, and the men-in-black myth that had sprung up around them tended to work in their favor.

But now they might prove more than nuisances; now they could ruin everything. Worse, they would destroy him on sight—if they recognized him.

"Let us consider this logically," Roma whispered. "We can assume they do not know that I am The One. If they did, they would have grabbed me at the first opportunity—they would not care where, public or private . . . while I was giving the welcoming address last night, for instance—and torn me to pieces in front of everyone."

"But they must know *something,*" Mauricio said. "Why else would they be here? Unless . . ."

"Unless what?"

"Unless they know what the Ehler woman discovered."

"Good thought, Mauricio. That might be it. Although, I will bet they know only that Melanie Ehler discovered *something,* and not what, and that is why they are here. They must have followed her husband right to our doorstep."

The slam of a door down the hall jolted Roma. It was

followed immediately by the chime of the elevator car heading down. Roma leaped inside and jabbed the LOBBY button until the doors closed.

"Now will you abandon this folly?" Mauricio said quickly—neither knew how much time they had before the elevator picked up another passenger. "As I've said all along, it is not yet your time. Too many things have already gone wrong, and even if they hadn't, the arrival of the Twins alone is reason enough to abort it."

Roma shook his head. "These are merely complications. We will go ahead as planned. The second and final delivery is tonight."

"But we haven't located the first yet!"

"Then you must keep searching, Mauricio. Find that device!"

The elevator doors opened, admitting a young couple. Roma was glad of that. He knew Mauricio had more to say but he didn't want to hear it. All he needed was another twenty-four hours, and he would be able to fulfill his destiny.

7

"Look at your scars," Gia said, tracing her fingers across his chest. "They're all inflamed."

Jack leaned against the tile wall of the shower stall with closed eyes. An hour of vigorous lovemaking had left him with partially vulcanized knees. The steam from the hot water was easing him into a pleasantly tranquil state of paralysis.

He opened his eyes and watched the water course

over Gia's pale, lithe body as she leaned against him. The flow had molded her short blond hair against her scalp. He reveled in the soft feel of her.

The bathroom was old-fashioned white tile with time-darkened grout. But the enclosed shower was relatively new and roomy.

At Jack's urging, Gia and Vicky had moved into the Westphalen townhouse on Sutton Square. It was unofficially Vicky's anyway—she was listed in her aunts' will as the final heir. She'd be the legal owner when Grace and Nellie Westphalen were declared officially dead, but just when that would happen—their bodies never would be found—was anyone's guess. Since there was no one to object to Gia and Vicky living in the place and keeping it up, they'd done just that.

With what seemed like enormous effort, Jack looked down at the three red lines running diagonally across his chest, starting near his left shoulder and ending at the lower border of his right ribs.

The scene strobed through his mind as if it had been yesterday. Battery Park . . . Kusum's ship burning in the harbor . . . the scar-lipped rakosh closing in on Gia and Vicky . . . Jack clinging to its back, trying to blind it . . . the creature peeling him off and slashing at him . . . the talons of its three-fingered hand raking fire across his chest. . . .

"Not *all* the scars," he said. "Just the ones made by that rakosh."

"Funny. They weren't red last time we made love."

"Yeah, well, they've been kind of itchy lately." At least he assumed they were the source of that itching out in Monroe the other day. "I dreamed about the rakoshi again last night."

"Again? Bad?"

He nodded, thinking: Please don't ask if you were in it.

Instead, she touched the scars again. "I'm hoping the whole thing will eventually seem like just a bad dream. But you'll always have these as reminders."

"I like to think of them as proof that we really did run up against those things."

"Who wants proof?" Gia said, snuggling tighter against him. "I want to forget them—forget they ever existed."

"But they were real, right? We didn't just imagine them."

She stared at him. "Are you serious? Of course they were real. How can you even ask?"

"Because of the people I've been hanging with at the conference. UFOs and aliens and Antichrists are real to them. If one of them said to a friend, 'Are the gray aliens real?' he'd get the same look you gave me just now, and the friend would say, 'Are you serious? Of course they're real. How can you even ask?' You see what I'm getting at? These people are absolutely sure these conspiracies, these beings, these secret organizations are real."

"Shared delusions," Gia said with a slow nod. She began soaping his chest, hiding the scars with lather. "I see what you mean."

"To me, they're nut cases. I mean, talk to any one of them for five minutes and you *know* that someone has stopped payment on their reality check. But what if you and I went around talking about the rakoshi? Wouldn't people think the same about us? And with good reason—because we can't prove a damn thing. We have no hard evidence except these scars of mine which, as far as anybody knows, could have been self-inflicted."

"It happened, Jack. We lived through it—just barely—so we know."

"But *do* we? What do we know of reality but what we remember? When it comes right down to it, who we *are* is what we remember. And from what I've read about memory lately, it isn't all that reliable."

"Stop talking like this. You're scaring me."

"I'm scaring *me*."

"At least we're not out there saying rakoshi are planning to take over the world, or responsible for everything bad that happens."

"No . . . not yet."

"Now cut that out," she said, landing a gentle punch on the chest. "We're different from them because we're not focusing on it. That awful experience happened, we've dealt with it, and we've put it behind us—believe me, I'm doing my best to *forget* it. But they make it the center of their lives; they extrapolate it into a worldview."

"Yeah. Why would anybody want to do that? Isn't reality complicated enough?"

"Maybe that's the problem," Gia said. "Most of the time I find reality *too* complicated. Something happens because of this, something else happens because of that, another thing happens because of a combination of this, that, and the other thing."

"And lots of times," Jack added, "things seem to happen for no damn reason at all."

"Exactly. But an all-encompassing conspiracy simplifies all of that. You don't have to wonder any more. You don't have to fit the pieces together—you've got it all figured out already. Everyone else might be in the dark, but *you* know the real skinny."

"Come to think of it, a lot of those SESOUPers do look kind of smug." Jack sighed. "But in spite of everything you've said, some of them almost remind me of . . . me."

"Get out."

"I'm serious. Consider: They're always looking over their shoulders, I'm always looking over mine."

"With good reason."

"Let me finish. They tend to be loners; until I met you, I was a loner—big time. They're outsiders, I'm an outsider."

"Way outside."

"They're considered weirdoes by mainstream society, I'll land in the joint if mainstream society ever finds out about me. Really, despite the fact that I'm keeping my mouth shut, how do I know I'm not just like them, or"—he held up his thumb and forefinger, a quarter inch apart "this far from being one of them?"

"Because I say you're not," Gia said, then kissed him.

If only that was enough, he thought, closing his eyes and holding her tight against him, needing her warmth, her presence, her very existence. Gia was his anchor to reality, to sanity. Without her and Vicky, who knew what wild shore he might be sailing toward.

He glanced down once more at the reddened diagonal streaks of his scars and suddenly the image of Roma was before him, from the cocktail party last night, his three middle fingers hooked into rakoshi-like talons, raking the air between them along the exact angle of Jack's scars.

"What's wrong?" Gia said as Jack's spine stiffened reflexively.

"Nothing," he told her. "Muscle spasm."

He held her tighter to keep her from seeing his expression, knowing it would give away his shock, his bafflement.

Did Roma know? What had he said? *How easily we forget.* But Jack had not forgotten. And no way Roma could know.

Then why make that weird three-pronged gesture, at just the right angle? Jack could think of no other way to interpret it. Roma knows. But how?

Jack had no idea, but he intended to find out.

But if Roma knew about the rakoshi scars, did he also know about Gia and Vicky? Could he have followed Jack here?

He reached past Gia and ratcheted the hot water handle up another notch. The temperature in the shower seemed to have dropped a few degrees.

8

After arranging with Gia to give Vicky a little coaching on baseball later in the afternoon, Jack returned to the hotel. As he entered he thought he sensed the tension building in the atmosphere again. He looked around for Roma—*Want to ask you a question or two, pal*—but didn't see him. When he reached the second floor he spotted a Mutt and Jeff pair standing in the common area outside the meeting rooms: Lew and Evelyn. He headed their way.

Evelyn was anxiously rubbing her tiny, pudgy Little Lotta hands together. She looked upset.

"Something wrong?"

"We still haven't found Olive?" she said. "No one's seen her since the reception last night? I'm getting worried?"

"You've checked her room?

Lew said, "I've called, I've knocked. There's no answer."

"Maybe you should get the hotel to open it, just to make sure she's not in there in a coma or something," Jack said.

Evelyn's hand fluttered to her mouth. "Do you really

think so? I never thought of that? But what if she just forgot? And she's out sightseeing or something? How will she feel when she finds out we've been searching her room?"

In any other case, Jack thought, the person in question probably would be touched by their concern. With this crew . . . it would all seem part of a sinister scheme.

"I think you've got to risk it."

Evelyn glanced at her watch. "I'll give her another hour? If I don't hear from her by then? I'm going to go to the management? I'll have them check? How does that sound?"

"Sounds like a plan," Jack said.

As Evelyn bustled away, Lew turned to Jack. "And I think I'll head back home for a while."

"All the way to Shoreham?"

"Yeah. I want to check and see if Mel might've come back, maybe left me a note or something." He blinked away tears. "First Mel, now Olive. I'm really scared. Anything new?"

"Nothing definite," Jack said, and saw Lew's face fall. "But maybe you can clear up something for me."

"Sure. Anything."

"Olive mentioned that Melanie had given her a set of computer disks. Why would Melanie do that?"

He shook his head. "I can't imagine. They weren't that close."

"Think she's making it up?"

"I couldn't say for sure. Maybe Olive is trying to make herself sound important. Or maybe Melanie did give them to her for safekeeping—you know, after she wiped out her GUT file. Perhaps she figured no one would think of Olive since she's a computerphobe."

"It's a thought," Jack said. "When Melanie shows up, we'll ask her."

"*If* she shows up." Lew took a deep, sighing breath. "I'll see you later," he said and walked off.

Jack decided to check his messages, then try to catch one of these panels . . . the elusive Miles Kenway was scheduled to moderate the next one. Jack wanted to get a line on him.

As he was heading for the lobby he noticed the red-haired guy sitting in his wheelchair in a doorway, staring at him again, just like last night. The intensity of the scrutiny bothered him.

What's so damn interesting? he wondered.

He used his calling card to check his voice mail. Just his father . . . again.

Okay, time to bite the bullet and call him. He found the number in his wallet and punched it in. He'd moved *way* down in Florida, someplace near Coral Gables with the Everglades practically in his backyard.

Dad was in. They made a little small talk—he always made sure you knew how nice and warm the weather was down there—then Jack got to the point.

"Are your travel plans pretty well set?"

"Yes," Dad said. "I've got my tickets and everything."

"Gee, that's too bad, because I'm going on a cruise for a couple of weeks and it falls right in the time you'll be up here."

A long silence on the Florida end of the line, during which hurt seeped through the receiver. Jack felt ropes of guilty perspiration begin to trickle down his face. Obviously Dad was trying to get closer to his wayward son in his sunset years, and Jack was giving him the cold shoulder.

I'm such a coward, he thought. A lousy lying coward.

Finally: "Cruise?" Dad said. "Where to?"

Oh, shit—where? "Alaska."

"Really? I've always wanted to cruise to Alaska, see

those glaciers and all. I wish you'd said something. I would have gone with you. Maybe I can still arrange something."

Oh no! "Gee, Dad. It's fully booked."

Another long silence.

Not only am I a lousy lying coward, I'm a rat.

"You know, Jack," Dad finally said, "I realize you may not want me in your life, or that there may be aspects of your life you don't want me to know about . . . but—"

Jack went cold. "What . . . what do you mean?"

"Look, Jack, if you're . . . if you're g-gay"—he seemed to have trouble getting the word past his lips—"or something like that, it's okay. I can accept it. You're still my son."

Jack sagged against the phone. Gay? Is that the worst he can think of?

"No, Dad. Guys don't do a thing for me. In fact, I can't understand what women see in them. I like *women.* Always have, always will."

"Really?" Jack could hear the relief in his voice. "Well, then why—?"

"I won't be around, really."

"Okay. I'll buy that. But you did say you'd come down for a visit, right? When's that going to be? Let's set a date."

"I can't set a date right now, but" . . . he couldn't turn him down cold again. . . "I promise I'll get there before the year is out. How's that?"

"Okay! It's a deal!"

He kept Jack on for a few more minutes of small talk, then let him go. Jack hung up and simply stood there, recouping his strength. He'd rather face any number of enraged monte grifters than a phone conversation with his father.

He banged his fist against the wall. What did I just

do? I promised to visit him, and I locked in a time frame: before the end of the year. Am I crazy?

He hated to travel anywhere, but . . . guilt springs eternal.

He was stuck. He'd promised.

Jack decided to go back to his room. He needed a rest.

9

Salvatore Roma sat staring at his room's TV, but was only vaguely aware of what was on the screen—a talk show featuring a panel of bizarrely coifed and accessorized males and females bemoaning their treatment by conventional society. His mind was elsewhere, imagining the near future, and the changes he would bring to this world. He smiled at the screen: You whine about your troubles now? Wait . . . just wait.

An insistent scratching at the door wrenched him back to the present. He pulled it open and Mauricio scampered in.

"I found it," he said, hopping onto the bed.

"It took you long enough."

"I could only get into the rooms when the maids entered for cleaning. I'd still be running around with no answer if I hadn't staked out one room for special attention."

Roma felt his fists clench of their own accord. "The stranger."

"Yes! The mysterious Jack Shelby. The delivery is sitting under the counter in his bathroom."

Roma squeezed his eyes shut. "Opened?"

"Yes, but I saw no sign that he'd attempted to assemble it."

"Not that it would matter. It is incomplete. And even after the rest of it arrives—"

"Let's just hope he hasn't damaged it or lost some crucial component. I think we should reclaim it as soon as possible."

"I disagree," Roma said. "Not with the Twins here. Besides, we have too many unanswered questions. Why did the delivery arrive in his room instead of the basement as planned? Was that his doing, or was it redirected from the other side? Who *is* this man?"

"If I hadn't spent the whole day searching for the shipment, I might be able to tell you."

"But why is he here? Is he connected to the Twins? If so, we might be playing directly into their hands by revealing ourselves if we make a move against him."

"I don't like it," Mauricio said. He scampered to the door and looked back. "Let me out of here."

Roma twisted the handle Mauricio couldn't reach in his capuchin form. "Where are you going?"

"I need to think."

As the monkey stepped out, it stared down the hallway and froze as if in shock.

10

The made bed in Jack's room indicated the maid had been through. He checked the bathroom and was relieved to see that no other crate had arrived. The original was still there, right where he'd left it.

He lifted the lid and looked again at the miniature girders and rods. Maybe he should take a shot at assembling the damn thing. He checked his watch: no time. Only forty or fifty minutes before Evelyn called in the cavalry to charge Olive's room. Jack had a bad feeling about her no-show at her panel. Out sightseeing? Olive? In Sin City? Hardly.

She'd told him yesterday she was in room 812.

Well . . . why not pay the room a visit? If she'd died in her sleep, he wanted to know. If she was alive and he found her hiding there for some reason, he'd just tell her he'd been worried about her. And if the room was empty, maybe he could find the disks she said Melanie had given her.

The more he thought about it, the better he liked the idea.

He grabbed a few goodies from his gym bag and headed up to the eighth floor. The hall was empty, and the maid was busy in a room down on the far side of the elevators. Now or never.

He found a "Do Not Disturb" sign on 812's doorknob. That would keep the maid out, but not him. Just to be sure, though, he knocked and softly called Olive's name. No answer.

Okay. He pulled out his own custom made slim-jim—a wafer-thin length of high-tensile steel, twelve inches by two, notched on one side about an inch from the end. He had his lock pick set, but this would be much quicker. He leaned on the door and slipped the metal between the jamb and the wood. The notch caught on the latch bolt. A wiggle, a pull, a slide, and the door was swinging inward—

But only an inch. The swing latch was in the locked position.

Jack froze. Those latches could only be flipped over

from the other side. That meant Olive was still in the room.

"Olive?" he said through the opening.

No voice answered, but he swore he heard movement in there.

Jack's heart picked up its pace. Something very wrong here. Someone—maybe Olive, maybe not—was sneaking around in Olive's room.

Jack pulled the door closed again and checked the hall. Still no one coming. He worked his slim-jim between the jamb and the door again, this time at eye level, felt it clink against the swing latch, then pushed. He heard the latch swing back. The he reopened the knob latch and pushed the door inward.

The breeze from an open window hit him immediately. He hadn't felt that a moment ago.

But before he did anything else, he pulled out the tail of his flannel shirt and wiped the doorknob clean. Then he stepped inside and closed the door behind him.

The bathroom lights were on. He glanced in. The shower curtain was pulled back—no one hiding in here. He moved into the room. The sheer curtains, billowing in the breeze from the open window, caught his eye first. One of those casement jobs that was supposed to slide back only a few inches. Someone must have pried off the safety stop. The window was open wide enough for someone to slip through.

A mental image of Olive leaping from the ledge was taking shape in Jack's brain when he saw open drawers, the clothing strewn about; and then the walls—pictures of Jesus had been taped over the framed prints; and crosses and crucifixes, at least a dozen of them, were taped to the walls, an especially large one over the king-size bed—

"Damn!" he blurted and jumped back when he saw Olive lying in it.

At least he was pretty sure it was Olive—or had been. The covers were pulled up to her neck but she wasn't sleeping. Her eyes had been removed, leaving empty red-crusted sockets staring at the ceiling. But worse, her lips had been cut off, and none too neatly, leaving her with a hideous permanent grin.

Wary, his stomach churning, Jack inched toward the bed. The pillows and spread were oddly clean—not a bloodstain in sight. Her face was a horror, but what had they done to her body? He had to know. Steeling himself, he gripped the edge of the covers and pulled them back.

"Aw, jeez."

At first Jack wasn't quite sure what he was seeing, but it repulsed him anyway. He saw wide cuts here and there on Olive's exposed skin—slices, gouges, pieces removed. If it was torture, it wasn't like any form Jack had ever heard of. Some sort of ritual maybe? But something beyond the slicing and dicing was terribly wrong. And then with a sledgehammer shock Jack realized what it was. He gasped and involuntarily retreated a step.

He was looking at Olive's back.

Her head was still connected to her body, but it had been wrenched 180 degrees around.

The sound of breaking glass made Jack jump. He whirled, hunting the source. From over there—the window.

He leaped to the drapes and fought them aside. All the glass was intact.

"I could have sworn—"

He poked his head outside and found himself looking over the rear of the hotel. A white flutter jerked his attention to the left: part of the neighboring room's curtain was flapping through a human-sized hole in the window there. Jack looked down. No corpse splattered on the rooftop of the next building three stories below. Had someone broken *into* the next window?

The sound of a slamming door echoed through the shattered glass.

Jack shoved away from the window and raced for the door, gathering his loose shirttail as he ran. He twisted the knob with his flannel-wrapped hand and charged into the hall.

To his left he saw Roma's monkey scamper out of one of the rooms and freeze at the sight of him; to his right, a retreating figure—black suit and hat—was three quarters of the way to the end of the hall, not exactly running, but hurrying, making damn good time. The guy glanced over his shoulder, flashing a pale face and dark glasses, then started to run.

One of the bogey-men in black, Jack thought as he sprinted after him. Okay, guy. Let's see how you handle someone a little tougher than a middle-aged lady.

The black-clad figure ducked through the exit door into the stairwell.

Jack burst through and paused on the landing, dimly aware of bare blocks, painted beige; steel rails, dark brown with a sick green showing through the chipped spots. He focused on the whispery echo of soft soles galloping down the steps a good two flights below.

He started after them. This guy was fast. And pretty damn agile if he was outside Olive's window while Jack was checking out the corpse. Had to be some sort of human fly.

Well, I can fly too . . . in a way.

He vaulted over the railing to the flight below, descending a few steps, then vaulted again. Dangerous—if he landed wrong he'd break an ankle—but it was the only way he'd ever catch this guy.

Jack reached the flight directly above the killer and he vaulted the railing between them. The guy glanced up. Jack saw pale skin, a small nose, and thin lips; he also saw the soles of his sneakers reflected in the black sunglasses just before he landed on the guy's head.

They both tumbled to the next landing, Jack on top. He was vaguely aware of the sunglasses skittering across the concrete as they hit. Even with the man in black's body cushioning Jack's fall, the impact was jarring. His elbow hit the wall, sending fiery tingles down his arm. Had to be a lot worse for the other guy, but to Jack's shock, he jumped up immediately, almost as if nothing had happened, and continued his descent, grabbing his shades as he went.

Wondering if this guy's pain threshold was somewhere out near the moon, Jack struggled to his feet—not quite so quickly—and resumed the chase. The next landing was home to a red door labeled "5"—Jack's floor. The man in black dashed past it, but as Jack arrived the door swung open and he found himself facing a mirror image of the guy he was chasing, except this one was wearing a black gimme cap.

And he was all set for Jack, already in mid-swing when the door opened. Jack was utterly unprepared for the black-gloved fist that rammed deep into his solar plexus.

The force of the blow slammed him against the cinderblock wall. Pain exploded in the pit of his stomach. He couldn't breathe. His mouth worked, struggling to draw air, but his diaphragm was paralyzed. He tried to keep his feet but they wouldn't cooperate. He crumpled like an old dollar bill, doubled over and grunting on the landing, helpless to stop the second man in black as he followed his buddy downstairs.

It took Jack a good fifteen-twenty seconds before he could breathe again. He lay there gasping, sucking delicious wind, waiting for the pain to go away. Eventually he was able to push himself up to a sitting position. He leaned back against the cinder blocks, groaned, and shook his head. No, he was *not* going to vomit, no matter how much his stomach wanted to.

Christ, that was some shot. Perfect placement, damn near went clear through to his spine. Must have been wearing a weighted glove—at least Jack hoped he was. Didn't like the thought of such a skinny guy packing that kind of wallop all on his own.

Finally he struggled to his feet. No sense in trying to catch up to them now; they were long gone. Jack got himself together, pulled open the door, and tried to look casual as he limped down the hall to his room.

▌▌

After splashing some water on his face, Jack pondered his next move.

Olive . . . dead. Christ. And not merely dead—mutilated.

Jack had seen his share of corpses, but never one like Olive's. One thing to kill somebody, but then to cut out her eyes, carve off her lips . . . jeez.

Why? Was there symbolism there? Had she seen too much? Talked too much? She'd told Jack about the disks. Had she told someone else—the *wrong* someone else? The room had been ransacked—in search of the disks, he'd bet. Question was: had they found them?

Not that Jack could go back for a second look. In another twenty minutes or so, Evelyn would be asking the management to open Olive's room. He didn't want to be around when the police started swarming through the hotel asking questions, but he didn't want to be on anyone's suspect list either. Except for the time he'd spent at Gia's, his whereabouts for most of the morning were pretty well accounted for. Better to hide in plain sight until the body was found, then lay low.

Which meant he should head downstairs and make sure Evelyn and anybody else around saw him.

When he reached the meeting area, he looked around for someone he'd met, but saw neither Zaleski, Carmack, nor Evelyn. He'd even settle for Roma—find out about his three-fingered high sign—but he wasn't in sight. Jack did spot the red-headed guy with the beard, staring at him again from his wheelchair.

All right, Jack thought. Let's make this a two-fer: establish my presence and find out what makes me so damn interesting.

He crossed the common area and stood over the guy. Close up Jack saw that he'd be on the short side even if he could stand. He was barrel-chested under his Polo golf shirt. Stick a horned helmet on his head and he'd pass for Hagar the Horrible. His pelvis and legs were wrapped in a loud red, black, and yellow plaid blanket.

"Do you know me?" Jack asked.

The man looked up at him. "Last night was the first time I ever laid eyes on you."

"Then why do you keep staring at me?"

"You wouldn't understand."

"Try me."

"You're the last one to hear from Melanie, I'm told."

That wasn't an answer, but Jack nodded. "Supposedly. News travels fast around here."

"Melanie and I go way back." He extended his hand. "Frayne Canfield."

Jack remembered Lew mentioning that name— Melanie's childhood friend from Monroe—but he shook his hand and played dumb.

"How far back?"

"We grew up together, and we've kept in touch. Hasn't Lew mentioned me?"

"Possibly," Jack said. "I've met so many people since I arrived." He shrugged.

"Well, if he hasn't, he probably will. We've stayed close, Melanie and me, and sometimes I think Lew's suspected us of having an affair." He smiled bitterly and pointed to his blanketed lower body. "But that, I'm afraid, is quite impossible."

Canfield's legs shifted under the plaid fabric, and something about the way they moved sent a chill across Jack's upper back. He felt he should make some sort of response but couldn't think of anything that didn't sound lame.

Canfield shrugged. "Ironic, in a way: The thing that keeps us close also keeps us from getting too close."

"I'm not following you," Jack said.

"Our deformities . . . they're a kind of bond unhindered people can't understand."

Jack was baffled. "Melanie has a deformity?"

Canfield looked smug. "You mean you don't know? Perhaps I shouldn't have said anything." He tugged on his red beard and stared at Jack. "You really haven't met her, have you."

"Why would I be lying?" Jack said, then had to smile. "But then, considering the nature of this gathering, why should I be surprised I'm not believed?"

Canfield nodded. "You've got a point."

Jack mentally reviewed the photos he'd seen both in Shoreham and in Monroe. Melanie had looked perfectly normal.

"What's Melanie's deformity?"

Canfield looked around. "Let's get out of the traffic." He started rolling his chair to the left. "Over here."

He stopped before a couch against the wall. Jack

sank into the too-soft cushions, so far down that he was now looking up at Canfield.

"I'm not going to discuss Melanie's particular deformity," Canfield said. "When you meet her you'll know."

At least he's optimistic, Jack thought.

"But I will tell you," Canfield went on, "that it shaped her life. It's the fuel powering her engine. She's searching for the cause of the Monroe Cluster."

"Cluster of what?"

"Deformities. Toward the end of 1968, half a dozen deformed children were born in Monroe over a period of ten days. The parents all got to know each other. That was how my folks met the Rubins, Melanie's folks. I remember others—the poor Harrisons, whose severely deformed daughter Susan didn't survive past age five, and the doubly damned Bakers, whose daughter Carly disappeared after murdering her brother. They and a few others formed a mini-support group, looking for answers, wanting to know, *Why us?*"

Jack glanced at Canfield's shrouded nether half, wondering what hid beneath that blanket.

"A radiation leak, maybe?" Jack offered.

Canfield shook his head. "An investigative team from Mount Sinai came out and puttered around, looking for evidence of just that. When that didn't pan out they tested the water and the ground for toxic contamination, but never found a thing. Melanie thinks they came up empty-handed because they were looking for a natural cause. She thinks the cause was *un*natural."

Canfield's legs shifted again under their blanket . . . something not quite natural about that, either.

"Like what?"

"Something else . . . something *other.*"

"Is this a secret code or something? You're losing me."

Canfield sighed. "Melanie and I have discussed it endlessly. She's been convinced that something 'unnatural' happened in Monroe in late February or early March of 1968 when her mother and my mother and all these other mothers were newly pregnant. Something happened that warped the fragile cell structures of the newly conceived fetuses. 'A burst of Otherness,' she calls it. She refers to us and the other deformed ones as 'Children of the Otherness.'"

Uh-oh, Jack thought. Do I sense another conspiracy theory in the making?

"All right," he said. "I'll bite: What's that supposed to mean?"

Canfield shrugged. "That's the question Melanie has spent her life trying to answer. But just a couple of weeks ago she told me that with Professor Roma's help, she was getting close . . . and that she soon might have the key to her Grand Unification Theory."

Back to Melanie's theory again. All roads seemed to lead to that particular Rome.

"I'd love to hear this theory," Jack said.

"You and me both. Believe me, if a single event has shaped your life—or *mis*haped your life—you want to know what it is."

"How exactly did it misshape Melanie?" Jack said.

"Sorry," Canfield said, shaking his head. "Better ask Lew. Good talking to you."

But I can't ask Lew, Jack thought. He's on his way out to Shoreham.

And then it occurred to him that the secret of Melanie Ehler's whereabouts—as well as her mysterious deformity—might not be here with the SESOUP loonies, but back in her home town. In Monroe.

Canfield had backed up his wheelchair and started to roll away.

"One more thing," Jack said. "What's your angle here?"

Canfield stopped and looked back. "Angle?"

"Yeah. UFOs? Satan and the End Days? The New World Order? The International Cabal of Bankers? The Cthulhu cult? Which is your baby?"

"Haven't you been listening?" Canfield said, then rolled away.

He knows something, Jack thought as he watched him go. The way he dodges the important questions—oh,yeah, he's definitely involved.

Jack looked across the common area and saw Evelyn step out of the hotel's business office and head for the elevators in the company of two suits with little brass name tags on their lapels. On their way to Olive's room, no doubt. Which meant the hotel would be crawling with blue uniforms in about ten minutes.

Maybe now was a good time to take another look around the missing lady's ancestral home.

12

Jack retrieved his rental car from the garage and backtracked out to the Long Island Gold Coast. He didn't have a map and wasn't sure of Monroe's exact location, but remembered it was somewhere at the end of Glen Cove Road. Along the way he spotted a road sign pointing him in the right direction. After that, he had no problem finding his way back to Melanie's family home.

He also found himself glancing repeatedly in his

rearview mirror, looking for a black sedan. He had a vague feeling that he was being watched, and he scrutinized every black car he spied along the way.

Melanie's old home was easily identified by the big oak and its oversize lot. Jack parked in the driveway this time, but went to the back door. The knob was a Yale; so was the dead bolt. Jack was good with Yales. Took him thirty seconds on the knob, less than a minute on the dead bolt, and he was in.

He wandered through the house again, rechecking all the photos. He began to see a pattern that had escaped him completely on his first pass: in not one photo was Melanie's left hand visible. In solo shots it was always behind her back; when with her mother or father she was always positioned so that her left lower arm was behind the other person.

A deformed left hand? That sort of jibed with the box full of dolls with mutilated left hands. . . .

But so what? What if anything did that have to do with her disappearance?

Jack went downstairs to the basement. Yeah, the rope ladder was still imbedded in the cement. Did *that* have anything to do with Melanie's disappearance?

He stood staring at it, as baffled as ever, waiting for some sort of epiphany that would explain everything.

The only thing that happened was the front of his chest started itching again.

Damn, he thought. Must be allergic to something down here.

Still scratching, he went over to the desk and checked out the large amber crystals. He held one up to the light but saw nothing unusual about it.

He sighed. Deformed children, a missing wife, a mutilated corpse, black-clad tough guys, a gathering of paranoids . . . were they linked? He couldn't buy them as random and unrelated. But where was the common thread?

Frayne Canfield had said that something "unnatural" had happened in Monroe in late February or early March of 1968. Was that the link?

Jack had passed a public library in town. As long as he was here, why not check out what he could?

He made sure he relocked both the knob and the dead bolt before he left.

13

"Why are you interested in that particular period?" the librarian asked, giving him a close inspection. Then she added, "If you don't mind my asking."

Mrs. Forseman was straight out of Central Casting with her frumpy dress, wrinkled face, lemon-sucking pursed lips, and pointy-cornered reading glasses dangling from a chain around her neck.

"Just curious."

He'd asked to see the microfilm files of the Monroe *Express* for the first quarter of 1968. She clutched the cartridge in her bony hand, but hadn't offered it to him yet.

"Curious about what? If you don't mind my asking."

I damn well do mind, Jack thought, then decided she looked old enough to have been around then. Maybe she could save him some time.

"I heard about something called the 'Monroe Cluster' and—"

"Oh, no," she said, rolling her eyes. "You're not some writer planning to go digging into those deformities, are you? This town has had more than its share of trouble, especially those poor people, so leave them alone. Please."

"Actually, I'm a geneticist," Jack said. "If I publish anything it'll be in a scientific journal. Do you remember anything about the incidents?"

"I remember a lot of panic around the time those poor children were born, especially in all the other pregnant mothers in town, all terrified that their babies might end up the same way. We didn't have all the tests then that we have now, so there were a lot of very frightened families. It was an awful time, just awful. A research team from one of the medical centers came through and did a thorough investigation for the State Department of Health. They didn't find anything, neither will you."

Jack held out his hand for the cartridge. "You're probably right, but I'll never know until I look, will I."

"Suit yourself," she said, shoving the cartridge into his palm. "But you're wasting your time."

Turned out she was right.

Jack situated himself before a viewer and began paging through the back files. The *Express* was a small town paper, devoted almost exclusively to local issues. Took Jack no time to scan through two months' worth.

February 1968 was an uneventful month, but March turned out to be a whole different story—not a good time at all for the Village of Monroe: violent storms, protest marchers, and a man named Jim Stevens dying an ugly accidental death outside some place known as "the Hanley mansion." And then a few days later, mass murder and mayhem inside the same house.

And that was it. Not a hint as to what might have caused the birth defects that popped up nine months later, and certainly nothing to back up Melanie's "burst of Otherness" theory.

Jack returned the cartridge to Mrs. Forseman at her desk.

"Should have listened to you," he said, trying to soften her up. "Couldn't find a thing."

It worked. She actually cracked a smile. A tiny one. "Just trying to save you some trouble."

"I guess any way you look at it, sixty-eight was a bad year for Monroe."

"A bad year for the whole country," she said. "The assassinations of Martin Luther King and Bobby Kennedy came in the spring, followed by the riots in Chicago at the Democratic convention. And then the Russians invaded Czechoslovakia and slaughtered people in the streets." Her eyes got a faraway look. "Almost as if a dark cloud passed over the world that year and turned everything ugly."

Jack hunched his shoulders to relieve a crawling sensation along his nape as he remembered Canfield's talk about a "burst of Otherness." You could almost make a case for something foul entering the world early in sixty-eight.

He shook it off. "Any children of the cluster still around?"

"Only two survived," she said, wary again. "But don't expect me to tell you who they are. They deserve their privacy."

"I suppose you're right. I've already spoken to Melanie Rubin and Frayne Canfield and I thought—"

"I saw Melanie recently myself. I hadn't seen her since her mother's funeral, but just last week I passed her old house and saw her standing outside with a very handsome man."

Jack knew she couldn't be talking about Lew. "What did he look like?"

She laughed. "Oh, I doubt very much I could describe him. My attention was too fixed on the monkey on his shoulder."

"A monkey, ay?" Jack said. Hadn't Roma told Lew yesterday that he'd been looking forward to meeting Melanie in person? "Isn't that interesting."

"Yes. Cute as a button."

Jack shrugged. "I guess that's it then. Thanks."

"Let those poor people be, young man," she said as he headed for the door. "Just let them be."

Jack found a pay phone in the library foyer and called Lew's home number.

When Lew recognized Jack's voice he gasped. "Have you found her?"

"Not yet," Jack said. "Any sign of her out there?"

"No," he said, his tone disconsolate. "Not a thing."

"I had a nice little chat with Frayne Canfield."

"Was he any help?"

"Not much. What's his story?"

"Still lives with his parents. Keeps to himself pretty much except for SESOUP activities. Debugs software for a living, but I don't think he's particularly successful at it. Why? You think he's involved?"

"It's a possibility." A very *good* possibility. "I'm going to be keeping an eye on him. But you didn't tell me he was wheelchair-bound. He described his legs as 'deformed' . . . which is also how he described Melanie's left arm." Not quite true, but Jack didn't want to let on that he'd broken into the Monroe house. "How come you never mentioned Melanie's arm?"

"I didn't think it mattered."

"It does if it's an identifying characteristic. Can I ask what's wrong with her hand?"

"Well . . . she doesn't really have one. According to the doctors, all the fingers on her left hand fused into a single large digit while she was a fetus. The same happened with the fingernails, leaving her with one large thick nail. She keeps it bandaged in public because it tends to upset people—they either stare or turn away."

"I'm sorry," Jack said, unable to think of anything to say.

Poor Melanie . . . imagine having to go through life hiding one of your hands all the time . . . and chopping the hands off your dolls. . . .

"Nothing to be sorry about," Lew said. "She leads a full life. People stop noticing the bandage after a while. And to tell you the truth, it never bothered me. I fell in love with her the moment I laid eyes on her. The only thing it *has* stopped her from doing is having children. She's too afraid she'll pass on her deformity."

Jack shook his head, remembering the wistful look in Lew's eyes this morning when he was playing with that toddler in the coffee shop.

"There's always adoption."

"Someday I hope we will." His voice teetered on a sob. "If she ever comes back."

"We'll find her, Lew," Jack said, only half believing it himself. "Just hang in there."

"Like I have a choice?" he said and hung up.

Don't fall apart on me, Lew, Jack thought as he replaced the receiver. You're the only one I've met in this thing who seems to be dealing from a full deck.

He turned and saw an aerial map of Monroe with the streets labeled. He found Melanie's family home. He remembered the address of the Hanley mansion from the articles and, just for the hell of it, located its approximate location. Not too far from Melanie's place. Jack could see no line of causality between the storms and the deaths at the mansion in March to the birth defects in December, but he was sure some of the SESOUPers back at the convention could find multiple ways to link them. Probably link them to the King and Kennedy assassinations and every other nasty occurrence that year as well.

But there couldn't be a connection. Just coincidence . . .

Shaking his head, he stepped outside and ambled toward his car. He was in no hurry to get back to the hotel. By now the SESOUP crew would be frothing at their collective mouths with theories about the ritualistic murder of one of their members.

Good a time as any to do some more work on the new Social Security number, and maybe even sneak in a little time to help Vicky with her baseball skills.

14

"They cut out her *eyes?*" Abe said around a mouthful of frozen mocha yogurt. His expression registered disgust. "You're making me lose my appetite."

"Wait," Jack said. "That's just the start. I haven't told you what they did to her lips and how they twisted—"

He waved his hand in Jack's face. "No-no-no! What I don't know can't nauseate me."

Just as well. Jack didn't want to talk about it anyway. He kept picturing himself finding Melanie in that condition and having to tell Lew.

He'd brought a pint of fat-free frozen yogurt as a gift in anticipation of Abe's aid in authoring a letter to the Social Security Administration in Trenton. He hadn't mentioned the letter yet. He'd also brought a packet of sunflower seeds for Parabellum, who was patiently splitting the shells with his deft little beak and plucking out the tiny meats.

Jack shrugged. "Okay. Bottom line is, she's dead."

"And those tough guys in black did it?"

"I'm assuming so. Never got the chance to ask. Tossed her room pretty well too."

Abe picked up the sweating yogurt container and peered at the label.

"Non-fat shouldn't taste this good. You're sure it's non-fat?"

"That's what it says. And less calories too."

"*Fewer* calories."

"Less." Jack pointed to the bright yellow flag on the container. "Says so right there."

"I should accept a yogurt label as my authority on grammar? Trust me, Jack, it's 'fewer.' Less fat—okay. But *fewer* calories."

"You see?" Jack said, slapping a black-and-white composition book down on Abe's counter. "That's why you're just the man to help me write a letter from a high school sophomore."

Abe's eyes narrowed. "Have I just been suckered?"

Jack blinked. "Why . . . whatever do you mean?"

Abe sighed. "Another letter to the SSA? Just rewrite the last one."

"Nah. You know I like a new one every time. And besides, it's all your fault. You're the one who got me started on plastic money."

"Had I but known what I would set in motion . . ."

When Abe finally had convinced Jack of the necessity of a credit card, he suggested adding Jack as an additional cardholder on his own pseudonymous Amex account. Jack chose the name Jack Connery—he'd been running some old James Bond films at the time—but needed a Social Security number to accompany the name.

For Connery's SSN he used Abe's new—at least it was new at the time—method: he made one up. But that didn't mean simply pulling random numbers out of the air. Under Abe's tutelage, Jack learned that the SSN was divided into three sets of digits for a reason. The first set, the three-digit "area" number, told *where* the number was issued. If Connery had a New York birthplace and a New York address, he should have an area number somewhere between 050 and 134, indicating the number had been issued in New York. The second set of numbers was the "block" pair, indicating *when* the number was issued. Since Connery was listing a birth date of 1958, Jack didn't want to submit a block number that said Connery's SSN was issued before he was born. As for the last four digits—the "serial number"—anything goes.

Abe submitted the information to Amex, a Jack Connery card was duly issued, and Jack joined the plastic money parade, making sure to charge a few items every month.

Sixteen months later he was holding not one but three offers for pre-approved cards. Jack Connery signed up for his own MasterCard and, shortly thereafter, Abe canceled him as an additional cardholder.

Jack Connery was on his own.

"Used to be so easy," Abe said morosely. "You'd go to the registry, pick out the name of a dead guy, copy down his dates and numbers, and send those into the credit card company. Instantly, you've got a card. But now, computers have ruined everything."

Jack nodded. "Got to love 'em, but they're a major pain in the ass too."

Abe was referring to the SSDI—the Social Security Death Index that credit report companies like TRW and Equifax had compiled to ferret out credit cheaters. People like Jack and Abe weren't out to cheat anyone—they paid on time, to the dime—but the SSDI put their fake identities at risk. Even Jack's made-up number for Connery—someone just might happen to have that same SSN. What if that someone died and his number went into the SSDI? Neither Abe nor Jack needed a fraud investigator sniffing their way.

So Jack had searched for a better way.

He'd found it in the registry of vital statistics. Children . . . the registry was filled with dead children, many of them infants, some gone from disease and birth defects, too many of them the victims of abandonment, abuse, or neglect whose immediate progenitors—to call them parents would be an insult to real parents everywhere—had cast them off like so much garbage. Jack collected a list of a dozen or so, all with the first name John, who had died ten to fifteen years before—*without* a Social Security number. For a small fee he obtained certified copies of their birth certificates . . . and adopted them.

As each reached his fifteenth or sixteenth birthday, Jack applied for a new Social Security number in that name.

Jack pulled out a pen and opened the composition book.

"Okay. This one's John D'Attilio. He'd have been sixteen next month. I've got Eddy working on the documents. The Hoboken drop is going to be his home address, so he'll be writing to the SSA office in Trenton. Let's make this a good one."

Since the Social Security Act allowed someone under eighteen to apply for a Social Security number through the mail, Jack took full advantage of it. Over the years, he and Abe had composed a series of letters from various kids. Abe had a real knack for sounding like a reluctant teenager forced into applying for a Social Security number because his inconsiderate parents wanted him to ruin his summer by getting a dumb job.

It took them about ten minutes to come up with a vernacular, handwritten request; Jack made a point of crossing out a word here and there along the way.

The application required certified copies of the birth certificate, which Jack already had, and a school ID, which Ernie would provide. Then he'd put them all together and send the package off to Trenton. In a month or so, John D'Attilio would be issued a bona fide Social Security number, and added to the Social Security Administration's computers: another American cow branded and allowed to join the taxpaying herd.

"How many times have we done this now?" Abe said.

"Eight, I think."

After Jack Connery had been spun off from Abe's Amex, Jack had added two additional cardholders—Jack Andrissi and John Bender—to the Connery MasterCard. A year and a half later, various banks and Amex were wooing Andrissi and Bender with preapproved offers.

He'd then spun off Andrissi and Bender and abandoned Connery. A new identity was added to each of the Andrissi and Bender cards. And so it went, an ongoing process of creating new identities and discarding old ones, leaving an increasingly attenuated, protracted maze that—Jack hoped—would be impossible to follow.

"Kind of morbid," Abe said. "And such a *megillah*."

Jack sighed. "I know about the morbid part—but I mean, I could be the only one in the world who's given one thought to some of these kids since the day they died—since the day they were *born,* maybe. They're almost like real family to me. And, in a sense, this gives them back some sort of life."

"A virtual life—in the databanks."

"So to speak. But as for the megillah . . . you've got that right."

He slumped against the counter as a dark cloud seemed to form up near the ceiling and trickle a cold drizzle on him.

"You know, Abe, I've spent most of my adult life trying to get to this place. And now . . . I don't know."

It had been a long hard journey, full of dangerous curves, to achieve sovereign statehood, to become a nation of one. At first it had been kind of fun—the artful dodging, the hide and seek, the daily buzz of staying on his toes and living by his wits. But the buzzes had grown fewer and further between. And without the buzz, all the dodging and hiding became work—a *lot* of work. Jack's was a high-maintenance lifestyle.

"Sometimes I get tired of all the upkeep . . . and I start asking, is it worth it?"

"You're just having a bad day."

"No . . . it's not just the day." He thought of seeing Vicky later and playing catch with her. "It's this schizoid life I'm leading."

"Well then, the question you've got to ask is, will merging with the global mega-conglomerate out there make you happier than remaining a closely held corporation of one? It's a decision only you can make."

"Tell me about it. But I'm beginning to see that it's not really a question of 'if'—more a question of 'when.' I mean, can you see me doing this thirty years from now? Who in his sixties has the energy for this?"

"I'm in my fifties and I can barely keep up. I should retire."

A shock of alarm pierced Jack. "What? And give up the gun trade? A lot of people out there depend on you, Abe. And what would you do? You couldn't get by selling just sporting goods, could you?"

Abe shrugged. "You never know. Take Rollerblades, for instance. Such a racket. You sell them these inline skates so they can go out and have some fun exercise. But then they have to buy helmets and shin guards and knee pads and wrist protectors so they shouldn't maim themselves while having said fun exercise."

"Hardly seems fair," Jack said.

Abe shook his head. "I know. Gun running is a much more honorable trade."

"Well, you could simply refuse to carry the skates."

"What, am I crazy? You have any idea what the markup is on that stuff? I should let someone else make all the profit?"

15

"Eye on the ball, Vicks. That's it. Watch it all the way into the glove."

Vicky did just that—watched it go into her glove and bounce right out. As she chased it across the tiny backyard, Jack had to admit that Vicky was a bit of a klutz when it came to baseball.

He looked around. A backyard in Manhattan, a stone's throw from the East River. A private oasis in a ferro-concrete desert. What a luxury.

The grounds had gone untended through the fall. Now Gia had already started weeding the flower beds, but the grass needed cutting, especially around Vicky's playhouse in the rear corner. Jack planned to buy a mower next week and take care of that. He hadn't cut grass since he was a teenager. Used to be his summer job. He found himself looking forward to mowing again. The city was filled with smells, but new mown grass wasn't one of them.

Despite the neglect, it was still pretty out here, especially near the rear wall of the house where the buds on the rose bushes were swelling, showing some pink as they prepared to bloom.

Gia had come out to paint. She was taking a break now, sitting at the white enameled table in the shade, nibbling delicate slivers of a bright green Granny Smith as she whittled them off with a paring knife. Her latest painting—the top of the Fifty-ninth Street Bridge glinting in the afternoon sun as it peeked over the townhouse roof—sat half finished on an easel by the playhouse. Jack liked it a hell of a lot better than any of Melanie Ehler's work, especially that one in her study. Gia, on the other hand, might go for Melanie's stuff. Her appreciation of art was so much wider than Jack's.

Vicky picked up the baseball and threw it—wild.

She throws like a girl, Jack thought as he raced to intercept it before it hit her mother. But then, what else did he expect?

Jack caught the ball a few feet away from a cringing Gia.

"Many athletes in your family?" he said in a low voice.

"Not that I know of."

"Didn't think so."

"Looks like you've got your work cut out for you," she said, batting her blues as she smiled up at him.

"But I'm up to it." Then, raising his voice. "Before I'm through with her, the Vickster will be the best ballplayer in the whole damn city!"

"Yay!" Vicky cried, pumping her fist in the air.

They tossed the ball back and forth a few more times, and then Vicky wanted a break.

"I'm hungry," she said.

Gia held up her Granny Smith. "Want some apple?"

"Wait," Jack said. "I've got just the thing."

He trotted over to the shopping bag he'd brought with him and produced a red paper box. He tossed it to Vicky.

"Animal crackers!" she cried, and tore open the top.

Jack watched Vicky munch and pick through the crackers to find her favorite animals. So easy to make her happy. She took such a disproportionate amount of pleasure from little things, and he took an equally disproportionate amount of pleasure from hers.

He looked around and knew he loved it here. So far from mutilated bodies and names stolen from dead children. At times like these he didn't want to leave. Ever.

Vicky turned to her mother. "Want a lion, Mommy?"

"Vicky!" Jack said in a shocked tone. "How can you *say* that? You know your mother doesn't eat meat!"

Gia winged her partially eaten apple at him.

It sailed wide. Jack reached out and snagged it, then took a sloppy bite and gave them both a big juicy grin. Vicky laughed. Gia smiled and shook her head as she bit into her lion cracker.

Life could be so good.

16

After a quick stop at his apartment to drop off the letter and pick up some extra clothes—and delay his return—Jack finally reached the hotel. As he walked up to the front entrance, he was struck by the absence of officialdom. He'd expected at least one blue-and-white unit to be hanging around.

The lobby looked pretty quiet too, although he could feel that strange tension again, coiling and building in the air. Most of the excitement should have subsided by now, but he'd expected to see at least one or two knots of people whispering and glancing over their shoulders.

He spotted Evelyn heading for the stairs on her Little Lotta feet. He hurried to catch up with her.

"I just got back," he said, slowing to match her pace. "Did Olive show up yet?"

She shook her head. "No one's seen her? And she hasn't contacted anyone?"

Jack repressed a groan. *Don't tell me they haven't opened her room yet.*

"What about her room?"

"She wasn't there? I had the managers—"

Jack froze. "What?"

"Her room was empty? I—" She stopped and looked at him with motherly concern. "Are you all right?"

Jack was mentally reeling. He knew if his face reflected half of the shock he was feeling, he must look terrible. He tried to compose himself.

"She wasn't in her room?"

She shook her head. "I can't tell you how relieved I am? I was so afraid? Like maybe we'd find her dead of a heart attack or a stroke or something?"

His mind raced, stumbling along as it tried to decide which way to go. *Not there? Impossible. He'd seen her . . . dead . . . mutilated . . . her head twisted around. . . .*

"You're sure you had the right room?"

"Of course? Eight-twelve? I was there? I searched the room myself? Olive's suitcase? And her clothes? They're all there in the drawers? But no Olive? Isn't that strange?"

"Yeah," Jack said. "Real strange."

"It makes you wonder? You know, about the End Days? When the faithful are taken away in the Rapture? Could this be the start? And Olive is one of the first to be taken?"

How do I—how does anyone—answer that? Jack wondered.

Evelyn smiled and patted his arm. "Rapture or not, the show goes on? I have to run? I'm introducing Professor Mazuko's panel on Japanese UFOs? See you later?"

"Sure," Jack said, still feeling dazed. "Later."

He wandered up to the common area and dropped into a chair. Olive's corpse . . . gone. How had it been spirited out through a hotel full of people?

Spirited out . . . swell choice of words.

And without leaving a trace of the murder.

This left him and the killers as the only ones who knew that Olive Farina was dead.

Or *was* she dead? *Did* he know that?

Jack was having a SESOUP moment here—he'd witnessed something but didn't have a shred of physical evidence to prove it.

Had to stop that kind of thinking. Olive was dead. No question about that. But who sliced her up? The two men in black he'd run into? Or someone else?

All of which made Jack intensely uneasy. This was supposed to be a quiet job, a safe job. No rough stuff.

But the condition of Olive's corpse had said loud and clear that someone was playing *very* rough.

Of course there was always the possibility that Olive's murder had nothing to do with Melanie's disappearance.

Yeah, right. I should be so lucky.

Olive gone without a trace . . . just like Melanie. Did that mean Melanie was hidden away somewhere with no lips, no eyes, and a broken neck?

A logical conclusion, seeing as Jack, like everybody else except the killers, would be thinking of Olive as simply missing—or taken by the Rapture, if you were into that—if he hadn't broken into her room. He was glad he hadn't told Lew about Olive. He'd jump to the same conclusion, and that might just kill the poor guy.

He looked around at the SESOUP folk streaming into one of the conference rooms. Maybe these people weren't as crazy as they seemed. And maybe he could learn something useful at one of these panels.

As he followed the crowd he spied a flyer taped to the wall. He stepped closer to read it.

CALL FOR
RESEARCH PARTICIPANTS

**If one of your parents is an alien
OR
If one of your siblings or one of your children is the
product of an alien sexual encounter
PLEASE CALL IMMEDIATELY!**

Then again, he thought, maybe SESOUPers are even crazier than they seem.

Even though Jack had been sure at times during his childhood that his older brother was part alien, he resisted copying down the phone number.

He filed inside and found a seat near the rear of the room. He fought an urge to shout out: "All those who believe in telekinesis, raise my hand!" Instead, he listened to Evelyn introduce Professor Hideki Mazuko of the University of Tokyo—what department, she didn't say—and was startled to learn that the man didn't speak any English. He did, however, speak French. So did Evelyn, and she would provide a running translation of Dr. Mazuko's address.

As a lantern-jawed middle-aged Asian in a gray suit, white shirt, red- and blue-striped tie advanced to the dais amid polite applause, Jack groaned and looked around for a way out. He realized he couldn't make it without stumbling over a lot of SESOUPers, so he grudgingly settled in and promised himself a trip to the bar immediately afterward.

Dr. Mazuko began speaking in French, saying a few words, then stopping for Evelyn to repeat it in English. Jack had always assumed water torture required water; here was proof that he was wrong.

After his interminable stop-and-go preamble, Professor Mazuko asked that the lights be turned down so he could show slides of recent photos of UFOs over Tokyo.

A progression of images of blurry blobs of light flashed on the screen, with the audience *ooh*ing and *aah*ing at each one. Jack wondered why, if UFOs were supposed to be such a secret, they were always lit up like the Fuji blimp?

When one particularly strange-looking glowing object appeared, the woman on Jack's right began to clap and others joined her.

"Incredible!" she said in a voice hushed with awe.

Jack wholeheartedly agreed: Incredible was just the word for it. Even eight-year-old Vicky would see that it was a kite. Or pie in the sky—literally.

Like Abe had said the other day . . . believing is seeing. Yes, sir.

"Shit, shit, *shit!*" Suddenly someone was shouting. "That does it! Turn on the lights! Turn on the goddamn lights!"

Jack thought the voice sounded familiar, and when the lights came up, he spotted James Zaleski striding toward the front of the room.

"What's the matter with you people!" he shouted. "These are the goddamn phoniest looking photos I've ever seen!"

Jack heard groans around him and muttered variations on the theme of "Oh, no, Jimmy's on a tear again."

Obviously this wasn't the first time he'd made a stink at a UFO panel.

"Dammit," Zaleski yelled, "you've got to be more discriminating! You've got to be *critical!* We know they're here, but are we so desperate for proof we'll accept *anything,* even these poorly doctored fakes, as real? We demand the truth from the government, but how are we ever going to be taken seriously if we don't demand honesty within our own ranks? We come off like a bunch of gullible cranks!"

Members of the audience had started rising to their feet during his impassioned plea and now they were shouting at him to be quiet and return to his seat and let Professor Mazuko finish.

Jack remembered Gia taking him and Vicky to the revival of *1776* when it had played at the Roundabout. This reminded him of the booming opening number when the entire cast rose and sang "Sit Down, John!" to John Adams.

Jack used the uproar to cover his exit. On the way out he saw Miles Kenway standing ramrod straight against the rear wall, staring at him. Jack felt like a school kid caught playing hooky. He matched Kenway stare for stare.

How do I get to talk to Kenway? he wondered as he reached the common area. At least he and Zaleski were still around. If someone was knocking off the top people in SESOUP, they hadn't reached the men yet. But was it just a matter of time before they did?

Just then two dowdy, silver-haired members of Professor Mazuko's audience emerged from the room, in heated discussion.

"You don't believe that, do you?" said the one wearing the *MK-Ultra Stole My Brain!* T-shirt.

Her friend nodded vigorously. "Of course I do."

"No," said the first, as they wandered away. "You can't *really* believe that."

I believe I'll have a beer, Jack thought.

He headed for the bar.

17

"He is our enemy, I tell you." Mauricio's voice grew louder with each word. "Just look at what he has done to the Farina woman! That man is out to destroy us!"

"Hush, please. You do not know that."

They stood in the bathroom of Roma's suite where Olive's mutilated corpse lay stretched out in the tub. They had partially covered it with ice to keep it from stinking.

"I *do!* I saw him in the hall outside her room!"

"And you also saw one of the Twins at the same time."

"And they both fled together."

"Or he chased the Twin."

"If he did, he's crazy."

"Have you ever known the Twins to work with anyone but each other?"

Mauricio looked away. "No," he said sullenly. "Not directly."

They had run down the hall after the stranger and the

Twin had disappeared into the stairwell, found Olive's corpse, and quickly moved her here.

"I think there is another explanation. I believe he discovered Olive, saw the Twin, and gave chase."

"Then why didn't he report the body?"

"Perhaps he is a thief and broke into her room to steal. Or perhaps he has a criminal record and was afraid he would be blamed. It does not matter. As far as I am concerned, the very fact that he did *not* report the body proves that he is not working with the Twins."

"I don't follow."

"Think, Mauricio: Why was Olive Farina mutilated in that fashion? Look at those wounds. Obviously meant to call to mind cattle mutilations and spread panic among our attendees. A discovery like that would disperse them, send them fleeing to the safety of their little homes all over the country."

Mauricio's dark monkey eyes widened. "Do you think the Twins know what we're doing?"

"No. Undoubtedly they know somebody is up to something, but they do not know who, what, or why. Under those circumstances, their best course is to break up the party. They tried, but failed."

"Only by the merest chance. If I hadn't stepped out into the hallway at that moment . . ." Mauricio let the rest of the sentence hang.

"True," Roma said, nodding. "But were we lucky . . . or guided?"

"We can speculate all day. The question is, what do we do about the stranger?"

"We watch him," Roma said.

"In other words, nothing!" Mauricio said, scorn ripe in his voice as he expanded to true form. He rose on his thicker, stronger legs, showing his fangs and fixing Roma with the ripe strawberries of his eyes. "The stranger calls the tune?"

"Watching is not 'nothing.'"

"And what of tonight's delivery? Do we to let that fall into his hands as well?"

"Do we have a choice?" Roma said. "The Otherness is in charge, do not forget. If the stranger received the shipment, it was not in error. I sense another purpose at work here, one that is compatible with our own."

"I do not," Mauricio said, his voice rising as he banged a large knotty fist on the black-furred barrel of his chest. "Something went wrong last night. I do not intend to allow that to happen a second time."

"Mauricio!" Roma said as the creature slouched toward the door.

"I know of only one way to settle this."

"Wait!"

But Mauricio ignored him. He reached up and turned the doorknob, then shrank again to capuchin form before stepping out into the hall.

"Do not do anything—!"

The door slammed, cutting him off. He hurried to the door and pulled it open, but Mauricio was nowhere in sight.

What was that creature thinking? He hoped he was not planning anything rash.

18

Jack felt better halfway through his second pint of Sam Adams. He was ready to polish it off and head for his room when he sensed someone behind him.

He turned and found Roma.

"Learn anything in Monroe?" Roma said.

Jeez, Jack thought, annoyed and chagrined, did someone follow me out there? Am I being watched?

"What makes you think I was in Monroe?"

Roma grinned. "I have contacts there. It's a small town, as you know. And when an outsider starts asking about 1968, it doesn't take long for word to get around."

Canfield had probably heard about his visit, and told Roma. That made Jack feel a little better . . . he preferred being on the Monroe grapevine to being shadowed.

"Then I guess you know what I found: *nada*."

"But how did you *feel* being there?" Roma asked, giving him an intense look.

"Feel? Like I'd wasted my time."

"No, no," he said. "In the air. Did you not feel a residual trace of something strange, something . . . Other?"

"'Other?' No. Why should I? First Canfield, now you. What's the story with this 'Other' and 'Otherness' business anyway?"

"It is something that has no rational explanation."

"Oh, well, thanks for clearing that up."

"Surely you've seen things that have no rational explanation."

"Maybe," Jack said, thinking of the creaking hold of a rustbucket freighter filled with cobalt-skinned, shark-headed creatures.

"Not maybe. Definitely. You are much more a part of this than you realize."

Something in Roma's voice stopped Jack, something unsaid. What was he getting at?

"You mean because of my experience?" And at that instant he realized that Roma was the only one who hadn't quizzed him on his cover story. Hadn't even mentioned it.

"Yes, but not the one you've been telling people about. Your *other* experience—the one that left you marked by the Otherness."

"Hey, let's not go tying me into any of that stuff."

"You already are."

"Like hell."

"Really? Then what left those scars on your chest?"

An arctic wind seemed to whistle through the bar; Jack could almost feel it rustle his clothes as it chilled his skin.

"How do you know anything about my chest?"

"The Otherness has left its mark on you, my friend. I sensed your contact with it the instant I saw you on the registration line. And when I am this close to you, I can almost see those scars glowing through your shirt."

Just as he'd done the night of the first reception, Roma raised this three middle fingers and hooked them into claws, then made a diagonal slashing motion in the air.

"Like that, yes?" Roma said.

Jack said nothing. His tongue felt like Velcro. He looked down at his shirt front, then back at Roma, remembering how his chest itched both times he'd been in Monroe.

Jack found his voice. "I think we need to have a nice long chat about this sometime."

To Jack's surprise, Roma nodded and said, "How about now?" He pointed to a tiny table in a darkened corner. "Shall we?"

Jack grabbed his beer from the bar and followed him.

As soon as they were seated, Roma said, "You were scarred by a rather formidable creature, yes?"

Jack didn't move, didn't speak. He'd never told a soul about the rakoshi episode. The people closest to him had been a part of it, and they were trying to put it behind them. Anyone who hadn't been part of it would think he was crazy . . . would think he belonged in SESOUP. So how the hell could Roma know?

He sipped his beer to wet his tongue. "You've seen one?"

"Seen one?" Roma grinned. "I was present when the Otherness conceived them."

Jack gave a mental whistle. This guy was as loony as the rest of them. Loonier, maybe. But he did know things he had no right knowing.

"Were you now?" Jack said. "You and this Otherness thing."

"The Otherness is not a thing."

"Then what is it? Besides a word, I mean?"

Roma stared at him. "You really don't know, do you."

"Know what?"

"Never mind. As for defining the Otherness, I doubt very much you can grasp the answer."

"Humor me."

"Very well. Let me see . . . one might describe the Otherness as a being, or a state of being, or even a whole other reality."

"That narrows it down."

"Try this then: Let us just say there is this dark intelligence, this entity somewhere that is—"

"Where?"

"Somewhere—somewhere *else*. Everywhere and nowhere. But put aside the *where* for the moment and concentrate on this force's relationship with humanity."

"Wait, wait, wait. You started out a step ahead of me and now you want to take another."

"How? How am I ahead of you?"

"*What* is this 'dark intelligence'? Is it just *there*? I mean, is it Satan, Kali, the Bogey Man, what?"

"Perhaps it is all of them, perhaps none of them. Why do you presume it must have a name? It is not some silly *god*. If anything, the Otherness is more of an anti-god."

"Like Olive's Antichrist?"

Roma sighed, his expression frustrated. "No. That is part of Christian mythology. Forget Olive's eschatological ravings, and every religion you have ever heard of. When I say anti-god, I mean something at the opposite pole from everything you think of when someone says 'god.' This entity does *not* want worshippers, does *not* want a religion set up around it. It has no name and does *not* want anyone assigning it a name."

"What is it then?"

"An incomprehensible entity, a huge, unimaginable chaotic force—it does not *need* a name. In fact, you might even say it wishes to *avoid* a name. It does not want us knowing about it."

"If it's so powerful, why should it care? And who's ever heard of a god that doesn't want believers?"

"Please stop using the word 'god.' You are only confusing yourself."

"Okay. Then why doesn't *it* want believers?"

"Because of its chaotic nature. Once you believe in it, once you acknowledge it, you give it form. Assigning it a form, a shape, an identity weakens its influence. Identifying it and giving it a name or, worst of all, converting a host of believers to worship it, would shrink its interface with this world and push it further away. So it masks itself as other religions and belief systems and lets them front for it."

"Sort of like a multinational conglomerate hiding behind lots of dummy corporations."

Roma nodded slowly. "A mundane analogy, but you seem to be getting the picture. This force is in this world in many guises, but all working toward the same end: chaos."

"A little chaos isn't so bad."

"You mean, a little randomness? A little unpredictability for excitement?" He laughed softly as he shook his head. "You have no idea, no concept of what we are discussing here."

"All right, what does *it* want?"

"Everything—including this corner of existence."

"Because why? We taste good?"

"Really, if you refuse to be serious—"

"Don't tell *me* to be serious when you've filled this hotel with a very serious group of otherwise sane adults who firmly believe that a horde of alien lizards is heading this way from space and is going to chow down on us big time when they get here. I didn't make that up— they did."

"Well, they are right and they are wrong. Something *is* trying to get here but the 'chowing down,' so to speak, will be of a more spiritual sort. If you would listen without interrupting you might understand."

Jack leaned back and folded his arms. "All right. I'll listen. But whenever I hear stuff like this I can't help thinking about how we all thought earth and humanity were the center of the universe. Then Galileo came along."

"Point taken. It does sound anthropocentric, but if you will hear me out, you will see it is not."

"Go."

"Thank you. I will try to come at this from a different angle: Imagine two vast, unimaginably complex forces at war. Where? All around us. Why? I do not pretend to know. And it has been going on so long, perhaps they themselves have forgotten why. But none of that matters. What does matter is that all existence is the prize. Notice I did not say 'the world,' 'the solar system,' 'the universe,' 'reality'—I said *existence*. That means that all other dimensions, other universes, other realities— which, trust me on this, do exist—are included as well.

This corner of reality is a minuscule backwater of that whole, but it *is* a part. And if you mean to call yourself the victor, you must have it all."

Jack resisted quoting Rodney King.

"Now," Roma continued, "one of these forces is decidedly inimical to humanity; the other is not."

Jack couldn't help it—he yawned.

"Am I boring you?" Roma said, his expression shocked.

"Sorry. Just sounds like the old Good versus Evil, God versus dat ol' debil Satan sort of thing."

"That is how some people interpret it, and Cosmic Dualism *is* rather trite. But that is not the case here. Please note that I did not say that the opposing side— the anti-Otherness, if you wish—is 'good.' I said it is not inimical. Frankly, I doubt very much that it gives a specific damn about humanity other than the fact that this territory lies on its side of the cosmic DMZ, and it wants to keep it there."

Wow, Jack thought. He'd heard some wild theories this week, and he'd become convinced that something—not aliens, not the Antichrist, not the New World Order, but *something*—was going on, but this . . . this Otherness stuff took the blue ribbon for being the farthest out.

"So . . ." Jack said. "We're all caught up in a giant game of *Risk.*"

Roma shook his head slowly. "You have an uncanny knack for reducing the empyrean to the mundane."

"So I've been told."

"But then," Roma said, "taking everything I've said into account, we must not overlook the big '*or.*'"

"Or?"

"Or . . . everything I have just told you is completely wrong because there is no way a human can understand the logic and motives of this totally 'other' reality."

"Swell," Jack said, wanting to scour the smug look off Roma's face. "Then all this talk's got nothing to do with"—Jack mimicked Roma's three-fingered gesture again—"this."

"On the contrary. Your scars were made by a creature of the Otherness."

"The ones you say you watched being conceived."

"Watched? A piece of my flesh was used in their genesis." Roma's expression clouded. "Not that I had much say in the matter. But they turned out to be rather magnificent creatures, didn't they."

"Magnificent isn't quite the word I'd choose."

But perhaps magnificent wasn't so far off. Magnificently *evil,* and so alien, so . . . *other,* that Jack remembered how his most primitive instincts had screamed for him either to run or to annihilate them.

Jack also remembered what he'd been told about the origin of the rakoshi. He could almost hear Kolabati's voice. . . .

"Tradition has it that before the Vedic gods, and even before the pre-Vedic gods, there were other gods, the Old Ones, who hated mankind and wanted to usurp our place on earth. To do this they created blasphemous parodies of humans . . . stripped of love and decency and everything good we are capable of. They are hate, greed, lust, and violence incarnate. . . ."

Could Kolabati's Old Ones be Roma's Otherness?

Roma rose from the table. "Well, I'm satisfied," he said.

"About what?"

"That all you know of the Otherness is what I've just told you. I thought you might be a threat, but I am now convinced you are not."

For some reason he couldn't quite grasp, Jack felt offended by that. "Threat of what?"

Roma went on as if he hadn't heard. "But there might

be others who are not so sure. You would do well to take care, Mr. Shelby. You might even consider returning to your home and locking your doors for the rest of the weekend."

The warning startled Jack, and before he could reply, Roma turned and strode away. Jack wanted to run after him, grab him, shake him, and shout *Tell me what you mean!* But he fought the urge. That would only cause a scene, and was unlikely to make Roma more talkative.

Feeling as if he'd been sucker punched, Jack headed for his room.

19

On the way back upstairs, Jack cursed himself for not telling Roma he'd been spotted in Monroe with Melanie last week. He would have loved to have seen his reaction. Damn. Why hadn't he thought of that?

What did Gia call it? *Esprit de l'escalier,* or something like that.

As soon as he stepped into the room he saw the red message light blinking on his phone. He followed the directions for message retrieval and heard a low, raspy voice: *"Wondering where Olive Farina is? Check the hotel basement."*

That was it. A mechanical sounding female voice announced the time the message had been recorded: 6:02. Seven minutes ago. Just about the time he'd left the bar.

He didn't recognize the voice, but he'd bet his last dollar it was one of the goons in black. Jack knew about Olive's death—he was probably the only one who did. That made him a loose end, one that needed tying up.

And they think I'm just going to go trotting down to the basement and into their tender loving arms?

He was insulted.

Of course, he was going—whoever spirited Olive away probably had something to do with Melanie's disappearance—but he wasn't going alone. Mr. Glock would come along.

He pulled the pistol from his gym bag and hefted it, considering a silencer, then discarding the idea. The increased length would make the pistol harder to handle in close quarters. If he needed to fire, he would, noise be damned. He slipped it under his belt, inside his shirt, then headed for the elevators.

He smiled and nodded at the SESOUPers who rode down with him. All but one got off at the second floor for the reception. The straggler departed at the lobby level, leaving Jack alone as he descended to the final stop.

He pulled the Glock and chambered a round as the car slowed, then held the pistol tight against his right thigh as the doors slid open. He stepped out into a narrow corridor. Its ceiling was tentacled with pipes and ducts, a closed door on either side, opening into a wider, darker space at its end where machinery clanked and whirred. Warm and dusty. The Clinton Regent was old enough to have boilers.

"Hello?" he called once, then again. No reply.

He raised his pistol as he edged up to the first door and tried the handle. Locked. With the Glock's muzzle ceilingward, he slid his back along the wall until he was opposite the second door. He reached over and tried that knob—also locked. But locked didn't mean unoccupied. Someone could pop out of either at any time.

Keeping his back to a wall, and an eye on those doors, Jack slid to the end of the corridor. Hotter here, darker and noisier too—a wide dim space, its floor lower than the corridor's. Light spilling from behind him glinted off hulking elephantine shapes snared in a maze of pipes and ducts.

Jack darted his head out and back, twice, checking left and right. Visibility was the pits, but at least no one was hovering just around the corner. And he'd spotted a light switch on the right. He reached his left hand around and flipped the single toggle.

The two naked bulbs that came to life far to the left and right in the ceiling did little to chase the gloom. Jack stepped onto a small platform that sat a couple of feet above the floor of the bigger space. Leaning against the low pipe railing, he scanned the walls for more switches. The place had to have better light than this. As he looked for more bulbs so he could follow the wiring back to a switch, he spotted a large dark lump attached to one of the pipes against the ceiling almost directly above him. He immediately moved to the side and peered up at it.

The way it was stuck to the pipe reminded him of some huge barnacle. But as his eyes adjusted to the dimmer light, he could see that it was covered with either fur or some sort of black fuzzy mold. No details, just a big lump of black fur. In fact, from this angle it looked like someone had attached a sable coat to the pipe.

Jack blinked and suddenly it was coming his way— not simply dropping from the ceiling, *catapulting* at him. With a hoarse bellow, a hurtling mass of bared fangs, extended claws, and bright crimson eyes was on him before he could raise his pistol for a shot. The Glock was knocked from his grasp, clattering away along the floor as he went down under the brain-jarring impact.

The thing was all sinew and muscle and utterly savage in its attack, raking him with its claws and snapping at Jack's face. He got his hands around its throat and held it off, but the first three seconds told him how this was going to go—he was going to lose. He needed a weapon or a way out. The Glock was gone and the Semmerling was out of reach in his ankle holster.

Jack tried to match the creature's ferocity, roaring at it as he pushed it to arms length. He bent his knees, got his feet against its torso, and kicked out with everything he had. The creature went flying, slammed against the platform railing, and slipped through, falling to the floor below. Jack looked around, spotted the Glock on the corridor floor, and dove for it. But the creature had already recovered and, screaming with rage, was on him again before he reached it.

The force of the impact against his back drove Jack to the floor. In that instant he felt strong fingers grab a handful of his hair and yank his head back, glimpsed extended fang-filled jaws gape wide and slash toward his exposed throat, and he knew he was done. No time for any thought other than sick dread and a silent *No!*

And suddenly the weight was off him. Jack hesitated through a heartbeat of confusion, then rolled over in time to see the creature hurtling through the air, slamming back first against the corridor wall.

What the—? How'd I do that?

The thing sprawled against the wall an instant, dazed, shaking its head, and now Jack had his first good look at it—a hellish cross between a rottweiler and a baboon, but bigger and heavier.

Then it was rushing at him again—

Only to hurl itself back against the wall before it reached him.

Jack had no idea what was going on and wasn't going to waste time pondering it. Get the Glock! He rolled toward the pistol as the thing came for him once more, only to veer away and slam itself against the wall a third time.

That seemed to be enough for the thing. As Jack reached the pistol, the creature turned and fled the corridor. Before he could take aim, it was gone, lost amid the pipes and tanks.

Jack sat alone in the middle of the floor, panting, almost retching. He'd been as good as dead less than a minute ago. What had happened? And what *was* that hell thing? Obviously it had been sent to kill him, but why hadn't it finished him off when it had the chance?

Shaken, weak, he struggled to his feet and staggered back toward the elevator.

20

Jack crouched among the rhodos in the Castlemans' backyard, trying to find a comfortable position.

I shouldn't even be here tonight, he thought.

Still rattled and hurting from his earlier encounter with that monkey-dog creature, the last thing he felt like doing tonight was babysitting the Castlemans. But he didn't exactly have anybody to sit in for him. So after soaking his wrenched muscles and ligaments in the tub in his hotel room, he'd dragged himself out to Elmhurst. He ran into traffic along the way, and Ceil was already home by the time he reached his post among the rhodos.

Even here, far away from the Clinton Regent basement, Jack couldn't shake the memory of the utter ferocity of that creature. He'd never seen anything like it. Not a rakosh, but just as bloodthirsty.

And why me, damn it? I'm not supposed to be a target. This isn't about me, it's about Melanie Ehlers.

Jack was spooked, he admitted it. Every shadow held menace now.

He forced himself to concentrate on Ceil. She was sipping what looked like a vodka but she wasn't slicing and dicing. The casement windows over the kitchen sink had been cranked out an inch or so, and music from the stereo seeped into the backyard. When Donna Summer and Barbara Streisand finished caterwauling "Enough is Enough," Laura Branigan started singing about "Gloria."

Jack grimaced. Disco . . . Ceil still listens to disco.

She took her drink upstairs. Jack couldn't see into the bedroom, so he waited. And then for a moment or two he had the feeling that *he* was being watched. That thing again? Coming back to finish the job? Carefully he studied the shadows but didn't see anything. Eventually the feeling went away, but it left him on edge.

Got to shake this, he thought. Got to focus here.

When Ceil reappeared, she had changed into a dress. Gloria Gaynor's "I Will Survive" was thumping now and Ceil did a little dance around the kitchen, her dress swirling around her skinny legs as she made quick graceful turns this way and that.

Remembering the good old days? Jack wondered.

Finally she finished her drink, put on a coat, and headed for the door to the garage.

Don't forget to turn off the stereo, Jack wanted to shout. *Please* don't leave that music on!

Her hand was on the doorknob when she stopped, turned, and hurried back to the stereo.

"Thank you, Ceil," he whispered as the music died.

She drove off, and Gus didn't show up, so Jack

assumed Ceil was meeting her husband for dinner or a party. He debated whether or not to pack it in and call it an early night, or hang on and wait.

Jack chose waiting. He'd leave after seeing them safely to bed.

Waiting. This was always the lousy part. It could be put to good use. A perfect time for deep cogitation—or ratiocination, as Sherlock Holmes would say—but he was tired of thinking about Melanie and Olive and the SESOUPers. His brain needed a rest.

Jack had trained himself to fall into a light sleep under almost any circumstances. Now was an excellent time for a catnap. Normally he'd adjust his gym bag under him, lean back, and close his eyes. But not tonight. No snoozing in the dark tonight.

21

Miles Kenway sat behind his steering wheel and wondered where the hell he was. Somewhere in Queens, according to his map, but exactly where, he couldn't say.

He'd started out following this Jack Shelby character and had wound up out here.

Jack Shelby . . . not likely. Miles didn't know who the man was, but he wasn't Jack Shelby.

One thing he did know for sure about the mystery man was that he was some sort of pervert.

And that irked Miles no end. He'd followed this character all the way out here thinking he was going to meet with whoever had sent him. And when Miles saw him creep into the shrubbery of a home down the street, that was exactly what it looked like he was doing. But then Miles sneaked around the other side for a look and found him watching some woman dance around inside her house.

The man was a goddamn Peeping Tom.

Miles would have been long gone by now if the background check he'd run had come up clean. But it hadn't.

Miles had pocketed the man's beer bottle from last night's reception and called his man in the FBI. Working quickly, he'd reported that three good sets had been retrieved from the bottle: one belonged to Lewis Ehler, one to the bartender, and the third set was not on record.

That could be a good thing, meaning Jack Shelby had never been arrested, never applied for a gun permit, never worked in any security-sensitive jobs. It could also mean that he was a member of either a government agency or a secret organization powerful enough to have his print set removed from the FBI's computers.

Miles became convinced it was the latter when a check revealed that no one named Jack Shelby lived at the address he'd given when he registered.

So who are you, Shelby, and who are you working for? Whoever you are, you've made a big mistake getting on the wrong side of me. I can and will make your life miserable.

Miles reflected on how far he had come since his birth. Who'd have dreamed that a callow South Dakota farm boy would end up on the country's first line of defense against the New World Order. Now it seemed almost providential that he had joined the Army out of high school, worked his way up in the ranks, and had been in the right places at the right times to hear whispers about the UN, about NATO, about his own government, and to have the internal fiber and wherewithal to put it all together and realize that not everything was quite what it seemed.

When he'd learned the truth, he immediately resigned. He had almost forty years in, so he took his pension, withdrew all his savings, and bought a fifty-acre parcel in Montana where he gathered others who knew the truth. There they lived and trained for the day when the One Worlders would try to take over America.

He dreaded that day, but he'd be ready for it—ready to fight to the death to protect his freedom.

Miles yawned. He hadn't slept well last night. He'd had a dream about that day of invasion, when the New World Order's black helicopters peppered the sky as they came for him and his militia. He shuddered at the memory. He often had nightmares, but this one had been his worst ever. He'd awakened at four-thirty shaking and sweating.

He shook himself to wakefulness. Had to stay alert and wait to see where this so-called Jack Shelby character went from here.

22

The sound of a car turning into the driveway alerted Jack. He straightened, stretched, and crossed the backyard in a hurried crouch, slipping into the foundation shrubbery around the garage. The automatic door rolled up and the car eased into the garage. Jack recognized Gus's voice as the car doors opened.

". . . just wish you hadn't said that, Ceil. It made me look real bad in front of Dave and Nancy."

"But no one took it the way you did," Ceil said.

Jack thought he detected a slight quaver in her voice. Too many vodkas? Or fear?

"Don't be so sure about that. I think they're just too good-mannered to show it, but I saw the shock in Nancy's eyes. Didn't you see the way she looked at me when you said that?"

"No. I didn't see anything of the sort. You're imagining things again."

"Oh, *am* I?"

Jack heard the jangle of keys in the lock in the door to the house.

"Y-yes. And besides, I've already apologized a dozen times since we left. What more do you want from me?"

"What I want, Ceil, is that it not keep happening like it does. Is that too much to ask?"

Ceil's reply was cut off as the garage door began to roll down. Jack returned to the rear of the house where he could get a view of most of the first floor. Their voices leaked out through an open casement window as Gus strode into the kitchen.

". . . don't know why you keep doing this to me, Ceil. I try to be good, try to keep calm, but you keep testing me, pushing me to the limit again and again."

Ceil's voice came from the hall, overtly anxious now.

"But I told you, Gus. You're the only one who took it that way."

Jack watched Gus pull an insulated pot-holder mitten over his left hand, then wrap a dish towel around his right.

"Fine, Ceil. If that's what you want to believe, I guess you'll go on believing it. But unfortunately, that won't change what happened tonight."

Ceil came into the kitchen.

"But Gus—"

Her voice choked off as he turned toward her and she saw his hands.

"Why'd you do it, Ceil?"

"Oh, Gus, no! Please! I didn't mean it!"

She turned to run but he caught her upper arm and yanked her toward him.

"You should have kept your damn mouth shut, Ceil. I try so hard and then you go and get me mad."

He saw Gus take Ceil's wrist in his mittened hand and twist her arm behind her back, twist it up hard and high. She cried out in pain.

"Gus, please don't!"

Jack didn't want to see this, but he had to watch. Had to be sure.

Gus pressed Ceil against the side of the refrigerator. Her face was turned toward Jack, her cheek flattened against the enameled surface. He saw fear there, and terror and dread, but overriding it all was a sort of dull acceptance of the inevitable that reached into Jack's center and twisted.

Gus began ramming his padded fist into Ceil's back, right below the bottom ribs, left side and right, pummeling her kidneys. Eyes squeezed shut, teeth bared with pain she grunted with each impact.

"I hate you for making me do this," Gus said.

Sure you do, you son of a bitch.

Jack gripped the window sill and closed his eyes, but he could hear Ceil's repeated grunts and moans, and he felt her pain. He'd been kidney punched. He knew the agony.

But this had to end soon. Gus would vent his rage and it would all be over. For the next few days Ceil would have stabbing back pains every time she took a deep breath or coughed, and would urinate bright red blood, but she'd have hardly a mark on her, thanks to the mitten and the towel-wrapped fist.

It *had* to end soon.

It didn't. Jack looked again and saw that Ceil's knees had gone rubbery, but that didn't stop Gus. He was supporting her sagging body with the arm lock, and still methodically pummeling her.

Jack growled under his breath. All he'd wanted was to witness enough to confirm Schaffer's story. That done, he'd deal with dear sweet Gus outside the home. Maybe in a dark parking lot while Schaffer made sure he had an airtight alibi. He hadn't counted on a scene like this, though he'd been aware all along it was a possibility.

He knew the smart thing to do in this situation was to walk away. But he also knew himself well enough to be pretty sure he wouldn't be able to do that. So he'd come prepared.

Jack hurried across the backyard and snatched his gym bag from the perimeter shrubs. As he moved around to the far side of the house, he pulled out a nylon stocking and a pair of rubber surgical gloves; he slipped the first over his head and the second over his fingers. Then he removed the special .45 automatic, a pair of wire cutters, and a heavy-duty screwdriver. He stuck the pistol in his belt. He used the cutters on the telephone lead, then popped the latch on one of the living room windows with the screwdriver.

As soon as he was in the darkened room, he looked around for something to break. The first thing to catch his eye was the set of brass fire irons by the brick hearth. He kicked the stand over. The clang and clatter echoed through the house.

Gus's voice floated in from the kitchen.

"What the hell was that?"

When Gus arrived and flipped on the lights, Jack was waiting by the window. He almost smiled at the shock on Gus's face.

"Take it easy, man," Jack said, holding up an open,

empty hand. He knew his face couldn't show much anxiety through the stocking mask so he put it all in his voice. "This is all a mistake."

"Who the hell are you?" Gus shouted. He bent and snatched the poker from the spilled fire irons. "And what are you doing in my house?"

"Listen, man. I didn't think anybody was home. Let's just forget this ever happened."

Gus pointed the poker at the gym bag in Jack's hand. "What's in there? What'd you take?"

"Nothing, man. I just got here. And I'm outta here."

"Omigod!"

Ceil's voice, muffled. She stood at the edge of the living room, leaning against the wall, half bent over from the agony in her kidneys, both hands over her mouth.

"Call the police, Ceil. But tell them not to hurry. I want to teach this punk a lesson before they get here."

As Ceil limped back toward the kitchen, Gus shook off the mitten and the towel and raised the poker in a two-handed grip. His eyes glittered with anticipation. His tight, hard grin told it all: Pounding on his wife had got him up, but he could go only so far with her. Now he had a prowler at his mercy. He could beat the living shit out of this guy with impunity. In fact, he'd be a hero for doing it. His gaze settled on Jack's head like Babe Ruth eyeing a high-outside pitch.

And Schaffer thought a few sessions with a psychiatrist was going to turn this guy into a loving husband? Right. When the Dodgers came back to Brooklyn.

Gus took two quick steps toward Jack and swung. No subtlety, not even a feint.

Jack ducked and let it whistle over his head. He could have put a wicked chop in Gus's exposed flank then, but he wasn't ready yet.

"Hey, man! Be cool! We can talk about this!"

"No, we can't," Gus said as he swung the poker back the other way, lower this time.

Jack jumped back and resisted planting a foot in the big man's reddening face.

"Whatta you tryin' t'do? Kill me?"

"Yes!"

Gus's third swing was vertical, from ceiling to floor. Jack was long gone when it arrived.

Gus's teeth were bared now; his breath hissed through them. His eyes were mad with rage and frustration. Time to goose that rage a little.

Jack grinned beneath the nylon. "You swing like a pussy, man."

With a guttural scream, Gus charged, wielding the poker like a scythe.

Jack ducked the first swing, then grabbed the poker and rammed his forearm into Gus's face with a satisfying crunch. Gus cried out and released his hold on the poker. He staggered back, eyes squeezed shut in agony, holding his nose. Blood began to leak between his fingers.

Never failed. No matter how big they were, a smashed nose tended to be a great equalizer.

Ceil hobbled back to the threshold. Her voice skirted the edge of hysteria.

"The phone's dead!"

"Don't worry, lady," Jack said. "I didn't come here to hurt nobody. and I won't hurt you. But this guy—he's a different story. He just tried to kill me."

As Jack dropped the poker and stepped toward him, Gus's eyes bulged with terror. He put out a bloody hand to fend him off. Jack grabbed the wrist and twisted. Gus wailed as he was turned and forced into an arm lock. Jack shoved him against the wall and began a bare-knuckled workout against his kidneys, wondering if the big man's brain would make a connection between what he'd been dishing out in the kitchen and what he was receiving in the living room.

Jack didn't hold back. He put plenty of body behind the punches, and Gus shouted in pain with each one.

How's it feel, tough guy? Like it?

Jack pounded him until he felt some of his own anger dissipate. He was about to let him go and move into the next stage of his plan when he sensed motion behind him.

As he turned his head he caught a glimpse of Ceil. She had the poker, and she was swinging it toward his head. He started to duck but too late. The room exploded into bright lights, then went dark gray.

An instant of blackness and then Jack found himself on the floor, pain exploding in his gut. He focused above him and saw Gus readying another kick at his midsection. He rolled away toward the corner. Something heavy thunked on the carpet as he moved.

"Christ, he's got a gun!" Gus shouted.

Jack had risen to a crouch by then. He made a move for the fallen .45 but Gus was ahead of him, snatching it from the floor before Jack could reach it.

Gus stepped back and worked the slide to chamber a round. He pointed the pistol at Jack's face.

"Stay right where you are, you bastard! Don't you move a muscle!"

Jack sat back on the floor in the corner and stared up at the big man.

"All right!" Gus said with a bloody grin. "All *right!*"

"I got him for you, didn't I, Gus?" Ceil said, still holding the poker. She was bent forward in pain. That swing had cost her. "I got him off you. I saved you, didn't I?"

"Shut up, Ceil."

"But he was hurting you. I made him stop. I—"

"I said *shut up!*"

Her lower lip trembled. "I . . . I thought you'd be glad."

"Why should I be glad? If you hadn't got me so mad tonight I might've noticed he was here when we came in. Then he wouldn't have took me by surprise." He pointed to his swelling nose. "This is *your* fault, Ceil."

Ceil's shoulders slumped; she stared dully at the floor.

Jack didn't know what to make of Ceil. He'd interrupted her brutal beating at the hands of her husband, yet she'd come to the creep's aid. And valiantly, at that. But the gutsy little scrapper who'd wielded that poker seemed miles away from the cowed, beaten creature now standing in the middle of the room.

I don't get it.

Which was why he'd made a policy of refusing home repairs in the first place. From now on, no more exceptions.

"I'll go over to the Ferrises'," Ceil said.

"What for?"

"To call the police."

"Hold on a minute."

"Why?"

Jack glanced at Gus and saw how his eyes were flicking back and forth between Ceil and him.

"Because I'm thinking, that's why."

"Yeah," Jack said. "I can smell the wood burning."

"Hey!" Gus stepped toward Jack and raised the pistol as if to club him. "Another word out of you and—"

"You don't really want to get that close to me, do you?" Jack said softly.

Gus stepped back.

"Gus, I've got to call the police!" Ceil said as she replaced the poker by the fireplace, far out of Jack's reach.

"You're not going anywhere," Gus said. "Get over here."

Ceil meekly moved to his side.

"Not here!" he said, grabbing her shoulder and shoving her toward Jack. "Over there!"

She cried out with the pain in her back as she stumbled forward.

"Gus! What are you doing?"

Jack decided to stay in character. He grabbed Ceil's shoulders and—as gently as he could—turned her around. She struggled weakly as he held her between Gus and himself.

Gus laughed. "You'd better think of something else, fella. That skinny little broad's not gonna protect you from a forty-five."

"Gus!"

"Shut *up!* God, I'm sick of your voice! I'm sick of your face, I'm sick of—shit, I'm so sick of everything about you!"

Under his hands, Jack could feel Ceil's thin shoulders jerk with the impact of the words as if they were blows from a fist. A fist probably would have hurt less.

"B-but Gus, I thought you loved me."

He sneered. "Are you kidding? I *hate* you, Ceil! It drives me up a wall just to be in the same room with you! Why the hell do you think I beat the shit out of you every chance I get? It's all I can do to keep myself from killing you!"

"But all those times you said—"

"How I loved you?" he said, his face shifting to a contrite, hangdog expression. "How I didn't know what came over me, but I really, truly *loooove* you with all my heart?" The snarl returned. "And you believed it! God, you're such a pathetic wimp you fell for it every time."

"But why?" She was sobbing now. *"Why?"*

"You mean, why play games? Why not dump you and find a real woman—one who's got tits and can have kids? The answer should be pretty clear: your brother. He got me into Gorland 'cause he's one of their biggest customers. And if you and me go kaput, he'll see to it I'm out of there before the ink's dry on our divorce papers. I've put too many years into that job to blow it because of a sack of shit like you."

Ceil almost seemed to shrivel under Jack's hands.

He glared at Gus. "Big man."

"Yeah. I'm the big man. I've got the gun. And I want to thank you for it, fella, whoever you are. Because it's going to solve all my problems."

"What? My gun?"

He wanted to tell Gus to hurry up and use it, but Gus wanted to talk. The words spewed out like maggots from a ripe corpse.

"Yep. I've got a shitload of insurance on my dear wife here. I bought loads of term on her years ago and kept praying she'd have an accident. I was never so stupid as to try and set her up for something fatal—I know what happened to that Marshall guy in Jersey—but I figured, what the hell, with all the road fatalities around here, the odds of collecting on old Ceil were better than Lotto."

"Oh, Gus," she sobbed. An utterly miserable sound.

Her head sank until her chin touched her chest. She would have fan-folded to the floor if Jack hadn't been holding her up. He knew this was killing her, but he wanted her to hear it. Maybe it was the alarm she needed to wake her up.

Gus mimicked her. "'Oh, Gus!' Do you have any idea how many rainy nights you got my hopes up when you were late coming home from your card group? How I prayed—actually *prayed*—that you'd skidded off the road and wrapped your car around a utility pole, or that a big semi had run a light and plowed you under? Do you have any *idea?* But no. You'd come bouncing in as carefree as you please, and I'd be so disappointed I'd almost cry. That was when I really wanted to wring your scrawny neck!"

"That's just about enough, don't you think?" Jack said.

Gus sighed. "Yeah. I guess it is. But at least all those premiums weren't wasted. Tonight I collect."

Ceil's head lifted.

"What?"

"That's right. An armed robber broke in. During the struggle, I managed to get the gun away from him but he pulled you between us as I fired. You took the first bullet—right in the heart. In a berserk rage, I emptied the rest of the clip into his head. Such a tragedy." He raised the pistol and sighted it on Ceil's chest. "Goodbye, my dear sweet wife."

The metallic click of the hammer was barely audible over Ceil's wail of terror.

Her voice cut off as both she and Gus stared at the pistol.

"That could have been a dud," Jack said. "Man, I *hate* when that happens." He pointed to the top of the pistol. "Pull that slide back to chamber a fresh round."

Gus stared at him a second, then worked the slide. An unspent round popped out.

"There you go," Jack said. "Now, give it another shot, if you'll pardon the expression."

Looking confused, he aimed at Ceil again, and Jack detected a definite tremor in the barrel now. Gus pulled the trigger but this time Ceil didn't scream. She merely flinched at the sound of the hammer falling on another dud.

"Aw, *maaaan!*" Jack said, drawing out the word into a whine. "You think you're buying good ammo and someone rips you off! Can't trust nobody these days!"

Gus quickly worked the slide and pulled the trigger

again. Jack allowed two more misfires, then he stepped around Ceil and approached Gus.

Frantically Gus worked the slide and pulled the trigger again, aiming for Jack's face. Another impotent click. He began backing away when he saw Jack's smile.

"That's my dummy pistol, Gus. Actually, a genuine government-issue Mark IV, but the bullets are dummies—just like the guys I let get hold of it."

Jack brought it along when he wanted to see what somebody was really made of. In the right situation, it tended to draw the worst to the surface.

He bent and picked up the ejected rounds. He held one up for Gus to see.

"The slug is real," Jack said, "but there's no powder in the shell. It's an old rule: Never let an asshole near a loaded gun."

Gus charged, swinging the .45 at Jack's head. Jack caught his wrist and twisted the weapon from his fingers. Then he slammed it hard against the side of Gus's face, opening a gash. Gus tried to turn and run but Jack still had his arm. He hit him again, on the back of the head this time. Gus sagged to his knees and Jack put a lot of upper body behind the pistol as he brought it down once more on the top of his head. Gus stiffened, then toppled face first onto the floor.

Only seconds had passed. Jack spun to check on Ceil's whereabouts. She wasn't going to catch him twice. But no worry. She was right where he'd left her, standing in the corner, eyes closed, tears leaking out between the lids. Poor woman.

Nothing Jack wanted more than to be out of this crazy house. He'd been here too long already, but he had to finish this job now, get it done and over with.

He took Ceil's arm and gently led her from the living room.

"Nothing personal, lady, but I've got to put you in a safe place, okay? Someplace where you can't get near a fire poker. Understand?"

"He didn't love me," she said to no one in particular. "He stayed with me because of his job. He was lying all those times he said he loved me."

"I guess he was."

"Lying . . ."

He guided her to a closet in the hall and stood her inside among the winter coats.

"I'm just going to leave you here for a few minutes, okay?"

She was staring straight ahead. "All those years . . . lying. . . ."

Jack closed her in the closet and wedged a ladder-back chair between the door and the wall on the other side of the hall. No way she could get out until he removed the chair.

Back in the living room, Gus was still out cold. Jack turned him over and tied his wrists to the stout wooden legs of the coffee table. He took two four-by-four wooden blocks from his gym bag and placed them under Gus's left lower leg, one just below the knee and the other just above the ankle. Then he removed a short-handled five-pound iron maul from the duffel.

He hesitated as he lifted the hammer.

"Consider this a life saving injury, Gus, old scout," he said in a low voice. "If you're not laid up, your brother-in-law will kill you."

Still Jack hesitated, then recalled Ceil's eyes as Gus methodically battered her kidneys—the pain, the resig-nation, the despair.

Jack broke Gus's left shin with one sharp blow. Gus groaned and writhed on the floor, but didn't regain con-sciousness. Jack repeated the process on the right leg. Then he packed up all his gear and returned to the hall.

He pulled the chair from where it was wedged against the closet door, and opened the door a crack.

"I'm leaving now, lady. When I'm gone you can go next door or wherever and call the police. Better call an ambulance too."

A single sob answered him.

Jack left by the back door. It felt good to get the stocking off his head. He'd feel even better to be far away from this house.

23

Jack took the Fifty-ninth Street Bridge back into Manhattan. Since that would drop him right in Gia's neighborhood, he figured he'd pop in on his way back to the hotel. Vicky would be asleep, but he hoped Gia would be up. After the grimness of the Castlemans, he needed a little sweetness and light.

He was about halfway across when he spotted the black sedan. He'd scanned the street when he'd left the Castlemans, but had seen no sign of it then. They must have been waiting somewhere along his return route.

Or . . . it simply could be a couple of guys who just happened to be heading into the city behind him, and just happened to be driving a black sedan.

Could be. But Jack wanted to know for sure.

When he reached the Manhattan side he took the downtown ramp, then made a full three-sixty loop around a single block. The black sedan stayed with him all the way, right behind him, not even bothering to hide its presence.

That did it. He'd been sucker punched on a stairwell, damn near killed by some sort of dog monkey, and clocked on the back of his head with a fireplace poker. It had been a bad day and he'd had it.

At the next red light, Jack slammed on the brakes, rammed the gearshift into PARK and jumped out of the car. Bursting with anger, he strode back to the Lincoln and yanked on the handle of the driver's door—locked. He pounded against the window.

"Open up, dammit!"

The window slid down and Jack found himself staring into the black lenses of a pair of sunglasses. He couldn't tell if this was the guy he'd chased or the one who'd punched him earlier today. They both looked alike and he could pick out no distinguishing marks on what little of their faces was visible.

Traffic was light on the street, but just then a red pickup truck pulled to a stop behind the black sedan. Jack waved him around—he didn't want any witnesses to the altercation he was sure was about to ensue, but the truck stayed put.

That bothered Jack a little. He thought he remembered seeing a red pickup in his rearview a couple of times since leaving the Castleman house, but couldn't be sure—he'd been concentrating on the black sedan. Who was it . . . backup for the jokers in the sedan, or just another late night traveler?

If it were a black pickup he'd definitely be worried but since it wasn't, he turned his attention back to the sedan.

"What's the story, guys?" he said, crouching slightly to look into the open window. "Who the hell are you and why're you following me? Is my life that much more interesting than yours?"

The driver merely stared up at him through his

shades, saying nothing, his lips a straight line, his pale face expressionless, as if he were deciding whether this man was worthy of reply.

That expression plus the memory of Olive's mutilated body stoked Jack's already topped-off anger.

"Didn't your mothers ever teach you to take off your hats in a car? And what's with the shades at night? Don't you know that's dangerous?"

Jack shot his left hand into the car, aiming to knock off the jerk's hat and grab his sunglasses, but before his fingers were through the opening, the driver's black-gloved hand grabbed Jack's wrist and stopped him.

Jack tried to push farther in, but could not. And when he tried to pull free, he found his wrist imprisoned in a steely grip. Alarmed, he struggled but couldn't break free.

The light had changed to green. A horn sounded, not from the pickup truck, but from some car behind it. The black-gloved grip on his left wrist remained tight as a manacle. The fourth car, a battered old Toyota hatchback, chirped its tires and squeezed through the narrow, barely passable space on the far side of the pickup, the sedan, and Jack's rental, honking angrily all the way. The pickup didn't honk, didn't budge. Maybe the driver didn't think it could fit.

As soon as the Toyota was gone, Jack heard the door open on the other side of the sedan. He looked up and saw the passenger emerge. A carbon copy of the driver. He stared at Jack across the black roof of the car.

"Where is Melanie Rubin Ehler?" the second one said in a hoarse, whispery voice.

"You're asking *me*?" Jack said. "Don't you know?"

The passenger held up a small cylinder in his black-gloved hand. His thumb pressed some sort of button, Jack heard a *snikt!* and an ice-pick-like needle suddenly jutted from the upper end. The green glow from the traffic light gleamed evilly along its narrow polished surface.

"Where is Melanie Rubin Ehler?" he repeated, and slammed the door.

As the passenger started to move toward the front of the car, Jack grabbed the little finger on the driver's hand; with no little difficulty he worked it free and pried it up until he got a firm grip on it. Then he bent it sharply back.

He heard the bone snap. But that was all he heard— no cry from the driver, and not the slightest lessening of the lock grip on his wrist. The driver was still looking up at him—no change of expression. Hadn't even flinched.

A quick cold thrust of shock stabbed Jack's gut. He *knew* he'd broken that bone—he'd felt it give way. Didn't this guy have any nerves?

Jack punched the driver's face as the passenger passed the right headlight. The sunglasses flew off as his hat slid down over his face; Jack punched the fedora, but the iron grip never slackened. A quick glance showed the passenger rounding the left headlight and coming Jack's way, his big needle held high.

Time to bring out the artillery, Jack thought as he flexed his right knee to bring his ankle holster with the Semmerling within reach. But before he touched it, someone began firing.

Jack looked around. The shots had come from the pickup. The driver door was open and a man was standing behind it, aiming a pistol in a two-handed grip through the window opening. Jack couldn't see his face, but that wasn't important right now. What mattered was he wasn't firing at Jack—he was aiming for the passenger.

With an almost snakelike hiss, the passenger ducked

into a crouch and jumped back into the car. The next bullet from the pickup went through the sedan's rear window.

"Whoa!" Jack shouted. "Easy back there!"

The driver still hadn't released Jack's arm, but that didn't stop him from throwing the car into gear and spinning the steering wheel.

"Hey!" Jack shouted, pounding on the roof as the car started to roll. "Hey, what the hell are you doing?"

"Where is Melanie Rubin Ehler?" said that same voice from inside the car.

"I don't know!" Jack said as he began to be pulled along by the car.

The sedan picked up speed, moving past the rear bumper of Jack's car, clearing it by a couple of inches— maybe. If Jack didn't free himself right now, his legs would be pinned between the cars. He tried to take another poke at the driver but, because of his position, couldn't reach him with his right fist.

To save his legs, Jack stepped on his own car's bumper, jumped up onto the trunk, and then the driver gunned the sedan, pulling Jack along.

Frantic now, Jack saw he had a choice between being dragged along the street or riding on the sedan's roof. Hell of a choice. He did a belly flop onto the roof as the car picked up speed.

Jack knew he wasn't going to last long up here. He stretched, reached down, pulled the Semmerling. The chamber was empty so he clamped his teeth on the slide, drew it back, then let it spring forward. Turning his head away, he fired a .45 caliber slug through the roof into the general area of the front seat below him. The angle of his wrist made for a wild recoil. The Semmerling was not an autoloader so he had to work the slide with his teeth for every shot. Only rarely did he load full-jacket slugs, and unfortunately this was not one of those times. But the frangibles must have done some damage down below because the sedan suddenly swerved and the grip on his wrist loosened a bit—just enough for Jack to twist free.

The car careened into a turn, its tires screeching as they slipped sideways on the pavement. It lost speed and Jack knew this might be his only chance. He pushed back, avoiding the shattered glass of the rear window as he slid off the roof onto the trunk, then slipped off onto the street. He hit the pavement running just before the car picked up speed again.

His forward momentum was still too fast for his sneakered feet. He went down, landed on his shoulder and rolled halfway back to his feet, then slammed against the side of a car, denting its rear fender. He felt a quick wave of nausea but shook it off.

At least he'd stopped moving. He stood and rubbed his sore shoulder as the black sedan continued down the street. Other cars passed. He saw curious faces looking his way, but no one stopped.

At least not until the red pickup pulled up. Jack recognized the fifty-something guy with the gray crewcut behind the wheel: Miles Kenway.

"You all right?" Kenway called through the open passenger window.

What the hell was he doing here? "I've been better."

"Get in. I'll take you back to your car."

Jack looked back. He'd barely traveled a block. "I can walk."

"Get in. We need to talk."

Jack hesitated, then figured, what the hell, the guy had probably saved his life—or at least his lips and eyes. Jack got in. The first things he noticed were Kenway's camouflage pants and jacket. Camo? In the city?

"Damn good thing I followed you tonight," Kenway said as he shoved the truck into gear.

"And why were you doing that?"

"Thought you might be working for them."

"Who? The men in black?"

"Don't call them that. That's what the UFO nuts call them. They're NWO operatives."

"NW—?"

"I'll explain later. Obviously you're not with them."

"Obviously."

"But then again, maybe that little scene was all a charade for my benefit, to suck me in, get me thinking of you as an ally."

"Could be," Jack said, nodding, and thinking, Hey, I can be paranoid too. "Or . . . your rescuing me from that little scene could have been a charade for *my* benefit, to suck *me* in, get me thinking of *you* as an ally."

Kenway glanced at him and gave him a slow smile. "Yeah, I guess you could look at it like that. But trust me, Shelby—you're riding with the New World Order's worst nightmare."

"Call me Jack."

"Okay, Jack," he said, pulling to a stop behind Jack's car. "Meet me back at the hotel. I need to debrief you. And don't try confronting these guys again without backup. They're *tough.*"

Tell me about it, Jack thought, rubbing his wrist. He jumped out of the pickup.

"Thanks."

Kenway gave him a thumbs-up and roared away.

Well, Jack had been looking for a way to get to Kenway. Maybe he could turn this "debriefing" into a two-way exchange.

As he turned toward his car, something crunched under his foot. Looked like sunglasses. The ones he'd knocked off the driver? He picked them up—no, not quite sunglasses, just the frames. Thick black frames. But where were the lenses?

He searched the pavement. The light wasn't great but he should have been able to spot black pieces among the glittery shards of shattered car window glass. He found nothing.

Odd . . .

24

Jack ditched the idea of dropping in on Gia. If he was being tailed, he didn't want the followers knowing anything about Gia and Vicky. Instead, he headed back to the hotel.

He found Kenway waiting for him in the lobby. He wasn't exactly standing at attention, but his spine was so straight, his bearing so erect, he might have been waiting for military inspection. His camo stood out among the more civilian types coming and going around him, but no one paid him much notice.

"All right," Jack said as he reached him. "What—?"

"My room," Kenway said, and marched off toward the elevators.

Amused, Jack followed the shorter man. For the first few paces he resisted the temptation to fall into lockstep directly behind him, then gave in. He even saluted a couple of passersby.

As they entered Kenway's room on the seventh floor, the older man stopped Jack just inside the door.

"Wait here."

All the lights were on. Jack gave the place a quick once-over. No shadows, no place for a big dog-monkey to hide. Good. He watched Kenway cross the room and take a little black box from atop the TV. He pressed a few buttons, then nodded with satisfaction.

"All right. Come in."

"What's that?" Jack said, pointing to the box.

"A little something of my own invention," he said proudly. "A motion detector-recorder. It records the time of any motion in the room. Right now it shows clear readings since the time I left until half a minute ago when we entered. That means no one's been in while I've been out."

"Pretty neat," Jack said, and meant it. He wouldn't mind having a few of those himself. "Anytime you decide to put them on the market, I'll be your first customer."

This seemed to please Kenway, which was one of the reasons Jack had said it. No harm in softening up the guy.

Kenway offered Jack a scotch from the minibar. Jack refused but that didn't deter Kenway from pouring himself a Dewar's, neat.

"Good thing you were traveling armed," Kenway said. "I saw you shoot through the roof. Good move. What are you carrying?"

Jack handed over the empty Semmerling and Kenway laughed.

"I've heard of these but never held one. Cute little baby." He reached under his camo top to the small of his back and came up with a 1911A1 Colt .45. "Here's it's daddy. Best damn handgun ever made."

Jack smiled. "I'll be glad to play 'mine is bigger than yours' some other time, but right now I'd like to know why you were following me."

Kenway pointed his .45 at Jack's chest. "I'll be asking the questions here."

"Ooh, scary," Jack said, broadening his grin. "We both know you're not going to fire that. Lose it now or I'm out of here."

Jack met and held Kenway's gaze. He didn't exactly *know* that Kenway wasn't going to shoot him, but he was pretty damn sure. A .45 makes one hell of a racket, especially indoors. Kenway had to know that the whole floor would hear it and someone would call the desk to see what was going on.

Finally Kenway sighed and stuffed his pistol back inside his shirt.

"You're a cool one," he said, handing back the Semmerling. "Whoever you are. And don't give me that Jack Shelby shit because I ran a background on you and you're not Jack Shelby."

Background . . . the very word sent snakes of dread crawling through his veins. He'd known from the start that a paranoid guy out of Army Intelligence would be trouble, but he hadn't counted on a full background check.

"Strange," Jack said, trying to keep cool, "that's what my First Annual SESOUP Conference badge says."

"Don't play cute."

"Well, if I'm not Shelby, who am I?"

"Damned if I know." He took a sip of his scotch. "Can't tell you your real name at this point, only that it isn't Jack Shelby. That's probably just something you pulled out of the air. But I'm willing to bet those NWO operatives know who you are."

New, bigger dread-snakes wriggling in Jack's veins.

"Maybe they came up empty too," Kenway said. "And maybe they were following you for the same reason as I was—to find out who the hell you are. What I found is you're some kind of creep—a lousy Peeping Tom."

"A Peeping Tom?"

"Don't play innocent with me. I saw you watching that woman out in Queens. Christ, fella, get a life!"

Jack ran a hand over his mouth to hide an incipient grin. *This guy follows me around and watches me watch the Castlemans—and he thinks I need a life.* He wondered if Kenway had seen the fight.

"You watched me all night?"

"Only for a few minutes," Kenway said, "Then I waited in my truck." He narrowed his eyes. "And I bet that story of your experience out in the Jersey pines is as bogus as your name."

"How do you know I didn't change my name because I don't want to be connected with that story? Maybe I have a job and a family and I just don't want everybody thinking I'm nuts. That ever occur to you?"

"Of course it did. Nobody knows better than me how people fear the truth. But some of us have the guts to stand up and be counted. If what you said is true, you probably stumbled on a New World Order outpost. They tend to set up in remote areas, especially in national parks. Did you see any black helicopters?"

"You asked me that the other night. I told you, it was dark—night, remember?"

"Oh, right. I do remember. But did you *hear* a helicopter?"

"Not that I recall." Jack wasn't interested in black helicopters. He wanted to turn the discussion toward Melanie Ehler. "Maybe you should ask Melanie. She seemed to know all about what happened to me."

"I wish I could. If there's an NWO outpost in the pinelands, I want to know about it."

"What about her Grand Unification Theory? You think—?"

"Frankly I don't give a damn about her theory. If it

doesn't center on the New World Order, then it's flat-out-wrong."

A little heat there, Jack thought. If he could get Kenway rolling, maybe he'd make a slip.

"What's this New World Order you keep mentioning? Wasn't George Bush talking about that after the Gulf War?"

Kenway nodded vigorously. "Damn right he was." He leaned forward, and Jack got the impression he'd been waiting for Jack to ask about the NWO. "Remember how he was the hero of the country then, of the whole damn so-called free world? His reelection looked to be a sure thing, didn't it. But he slipped up, got carried away and spilled the beans about the New World Order. That was a no-no. Not bad enough to be punishable by death, but they had to take him out of the lime-light. And that's why 'the guy who couldn't lose' was not reelected. When people talk about the 1992 Presidential race, they always mention Bush's lame, lackluster campaign. That's because he'd been told he was going to lose."

"So who's behind this New World Order?" Jack said. "Aliens?"

"Aliens?" Kenway said with the expression of someone who'd just stepped into a Portapotty at the National Chili Eating Contest. "I see Zaleski has been bending your ear. Look, Jim and his kind mean well enough, but the UFO types who aren't outright kooks are dupes. These flying saucers they're seeing aren't from outer space—they're from right here on Earth, experimental craft built by the One Worlders."

"What about Roswell and—?"

"Staged—all staged. That alien saucer crash baloney is all disinformation to distract people form the real truth. And I've got to hand it to them, they've done a masterful job—that intentionally clumsy fake cover-up at Roswell was a work of genius. But if you want the real skinny, you've got to go back to the nineteenth century." He finished his scotch. "You sure you don't want one?"

"Well, if we're going back to the eighteen hundreds . . . maybe a beer."

"Good," Kenway said, pulling a Heineken from the bar. "It all starts with a guy named Cecil Rhodes. You remember Rhodesia? He's the *Rhodes* in Rhodesia. A British financier and statesman. A true believer in the Empire. He formed a secret society called the Round Table whose members were dedicated to seeing the entire globe under one world government. And to their minds at the time, the ideal One World government was the British Empire. Rhodes's special interest was Africa. Wanted to add the whole continent to the Empire, became a small-scale tyrant in the process, but ultimately failed. His One World legacy lives on, however."

Kenway popped the top on Jack's beer and handed it to him.

"After World War One, the British Empire fell apart, so Rhodes's heirs had to try a different tactic. They formed two front organizations: the Council on Foreign Relations, then the Trilateral Commission. You've heard of those, I take it?"

"Heard of them," Jack said, sipping his beer. "But damned if I know what they do."

"Hardly anyone knows what they *really* do. But in a 1975 report the Trilateral Commission said that there could be, in certain situations—and I quote—'an excess of democracy.' Can you believe that?"

"Can you believe how little I'm surprised?" Jack said. "Or care?"

"You damn well should care. Between NATO and the

EC, they've got Europe pretty much in their pocket. And the UN—which they run—has the Third World sewn up. The only piece missing is the old US of A and they're making great headway here. Just consider: nearly every president and secretary of state is or was a member of the CFR and/or the Trilateral Commission. Bill Clinton's an even better example: he's with the Trilateral Commission, the CFR, and he's a *Rhodes* Scholar! He went to Oxford on Cecil Rhodes money! That's why he was tapped to replace George Bush."

"This is a little scary," Jack said, and meant it. Kenway's scenario wasn't quite as easy to dismiss as aliens and antichrists.

"A *little* scary? You don't know the half of it. Europe has pretty much surrendered, but the American people aren't playing ball. That means it's dirty tricks time, and the all-time masters of dirty tricks work for the CIA—which the NWO has controlled since its inception. It's public knowledge now that the CIA has been running mind-control experiments since the fifties. MK-ULTRA is the best-known. That one was exposed in Congress and the government has had to pay off the victims of those early LSD experiments."

"I read something about that a while ago," Jack said.

"*Big* embarrassment. They slipped up on that one. But there are so many other projects that've remained secret—remote viewing, HAARP, mind-control implants, brainwashing. The agents you dealt with tonight are the results of their mind-control and programming experiments."

"Yeah?" Jack said, rubbing his sore wrist. Something more going on with those two than mind control.

"Trust me: they were. The NWO has been dabbling in programmed suicide too—the Jonestown and Heaven's Gate mass suicides are their most successful tests—but they've generally failed in their quest to program the whole country. So lately they've been concentrating on the US military."

"You're ex-military, I'm told."

"With the emphasis on *ex*," Kenway said. "I got a look at some NATO papers that scared the shit out of me. That's why I retired. You see, the New World Order bosses have resigned themselves to the fact that force will be necessary to tame America. But first they have to soften us up. The plan is to weaken the American economy by shipping jobs out of the country with treaties like NAFTA, and hamstringing industry with whacked-out environmental restraints. Then they'll try to push us toward Kosovo-style anarchy with church bombings, and more Ruby Ridge- and Waco-type incidents. When all hell finally breaks loose, United Nations 'peacekeepers' will be called in to 'quiet' things down. But the forces won't have to be shipped in because they're already here. As I mentioned before, foreign UN troops are secretly camped out in our national parks and in wildernesses like the pine barrens, and when they charge out, our own soldiers will put on blue UN helmets and join them. Why? Because they've all been brainwashed by the CIA mind-control projects I told you about."

Kenway paused for breath and unlocked the briefcase on the desk. He pulled a map of the United States and handed it to Jack. Little hand-drawn stars were scattered across the country.

"These are confirmed UN troop locations and planned concentration camp sites. Black helicopters will darken the skies and people like me will be rounded up and placed in concentration camps where we'll be 're-educated.' But not without a fight, brother. I and others like me will fight to the death to keep America from becoming enslaved."

Jack handed back the map and said nothing. It would

be so easy to get sucked into Kenway's world—the reasoning and pseudologic were so convincing on the surface—but he wasn't buying.

"Well?" Kenway said. "Want to join me? I saw the way you handled yourself tonight. We can always use someone like you."

"I'll think about it," Jack said, hoping to avoid a sales pitch. "But I can't help wondering why these New World Order types should bother with an armed takeover. I mean, considering how nowadays people are slugging away at two and three jobs to make ends meet, how Mr. and Mrs. Average American are working until mid-May every year just to pay their federal income tax, and then on top of that they pay state and city income taxes, and then *after* those they've got to fork over sales taxes, property taxes, excise taxes, and surcharges, not to mention all the hidden expenses passed on in day-to-day prices jacked up by license fees and endless streams of regulations from OSHA and all the other two-bit government regulatory agencies. By the time Mr. and Mrs. Citizen are through they've surrendered seventy-five percent of their earnings to the bureaucracy. Seems to me like the NWO boys have already got you right where they want you."

"No, no, *no!*"Kenway said, his face reddening as he vigorously shook his head. "An armed takeover! That's how it will happen! That's how they'll take away our freedoms and make us slaves, make us *property!*"

A little touchy, aren't we? Jack thought as he finished his beer. Let's try one extra nudge.

"As I see it, that's pretty much what you already are. If and when this takeover comes, the only difference will be you'll no longer be able to kid yourself that you're *not* property."

Kenway stared at him, mouth slightly parted. Then

his eyes narrowed. "You keep saying 'you,' as if you're not involved."

Uh-oh. This was veering into areas Jack did not want to go. His own lifestyle was off limits.

"Just a way of putting it," he said, rising. "Time to go. Thanks for the help tonight, and the beer."

"No, wait," Kenway said. "There's so much more to discuss."

"Thanks, but I need my beauty sleep." He turned toward the door, then turned back. "By the way . . . you said you checked me out. Ever check out Roma?"

"Damn straight—six ways from Sunday, and Professor Salvatore Roma of Northern Kentucky University passed with flying colors. I don't particularly like the fellow, but he's the real deal."

"Yeah?" He kept thinking about Roma being spotted in Monroe with Melanie before she disappeared, and then lying about having never met her.

"Ever see a picture of him?"

Kenway laughed. "Why should I want to? I know what he looks like. I've been looking at his pretty puss for two days now."

"You know what the guy calling himself Professor Salvatore Roma who started SESOUP looks like. But does he look the same as the professor you checked out at Northern Kentucky U?"

Kenway's smile vanished like a coin in a magician's hand. "What are you saying?"

"Just wondering. Does SESOUP mail go to Roma's faculty office, his home, or a post office box?"

"A P.O. box."

Jack smiled and shook his head. "I think you'd better get that faculty photo."

Miles's eyes widened. "You mean they're different people?"

Jack held up his hands. "Didn't say that. It's just you never know till you check. Usurping someone's identity is surprisingly easy."

"Oh, really?" Kenway's eyes narrowed. "How do you know so much about it?"

"Gotta go," Jack said, heading for the door.

"All right, some other time then," Kenway said. "But just to be sure, I'm going to get a picture of the university Roma."

"You can do that?"

"I'll have it within twenty-four hours, tops."

"Love to see it when you get it."

Kenway started following Jack to the door, but stopped at the desk to scribble on a hotel pad. He tore off the sheet and handed it to Jack.

"Think about what I said. Here's my pager number. Any time you want to talk about joining us, call me. I like the way you think."

He unlatched the door and used the peephole before opening it. Then he stuck his head out and peered up and down the hall.

"And be careful," he said. "They're watching you."

Jack stepped out into the hall. He could feel Kenway's eyes on his back as he walked away.

And so are you, he thought. Lately it seems like everybody's watching me.

IN THE WEE HOURS

Roma . . .

"Feel it?" Roma said as he and Mauricio waited in the basement. "It is beginning again."

"To what end?" Mauricio said sourly. "To send the rest of the device to the stranger?

Roma sensed that Mauricio was troubled . . . much more so than usual.

"What is wrong?"

Mauricio looked away. "I must tell you something. Earlier tonight I tried to eliminate the stranger."

"What?" Roma cried, suddenly furious. He'd half-suspected the creature would do something foolish, but had hoped his better judgment would prevail. "Without checking with me?"

Mauricio still did not make eye contact. "I felt it the safest course."

"You said 'tried.' I assume that means you failed?"

"Yes. And that is what is most disturbing. I had him down. I was about to deliver the death blow, when suddenly I was pushed away from him."

"Pushed? By whom?"

"By myself—or rather by some strange sudden impulse within that would not allow me to kill him."

Roma's anger evaporated. He did not like the sound of this at all. "Did you sense the enemy protecting him?"

"No. That is the strangest part. It seemed to be the work of the Otherness. I am very confused."

So am I, Roma thought. Why would the Otherness protect the stranger? It made no sense. Perhaps Mauricio was mistaken.

"You shouldn't have acted without my approval in the first place," he said. "I will tolerate no more of that, understood?"

Mauricio said nothing.

"I had a long talk with the stranger earlier. He is blissfully ignorant of the Otherness and anything connected with it. We have nothing to fear from him. When the second half of the shipment arrives, we will relieve him of both packages."

"In light of my experience with him, that may not be so easy."

Roma pondered that. He would *not* allow these anomalous events to rattle him. He would remain in control.

"That is why we must learn who he is and, as I said before, who he *loves*. With the proper leverage, we can move him in any direction we wish." Roma closed his eyes and breathed deeply. "Ah. Feel it?"

Right now he could almost smell the charge in the air. Once again he congratulated himself on his cleverness at being able to concentrate all these sensitives in one spot. They were lightning rods, so to speak, attractors for the influence of the Otherness, and as they slept they would draw it in and funnel its power through the building, weakening the barrier between this plane and the Otherness just long enough to allow something to slip through from the other side.

The second delivery was on its way now . . . he could feel the barrier thinning, the tiny rent beginning. . . .

And once again, just like last night, that seepage from the other side would gift these sensitives with the worst nightmares of their lives.

James . . .

. . . awakens squinting in the white glare that pours through his room window, creating a brilliant rectangle on the carpet.

The light blazes intolerably, searing his retinas, so bright it seems solid.

Jim could swear he pulled the curtains before knocking off, but now they're wide open, as if pushed aside or burned away by this beam from above.

Where's it coming from? Sure as hell ain't the moon, and it's too white for sunlight.

He doesn't want to move, doesn't want to leave the security of his bed, but he's got to know the source. Like a reluctant moth wise beyond its genus, knowing its wings will be fried but slave to a hardwired compulsion, Jim is drawn inexorably toward the shaft of brilliance. Without allowing the light to touch him, he peers through the window at an angle but cannot find the source. Finally he takes the plunge and steps into the shaft—

—and *screams* as the light pierces him. It is a physical thing, lancing through skin, fat, bone and organ, spearing every cell of every tissue. He feels the birdshot sting of each photon as it shoots through him.

And once he is firmly and irretrievably spitted, the light lifts him like a speared fish and hauls him toward the window. He cringes in fear as he sees the glass rushing toward him. He raises his arms across his face and howls as he hits the glass . . . but his wail fades as he passes through it, leaving both window and flesh unscathed.

He's afraid—shit, he's one absofuckinglutely terrified little boy who wants to go home to Mama—but he's filled with awe and wonder as well. He's not trapped in the light, he's part of it, one with it. And as he looks up he sees its intolerably bright source, a circular doorway into the blazing heart of the Cosmic Egg at zero-point-one nanoseconds before the Big Bang.

He's not drifting toward it, he's careening upward at near light speed, far beyond escape velocity. He leaves behind the moldy apple of Earth, flashes past the moon, and hurtles through interplanetary space, past Mars, straight through the tumbling asteroid obstacle course, and on toward the red-eyed beach ball of Jupiter.

But Jim doesn't reach Jupiter. He's drawn into a huge saucer-shaped mothership hovering off Io. He flashes through the searingly bright portal. His universe dissolves into blinding liquid brilliance. . . .

When he can see again, he finds himself naked, strapped facedown upon a gleaming block of polished steel in an oblong room with mirror walls. The surface of the block is cold and hard against his bare flesh.

He is not alone in the room.

The grays are here, perhaps a dozen of them, but it's hard to tell with all the reflections off the walls. They're not quite like the drawings he's seen, but close enough. They're big-headed, small-bodied, and three to four feet tall; their hairless gray skin is wrinkled, as if they've been left in the water too long. They float through the air, whether by levitation or zero gravity, Jim can't say. Probably levitation, because those puny legs don't look strong enough to support an infant. And nothing between those legs to give any hint whether they're male or female. Long skinny fingers at the end of long skinny arms, big, lidless slanty black eyes over a rudimentary nose and a slit mouth.

The wonder is gone, leaving only the terror. Jim feels something warm and wet pooling around his pelvis as his bladder cuts loose.

His voice echoes off the shiny walls as he cries out—inanely—in dread. "Who are you? What do you want?"

He knows damn well who they are. And he's afraid he'll have the answer to the second question long before he wants it.

None of the aliens pauses or even looks his way. They float on, going about their business as if he were a fixture.

Suddenly something cold is thrust between his buttocks, and a whirling searing pain shoots into his rectum. As Jim screams, a gray floats into view and hovers near his head. Nothing in those black eyes as they stare down at him. The gray lifts something in its hand: a slender instrument with a thin, needle-like probe attached to its tip. The alien extends it toward Jim's face, taking dead aim at one of his nostrils.

Jim screams again, writhing and twisting frantically within his restraints.

No! Please! Not a mind-control probe! Anything but that!

But he's utterly helpless, a test animal in a vivisection clinic. He can't even turn his head. All he can do is watch in crosseyed horror as the probe enters his left nostril. But instead of a stab of pain in his nose, Jim feels a sharp blow to the side of his head—

"What the fuck?"

He was on the floor of his hotel room, mummied in his sheets, his left temple throbbing with pain.

Damn, that hurts.

He wriggled an arm free and rubbed the spot, then reached out and felt the corner of the night table, inches away.

Must have fallen out of bed.

He unwound himself from the sheets and crawled back up on the mattress.

Kee-rist, another wild-ass dream.

He glanced at the clock: 4:32. Same time as last night. What was going on here?

He lay back, sweaty and trembling. Awfully fucking real, that dream. How could he be sure it *was* a dream? He felt his nose—no tenderness there.

And yet . . .

James Zaleski lay in the dark, trembling, staring at the shadows on the ceiling, afraid to go back to sleep.

Miles . . .

. . . awakens with a start to the sound of gunfire.

A dream, or real? And where did it come from?

Another burst of automatic fire—from the hall.

Miles leaps out of bed, pulls open the night table drawer, and reaches inside for his .45.

Gone! Panic nibbles at his entrails as he runs frantic fingers over the entire interior of the drawer—except for the Gideon Bible, it's empty.

Leaving the lights off he feels his way to his suitcase where he always carries a spare. But that's gone too. Miles jumps at the sound of an accented voice behind him.

"Don't waste your time, Kenway."

The lights go on and he sees a man in full military battle gear, all in black except for his pale blue helmet. He looks Japanese or Chinese, or maybe even Vietnamese.

"Who the hell are you?"

Miles knows full well who he is—not his name, but who sent him. He recognizes the uniform, and cold dread seeps through his soul. It's finally happened—the New World Order has begun its takeover.

"Your new master," the trooper says. He's pointing an AK-47 at Miles's gut. "Out into the hall."

Miles looks down at his undershirt and boxer shorts. "At least let me get—"

Without warning, the automatic rifle bursts to life. Miles cringes as it stitches a row of holes across the wall of the room.

"Move!"

Miles moves. Barefooted, he raises his hands above his head and pads toward the door. His heart thuds against his chest wall like a mailed fist. Where are they taking him? To a mass execution area? Or to a detention camp? Better a quick death here than a slow death in a camp.

With that thought powering him, he lowers his hands and grabs the doorknob. He pretends it won't turn.

"Something's wrong," he says. "It's locked."

The NWO trooper shoves the stock of his rife against Miles's back and barks: "Open it!"

"It won't turn, I tell you."

The trooper shoves him again and reaches past him . . . and that leaves only one hand on the rifle.

Do I have the guts to do this? Miles wonders. His bladder feels ready to explode and he's got so much adrenaline flowing through him now he feels like he's floating. *Do* I?

Guts or not, this may be his only chance, so that leaves him no choice.

Miles twists and drives his right elbow into the trooper's throat as he grabs the AK-47. The trooper lets out a strangled cough and staggers back, clutching at his throat. Miles knees him in the balls as he gets a two-handed grip on the rifle and rips it free. Without hesitation he aims and fires a short burst. The rifle kicks and bucks and blows the bastard through the window onto the street below.

Miles stares at the ragged hole in the glass. Jesus, he did it! All that training paid off! He blew the son of a bitch away!

Suddenly the remaining glass is shattered by a barrage from below. Miles turns, ducks, and dives for the door. They'll be after him now. No time to get dressed. He runs out into the hall and automatically turns toward the elevators. He stops. No. Too easy to trap him there. He whirls and runs for the stairs.

As he reaches the door he hears a commotion behind him. He looks back and sees a squad of NWO troopers rush out of the elevator foyer.

"Damn!" he whispers and pushes through into the stairwell.

He starts down but hears the sound of running feet echoing from below. He's got only one option now, and since there's only one floor above him, that doesn't leave him far to go.

He bounds up four flights to a red door. The sign says:

**FOR EMERGENCY ONLY
ALARM WILL SOUND**

He pushes through and, just as promised, the alarm starts ringing. And now he's on the roof and he knows it's Alamo time. He won't get out of this alive, but he'll take as many of the bastards as he can with him before he dies.

The oblivious city is lit up around him. In how many other buildings is this same scene being played out?

He finds an air conditioning vent and crouches behind it, points the AK-47 at the door, and waits.

Suddenly a nylon rope whips around his upper body and tightens like a noose, pinning his arms at his sides. He drops the rifle as he is yanked off his feet and into the air.

He looks above and sees a giant black helicopter reeling him in like a cheap toy in an arcade game. Why can't he hear it? Why doesn't he feel the wash from its rotating blades?

Rough hands haul him into the black maw in the side of the craft. As the rope is loosened and pulled over his head, an accented voice, much like that of the trooper he killed, whispers in his ear.

"We've been looking for you. You're too valuable to kill, so we've got a special spot reserved in one of the re-education camps. You'll make a fine addition to one of our units."

No! He won't be brainwashed!

Miles kicks out and leaps from the helicopter. Death first!

But a hand grabs the back of his shirt, and a different voice, a very American voice, starts shouting. . . .

"Easy, now. Easy. You don't want to hurt yourself."

Miles looked down and saw the street eight stories below. With a cry of alarm, he turned and lurched away—

—into the arms of a large black man in some sort of uniform.

"Hey, now, that's better!"

It took Miles a second to recognize him as a hotel security guard.

"Where am I? He said, shakily pulling free of the guard's grasp.

"Up on the roof."

"How—how'd I get here?"

"Sleepwalking, I think. You sure didn't look completely awake when you passed me in the hall a few minutes ago. And since it's my job to be on the lookout for things like people wandering around dressed in their skivvies at four-thirty in the morning, I decided to follow you. Good thing I did or you'd be splattered on the sidewalk by now."

Miles shuddered. "But I never sleepwalk."

"Well, you did tonight. Come on," he said, gesturing toward the door to the stairs. "Let's get you back to your room."

Shakily, Miles led the way.

"We don't have to tell anyone about this do we?"

"I'll have to put it in my report," the guard said, "but it won't go beyond that."

"Good," Miles said, relieved. "Thank you. I have a reputation to uphold in this organization."

"I hear you. It's just a good thing I was upholding your ass a few moments ago or you wouldn't be worrying about your reputation or anything else."

The guard laughed good-naturedly. Miles saw nothing funny about it.

Jack . . .

. . . feels his bed move and opens his eyes.

His eyes search for the clock's red numerals and can't find them. The room is dark . . . too dark. Light from the street lamps below usually leaks around the edges of the drapes, but not now. A sound leaks through instead . . . a deep basso rumble shuddering through the floor and walls.

His bed trembles as the rumble grows, mixing with frightened cries and wails from outside.

Jack rises and pads across the vibrating floor to the window where he pulls back the drapes. The moon is high and full in a pristine sky, bathing the world outside with glacial light. The street is clogged with crawling cars and frantic people screaming, running, clawing over each other in a scene out of every giant monster film ever made. It's *The Beast from 20,000 Fathoms* times ten, but this is no movie; this is real. Even up here on the fifth floor he can smell the raw-edged panic as the mob struggles downhill, west, toward the river. He scans his limited view to the east to see what's driving them. All he can tell is that the rest of the city is dark.

Power failure, he thinks, and then blinks. An icy phantom breeze ripples his nape hairs as he cups his hands around his eyes and squints through the glass . . . it's *too* dark. Even with the power gone and the lights out, the moonlight should pick up *something*.

Jack slides the window back and pokes his head

through the opening for a better look. If nothing else, the metallic top of the Empire State Building should be visible. But the sky is empty there, stars twinkle where buildings stood.

And that rumble, growing ever louder, deafening now, jittering the entire building on its foundation.

And then, still staring east, Jack sees an office building tilt, then fall away, disappearing behind the structure before it. And now that building is collapsing, and then the one in front of it follows, a wave of destruction coming his way.

Jack is about to pull his head inside and run downstairs to join the crowd below when he sees it, moving inexorably along the street at the speed of a brisk walk, devouring everything in its path. Not a ravaging behemoth from another age, something much simpler and much, much worse.

A hole . . . so wide the moonlight can't find its far edge, so deep Jack can't hear the buildings hit bottom when they tumble into its ever-expanding maw. If the world were flat, a dirt pancake floating in space, and its edge began to crumble and fall away, this is what it would be like on that edge.

Part of Jack is saying this is a dream, it has to be, but another part is saying you *wish* it was a dream: this is too real to be a dream. Either way, he knows he can't escape, knows the hole will swallow the hotel well before he reaches the lobby. So he watches in fascinated dread as Hell's Kitchen crumbles and disappears into the approaching edge of infinity. Panic reigns supreme below as the marching rim undermines the pavement, sending cars and screaming bodies tumbling into the void, but Jack feels an unnatural calm. Gia and Vicky are already gone, swallowed with the rest of the East Side; soon he will be following them and there is nothing he can do about it, nothing he *cares* to do about it.

The rim is almost to the hotel now. Jack grabs a chair and uses it to smash the window. Then he climbs out onto the ledge and strains to see into the depths, but the bottom is lost in midnight shadow. He feels the building shudder and tilt to a crazy angle. As the hotel leans, poised on the rim, Jack leaps from the ledge. If he's going to fall, he'll fall his way.

He swan-dives into the abyss. . . .

And hears a loud CRASH! It's not the hotel . . . it's something else . . . something smaller . . . closer. . . .

Jack blinked in the darkness. Not complete darkness. The glowing red numerals on the clock read 4:33; light from the street filtered around the drapes. No cosmic rumble or sound of mass panic in the street outside.

He let out a deep breath. Another nightmare. But what was that noise? Sounded like it had come from—

"Aw, no."

Grabbing his pistol from under the pillow, he jumped out of bed and crept toward the bathroom. The only light at this end of the room was a narrow strip from the hallway leaking past the bottom edge of the door. The bathroom was dark . . . and the cold air flowing from it chilled his feet.

"Not again."

He reached in and turned on the light. Squinting in the glare, he saw the first crate under the sink where he'd left it. But now a new box of the same dark green material, smoking like dry ice, sat in the middle of the floor.

Jack checked the room door. This time he'd leaned the desk chair under the doorknob before hitting the sack. The chair was still in the wedged position.

Back to the bathroom: the second box had obviously arrived by the same route as the first. Which was . . . how?

He stepped back to the desk and retrieved a hotel pen from beside the phone, then used that to flip off this crate's lid.

No mini girders this time. The new crate was filled with curved metal plates and copper spheres, all collecting a rime of frost as moisture from the air condensed and froze on their surfaces. He checked out the underside of the lid and saw more construction plans—an exploded diagram of whatever it was, plus an illustration of the completed structure: Looked like an oil rig with a warty dome on top. As before, the directions appeared to have been seared into the material of the lid. He even thought he saw something that looked like lettering in one corner, but couldn't decipher it through the thickening layer of frost. He could check that out later. Right now . . .

Jack shivered—with cold as well as uneasiness. It was damn near freezing in here. He turned off the light and closed the bathroom door behind him.

He checked the clock again: 4:35 A.M. This second crate had arrived about the same time as the first. What was all this? Some weird equivalent of the "interociter" from *This Island Earth?* Was that it? Was he supposed to assemble the damn thing?

"Don't hold your breath, whoever you are," he muttered as he sat on the bed.

Jack had a bad feeling about that gizmo in there, a sense that putting it together might not be such a good idea. But even if he were gung-ho to do the Erector Set thing with it, he didn't have any tools with him.

He wondered if Lew had come back to the hotel. Wouldn't hurt to get his input. Maybe he'd seen something like this before.

An ungodly hour to get a call, but so what? Lew had got him into this. He rang Lew's room but no answer.

Still out in Shoreham, he guessed. It could wait till morning.

Jack got back under the covers but knew he wouldn't sleep. He tried not to think of those crates or the dream . . . a giant hole again, sucking him down. Why did it feel more like a premonition than a dream?

His thoughts drifted to Ceil Castleman and the lost, utterly crushed look in her eyes as he'd led her to the closet. And that called up another vision—Lewis Ehler, who seemed rudderless without his missing Melanie.

He lay still, thinking about lost souls as daylight grew beyond the pulled curtains.

Roma . . .

"Once again we come up empty-handed," Mauricio said from his place on the basement shelf.

Roma saw no need to acknowledge the obvious. He had a sinking feeling as to where the second delivery had come to rest.

"What I do not understand is *why*. Why is the Otherness directing the components elsewhere?"

"Maybe the stranger has found a way to influence the Otherness?"

Roma snorted in derision. "That man, controlling the Otherness? I hardly think so."

"But what other explanation is there?" Mauricio said, rising and pacing along the shelf. "You are The One. The device is for your use. Why would the Otherness direct it to anyone else? Unless . . ."

"Unless?"

"Never mind. It was a fleeting, ridiculous thought."

"Say it."

"Very well: Unless you are not The One."

The words staggered Roma. His terror-clenched jaw blocked speech. He locked his knees to keep from sagging. Not The One? Unthinkable! He had been preparing for ages! It could be no one else. There *was* no one else!

"You can see why I might think that," Mauricio said quickly. "After being prevented from killing the stranger, I had to wonder: Could he be The One? But of course that is impossible. I would not have been sent to you if you were not The One. The stranger has been marked by the Otherness, but he is not The One."

Mauricio was right. He had to be. The Otherness was not capricious. It was infinitely patient and glacially deliberate. It would not suddenly designate another over him without sufficient cause. And he had given it no cause.

Roma felt his muscles relax as the terror oozed away. Still, it left him feeling strangely weak.

"I believe the Otherness has plans for the stranger. In good time we will know. If it has delivered the device to him, it is no doubt for a good reason. We will not interfere."

"Your faith is admirable," Mauricio said. "But the Otherness is not infallible. It has made mistakes before, as you well know."

Roma nodded. "Mostly by underestimating the opposition." And he had often paid the price for those mistakes. "But these are different times. The opposition is all but non-existent these days."

"Let us hope you are right," Mauricio said.

Yes, Roma thought with a sharp pang of uneasiness. Let us fervently hope so.

SATURDAY

THE 1ST ANNUAL CONFERENCE OF THE SOCIETY FOR THE EXPOSURE OF SECRET ORGANIZATIONS AND UNACKNOWLEDGED PHENOMENA

SCHEDULE OF EVENTS
SATURDAY

Registration Desk Open:	8:00 A.M.–8:00 P.M.
Exhibits Open:	8.00 A.M.–8:00 P.M.

8:00–9:20 A.M.: **Experiencers' Panel**

9:30–10:20 A.M.: **Horns of Abuse:** A former FBI agent (now a Capuchin monk) tells how the Bureau is covering up evidence of a widespread Satanic cult underground

10:30–NOON: **MK-ULTRA Is Not Dead:** A survivor of CIA mind control experiments tells of the harrowing story of his dangerous corrective surgery, and demonstrates the control devices removed from his brain

NOON–1:30 P.M.: Lunch Break

1:30–2:50 P.M.: **El Niño:** A natural phenomenon? Or the result of UFO exhaust?

3:00–5:00 P.M.: **The 666 Chip**—how it is implanted during ritual abuse, how to locate it, how to deactivate it.

5:00–7:00 P.M.: **Cocktail Reception**—meet the panelists

9:00 P.M.–??? **Films:** *Communion, Red Dawn, Exorcist II: The Heretic*

I

Still a little shaky and unsettled from the night before, Jack balanced his cup of coffee atop the lobby pay phone and dialed Gia. Everything was fine there. No signs of anyone lurking about. That was a relief. Next he checked his voice mail. Only one call and—cheers—not from his father. Oscar Schaffer had left him a terse message.

"I've got the rest of your money. Just tell me where you want me to drop it."

Jack dialed the number and Schaffer picked up.

"Good morning. It's Jack."

"Oh. Where do you want me leave the money?"

And a gracious good morning to you too, Jack thought, wondering at Schaffer's tight, brusque tone. Go back to bed and get up on the other side.

"Drop it off at Julio's this morning. What's the story with—?"

"You going to be there?"

"Probably not."

"Good. 'Cause I don't even want to be in the same building as you, you sick, perverted bastard. I'll drop off your money, and then I don't want to see or hear or even think of you again!"

And then he hung up.

What's his problem? Jack wondered as he cradled the receiver. Schaffer should be one happy guy this morning. His sicko brother-in-law was in the hospital by now, and his sister was on vacation from her job as part-time punching bag.

Jack got a sour feeling in his stomach. Had Gus come to and managed to hurt Ceil worse than he had before? Jack couldn't see how—not with two broken legs. Had to be something else. He decided to hang out at Julio's this morning and find out firsthand what was bugging Oscar Schaffer.

He was almost to the lobby door when a familiar gangly figure limped through.

Lew. Jeez, he'd almost forgotten about him. Sometimes Jack became so immersed in a job that he lost sight of why he'd got involved in the first place. This missing Melanie thing wasn't the first gig that had taken on a life of its own, engulfing and carrying him along.

Lew looked terrible—pale, bags under his eyes, clothes wrinkled enough to look like he'd slept in them, except Jack had a feeling the guy wasn't sleeping much. Or showering much either: He needed a shave and his presence wasn't exactly a breath of fresh air.

"Lew. I thought you were out on the island."

Lew blinked heavy-lidded, red-rimmed eyes as he focused on Jack.

"I just got back. I stayed up all night out there, sitting in front of the TV, and then first thing this morning I was overcome with this feeling that I shouldn't be there. I should be . . ." His voice trailed off, followed by his gaze, settling somewhere over Jack's right shoulder.

"Should be where, Lew?"

He shrugged, still staring at some far corner of the ceiling. "I don't know. Somewhere *else*. So I came here." He focused on Jack again. "Any progress? Any news?"

Yeah, Jack thought. Something tried to kill me. But the call luring him to the basement yesterday had mentioned Olive instead of Melanie, so maybe there was no connection.

On the other hand, someone else *had* mentioned Melanie's name.

"Well," Jack said, "I discovered last night that I'm not the only one looking for Melanie."

Lew blinked and straightened. "Who? Who's looking for her?"

Jack told him about his run-in with the black-clad men in the black Lincoln.

"Men in black," Lew said, rubbing a hand over his rubbery features. "Everybody's heard of them, but . . . despite all the stories, I've never believed they were real. Maybe these were just guys dressed up and trying to scare you."

"Maybe. But I'll tell you this, if they were just hired meat, they were good actors; and if they were just actors, they were pretty damn tough meat. And they weren't trying to scare me off; they wanted to know where she was." He changed his tone to imitate the voice from last night. "'Where is Melanie Rubin Ehler?'"

Lew stiffened. "'Melanie *Rubin* Ehler?' They said that? They used her maiden name?"

"Every time. Something wrong with that?"

"I don't know about wrong, but it's certainly odd. Melanie never used her maiden name. She hardly ever used a middle initial."

"Well, whoever they were," Jack said, trying to boost Lew's spirits, "at least they think she's still alive—and findable."

He brightened. "Hey, that's right. That's right. Jack, I think you just made my day."

"Great, Lew. Why don't you go to your room and crash for awhile. You look dead on your feet."

"I think I'll do just that."

Jack watched Lew limp off, and couldn't help thinking of the other husband he'd dealt with in the past twenty-four hours. Could any two people be more different? Maybe someday Ceil would find herself a Lew to help her forget Gus.

As he was turning toward the door, Jack caught Roma staring at him from the other end of the lobby. Roma raised his hand, and for an instant Jack thought he was going to wave. But no—he made that three-fingered clawing gesture again.

Jack was tempted to make a gesture of his own, a more economical one employing only a single digit, but thought better of it. Instead, he held Roma's dark gaze until the monkey jumped up on his shoulder and added his own stare to his master's.

That was enough for Jack.

Later, Roma, he thought as he turned and pushed through the revolving door. We're not finished yet.

2

Roma watched the stranger leave, wondering where he was headed with such purpose at this early hour.

"Why did you do that?" Mauricio whispered when no one was looking.

"I wanted to rattle his cage, as they say."

"To what end?"

"To keep him off balance until we know the part he plays in this. Did you check his room?"

"As we assumed: the rest of the device is there."

Roma had expected this, would in fact have been shocked if Mauricio had reported otherwise, yet still it elicited a pang of dismay in his gut. Why, why, *why*?

"Undamaged?"

"Yes, but still, I am worried."

"No need to be," Roma said, forcing a casual tone. "As I told you, he knows nothing of the Otherness. And yet the Otherness seems to want him involved. Else why deliver the device to him—and protect him from you? No, my friend. We must watch carefully and see how this plays out . . . before another sunrise we will know what part this stranger is to play."

Mauricio growled his dissatisfaction, then said, "By the way, I ran into Frayne Canfield this morning. He's looking for you. Says he has something important to tell you."

"That despicable little hybrid always thinks he has something important to tell me. He will have to wait. I have better things to do than listen to his prattle."

Much more important, Roma thought, feeling his excitement grow. Less than twenty-four hours until his hour came round. He needed solitude. The growing anticipation made further human contact almost unbearable.

3

Jack was on his second coffee in Julio's when he spotted Schaffer through the front window. He was moving fast, no doubt as close to a run as his portly frame would allow. Jack had told Julio that Schaffer was coming and to do the usual interception, but tell him Jack wanted a word with him.

Schaffer entered clutching a white envelope. Perspiration gleamed on his pale forehead. His expression was strained. Here was one very upset real estate developer. He handed Julio the envelope; after they exchanged a few words, Schaffer glanced around like a rabbit who'd just been told there was a fox in the room, spotted Jack, and bolted out the door.

Jack got up and started after him. He passed Julio along the way.

Julio was grinning as he handed Jack the envelope. "What you do to spook him like that?"

Jack grabbed the envelope and kept moving. "Don't know, but I'm going to find out."

Out on the sidewalk, where spring was reasserting herself, he stopped and scanned the area. Quiet and sunny this morning, almost deserted. New York City is a different town on weekend mornings. Cabs never completely disappear, but only a few are on the prowl. No commuters, and the natives are sleeping in. Most of them, anyway. To his left, a guy stood with a pooper scooper in one hand and a leash in the other, waiting patiently while his dachshund relieved himself in the gutter. Far down to his right a young guy in a white apron was hosing last night off the sidewalk in front of a pizza shop.

But where the hell was Schaffer?

There—across the street off to his left, a bustling portly form hurrying away. Jack caught the developer as he was opening the door to his Jaguar.

"What's going on?" Jack said.

Schaffer jumped at the sound of Jack's voice. His already white face went two shades paler.

"Get away from me!"

He jumped into the car but Jack caught the door

before he could slam it. He pulled the keys from Schaffer's trembling fingers.

"I think we'd better talk. Unlock the doors."

Jack went around to the other side and slipped into the passenger seat. He tossed the keys back to Schaffer.

"All right. What's going on? The job's done. The guy's fixed. You didn't need an alibi because it was done by a prowler. What's your problem?"

Schaffer stared straight ahead through the windshield.

"How *could* you? I was so impressed with you the other day. The rogue with a code: 'Sometimes I make a mistake. If that happens, I like to be able to go back and fix it.' I really thought you were something else. I actually envied you. I never dreamed you could do what you did. Gus was a rotten son of a bitch, but you didn't have to . . ." His voice trailed off.

Jack was baffled.

"You were the one who wanted him killed. I only broke his legs."

Schaffer turned to him, the fear in his eyes giving way to fury.

"Who do you think you're kidding? You really think I wouldn't find out?" He pulled a couple of folded sheets of paper from this pocket and tossed them at Jack. "I've read the medical examiner's preliminary notes!"

"Medical examiner? He's dead?" Clammy shock wormed through him. Dead hadn't been in the plan. "How?"

"As if you don't know! Gus was a scumbag and yes I wanted him dead, but I didn't want him tortured! I didn't want him . . . *mutilated!*"

Confused, Jack scanned the notes. They described a man who'd been beaten, bludgeoned, bound by the hands, and had both tibias broken; then he'd been tortured and sexually mutilated with a Ginsu knife from his own kitchen before dying of shock due to blood loss from a severed carotid artery.

"It'll be in all the afternoon papers," Schaffer was saying. "You can add the clippings to your collection. I'm sure you've got a big one."

Jack squeezed his eyes shut for a few heartbeats, and reread the second half of the notes. His first reaction was relief of sorts—he hadn't killed Gus. Then he thought of Olive's mutilated body. A connection? No, this seemed different. Olive's mutilation had been almost ritualistic, Gus's sounded far more personal, a revenge thing, fueled by boundless rage and betrayal.

Jack tossed the report onto Schaffer's lap and leaned back. He lowered the window. He felt the need for some air.

Finally he looked at Schaffer. "How'd you get those notes? Are they the real thing?"

"Who do you think you're dealing with? Half the new construction in Queens is mine! I got connections!"

"And where was Ceil supposed to be when all this"—Jack waved the notes—"was happening?"

"Where you left her—locked in the hall closet. She got out after she heard you leave. And to think she had to find Gus like that. Poor Ceil . . . no one should have to see something like that. Especially her. She's been through enough." He slammed his fist against the Jag's mahogany steering wheel. "If I could make you pay—"

"When did she phone the cops?"

"Don't worry about the cops. I paid you and that puts me in this as deep as you, so I won't be saying anything."

Jack was getting a little tired of Oscar Schaffer. "Answer me, dammit. When did she call the cops?"

"Right before calling me—around three A.M."

Jack shook his head. "Wow. Three hours . . . she spent more than three hours on him."

"She? She who?"

"Your sister."

"Ceil? What the hell are you talking about?"

"When I left their house last night, Gus was on the living room floor, trussed up with two broken legs—out cold, but very much alive."

"Bullshit!"

Jack gave him a cold stare. "Why should I lie? As you said, you're not going to dime me. And someday when you have time you should try to imagine how little I care what you think of me. So think hard about it, Oscar: why should I lie?"

Schaffer opened his mouth, then closed it again.

"I left Gus alive," Jack said. "When I was through with him, I opened the door to the closet where I'd put your sister, and took off. That was a little while before midnight."

"No," he said, but there was no force behind it. "You've got to be lying. You're saying Ceil—" He swallowed. "She wouldn't . . . she couldn't. Besides, she called me at three, from a neighbor's house, she'd only gotten free—"

"Three hours. Three hours between the time I opened the closet door and the time she called you."

"No! Not Ceil! She . . ."

He stared at Jack, and Jack met his gaze evenly.

"She had Gus all to herself after I left."

Slowly, like a dark stain seeping through heavy fabric, the truth took hold in Schaffer's eyes.

"Oh . . . my . . . God!"

He leaned his forehead against the steering wheel and closed his eyes. He looked like he was going to be sick. Jack gave him a few minutes.

"The other day you said she needed help. Now she really needs it."

"Poor Ceil!"

"Yeah. I don't pretend to understand it, but I guess she. was willing to put up with anything from a man who said he loved her. But when she found out he didn't—and believe me, he let her know in no uncertain terms before he pulled the trigger on her."

"Trigger? What—?"

"A long story. Ceil can tell you about it. But I guess when she found out how much he hated her, how he'd wanted her dead all these years, when she saw him ready to murder her, something must have snapped inside. When she came out of the closet and found him helpless on the living room floor . . . I guess she just went a little crazy."

"A *little* crazy? You call what she did to Gus a *little* crazy?"

Jack shrugged and opened the car door.

"Your sister crammed ten years of payback into three hours. She's going to need a lot of help to recover from those ten years. *And* those three hours."

Schaffer pounded his steering wheel again. "Shit! Shit! Shit! It wasn't supposed to turn out like this!"

Jack got out and slammed the door. Schaffer leaned over the passenger and looked up at him though the open window.

"I guess things don't always go according to plan in your business."

"Hardly ever," Jack said.

"I gotta get back to Ceil."

Jack listened to the Jag's engine roar to life. As it screeched away, he headed for Abe's.

4

"Occam's what?"

"Occam's Razor," Abe said.

Jack had picked up half a dozen raisin bran muffins along the way. He'd also brought a tub of Smart Balance margarine in a separate bag. Abe had spread the sports section of the morning's *Times* on the counter and the two of them were cutting up their muffins. Parabellum hopped about, policing the crumbs.

"Kind of flaky, these muffins," Abe said. "They fresh?"

"Baked this morning." Jack didn't want to tell him they were low fat.

"Anyway, Occam's Razor is named after William of Occam, one of the world's great skeptics. And he was a skeptic back in the fourteenth century when it could be very unhealthy to be a skeptic. Such a skeptic he was, one of the popes wanted his head. Occam's Razor is something your friends in that chowder club—"

"SESOUP," Jack said.

"Whatever—it's something everyone of them should memorize by heart, and then *take* to heart."

"How do you memorize a razor?" Jack said.

Abe stopped sawing at the muffin and stared at him. He raised the knife in his hand.

"Occam's Razor is not a cutting instrument. It's an aphorism. And it says, 'Entities ought not to be multiplied without necessity.'"

"Oh, well, I'm sure that will make everything clear to them. Just tell them, 'Necessity cannot be multiplied unless you're an entity,' or whatever you said, and all talk about antichrists and aliens and New World Orders and Otherness will be a thing of the past."

"Why do I bother?" Abe sighed, glancing heavenward. "Listen carefully to the alternate translation. 'It is vain to do with more what can be done with fewer.'"

"Fewer what?"

"Assumptions. If you've got two or more possible solutions or explanations for a problem, the simplest, most direct one, the one that requires the fewest assumptions, tends to be correct one."

"The shortest distance between two points, in other words."

"Something like that. Let me illustrate: You and I are walking down a country road in Connecticut, and all of a sudden we hear lots of hoofbeats around the bend. When we reach the bend, however, whatever was making those hoofbeats is now out of sight, so we must make assumptions on what they could have been. What's the most logical assumption?"

Jack shrugged. "A horse, of course. What else?"

"What else, indeed. But I bet that some of your friends in Paella—"

"SESOUP."

"Whatever—would probably imagine a herd of zebras of wildebeests, am I right?"

"Or UN invaders on horseback . . . or hoofed aliens . . . or the legions of hell. . . ."

"That far out we won't go," Abe said. He'd finished slicing his muffin in half and was reaching for the bag with the margarine. "Wildebeests will serve fine. But you see my point? We're in the country in Connecticut where a lot of people keep horses. I should expect wildebeests? No. Horses require very few assumptions.

Wildebeests, however, require assumptions like some-one has been importing the creatures and keeping their existence secret—I don't know about you, but I haven't seen any stories in the paper about a black market in wildebeests. So Occam's Razor demands we assume, until proven otherwise, that the noise was made by horses and—"

Abe had pulled the Smart Balance from the bag and was staring at it like a wino contemplating a bottle of O'Doul's.

"What on earth is this?

"It's a kind of margarine."

"Margarine? So? What happened to my Philly? Or my nicely salted Land o' Lakes?"

"This is supposed to be good for your heart."

Outwardly Jack remained casual, but inwardly he cringed, waiting for the explosion. This was sacred ground. Not counting a few friends like Jack, Abe didn't have a hell of a lot in his life beyond his business and his food.

Yeah, he had every right to eat himself into an early grave, but Jack had just as much a right to refuse to shorten that trip.

"My heart? Who should be worried about my heart?"

"You," Jack said.

"And I suppose this is a low-fat muffin?"

"*No* fat, actually."

Abe looked at him, his face reddening. "Since when do you worry about my heart for me?" Before Jack could answer, he added, "Maybe *I* should worry about *my* heart, and *you* should worry about *yours*."

"That would be fine if you seemed to give a damn, but—"

"So now my doctor you've become?"

"No," Jack said levelly. He was acutely uncomfort-able with this role, but wasn't going to back down. "Just your friend. One who wants you around for a long time."

Abe stared down at the Smart Balance, and Jack waited for him to toss it across the store. But Abe surprised him. He flipped the lid, peeled back the seal, and dug his knife into the yellow contents.

"Well," he said with a sigh. "Since there's nothing else . . ."

Jack felt his throat tighten as he watched Abe spread a glob on the muffin. He reached across the counter and clapped Abe on the shoulder.

"Thanks, Abe."

"You should be thanking me? For what? For poisoning myself maybe? Probably full of artificial ingredients. Long dead and in the grave I'll be from chemical preservatives and toxic dyes before my cholesterol even knows I'm gone."

He bit into his muffin, chewed thoughtfully for a moment, then swallowed. He picked up the container and stared at it.

"This I hate to say, but . . . not bad."

"Keep this up," Jack said, "and maybe someday you'll die of nothing too."

They finished their muffins in silence.

"Nu?" Abe said finally. "You next look where for this missing lady?"

"That's the million-dollar question. I get dizzy and disoriented whenever I talk to these people. They've got an elaborate answer for everything except where Melanie Ehler might be." He shook his head. "Isn't life complicated enough without seeing a conspiracy behind everything? I mean, why is everybody so into conspiracies lately?"

"Lately?" Abe said. "What's lately about it? Conspiracy theories have been with us since humans could organize thought. What were the first religions but conspiracy theories."

"You mean like Olive's Satan and the Antichrist conspiring to take over America?"

"No. Long, long before the Bible was dreamt up. Cavemen I'm talking. Hut dwellers. Gods were created to make sense of the seeming randomness of nature and everyday life. Why did the lightning spare the tall tree but strike my hut and kill my wife and children? Why did it not rain during the growing season, and then pour after the meager harvest? Why was my child stillborn? Powerful supernatural beings explain it all very nicely, so early humans created a pantheon of cosmic kibitzers—a god of thunder, a god of trees, a god of wine, one for each aspect of the world that affected them—and imagined them conspiring against humanity. You think these Finnan Haddie people—"

"SESOUP."

"Whatever—you think their conspiracies are elaborate? Feh! Look at the old mythologies—Babylonian, Greek, Roman, Norse—so rife with divine plots, either against each other or against humans, your head will spin."

Jack nodded, remembering tales from *Bullfinch's* in high school. "The Trojan War, for instance."

"Right. Gods conspiring with gods, gods conspiring with humans, such a mess. But no matter how many entities we humans created, the purpose was the same: When something went wrong, we had an explanation. Bad things happened because a certain good deity was angry or displeased, or an evil deity was at work. We might be at the mercy of these entities, but at least we've ordered the randomness, we've appended a name to the darkness, we've created symmetry from chaos."

"Sort of like the old fairy tale thing that if you know someone's name you can control them."

"Control is the key. Once we identified the deity, we tried to control it—sacrifices, chants, dances, rituals anything you could dream up was tried. And sometimes certain actions did appear to work. If slaughtering a lamb at the vernal equinox seemed to convince the deity to bring rain for the growing season—or stop the recurrent floods that were plaguing the area—suddenly a lamb was not such a healthy thing to be."

"But dead lambs have no effect on El Niño."

"They can seem to if the timing is right. And I'm sure knowledge of El Niño would have done wonders for the lamb population. Still, we now have to wonder what causes El Niño."

"UFO exhaust," Jack said. "I have it on good authority."

"Then someone should inspect those things. Fit them with catalytic converters, at the very least."

"Could also be CIA solar mirrors."

"The CIA," Abe said, shaking his head. "I should have known. But the point is, the effect of thousands of years of accumulated knowledge is a general pushing back of the darkness. As we discover more and more non-supernatural explanations for the formerly inexplicable, the gods and demons recede. The magic goes away. *But*—a certain amount of randomness remains."

"Shit still happens."

"How eloquent you are today."

Jack shrugged. "It's a gift."

"I envy you. But as you say, shit does indeed still happen. So, people who don't use Occam's Razor tend to go two ways. Some drop into denial and reject all our centuries of rational and scientific evidence; they seek shelter in orthodoxy and cling to potty beliefs like creationism."

"Some of them must belong to SESOUP. I saw a flyer about a book exposing 'the Evolution Hoax.'"

"With Darwin as the chief conspirator, I'm sure. But if you're Occam-impaired and choose to keep your head out of the sand, you must come up with new brief systems to explain what's wrong with your world and who's pulling the strings attached to your life. For half a century international communism was such a wonderful bad guy, but when the USSR went kaput it left a huge vacuum that had to be filled—because we all *know* there's something in those shadows. King and the Kennedy brothers weren't killed by lone meshuggeners, the changes in family life and society aren't part of long processes—they're all part of a plan. The result is that fringe groups, with the help of a jaded, sensation-hungry public and accommodating mass media, get mainstreamed. We find comfort in the wackiness."

"I don't know," Jack said. "Aliens, antichrists, New World Orders . . . that's comforting?"

"For lots of people, most certainly yes. There's a certain comfort in being able to point a finger and say '*That's* why,' in being able to *explain* events, no matter how scary the explanation. If the cause is a conspiracy, then it can be identified, it can be broken up, and the world will be on track again."

"Which brings us back to control. You know," Jack said, remembering his conversations with various SESOUPers, "the fear of mind control seems to play a big part in all their theories."

"And shadow governments. A shadow government you need, subverting the will of the electorate in order to implement mind control."

"Yeah. Olive worried about the 666 chip, Zaleski talked about mind-control devices implanted by aliens, and Kenway went on about the CIA's mind control programs."

"That you should lose control over your thoughts and actions is a terrible fear. You would think about things that frighten you, you could injure or hurt people you love."

"Start talking about mind control and I start thinking about Dirty Eddie," Jack said, referring to a homeless guy of indeterminate age and race who used to wander Columbus Avenue.

Abe smiled. "Eddie . . . where is he these days? Haven't seen him for a year at least."

"Me neither, but you remember the aluminum foil cap he used to wear? Told me it was to keep out the voices that kept telling him to do things."

"I'm sure any conspiracy theory has its paranoid schiz mavens; that sort of stuff is tailor-made for them. But for the rest who haven't completely broken with reality, the cult aspect is probably as important as the conspiracies themselves. Fellow True Believers form a sort of intellectual commune. Not only do you share The Truth with them, but appreciation of that common knowledge sets you apart from the workaday schlmiels who remain in the dark. You form an elite corps. Soon you're associating only with other True Believers, people who won't challenge The Truth, which in turn reinforces The Truth over and over. I'm sure no small number of people are involved for fun and profit, but the core believers are searching for something."

"Control."

"Yes . . . and something else, maybe. Something they're not finding in modern society. Family, I think. Fellow believers become a family of sorts. And in this rootless, traditionless, culturally challenged society America has become, family is hard to find."

Family . . . Jack thought about how violent death had hurled him on a tangential arc from his own family, how his father and sister and brother were scattered now up and down the East Coast. And he thought of how Gia and Vicky and Abe and Julio had become a new family of sorts. Anchors that kept him from drifting into a dark no-man's land.

"Yeah," he said. "I guess everybody needs a family of some sort."

"And this *fish yoich* group—"

"SESOUP."

"Whatever—is a sort of extended family. And like any family, they have squabbles."

"*Deadly* squabbles?" Jack said. "Neck-twisting, eye-gouging, lip-removing squabbles?"

Abe shrugged. "Hey. When the police find a dead body, who's the first suspect? Someone in the family. And here you're dealing with one meshugge family."

"Yeah, maybe," Jack said. "But I've got to tell you, Abe, after what's been happening, I'm starting to wonder."

"Oy, you're not serious? I'm starting to think maybe you've been hanging around these people too long."

"*Something*'s going on, something a lot bigger than a bunch of conspiracy nuts sitting around and trading theories. I sense it, Abe. Someone's moving around behind the scenery. I don't know if it's one of these fabled secret organizations or a government agency—"

"If it's a government agency, then you should include yourself out of this mess immediately, if not sooner. You and government weren't meant to mix. Let someone else find the missing lady."

"But I can't," Jack said, wishing he could get out, but haunted by what Melanie Ehler had told Lew.

"Why the hell not?"

"Didn't I tell you? Because only I can find her. Only I will understand."

5

Jack closed his apartment door behind him and froze. He scanned the front room as he snatched the Semmerling from his ankle holster.

Something wrong here.

He listened. No sound except the hum from the computer's CPU fan and the ticks and tocks from the various pendulum clocks—a Shmoo, Felix the Cat, Sleepy the Dwarf—on the walls. No unusual odor.

He didn't sense anyone in the apartment, yet something was not right. With his pistol against his thigh, he did a quick search of all the rooms—he knew every possible hiding place, and each was empty. All the windows were double-locked with no sign of forced entry. Times like this he wished he'd put bars on the windows; trouble was, bars worked both ways, and there might come a time when he wanted to go *out* one of those windows.

Jack and his fellow tenants had a mutual watchdog society and were extremely careful who they buzzed in. A four-way bar-bolt secured his door. No one was going to break it down, but as he well knew from experience, no lock was bypass-proof. No system was perfect.

Long ago he'd considered and rejected an alarm system; that would bring the police, and the last thing he wanted was a couple of cops—city or private—snooping through his place looking for an intruder.

He thought of Kenway's motion recorder and wished

he had one. That would have settled the question once and for all.

Jack turned in a slow circle. He was the only one here now. And from all appearances, he was the only one who had *been* here since he'd locked up and left yesterday.

But he didn't put the Semmerling away. His hackles were up and his nervous system was on full alert.

Why?

He couldn't put his finger on it, but the apartment and its contents seemed subtly out of kilter, just the tiniest bit askew.

He checked his computer, the filing cabinet, riffled through the papers on his desk, did a count in the weapons cache behind the secretary. Nothing appeared to be missing, everything seemed to be just where he'd left it. He checked his shelves, still crammed with all his neat stuff. Nothing had been disturbed—

Wait. At the base of the Little Orphan Annie Ovaltine shake-up mug . . . a crescent of clean wood reflecting the sunlight from the window. The rest of the shelf's lacquered surface—what little wasn't obscured by the crowded mementos—sported a down of dust. Jack had never been one to expend much energy in the house-keeping department, tending to wait until the situation reached crisis proportions, and now he was glad of it. Because that bright sliver of polished wood meant the mug had been moved.

If Jack were searching this room, he knew he'd want to know if anything was hiding in that old red domed mug. And since it sat at eye level, the only way to check would be to take it down, lift the cap, and look inside, then replace it.

No question—the mug had been moved. But by whom?

Me?

Had he adjusted the mug or looked at it when he'd bought the Daddy Warbucks lamp? After all, Daddy and Annie were connected. He couldn't remember.

Damn. If he'd known it was going to matter, he would have paid more attention at the time.

Or was all this simply his imagination? Maybe all the hours he'd been spending with the SESOUP crowd were having an effect.

Is this what it's like? he wondered. Is this how Zaleski and Kenway live, suspicious of every little inconsistency, always looking over their shoulders and under the bed?

Had somebody been here or not, dammit?

He was surprised at how rattled he was by the mere hint that the seal on his sanctum had been broken. And rage accompanied the rattle. He had to get back to the hotel, but he didn't want to leave. He wanted to hunker down in the easy chair with a scattergun across his knees and wait. Anybody came in—men in black, men in blue, men in chartreuse or paisley, Jack didn't care— they'd get bellies full of magnum double-O buck, fifteen pellets per round, one after the other.

But he had to find a missing lady . . . and talk to a weird guy with a monkey.

He holstered his pistol and stepped into the bathroom. Positioning himself before the mirror, he pulled up his shirt, exposing his chest. He stared at the three ragged lines, angry red now instead of pale, running diagonally across his chest.

How could Roma possibly know about these scars?

And what was it he'd said? Something about being "marked by the Otherness."

They're not *marks,* Jack thought. They're ordinary scars. No big deal. I've got lots of scars. These are just part of the collection.

You are much more a part of this than you realize.

No. I'm not part of anything, especially this Otherness junk. And you're not sucking me in. I'm not like you people.

But were these scars why Melanie had said that only Repairman Jack could find her . . . that only he would understand?

And he remembered something else Roma had said yesterday, just minutes before that creature had attacked him.

You would do well to take care, Mr. Shelby. You might even consider returning to your home and locking your doors for the rest of the weekend.

Had Roma known he was going to be attacked?

Too many questions . . . and he could think of only one man who might be able to answer them.

Roma.

Jack tucked in his shirt and—reluctantly—left his apartment. But in the hall, after locking the door, he pulled a hair from his scalp, wet it with saliva, and stretched it across the space between the door and the jamb. After the saliva dried, it would be invisible. A crude little telltale, but very effective.

He headed back to the hotel, glancing over his shoulder all the way.

6

Jack sat on one of the benches in the common area on the second floor as various SESOUPers wandered in and out of the huckster room and the MK-ULTRA panel. He watched them smile and greet each other, laugh at an in-joke, throw a friendly arm over another's shoulder, and he thought about what Abe had said. They truly were like a family, not genetically related, maybe, but they did share a heritage of sorts. He'd bet the majority of them spent a lot of time alone, their contact for most of the year limited to newsletters and the Internet, and maybe an occasional phone call. This conference was a family gathering of sorts . . . a gathering of loners, mostly.

Loners . . . Jack knew the Loner family . . . he was a charter member.

But one member of this particular branch was dead. Maybe two, if Melanie already shared the same fate as Olive.

"Working hard?"

Jack looked up and saw Lew Ehler standing over him.

Lew looked worse than he had this morning. Wasn't he sleeping at *all*?

"Sit down, Lew" Jack said, patting the spot next to him on the bench. "Want to ask you a couple of questions."

Lew wearily slumped his gangly frame onto the bench. "Have you learned anything since this morning?"

"Nothing useful."

"Sitting here daydreaming isn't going to improve that situation."

Jack gave him a raised-eyebrow look.

"Sorry," Lew said, looking away. "I'm a wreck, just a wreck. With each passing hour I become more and more convinced I'll never see her again." He bit his lip. "I'm going out of my mind."

"You were feeling better when I left you this morning."

"For a while, yes. The men in black . . . I figured that's why she's missing, and why she doesn't contact me—she's hiding from them." He slumped further. "But then I started asking myself, How can I be sure? And if she *is* hiding, *where* is she hiding? I can't bear to think of her huddled somewhere alone and afraid."

Jack sensed Lew was going to puddle up again. "It may not be that bad. She may be holed up in a motel—"

"How? Using what for money? I checked our bank account and she hasn't made any ATM withdrawals. I called our credit card companies and there've been no charges on her cards. It's like she dropped off the face of the earth."

"Maybe she's with a friend," Jack offered.

"Olive, maybe?" he said, brightening just a little. "She's still missing, you know."

"I'd assumed as much," Jack said carefully.

"She still hasn't contacted anyone—just like Mel. Do you think Olive could be with Mel, maybe helping her?"

Jack debated telling him about Olive. Did Lew have a right to know? Maybe. Would it make his life any easier at the moment? After seeing the flicker of hope the mention of Olive had lit in his eyes, Jack was certain the truth would sink him.

Some other time, Jack decided.

"I don't know what to tell you about Olive," Jack said.

Not an answer, he admitted, but at least it's true.

"I keep thinking about that rope ladder in Mel's folks' basement," Lew said. "It's so bizarre . . . I can't seem to get it out of my head. Don't ask me why, but I just know it has something to do with Mel's disappearance."

"All right," Jack said, grasping at anything to steer the subject away from Olive. "Maybe we'll go take another look at it."

"Now?" Lew said eagerly.

"Well, no. Not right now. I want to have a talk with Professor Roma first."

"How can he help?"

"You said he was in contact with Melanie a lot before she disappeared. Do you know if they ever met?"

"No. I'm sure they didn't. Why?"

He told Lew about his trip to Monroe yesterday, and what the librarian had said about seeing Melanie last week with a man who had a monkey on his shoulder.

Lew looked stunned. "Professor Roma?"

"Do you know anyone else with a pet monkey?"

Lew shook his head. "I don't understand."

"Neither do I. That's why I'm looking for him."

Jack looked away. He didn't mention that his interest in Roma was of a more personal nature. Sure, Roma might know something about Melanie, but that wasn't the only reason now. Jack wanted to find out how much he knew about Jack, and how he knew it.

"Don't forget Frayne Canfield while you're at it," Lew said. "He and Mel were close. They shared a bond that excluded me."

Jack looked at him now. Was that a hint of jealousy in Lew's voice?

"But I guess it's to be expected," Lew went on. "They grew up near each other in a small town, both disabled. . . ." He shook his head. "For a while there I suspected they might be having an affair, but . . . I realized I was wrong. Mel wouldn't do that to me."

"By the way, what's wrong with his legs?"

"I don't know. I've never seen them . . . but Mel has."

"How do you know?"

"Because I asked her just what you asked me. 'What's wrong with Frayne's legs?' She told me, 'You don't want to know.'"

7

Jack spent the rest of the morning and some of the early afternoon looking for Roma, but man and monkey seemed to have vanished. No one at the hotel knew his whereabouts. He tried to listen to some of the El Niño panel but found it so lame he fled after a couple of minutes. It irked him that he could have been using the time to coach Vicky on her baseball basics.

Finally he went outside in search of a phone. A sunny spring Saturday greeted him. And what did New Yorkers do when the sky was bright and the air balmy? Without lawns to mow or gardens to weed, they were free to hit the streets. And today they were hitting with a vengeance—strolling, jogging, shopping, snacking, parents pushing baby carriages, couples in shorts and sun dresses walking arm in arm or hand in hand, kids chasing each other along the sidewalks.

An abundance of navels on display, many of them pierced.

And all these pretty girls with really ugly guys . . . almost as if they were dating outside their species. Then Jack wondered if people thought the same when they saw Gia with him. Probably.

The people-watching served only to make Jack long all the more to be with Gia and Vicky. But he knew that even if he'd already found Roma and finished questioning him, he'd probably be keeping to himself today.

He couldn't shake the feeling that Gia and Vicky might be safer if he stayed away.

He found a pay phone at the corner of Ninth and Fiftieth. A huge painting of the Toxic Avenger grinned at him from the side of the building half a block down the street where Troma Films had its offices. He called Gia, cupping his hand over the buttons as he tapped in her number.

Dammit, he thought. Why don't I just become a card-carrying member of SESOUP? I'm becoming just like them.

Except I'm *really* being watched.

Which was no doubt how Kenway and Zaleski saw themselves too.

What next? Start getting myself X-rayed for mind-control implants?

Jack could not remember ever feeling this spooked.

"Hey, it's me," he said when Gia answered.

"You're late," she said. "Vicky's been waiting for you."

He hated the thought of disappointing Vicky. "I'm afraid I'm going to have to cancel out of baseball practice, Gia."

He heard her sigh. "You shouldn't have promised if you weren't sure you could make it."

"I was sure I could get away for a couple of hours, but . . ."

"Tomorrow, then?"

"I don't think so. I—"

In the background he heard a little voice saying, *"Is that Jack? Is that Jack?"* And then Gia saying, "Yes, hon, and he has something to tell you."

"Hi, Jack!" Vicky said, and rattled on with her usual ebullience. "How come you're not here yet? I've had my glove on since one o'clock and it's getting all sweaty inside while I've been waiting. When are you coming?"

The image she conjured tore at his heart.

"Uh, I'm, sorry, Vicks, but I have a job that's going to keep me away for a while. I'm really sorry, but—"

"You're not coming?" she said at about half her previous volume.

"I promise I'll make it up to you," he said quickly. "We'll have a nice long practice as soon as I can get away."

"But tryouts are next week."

Please, Vicks, he thought. Please understand.

"Vicks, I'll be there for you. I won't let you down. I promise."

"Okay." She was at quarter volume now. "Bye."

Jack leaned against the phone booth's shielding and stared at the pavement. An ant was crawling along the curb. He felt low enough to challenge it to a foot race.

"Really, Jack," Gia said, her voice taking on a vague scolding tone, "is what you're doing right now so all important that you can't come by and see her?"

"It's not that. It's just that I don't like the way things are going here."

"Meaning?"

"I'm being followed."

"By whom?"

"Not sure, and that's what worries me. I don't want them to know about you and Vicks, so I'm thinking it might be best for you two if I keep my distance until this job was finished."

"Oh," she said. "And when will that be?"

"Real soon, I hope."

Another sigh. "Jack, when are you going to give this up?"

"Please, Gia. Not now. A pay phone on a crowded sidewalk in Hell's Kitchen is not where I want to discuss this."

"You never want to discuss it."

"Gia . . ."

"Don't you see what this Repairman Jack stuff does? It doesn't involve just you. It affects all of us. And now you're afraid to see us because of it."

"I hate it when you're right."

That seemed to mollify her. "All right. To be continued. Please be careful, Jack."

"Always. Love you."

"Love you too."

His insides roiling, Jack hung up and stood staring at the phone. Gia was right. He should be more careful with the kinds of jobs he took. He guessed this was the price of caring, of close attachments. None of it had entered the picture in his lone wolf days when he'd done his share of rough-and-tumble gigs. But now . . . what was worth disappointing Vicky—or possibly endangering her?

What irked him was that he'd been so darn choosy lately. This gig, for instance—a missing wife should have been a no-risk, no-sweat fix-it. How had everything spun so damn far out of control?

Sooner or later he was going to have to face it: He couldn't have it both ways. Some hard choices were coming.

But he couldn't think about that now.

He picked up the receiver as if he were about to make another call, then whirled—

—and startled a young woman waiting behind him.

She wore jeans and a chopped Orioles T-shirt, had buzz-cut hair, and at least a dozen rings in her left ear. She recovered quickly.

"You finished with that?"

He scanned the area to see if he could catch someone watching him.

No one . . . at least no one he could see.

He handed her the phone and moved on. He wished he were done with this job. It was making him crazy.

8

Jack returned to his hotel room and hauled the crates out of the bathroom. He propped the lids against the headboard of his bed and made a stab at assembling some of the Erector Set-type struts, but soon realized the job required an extra pair of hands. He tried to decipher the scrawl in the corner of the smaller lid but it didn't make much sense.

Frustrated, he sat on the bed and stared at the two crates full of puzzle parts. He thought of Vicky. She loved puzzles. Under normal circumstances, this might have been a fun project to tackle with her, but something in his gut didn't want Vicky anywhere near these crates.

After a few more hours of haunting the conference areas, he was hungry. He couldn't bear the thought of another meal in the coffee shop, so he wandered out and found a place on Tenth called Druids. A pint of Guinness and a steak had him in a somewhat better state of mind and body by the time he returned to the hotel.

He was halfway to the escalator when he saw Frayne Canfield rolling toward him across the worn carpet of the lobby. He wore a bright green shirt that, along with his red hair and beard, gave him a Christmas look.

"Have you found Sal yet?" Canfield said.

Jack tried to look barely interested. "You mean Professor Roma? Who told you I was looking?"

"Evelyn. Lew. I've been looking for him too. Any luck?"

"Nope."

"Maybe we can look together."

Is he really looking for Roma, or trying to keep an eye on me? Who's he working for?

Then he remembered that Canfield had been the first to mention this Otherness stuff. Maybe Jack could pump him about it, and maybe he'd slip—maybe he'd drop something about Melanie in the process.

"Maybe," Jack said. "We had a long discussion about the Otherness yesterday, and I wanted to get back to it."

"The Otherness, ay?" Canfield's bulging eyes narrowed as he looked up at Jack. "And how you're tied into it?"

Jack fought to hide his shock. What have I got— some sort of sign around my neck?

"We, uh, never got that far into it."

Canfield looked around. "Well, if you want to discuss it, this isn't the place. My room or yours?"

Jack considered that for a second. If he went off with Canfield, he might miss Roma. But finding Roma was looking pretty iffy; Canfield was a sure thing. He didn't want Canfield to see the mystery crates and their contents, however.

"Yours," he said, and didn't offer an explanation.

As Jack followed him to the elevator, he glanced up and saw Jim Zaleski and Miles Kenway huddled in a corner, heads close in deep conversation. They stopped talking as they spotted Jack.

Kenway called out, "I'm expecting a photo to be faxed to me any time now."

Jack gave a thumbs-up and kept walking.

So Kenway had taken his advice about getting visual confirmation on the Roma here and the Roma in Kentucky. That could be very interesting.

"What photo?" Canfield asked.

"Just a mutual acquaintance," Jack said.

Jack and Canfield rode up in silence, with Canfield busily gnawing at a fingernail, and Jack trying to avoid looking at his flannel-wrapped legs and the disconnecting way they moved beneath the blanket. He couldn't help thinking about what Melanie had said to Lew about what was wrong with those legs. . . .

You don't want to know.

Canfield's room was laid out exactly like Jack's. In fact, it could have been Jack's . . . except it had no weird green crates lying about.

"Let's see now," Canfield said, grinning through his Hagar beard and motioning Jack to one of the chairs. "Where were we?"

He sat there snacking on fingernail and cuticle crudités as he regarded Jack with too-bright eyes. He seemed more wired up than usual. Salt-rimmed crescents darkened the armpits of his shirt.

"Yesterday you and I were in the 'Children of the Otherness' zone—inhabited by you and Melanie Ehler," Jack said. He settled into the chair, dropping to eye level with Canfield. "Later Roma said something about my supposedly being 'marked by the Otherness.'"

"Not supposedly—the mark is there and you know it."

You can see it too? Jack thought, stiffening. He

shrugged with as much nonchalance as his tight muscles would allow.

"Do I?"

"Of course you do. Open your shirt and I'll prove it."

"Sorry. Not on a first date."

Canfield didn't laugh. "What's wrong? Does it disturb you that your scars might link you to me and my birth defects?"

Jack repressed a shudder as Canfield's legs stirred under the blanket.

"Whatever scars I have came along long after my birth. You told me yourself that your defects happened before you were born. I don't see any connection."

"Ah," Canfield said, raising a well-chewed index finger. "But what made your scars? A creature, right?"

Jack stared at him. *He knows too?* Finally he said, "Where do you get your information?"

"About the Otherness creatures?"

Why doesn't he call them by name? Jack wondered.

"Yeah. How do you know about them?"

"Melanie and I sensed their presence last year. Just as I sensed those scars on your chest, we became aware of the Otherness creatures approaching from the east."

That's right, Jack thought. *The rakoshi had come from the east . . . from India . . . by freighter.*

"I get the impression you never saw one."

"I never had the honor. We searched, but we never could locate them."

"Lucky for you."

"I don't see it that way. I could consider them almost . . . brothers. After all, they too were children of the Otherness, like Melanie and me, although they contained far more of the Otherness than either of us."

"The Otherness . . . I'm getting real tired of that word."

"Well, it's a perfect name, really. The Otherness represents everything that's not 'us'—meaning the human race and the reality we inhabit. Melanie thinks it's vampiric in a way, sucking the life—the spiritual life—out of everything it encounters. Monstrously dark times will ensue if and when it takes over."

"And how would it manage that?"

"Sneak in when the other side's not looking. It can't charge in because the current landlord's got it locked out, but it's always there, hovering just beyond the threshold, keeping an eye on us, making tiny intrusions, creating strange, fearful manifestations, using its influence to sow discord, fear, and madness wherever and whenever it can."

"Like through the folks downstairs?"

Canfield nodded. "Some people are more aware, others less, but each of us *knows*—I don't care whether it's in our preconscious, post-conscious, subconscious, in the most primitive corners of our hindbrains, in the very cells of our bodies, we all sense this battle raging. And that subliminal perception has been reflected in human religions since earliest recorded history: Horus and Set, the Titans and the Olympians, God and Satan. The war is out there, and it's been going on since the beginning of time. We're aware of it. We can sense the Otherness on the far side of the door, we can smell its hunger."

"Okay. Fine. Let's just say that's true. How's this . . . this evil Great Whatever screwing with things now?"

"It can influence certain susceptible individuals—'touched by the Otherness,' as Melanie used to say."

"Touched is right," Jack said.

Canfield smiled. "Interesting, isn't it, that 'touched' has two meanings."

Jack hadn't thought of that, and thinking about it now was no comfort.

"Keep going."

"The willing susceptibles give in to the influence and go to work for it—they're the ones behind all the discord and cover-ups."

"Controlled by the Otherness."

"Not so much controlled, as simpatico. They're not taking orders, per se, but they feel a certain solidarity with its ethic."

"Ethic? What ethic?"

"All right, perhaps ethic isn't the best term. How about 'esthetic'? Does that sit better? Whatever the term or the reason, they're quite willing to inject as much chaos and discord as possible into everyday life. The unwilling fight back, but not without paying a price."

"SESOUP folk, in other words."

"Yes. They're what we call 'sensitives.' For better or worse, their nervous systems are more attuned to the Otherness. Their minds have to make sense of the external will impinging on them and so they think they're hearing voices, or come up with these wild-sounding theories."

"Like gray aliens, reptoids, Majestic-12, the New World Order—"

"You're thinking small: from Christianity and its Book of Revelations to the Hebrew Kaballah, to the Bhagavad Gita, they all come from the same place."

"So in other words, there's no shadow government trying to control our minds."

Canfield shook his head. "You're missing my point. I believe there *is* a shadow government with our worst interests at heart, but it's not controlled by aliens or the UN or Satan, it's run by people under the influence—note I said 'influence,' not 'direction'—of the Otherness. Aliens, devils and the NWO are simply some of the masks worn by that single, nameless chaotic entity . . . the many faces of a single truth."

"Melanie's Grand Unification . . ." Jack said.

"Exactly. But this conference is a unification of sorts too. The members of SESOUP are particularly sensitive to the Otherness, that's why membership is so selective. And now they're all gathered here, packed into a single structure, each one of them a lens of sorts, perceiving the Otherness, and focusing it, distilling it. Surely you've noticed the charged atmosphere in the hotel?"

"Sort of. But focusing it for what purpose?"

"Only time will tell. We must believe now, but soon we shall have proof."

"Proof?" Jack said. "Real hard proof? That'd be refreshing."

"Your scars are a form of proof, wouldn't you say?"

Jack was glad to get back to the subject of his scars. He remembered something Canfield had said.

"You mentioned that you and Melanie 'sensed' the creatures. You 'sensed' they were in New York but you didn't know where they came from."

"Of course we did. They came from the Otherness."

"I mean, what country."

"Country? What is a country but an artificial boundary agreed on by ephemeral governments."

"And I'll bet you don't know what they were called, either."

"What's in a name? Just a label attached by some primitive people. All that matters is that the creatures were fashioned ages ago by the Otherness, and they carry the Otherness in them."

Odd. He seemed to know the big picture, but not the details.

"Carried," Jack said. "Past tense. They became fried fish food at the bottom of New York Harbor."

Canfield nodded. "Yes. I remember waking from a nightmare about their death agonies. When I read about the ship that had burned in the harbor, I guessed that was what had happened." He shook his head. "Such a shame."

"Shame, hell. Probably the best thing I ever did."

Canfield stared at him. Jack couldn't read his expression through all that hair. When he spoke his voice was just above a whisper.

"*You?* You're the one who killed the Otherness creatures?"

Something in Canfield's wide eyes made Jack uneasy.

"Yeah, well, somebody had to do it. They happened to pick on the wrong little girl for their next meal."

"Then it's no wonder you're here. You *are* involved . . . more deeply than you can possibly imagine."

"Involved in what?"

"In Melanie's Grand Unification Theory. The Otherness creatures are part of it, I'm sure, and therefore so are you."

"Whoopee," Jack said. "And does her theory involve weird contraptions as well?"

"You mean machines? I don't think so. Why?"

"Well, I've got a couple of crates of parts sitting in my room. I don't know why they're there—I don't even know how they got there—but I've got a funny feeling their appearance is somehow connected to Melanie's *dis*appearance."

"I can't imagine how. You mean, you don't know who sent them or where they're from?"

"Tulsa, I think. North Tulsa."

Canfield grinned. "Ever been to Tulsa?"

"No."

"I have. It's not big enough to have a 'north.'"

"Maybe it was something else then. All I know is the plans for assembling this gizmo are printed inside the lid, and I saw 'N. Tulsa' scribbled along an edge."

"N. Tulsa . . ." Canfield said softly. "N. Tul—" Suddenly he straightened in his wheelchair. "Dear God! It couldn't have been 'Tesla,' could it?"

Jack tried to picture the lid. "Could have been. It was kind of scrawled and I didn't pay that much attention because—"

Canfield was wheeling toward the door. "Let's go!"

"Where?"

"Your room. I want to see this myself."

Jack wasn't crazy about a guest in his room, but if Canfield knew something about those crates . . .

"Where's Tesla?" Jack said as they took the elevator down one stop.

"Not where—who. I can't believe you've never heard of him."

"Believe it. Who is Tesla?"

"A long story, not worth telling if I'm wrong."

Jack followed him to his own room. A disturbing thought struck him as he was unlocking the door.

"How come you know where my room is?"

Canfield smiled. "After I sensed those scars on you, I made it my business to find out. And I'm sure I'm not alone. Probably half the people here know where you're staying."

"Why the hell should they care?"

"Because you're an unknown quantity. Some may suspect you're with the CIA, some may think you were sent by MJ-12, or maybe even an agent of the devil."

"Swell."

"You're surrounded by people who believe that nothing is as it seems. What did you expect?"

"You've got a point there."

That does it, he thought. This was like his worst nightmare. First thing in the morning, I'm out of here.

Jack had left the lights on, and allowed Canfield to precede him into the room. The crates lay open on the floor dead ahead, and Canfield rolled directly to them. He picked up one of the lids, scanned its inner surface.

"The other one," Jack said.

Canfield checked that one and slapped his hand against it when he found what he was looking for.

"Yes!" he cried, his voice an octave higher than usual. "It's him! Nikola Tesla!"

Jack read over his shoulder. Now that he really looked, he could see that the scrawl was "N. Tesla."

"Okay. So who is Nikola Tesla?"

"One of the great geniuses and inventors of the last three or four generations. Right up there with Edison and Marconi."

"I've heard of Edison and Marconi," Jack said. "Never heard of Tesla."

"Ever had an MRI?"

Jack leaned back against the writing table. "You mean that X-ray thing? No."

"First off, it's not an X ray. It's magnetic resonance imaging—M-R-I, get it? And the units of magnetism it uses are called 'Teslas'—one Tesla equals ten thousand Gauss—named after Nikola Tesla."

Jack was trying hard to be impressed. "Oh. Okay. But why is this genius inventor sending me stuff?"

"He's not. He died in 1943."

"I'm not happy to hear that a dead man is sending me boxes," Jack said.—

Canfield rolled his eyes. "*Somebody* sent you these crates, but I don't believe for a moment it was Nikola Tesla. He was unquestionably a genius, but he didn't invent a way to come back from death. He was in his late twenties in the 1880s when he arrived here from Yugoslavia, and barely into his thirties when he perfected the polyphase alternating current power system. He sold the patents to Westinghouse for a million bucks—*real* money in those days, but still a bargain for Westinghouse. Today, every house, every appliance in the country uses AC power."

Now Jack was impressed. "So this was a real guy, then—not one of these make-believe SESOUP bogeymen?"

"Very real. But as he got older his ideas became more and more bizarre. He started talking about free energy, cosmic ray motors, earthquake generators, and death rays. Lots of fictional mad scientists were inspired by Tesla."

Something about death rays and mad scientists clicked in Jack's brain.

"The Invisible Ray," he said.

"Pardon?"

"An old Universal horror flick. Haven't seen it in ages, but I remember Boris Karloff playing a mad scientist with a death ray."

"Was he made up with bushy hair and a thick mustache?"

"As a matter of fact, yes. And he had an Eastern European name—Janos, or something."

"There you go: That was Nikola Tesla all the way. He lived in the Waldorf and had an experimental lab out on Long Island at the turn of the century where he was trying to perfect broadcast power."

"Broadcast power?" Jack said.

"Yes. You've heard of it?"

Jack only nodded. Heard of it? He'd seen it in action.

"Anyway," Canfield continued, "Tesla starting building this tower way out on Long Island in a little town called Wardenclyffe. . . ."

Canfield's voice trailed off as his face went pale.

"Wardenclyffe, Long Island?" Jack said. "Never heard of it."

"That's because it doesn't exist anymore," Canfield said slowly. "It was absorbed by another town. It's now part of Shoreham."

Jack felt a cold tingle rush down his spine. "Shoreham? That's where Lew and Melanie live."

"Exactly." Canfield slapped a palm against his forehead. "Why didn't I see this before? All these years I've never understood why Melanie left Monroe to live in Shoreham, but now it's clear. She's been living near Tesla's old property. She must have thought some of his wilder theories and never-executed plans had to do with the Otherness."

Jack remembered what Lew had told him that first day out in their house in Shoreham.

"Lew said she was buying and selling real estate, saying it had something to do with her 'research.'"

"I *knew* it!"

"He said she'd buy a place, hire some guys to dig up the yard, then resell it."

Canfield was leaning forward. "Did he say where she'd buy these places?"

"Yeah. Always in the same development . . . along some road. . . ." Damn. He couldn't remember the name.

"Randall Road?"

"You got it."

"Yes!" Canfield pumped his fist in the air. "Tesla's property ran along Randall Road in Wardenclyffe! That's where he built his famous tower. The old brick building that housed his electrical lab is still standing. No question about it. Melanie was definitely searching for old Tesla documents."

"You think she found something?"

"Most definitely." He nodded and pointed to the crates. "And I think it's sitting right in front of us."

"You think Melanie sent this stuff?"

"I do."

"But why to me? Why not to you?"

Only Repairman Jack can find me. Only he will understand.

Was that why?

"I wish I knew," Canfield said. He sounded hurt. "I certainly wouldn't have left it sitting around for days. I can tell you that."

"Really. What would you have done?"

"Assembled it, of course."

"Maybe she thought you might have . . ." He glanced at Canfield's blanket-wrapped lower body. "You know . . . trouble putting it together."

"Maybe," he said. He seemed cheered by the thought. "And she was probably right. But now there's two of us, so let's get to it."

"Whoa. We don't know what this thing is, or what it does. We don't know how it got here and we don't even know for sure it's from Melanie."

"It's from Melanie," he said. "I'm sure of it."

Jack wasn't sure of anything about these crates. Assembling the pieces might seem like the next logical step, but something inside him wasn't too keen on taking it.

"I only have one wrench and a couple of screwdrivers. We'll need—"

"Never fear," Canfield said, reaching around the back of his wheelchair. He removed a tool kit from the pouch back there. "I never travel without this. Let's get to work."

Still Jack hesitated. He could buy that this contraption was linked to Melanie, but he was far from convinced she'd sent it. Figuring there was safety in numbers, he decided to get some other people involved.

He pulled Kenway's pager number from his wallet and started dialing.

"What are you doing?" Canfield said.

"Calling in some help."

"We don't need help."

"Look at all those pieces. Sure we do."

"Who are you calling?"

"Miles Kenway."

"No!" He seemed genuinely upset. "Not him!"

"Why not? What's that old expression? Many hands lighten the load."

"He won't understand."

"Then we'll explain it to him."

When Kenway's beeper service picked up, Jack left a simple message: "Call Jack. Urgent." He was sure Kenway knew his room number. Everyone else seemed to.

"You shouldn't have done that," Canfield said, almost sulking. "Kenway doesn't belong here."

What's his problem? Jack wondered.

"He doesn't, but you do? How'd you reach that conclusion? The crates wound up in *my* room, remember?"

"He isn't part of this. We are."

"If what you've said is true, we're all part of this— whatever 'this' might be."

The phone rang. It was Kenway.

"Get up to my room," Jack told him. "I've got something to show you."

"Be right up," Kenway said. "And brother, have I got something to show *you*."

"Bring Zaleski," Jack told him. "And if you've got any tools, bring them along too."

"Will do."

Canfield groaned as Jack hung up the phone. "Not Zaleski too!"

"The more the merrier, I figure," Jack said as he dialed Lew's room number.

"Who now?" Canfield said. "Olive Farina?"

"Olive?" Jack said, watching Canfield closely. "She's been found?"

"No. Where have you been? She still hasn't shown up. A missing person report has been filed. Everybody's still looking for her."

Jack sensed that Canfield didn't know any more about Olive than he was saying.

No answer at Lew's room.

"I was going to ask Lew Ehler too," Jack said, hanging up. "But I guess he's gone back to Shoreham."

"Just as well." Canfield grunted with annoyance. "Zaleski and Kenway will be more than enough to handle. Whatever you do, don't mention the Otherness or that this device may be a link to it."

"Why not?"

"Because proof of the existence of the Otherness will expose Zaleski's UFO's and aliens and Kenway's New World Order for the shams they are. Who knows how they'll react. They might not be able to handle it." He pounded his fist on the armrest of his wheelchair. "I *wish* you hadn't called them!"

"Relax," Jack told him. "We'll order pizza and beer. We'll make this a party. Like a mini barn raising. You'll see. It'll be fun."

9

Kenway and Zaleski arrived less than fifteen minutes later. They both knew Canfield who finally seemed to have resigned himself to sharing the stage with the two newcomers.

"Take a gander at *this*." Kenway said, holding out a folded sheet of fax paper.

Jack opened the flimsy sheet and stared at the photo of a portly young man, blond, with a fuzzy attempt at a beard.

"Our mutual friend, I presume?"

"Exactly!" Kenway's grin was shark-like, his gray crewcut more bristly than ever as he took back the fax. "Oh, brother, is the shit ever gonna hit the fan when I pass this around tomorrow. I knew there was something phony about our fearless leader!"

Zaleski tried to get a look. "Who? Roma? What've you got there?"

"You'll find out tomorrow," Kenway said.

Jack's thoughts drifted as they argued. If Roma was a bogus identity, who was the guy running the show? Why had he created SESOUP and organized this meeting? Was he connected to Melanie's disappearance? To these boxes? And if so, why had they wound up with Jack, when he hadn't even known he was coming until the night before?

Jack's head was spinning.

"Whatever," Zaleski finally said to Kenway, then

grinned at Jack as he displayed an elaborate ratchet set. "You want tools, man? We got tools. What the fuck for?"

Jack explained what he could. Neither of them needed any introduction to Nikola Tesla, it seemed. Zaleski and Kenway were awed by the prospect of assembling a contraption designed by him.

They divided the workload. Jack and Zaleski would assemble the base while Kenway and Canfield tackled the dome. The contents of each crate were dumped onto one of the two double beds, and they had just begun to work when Canfield lifted his hand.

"Shhh! What's that?"

Jack listened. Something scratching at his door. He went to the peephole but saw nothing. Yet the sound persisted. He pulled open the door—

And Roma's monkey scampered in.

"Get that fucking oversized rodent outta here!" Zaleski shouted, tossing a pillow at the monkey.

It screeched and dodged the pillow, scampered a single circuit of the room, then fled. Jack slammed the door after it.

"Don't let that damn thing in again!" Zaleski cried, brushing his hair off his forehead. "Little fucker gives me the creeps."

"For once we agree on something," Kenway said. "It shouldn't be allowed to run free."

Jack was remembering what Olive had told him about that monkey, how she'd overheard it talking to Roma . . . or whoever he was.

"Let's get back to business," Canfield said.

"Tesla got royally screwed by J. P. Morgan, you know," Kenway said after a few minutes. "Morgan promised to fund his broadcast power project back at the turn of the century. He let Tesla get the Wardenclyffe tower three-quarters built—"

"That would be out on Long Island?" Jack said, glancing at Canfield.

"Yes, of course," Kenway said. "Morgan let him get to a certain point, then suddenly pulled the financial rug out from under him."

"Why do that?" Jack said. "Broadcast power would be worth zillions."

"Because Morgan was one of the bankrollers of the One World conspiracy, and he and his fellows came to realize that a cheap energy source like Tesla's broadcast power would rev all the world's economies into high gear. They figured that once the secret was out, they'd lose control of those economies. Tesla had a mysterious breakdown somewhere around 1908 and was never quite the same after."

"Bullshit," Zaleski said from the other side of the room. "He had a breakdown in 1908, but it wasn't caused by no J. P. fucking Morgan. Tesla had an in on alien technology, that's why he made all his breakthroughs."

Jack glanced again at Canfield who mouthed, *I warned you.*

"Back in 1908, with Morgan pulling the plug on his finances, Tesla needed a dramatic demonstration that his Wardenclyffe tower worked. Peary was making a second try to reach the North Pole at the time, so Tesla contacted the expedition and said they should be on the lookout for an unusual occurrence. On June 30, he aimed a beam of energy from Wardenclyffe to an arctic area where the explosion would be seen by the Perry team. But nothing happened. He thought he'd failed. Then he heard about Tunguska."

"What's Tunguska?" Jack asked.

"A place in Siberia," Canfield said. "Half a million square acres of forest were utterly destroyed by a mysterious cataclysmic explosion on June 30, 1908."

"Right!" Zaleski said. "The *same day* as Tesla's demonstration. *And* Tunguska is on the same longitudinal line as Peary's base camp."

"Researchers have estimated the force of the blast at fifteen megatons," Canfield added. "The boom was heard over six hundred miles away. It's never been explained."

Zaleski grinned. "But Old Nik knew the truth. His beam had overshot its mark."

"It was a meteor!" Kenway said.

"Really?" Zaleski's eyebrows floated halfway to his hairline. "Then how come no meteor fragments were ever found?"

"An antimatter meteor," Kenway said, not backing down an inch. "When antimatter meets matter, there's cataclysmic destruction, with total annihilation of one or the other."

"Uh-uh, Miles, old boy. Tesla did it, and the total awesomeness of the destructive power he'd unleashed blew his circuits. He had a nervous breakdown."

"Wrong," Kenway said. "J. P. Morgan's betrayal caused the breakdown."

"Gentlemen, please," Canfield said. "We're not going to decide this here. Suffice it to way that something happened to cause Tesla to stop communicating with people for a while and to sell his land and dismantle his tower. Let's just say that Nicola Tesla was never the same after 1908 and leave it at that."

"All right," Kenway said. "As long as there's no more talk about alien technology."

"Or New World Order bullshit," Zaleski said.

"Can we just build this damn thing!" Jack snapped. "I don't want to be at it all night."

He avoided looking at Canfield. Maybe he'd been right. Maybe including these two had been a bad idea.

10

"They're assembling it!" Mauricio cried as he rushed into the room. "And as I was listening at the door I heard Miles Kenway say something about a 'our fearless leader' being a 'phony!' It's all falling apart!"

"Keep calm," Roma said. "We knew the deception would not last forever."

Sal Roma—he'd immersed himself in the character so deeply that he'd become comfortable with the name. Might as well keep up the pretense. He didn't care what name he was known by, as long as it was not his own.

"But this is too close. And we do not have the device—*they* do!"

"Just who is 'they?'"

"Canfield, Kenway, Zaleski, and the stranger."

"Quite a crew. I wonder if this was what Canfield wanted to see me about—that he had learned about the device?"

"Who *cares* why he wanted to see you?" Mauricio screeched. "The device is *ours*! *We* are supposed to use it!"

"And we shall, dear friend. Without the bother of assembling it ourselves. This is all working out very nicely."

"You are insane! The plan was—"

"Hush now, Mauricio, before you anger me. The plan is heading for the right place, it is simply taking a different course—I do not know why that is, but in good time I am sure I shall. We need only watch and follow, and step in when it is to our advantage."

Mauricio crouched on the bedspread, and wrapped his thin arms around his folded legs. His sulking pose.

"This will come to a bad end, I tell you."

"A bad end . . ." Roma smiled. "That is the whole point, is it not?"

SUNDAY

1

Assembling the Tesla gizmo turned out to be a much more complicated chore than Jack had anticipated, especially the dome. It was close to two A.M. when they finished.

The beds had been pushed aside and now a five-foot oil derrick topped with a giant, warty mushroom cap stood in the middle of the floor.

One weird-looking contraption, Jack thought.

Something about it gave him the willies.

Nothing terribly strange about the eight-legged base. A bitch to assemble with all those crisscrossing struts, but it functioned as nothing more than a supporting framework. The dome was a whole other story. Curved sheets of shiny copper studded with dozens of smaller copper globes, larger toward the perimeter, and getting progressively smaller as they neared the center.

Jack could almost go along with Zaleski about its having been inspired by alien technology. He'd never seen anything like it.

"This looks a lot like the Wardenclyffe tower," Zaleski said in an awed tone.

"Tesla never finished the tower," Kenway said.

"So we've been told," Zaleski replied. "But I've seen renderings of how it was supposed to look, and this is it."

"Swell," Jack said. "But what's it supposed to do? Broadcast energy? Blow up Siberian woods? What?"

"I doubt we'll know that until it's finished," Canfield said.

Kenway tapped one of the gizmo's legs with his booted toe. "What do you mean? It *is* finished."

"Not according to this." Canfield held up one of the lids and pointed to the diagram of the dome. "See here? There's supposed to be some sort of light bulb or something in the top center of the dome. Has anybody come across anything like that tonight?"

Jack shook his head, and saw Zaleski and Kenway doing the same.

"Kee-rist!" Zaleski said. "Isn't that fucking typical? Just like the model kits I used to get when I was a kid—always a piece missing."

"You sure that's a bulb?" Kenway said, taking the lid from Canfield. He pulled out a pair of reading glasses and studied the diagram more closely. "Looks more like some sort of crystal to me."

"Lemme see that," Zaleski said. He peered closely, tilting the lid back and forth. "For once I agree with you, Miles. Look at the facets there. That's definitely some sort of crystal. Big one, I'd guess."

"Anyone seen a large crystal anywhere?" Canfield said, lifting and shaking the spread on the nearest bed.

"I have," Jack said, wondering at the surges of excitement suddenly pulsing through him as he remembered a basement . . . and an old desk . . . and on it, three large, oblong, amber quartz crystals. . . .

"Where?" Kenway said.

"Out on Long Island . . . in a little town called Monroe."

2

Jack checked out the moonless sky as he followed Kenway's pickup truck north along Glen Cove Road. Dawn was still hours away and they were all headed for Monroe.

But what a job to get to this point.

First the debate on whether or not to send someone out to fetch a crystal and bring it back. Eventually it was decided that that would take too long, so they all agreed to haul the mini Tesla tower out to Monroe. Canfield, still convinced that the crates had come from Melanie, said that seemed fitting.

But how to get it there?

Canfield reluctantly volunteered the back of his specially outfitted van—reluctantly because he didn't see any need for Kenway and Zaleski to come; he and Jack could handle everything just fine.

But no way were Kenway and Zaleski going along with that.

So they separated the dome from the tower and loaded both sections into the back of the van.

But that wasn't the end of it. Zaleski didn't want to ride in Kenway's truck, Kenway didn't want to ride in Zaleski's car. Neither wanted to ride in Canfield's van, and Jack had had enough of them all for one night.

Finally they got underway—a four-car caravan with Canfield in the lead, chugging through the wee hours of

Sunday morning. At least they had the road pretty much to themselves.

Jack felt a raw uneasiness wriggling through his gut, a vague awareness that he was riding toward big trouble. But he couldn't turn back now. He sensed that the end game was at hand, and wanted this crazy weird gig over and done with—tonight.

He'd tried to call Lew out in Shoreham to tell him where they were going and ask him if he wanted to meet them in Monroe. But all he'd reached was the Ehler answering machine. He'd tried Lew's hotel room again, but still no answer.

So where was Lew? Not with Olive, Jack hoped.

3

The first thing Jack noticed about Melanie's family home was that the lights were on. The second was Lew's Lexus by the garage—he spotted that when Canfield's headlights raked the front yard as he turned his van into the driveway.

As Zaleski and Kenway pulled into the curb, Jack drove past the house and parked at the corner of the property, near where he'd spotted the black sedan pulling away after his first visit to the house. He got out and looked around, zipping his warm-up top against the chill. No other cars on the street besides the ones he'd come with.

Satisfied they hadn't been followed, he walked over to Zaleski and Kenway who were watching Canfield lower himself and his wheelchair to the ground on the special elevator platform built into his van.

"Wait here," Jack told them. "I think Lew's in the house. Let me check first."

He stepped up to the front door and found it unlocked. He pushed it open and entered the living room.

"Lew?" he called.

No answer. He started forward, but a sound—an odd, rasping clink—stopped him. He paused, listening, and heard it again. And again. Slow and rhythmic . . . coming from below. . . .

Jack slipped through the dining room and kitchen and stopped at the head of the cellar steps. The lights were on below, and no doubt about it—the clinking was coming from down there. Along with another sound.

Sobbing.

Just to be on the safe side, Jack pulled the Semmerling as he crept down the stairs. He pocketed it when he saw Lew Ehler kneeling on the basement floor. Lew's back was to Jack, he clutched a heavy pickax, and was chipping away at the concrete around the embedded rope ladder.

He jumped when Jack touched his shoulder.

"Wha—?" he cried, looking up at Jack with a tear-streaked face.

"Hey, Lew," Jack said softly. "What's up?"

"It's Melanie," he sobbed. "She's down there! I know she's down there and I can't reach her!"

"Easy, guy," Jack said, hooking a hand under Lew's arm and helping him to his feet. "Come on. Get a grip, okay. You're not going to find her that way."

He felt the scars on his chest begin to itch again. What was it with this cellar?

Lew let the pickax fall into the shallow depression

he'd chipped in the concrete. As Jack bent to retrieve it, he noticed again the scorch marks around the ladder . . . eight of them. . . .

And eight legs on the Tesla contraption.

Suddenly excited, he guided Lew to the chair by the desk—and yes, the big amber crystals were still there, all three of them—then ran upstairs to find the others.

Outside in the front yard, it took Jack's eyes a few seconds to adjust to the darkness. He saw that Canfield's van had been backed onto the lawn. Canfield was watching Kenway and Zaleski as they off-loaded the mini tower from the rear.

"Where we going to set this up?" Zaleski said.

"I think I know just the place. Come inside and see if you agree."

They left the tower in the van and headed for the house. The three of them lifted Canfield and his wheelchair up the front steps and inside.

"Boy, does this bring back memories," he said as he rolled through the living room. "Where to?"

"The basement," Jack said.

"There's nothing down there."

Canfield's voice didn't ring quite true. Did he know more about this than he was letting on?

"You're sure of that?" Jack said.

They carried Canfield and his chair down the stairs. Lew leaped to his feet when he saw them, his expression shocked.

"What's going on?" he said.

"I'll explain in a minute, Lew," Jack told him.

He led the others over to the spot where Lew had been working with the pickax.

"What the fuck?" Zaleski said, squatting and tugging on the rope ladder where it disappeared into the cement.

Kenway stood next to him, hands on hips. "Most unusual."

"But that's only part of it," Jack said. He touched a number of the scorches with the toe of his sneaker. "Check this out. Eight marks in a rough circle. Can anybody think of anything we've seen recently with an eight-legged, roughly circular base?"

Canfield cried, "I knew it was from Melanie!"

"Melanie?" Lew said, pushing his way into the ring. "What's from Melanie?"

"Explain it to him," Jack told Canfield, "while we get the gizmo."

He led Zaleski and Kenway back to the van. Zaleski carried the dome on his own, while Jack and Kenway shared the larger, heavier, ungainly load of the derrick-like base.

Lew grabbed hold of the base as they eased it down the basement steps.

"Can it be true?" he said to Jack. He had hope in his eyes, and his face wore the closest thing to a smile Jack had seen for days. Obviously Canfield had given Lew his own slant on the origin of the crates. "Is this really from Melanie?"

"I'm going to have to reserve judgment on that, Lew."

Zaleski leaned the dome against the couch, then he helped Jack and Kenway guide the tower base toward the chipped concrete and set it down over the end of the ladder. A few minor adjustments in positioning and . . .

"I'll be damned," Kenway said. "You were right."

The feet of the tower's eight vertical supports fit perfectly over the eight scorch marks.

"Yeah," Jack said, feeling a growing uneasiness. "But I'm not sure I'm all that glad."

"Why not?" Canfield said. He cradled the big amber crystals in his blanketed lap.

"Well, for one thing, it's kind of obvious that another contraption just like this one was positioned here before. Where is it now? The question wouldn't bother me except for the fact that all we have left of the first are these marks that have been *burned* into the concrete."

"No scorch marks on the ceiling, though," Canfield said. "Nor on the furniture."

Good point, Jack thought. It made him feel a little better, but not a whole hell of a lot.

Zaleski stepped over to the couch and hefted an edge of the dome. "Let's get this sucker attached and see what happens."

Jack removed his warm-up jacket and dropped it onto the couch. He gripped the other side of the dome; together they raised it and set it on the base. A few minutes of tightening nuts and bolts, and the mini Tesla tower was reassembled. Light from the naked incandescents overhead gleamed off the dome's rows of copper globes.

"And now for the final piece," Canfield said, holding up one of the crystals.

"You really think that's all it'll take?" Jack said.

Canfield looked at him. "You have doubts?"

Jack pointed to the tower. "Where do we plug it in?"

"Tesla theorized that energy could be gathered free from the atmosphere," Kenway said. "That was why he was such a threat to the One-Worlders."

"Fine," Jack said, shrugging. "But a crystal? It seems so . . . so New Agey. It's just a pretty rock."

"Not just any rock," Canfield said, twisting the crystal back and forth to catch the light. "It's quartz—which has piezoelectric properties. You've heard of crystal radios, I assume?"

"Sure."

"And how many rocks do you know that can rotate the plane of polarized light? Trust me, a crystal is a lot more than 'just a pretty rock.'"

"Enough bullshitting," Zaleski said, grabbing the crystal from Canfield's hand. "Let's do it."

Standing on tiptoe, he inserted the crystal into the top center of the dome.

"Perfect fit," he said, then stepped back.

Jack did him one better. He retreated all the way to the steps. He didn't trust this thing. All he knew about this Nikola Tesla guy was what he'd been told, and one of the stories involved destroying half a million acres of forest on the far side of the North Pole.

Come to think of it, the stairs weren't nearly as far away as he would have liked. Albany might not even be far enough. But he stayed where he was and watched.

Nothing happened.

That didn't seem to faze the others. They kept waiting patiently in a rough semicircle.

Jack backed up a little more and seated himself on one of the steps.

How long do we wait before we call this a bust? he wondered.

Then he sensed a change in the cellar. He wasn't sure what was happening, but he could feel the hairs rising along his bare arms. Not from fear or alarm, but from the charge that seemed to fill the air. A little like what he'd felt in the hotel, but stronger, more concentrated.

Jack wasn't the only one to notice. He saw Kenway rubbing his arms, tugging at his shirt collar.

"Do you feel it?" Canfield said, grinning.

The lights flickered.

Lew looked around. "Did anyone just see . . . ?"

The others nodded silently.

Then all four sixty-watt bulbs in the ceiling dimmed to about thirty—and stayed dimmed. As they lost power, the crystal atop the dome began to pulse with a faint amber light.

The air became more highly charged, and then the mini tower began to hum, low at first, but steadily rising in pitch. Jack saw the semicircle widen as all but Kenway eased back.

Where's that thing getting its power? he wondered, tensing on the steps. He didn't like this one bit.

The crystal pulsed more brightly, strobing distorted shadows against the walls; the hum rose further in pitch as the pulses cycled faster and faster, finally merging into a steady glow.

And then the tower began to rise off the floor.

"Holy shit!" Zaleski said. "This is too fucking much!"

Kenway looked grim, Lew looked puzzled, and Canfield . . . Canfield looked absolutely rapt.

It continued to rise—one inch . . . two . . . six . . . a foot . . .

Jack sat frozen, bloodless. This was no trick. No invisible wires on that thing. He'd set it up himself. The tower was really and truly floating in the air.

"Didn't I tell you, soldier boy?" Zaleski said, clapping Kenway on the shoulder. "Alien technology! This is how they make their saucers go!"

Kenway said nothing, but his quick glance at Zaleski was pure malice.

Jack fought the urge to pack it in and head for his car. The crawling sensation in his gut was more intense than ever, telling him he wasn't needed here, and didn't even belong here.

This isn't what you were hired for. Get out while you can.

The tower rose until the blazing crystal set in its dome was poised between two rafters. And then it simply hung there.

Jack felt a cool breeze against this back. Had somebody opened a door upstairs? He was about to get up to go look when Canfield's shout stopped him.

"Look!" he cried. He was pointing at the floor.

"Good Lord!" Kenway said, finally retreating a step.

A hole was opening. The concrete wasn't melting or crumbling, it was simply fading away. But no dirt was visible beneath, just . . . hole. And the wider it got, the stronger the breeze against Jack's back, rushing toward the opening.

"Good God!" Lew said. "What is it?"

"What's it look like?" Zaleski said without looking up. "A pizza? It's a fucking hole."

A hole . . .

Jack gripped the edges of the step that supported him. His dreams the past two nights had been nightmares about a hole . . . one that looked like it wanted to gobble up the world.

"Hey, guys," he said, "I think we should call this off."

"Relax, Jack," Kenway said. "You won't fall in from there."

Idiot, Jack thought. "What if it keeps enlarging?"

"I gotta feeling this ain't the first time this hole has opened," Zaleski said. "And the house is still here, ain't it?"

Jack watched with mounting alarm as the hole kept expanding, widening until the concrete entrapping the rope ladder disappeared, leaving it hanging free over the rim and dangling into the opening.

And then it stopped enlarging.

Jack sagged with relief.

"I think that's it," Zaleski said.

Kenway leaned his body forward but kept his feet where they were. "How deep, I wonder?"

Zaleski inched forward, shuffling his feet nearer and nearer to the edge. "Only one way to find out."

He stopped with his toes perhaps half a foot from the rim, then craned his neck to peer over the edge.

"I see some light way down there and—holy shit!" He jumped back from the edge.

"What?" Lew said. "What's wrong?"

"Look!" Canfield said, pointing to the ladder.

The ropes were moving, vibrating as they stretched over the rim.

"Something's coming," Zaleski said. "Climbing the ladder."

I hope he means some*one,* Jack thought, backing up another tread on the steps.

He sensed something ugly, something sinister slipping from that hole and coiling through the cellar. He held his breath as the gyrations of the ropes grew more pronounced, and then a single black talon rose above floor level and hooked onto the concrete . . . followed by a head . . . a dark-haired human head . . . with a woman's face. . . .

"Melanie!" Lew cried and rushed forward.

He grabbed her arms and lifted her from the opening. Then he wrapped her in a bear hug that left her shoes a good foot off the floor.

"Oh, Mel, Mel!" he sobbed. "I've been so worried. Thank God, you're back! Thank *God!*"

Jack couldn't see Melanie's face, but her arms didn't seem to be returning Lew's hug with anywhere near his fervor. Especially the left arm . . .

This was the first time Jack had seen Melanie's deformed forearm, and it wasn't what he'd expected. It seemed a little thinner than the right as it tapered down to the wrist; beyond that it stayed rounded instead of flattening into a palm. Lew had told him that all the fingernails had fused, leaving her with one large thick nail. But Jack hadn't pictured this big, sharp, black claw.

She'd supposedly kept it bandaged in public, and now Jack could see why. It was wicked looking.

"Lewis, please," Melanie said in a strained voice. "You're crushing me."

He released her. "Sorry," he said, wiping his eyes. "It's just that I've missed you so."

"You two can snuggle later," Zaleski said. He indicated the hole and the still floating tower. "What is all this, Melanie? And where the hell have you been?"

"Home," she whispered. A strange fevered glow lit in her eyes as she said the word.

Jack eased down the steps for a closer look. Finally he was getting to see the notorious Melanie Ehler in the flesh. She seemed far more intense than her photographs had indicated. Her hair was darker, her black eyebrows thicker, and her thin lips were split into the rapturous grin of a zealot who'd just heard the voice of God.

"Not here," Kenway said. He pointed to the hole. "What's down *there?*"

"Home," she repeated, then turned to Frayne. "It worked. I've found the way to the Otherness. We can go home now."

Canfield clasped his hands together and looked as if he was going to puddle up along with Lew.

"Mel," Lew said, pointing to her arm. "What happened to your nail?"

"It changed," she said, raising her black talon to eye level. "As soon as I got there it changed shape and color . . . to the way it's supposed to look."

She looked around and Jack felt something like an electric shock as her gaze locked on him.

"And you must be Repairman Jack," she said.

Jack stepped off the steps onto the floor. "Just Jack'll do."

He glanced at the others, but the "Repairman"

remark didn't seem to have registered. They were all still fixated on that hole. Good.

"Thank you so much," she said, stepping forward and extending her hand. "I knew you were the right man for the job."

Jack was about to protest that he'd done very little when Melanie's touch stopped him. Her hand was *cold*.

"Come on, Melanie," Zaleski said. "Enough with this 'home' shit. What's going *on?*"

She stepped back to where she could face everyone. "I've found a gateway to the Otherness," she said.

Kenway snorted. "The *what?*"

"It would take too long to explain fully," she said, "and I've neither the time nor the inclination. Suffice it to say that the single solution to all the mysteries that have plagued you, the answer you've spent so many years searching for, lies on the far side of that opening."

Jack had heard all this from Roma and Canfield. Hadn't believed a word of it before, but now . . .

He hooked his arm around the support column at the foot of the stairs and looked around. He still sensed something nasty in the air. Was he the only one?

"Is this that 'Grand Unification' thing you've been talking us to death about?" Zaleski said.

"Yes, Jim," she said with a small, tolerant smile. "It's all there. The secrets behind your UFOs and Majestic-12."

"Yeah, right."

She turned to Kenway. "And for you, Miles . . . the identity—and the *real* agenda—of the power behind the New World Order conspiracy."

"I sincerely doubt that," he said huffily.

She looked around. "If only Olive were here."

"She's been missing for days, Mel," Lew said.

Jack watched her closely. She seemed genuinely puzzled and disappointed. Didn't she know?

"That's too bad," she said. "The truth behind her cherished Book of Revelations is on the other side as well."

"All down there?" Zaleski said.

"'Down' isn't quite right. 'Over' there would be more accurate."

"But how?" Lew said. His face had a hurt look. "And why?"

"How?" she said. "I learned from talking to some old timers out in Shoreham, people who had relatives who'd worked in the Tesla lab, that before he sold his property and dismantled his tower, Tesla had buried mysterious steel canisters here and there around his property, and even beyond it."

"After the Tunguska explosion!" Zaleski said. "Must have scared him shitless."

Jack had already heard enough about Nikola Tesla and Tunguska to last a lifetime, but he couldn't bring himself to leave just yet . . . not with that tower floating in the air and the hole yawning in the floor. He remembered the holes in his recent nightmares, and wanted to see this one closed before he headed home.

Melanie said, "I don't know if Tesla caused the Tunguska explosion, and I don't really care. But I can tell you this: Nikola Tesla was not the type of man to be frightened by a mere explosion, no matter how powerful. I've suspected all along that something else was at the root of his breakdown. And now I know."

"This . . . Otherness?" Kenway said.

Melanie nodded. "Yes. During the year I spent searching for those canisters, I found three. One of them confirmed my suspicions. I gave the others to Ron Clayton and—"

"Clayton?" Jack said. That name rang a bell. "You knew Ronald Clayton?"

Melanie shrugged. "We shared an interest in Tesla. Ron was more interested in his electronics theories."

"I'll bet he was," Jack said, remembering the transmitter he'd seen on a hilltop upstate. Apparently the creep hadn't been the great innovator he'd wanted everybody to believe.

"Whether Tesla's tower was able to broadcast energy is irrelevant," Melanie said. "What I do know, or rather what I have proven"—she gestured toward the hole— "is that it can open a gateway to the Otherness. And I think that's what unhinged Tesla. He made contact, saw what was on the other side, and immediately slammed the door."

"It's that bad?" Lew said.

"Not for me," she said. "And not for Frayne. But for the rest of you . . ." She slowly shook her head.

"Hey!" Zaleski said. "How bad can it be?"

"It is the truth . . . and the truth at times can be unbearable."

Somewhere in the back of Jack's head another Jack shouted, *You can't* handle *the truth!*

Zaleski stepped to the rim of the hole and peered over the edge. "And you were down there how long?"

"What day is it?" Melanie said.

Jack glanced at his watch. "Just about four A.M. Sunday morning."

"You've been gone almost a week, Mel!" Lew cried.

She shrugged. "Time is different there. It seemed like barely two days."

"Well, if you can fucking handle it," Zaleski said, "so can I." He turned to Kenway. "Whatta y'say, Miles? Want to get up close and personal with Melanie's Grand Unification Theory?"

"I don't know," Kenway said slowly. He sidled to the edge and looked down. "Awfully dark down there."

"You can see some light way down. Besides, you're carrying aren't you?"

Kenway stared at him.

Zaleski snorted a laugh. "Look who I'm asking! Does the Pope wear a cross? Come on, Miles. You're armed and dangerous. Don't be a pussy."

Kenway glared at him, then hitched up his belt. He pointed to the rope ladder. "After you."

Zaleski gave Kenway a thumbs up, then squatted next to the ladder. He grabbed the two ropes, swung his leg over, then started down.

"Is this such a good idea?" Jack said.

"It's a great idea, Jack. You're coming right? Maybe you'll find those missing hours."

"You can have them," Jack said. "Kind of late for spelunking. My job's done here. I think maybe I'll be heading home."

"No!" Melanie said quickly. "I mean, not just yet. I need to talk to you first."

"All right," Zaleski said. "Suit yourself. Here goes nothing."

He started down and disappeared below floor level.

After a few seconds, his voice echoed up from below. "Come on, Miles, you chickenshit bastard. Let's go."

Kenway pulled his .45 automatic from under his sweater, flicked off the safety, then put it away again. He sighed, looked around, and—with much less enthusiasm than Zaleski—started down.

Jack stepped to the edge of the hole and watched the bristling hair atop Kenway's head recede into the depths. Damn, that looked deep.

Lew came up beside him. "I'll be. There *is* some light down there."

"*Way* down," Jack said, spotting the faint flickers.

"Are you sure you don't want to go too?" Melanie said, looking at Jack. She sounded almost . . . hopeful.

Jack wondered about that. A moment ago when he'd said he was leaving, she wanted him to stay. Now she seemed to be encouraging him to leave by another route.

"I'm very sure," Jack said. "In fact, I don't think I've ever been so sure of anything in my life. But you said you wanted to talk to me."

Lew jumped in before Melanie could answer. "Before we go any further, I need an answer to something. When I asked you if it was so bad down there, you said, 'Not for me and Frayne.' What did you mean by that?"

Melanie sighed and looked away. Jack saw a touch of sadness and regret in her eyes.

"Lewis . . . when I called it 'home,' I wasn't exaggerating. When that gateway opened, and I entered the Otherness, that's exactly what it felt like—coming home. For the first time in my life I felt like I *belonged*. And Frayne will feel it too."

"But I won't?" Lew said, his voice full of hurt.

Zaleski's voice echoed up from the hole then.

"Hey! Something weird down here . . . like everything's floating."

Melanie went to the edge and called down. "That means you're almost there. Gravity reverses at the transition point. You'll have to climb *up* the rest of the way."

She waited, and a few seconds later Zaleski's voice came back, tinged with wonder and excitement, teetering on the verge of hysterical laughter.

"Fucking-ay, you're right! This is the weirdest shit I've ever seen!"

"Never mind them," Lew said. "What about me? Why won't I feel like I belong there?"

Melanie turned back to her husband. She spoke matter-of-factly, as if explaining the obvious to a child. "Because you'd be an outsider there, Lewis. You have no Otherness in you."

"Sure I do," he said, pointing to his leg. "I'm not normal. I'm different too. Not as different as you, maybe, but—"

"Different *inside*," she said. "Frayne and I are different right down to our genes. You're completely human, Lewis. We're not. We're hybrids."

Lew looked stunned. His jaw worked a few times before he could speak. "Hybrids?"

"Yes, Lewis. Hybrids." She walked over to Canfield's wheelchair and rested her claw on his shoulder. "Neither of us really belongs here."

Jack noticed how Lew's eyes locked on the spot where his wife was touching Canfield. His heart went out to the guy, but he couldn't help him. Lew was pushing for answers and Melanie was giving them to him.

She could take it a little easier on him, though.

"How?" he said. "When?"

"Late in the winter of 1968, right here in Monroe, the Otherness spawned something in this plane. Frayne and I were just tiny, newly formed masses of cells within our mothers at the time. We were vulnerable to the influence of the Otherness then—our DNA was altered forever as it made its beachhead."

"What beachhead?" Jack said.

Obviously she was referring to the "burst of Otherness" Canfield had mentioned. But what exactly were they talking about?

"It was not something anyone would take notice of. But the fate of this plane was sealed in that instant." Her eyes fairly glowed as she spoke. "A child was conceived. A special child—The One. He is grown now, and soon he will make his presence known."

"Sounds like Olive's Antichrist," Jack said.

Melanie smirked. "Compared to The One, Olive's Antichrist would be a fitting playmate for your children. When he comes into his own, everything will change.

The very laws of physics and nature as you know them will be transformed. And after the cataclysm . . . Otherness will reign."

Ooookay, Jack thought. Time to go.

"Sounds like fun," he said, turning toward the couch to retrieve his jacket. "But I've got to get moving."

"No, please," she said, moving away from Canfield and gripping his arm—Jack was relieved she used her hand instead of her claw. "Not yet. I must speak to you."

"Hey, that thing's getting hot," Lew said, holding up his palm to the Tesla device but not touching it.

Jack could feel the heat faintly from where he was standing.

"Lewis," Melanie said, "I wish to speak to his man alone."

"Alone?" Lew said. "Why alone? What have you got to say to Jack that I can't hear?"

"I'll tell you about it later, Lewis. Wait for me outside, in the car."

He stared at her. "You've changed, Mel."

"Yes . . . I have. I finally know who I am, and I've learned why I'm the way I am. And I'm proud of it. Please, Lewis. Wait for me in the car. I'll be up in a few minutes and we'll go home together."

His eyes widened. "Really? We're going home?" He glanced at the hole. "But I thought . . ."

"The gateway will be closing soon. I have some things I must do before it does, and then I'll join you."

Jack didn't believe it for a minute, but Lew seemed to be swallowing the whole package.

"Sure, Mel," he said, nodding as he started toward the steps. "I'll wait for you outside. For a minute there . . ."

"I would never hurt you, Lewis. Surely you know that."

"I do, Mel," he said. "I know you wouldn't." He hurried up the steps.

Canfield rolled over to the stairway and peered up, then wheeled around to face Melanie.

"Why did you tell him that?" he said in a low voice.

"Because I don't want him hurt," she said.

"How can he not be?" Canfield was twisted half around. Clinking noises rose from the pouch behind his seat back as he fumbled inside it.

"I mean physically. He was good to me, Frayne. He treated me like a human being instead of a freak. I owe him for that."

Jack felt like he was eavesdropping on a private conversation.

"Should I be hearing this?" he said. "Because frankly, I don't care to."

He glanced at the Tesla device and was sure its dome was starting to glow. He wanted out of here. The growing heat was only part of it; the whole scene was starting to annoy him. Especially Melanie and her hybrid buddy Canfield—something going on between those two, something that made him queasy.

Melanie turned to him and smiled . . . not a smile to be particularly trusted. "Everything will be made clear in a minute or two."

"Jack," Canfield said, still over by the steps, still rattling around in his chair's rear pouch, "could you help me with this a minute?"

The Tesla device's dome was glowing a dull cherry red now. Jack was glad to get away from the heat.

Jack came around behind the wheelchair. He noticed a length of sturdy chain running out the rear pouch, around the support column, and back into the pouch.

"Right here," Canfield said, indicating the pouch. "It's stuck. Could you just yank that the rest of the way out?"

Jack reached in next to Canfield's hand, grabbed a fistful of links—

—and felt something cold and metallic snap around his wrist just before Canfield dove out of the wheelchair and slithered—*slithered*—away across the floor.

"What the—?"

Jack yanked his hand out of the pouch and stared at the chrome handcuff around his right wrist. The second cuff was closed through the links of the chain looped around the support column.

Sudden panic at being trapped rippled through his veins, just as revulsion rippled through his gut at the sight of Canfield's boneless legs jutting from his pant cuffs; they seemed more like tentacles than real legs.

"Good job, Frayne," Melanie said as Canfield squatted beside her like a dog. Jack almost expected her to pat Canfield's head. Instead she turned toward Jack. She was positively beaming now. "It would have been so much easier if you'd chosen to climb down the hole."

Jack ignored her and calmed himself. He wasn't Houdini, but he could get out of this. Lots of options . . .

He tugged on the chain. The links were made of eighth-inch steel, and welded closed. He wrapped his hands around the column and tugged—not even a hint of give.

"Don't waste your time," Melanie said. "That column is a cement-filled steel pipe, set into the cement floor and bolted to a six-inch beam above. It's there to stay."

She was right. The column wasn't going anywhere. What about the cuffs, then? Top-grade Hiatts—a heavy-duty hinge model. If he had his pick set, he could have them open in thirty seconds. But the set was back in his hotel room.

Okay—he'd have to shoot himself free.

As he reached for the Semmerling he remembered it was in his jacket . . . out of reach on the couch across the room.

Jack's mouth went dry. He felt the entire weight of the house pressing down on him.

Trapped. He looked at them.

Canfield's eyes shifted away. "Sorry, Jack," he said. "It's not personal. Actually I kind of like you. But Melanie's calling the shots here."

"Is that so?" said a voice from the top of the stairs. "Since when?"

Jack recognized the voice, but it was Canfield who announced him. "That sounds like Professor Roma! Professor, I've been trying to reach you all day!"

Melanie, however, was suddenly agitated. "He's not Professor Roma." Her voice dropped to an almost reverential tone. "He's The One!"

Canfield sucked in a breath. "The One? *He's* The One?"

Jack turned and stared up the steps to where Roma stood in the doorway, his monkey perched on his shoulder as usual.

"The One what?" Jack said.

"The One who will soon be lord and master of this world," Melanie said.

"Oh, brother," Jack muttered.

Roma said, "You have not answered my question, Melanie."

"This man is wanted on the other side, sir," Melanie said. "Some entities there feel they have a score to settle with him."

Jack didn't like the sound of that at all.

"*Do* they?" Roma sounded like a chef who's just been told that some of the customers think he should add more chocolate to his mousse.

"Yes, they—"

Her reply was cut off by terrified shouts, then gunfire—half a dozen pistol shots—echoing up from the hole. Above it, the dome of the mini-tower was beginning to smoke.

"What's happening?" Jack said.

Roma said, "I imagine James and Miles have found the answers they've been seeking . . . and they don't like them."

More shots. Jack noticed the rope ladder begin to vibrate. The shouts turned to agonized screams . . . and then the ladder was still.

Above the opening the Tesla device's legs and struts were beginning to glow. Jack could feel the growing heat.

"They've also learned the painful truth," Melanie said, staring at the opening, "that the Otherness has no use for ordinary humans." She turned back to Jack. "Except for you."

Jack yanked futilely on his chains, diluting his fear with anger. "*Why,* damn it! I never even heard of this Otherness crap until last week!"

"Yes," said Roma—or The One. "Why?"

"The Otherness creatures—they were known as rakoshi, rakshashi, and various other names. They were children of the Otherness, and events were manipulated to have them brought here, to New York, to have them at your side for the Time of Change, but this man killed them. Certain entities in the Otherness went to great lengths to create those creatures, and now they want him brought across so they can do to him what he did to their creations."

"Why was I told none of this?" Roma bellowed, obviously angry now.

Melanie took a step forward but was careful to stay beyond Jack's reach. She bent and looked up the stairs.

"I cannot say, sir. One such as myself cannot contact The One. But I told Frayne and he was supposed to—"

"I couldn't find you!" Canfield blurted. "I searched all day and—"

"Never mind," Roma sighed.

Melanie said, "You see, sir, though I am part Otherness, it is only a small part. Not enough to be welcomed as a lost member of the family. I have to buy my way in. And Repairman Jack is my ticket."

"You mean *our* ticket," Canfield said.

"Yes." She turned and smiled down at him. "Ours."

"Have done with it then," Roma said—he sounded impatient. "I am going outside to wait."

"Yes, sir," Melanie said, all but kowtowing. "Thank you for your patience."

Jack glanced up at the now empty doorway, then back to Melanie.

"Your ticket?" he said, holding up the cuffs and chain. "I don't think your ticket is going anywhere."

"Don't worry. The Otherness will take care of that. All I had to do was get you this far. You see, while I was on the other side I learned my own painful truth—that I could not stay in the Otherness unless I earned my place there. So I contacted Lewis and told him to hire you. But I didn't tell him why. The plan was to draw you in through the assembly of the Tesla device, to lure you here to help reopen the gateway to the Otherness. In a way, you helped build your own gallows."

Jack ground his teeth in frustration. So goddamn *stupid!* How had he let himself get hooked and reeled in like this?

Melanie's smile broadened. "You might even say, Repairman Jack, that you are the victim of . . . a conspiracy."

Jack tugged again at the chain as she and Canfield grinned at each other.

"Why kill Olive then?" he said.

Their smiles vanished.

"She's dead?" Canfield said. "How do you know?"

"Don't give me that," Jack said. "You had a couple of your men in black mutilate her back in the hotel, then make her body disappear."

Melanie shook her head as Canfield stared up at her. She looked worried. "I don't know anything about men in black. Whoever they were, I doubt they were from the Otherness. But then, there's so much I don't know. What did—?"

She cut off as the Tesla device began to vibrate. The whole thing was aglow and beginning to drift back toward the floor.

"We don't have much time!" Melanie cried. "Quick! Into the gateway!"

Canfield hesitated, frowning as he stared at the yawning pit. "I don't know . . ."

"Trust me, Frayne," she said, beckoning to him with her talon. "You'll see—as soon as you step into the Otherness, all will be made clear. You'll *know*. You'll understand all its plans. You'll be part of it. You'll feel . . ." Her eyes fairly glowed as she looked down into the gateway. ". . . *wonderful*!"

"But will . . . will I be welcome?"

Melanie was already lowering her legs into the opening. "Yes." She glanced at Jack. "As long as we have him."

"But we *don't* have him."

"The Otherness will handle it. And trust me, you don't want to be on this side when it does." Her voice echoed up as she descended below floor level. "Hurry!"

Even as low as Canfield was, slithering on his boneless legs, he had to duck to make it under the descending base of the Tesla device. He wrapped his legs around the rope ladder and slipped over the edge. Before he disappeared, he looked Jack's way.

"See you on the Other side," he said, and was gone.

The device came to rest as Canfield disappeared, the feet of its glowing legs scorching the concrete where they touched down. Almost immediately the legs and struts began to bend like Twizzlers, sinking under the weight of the dome. Slowly they collapsed into the hole. The glowing dome caught on the rim for a few seconds, then it buckled, folded, and disappeared.

Saved! Jack thought.

Almost weak with relief, he slumped against the column. Melanie and Canfield had gone to their new home without an admission ticket. He smiled. He hoped they got a nice warm welcome. Without the Tesla thing to keep it open, the hole would close just as before, leaving the rope ladder embedded in the concrete just as before.

Now to get out of the damn cuff. . . .

4

"You see, Mauricio? All your fretting was for nothing. The gateway is open, just as planned. My time has come."

"Admit it, though," Mauricio said from his shoulder as they crossed the yard. "Even you must have had moments of uncertainty."

True enough, he thought. But he would never admit it.

"When I learned from the Ehler woman what she had

found in one of the buried Tesla caches, I suspected that my time was near. When I saw the plans and read Tesla's notes, I *knew*."

But the plans had been incomplete. The device they depicted could open the gateway for but a few minutes. Melanie had gone through to the other side to have a completed device sent back from the Otherness, one that would open a permanent gateway.

What matter if forces within the Otherness had directed the device to the stranger instead of him? The first gateway was open . . . more would follow, opening spontaneously around the globe. Now that the process had begun, nothing could stop it. The Otherness would seep through, engulfing this world, reshaping it in its own image.

And I will be the instrument of that process.

"Still," Mauricio said, "I would have thought that when your time was truly here, you would need no devices. The gates would open on their own."

He had always thought the same, but the device had presented an opportunity he could not ignore. After all the years, all the ages he had waited, he had grown weary of biding his time until all the signs were right, until something simply happened on its own. He had seen the discovery of the plans as a sign in itself, a chance to *make* it happen, and so he'd leapt for it.

"And there is still the matter of The Lady."

"Forget her! You can await your destiny, Mauricio, or you can go to meet it."

"At least now I know why I could not kill the stranger," Mauricio said. "I didn't know what stopped me or why. It might even have been the Enemy. Now I know. The Otherness wants the stranger for itself." He bared his sharp teeth. "Better for him if I had succeeded."

They paused by the big oak and faced the house. To

his right he saw the Ehler woman's husband sitting in his car, waiting in the darkness for his wife. How pathetic.

You will be reunited with her soon, he thought, but not in any way you can imagine.

He returned his attention to the house. His vibrating nerves sang with joyous anticipation. At last, after all this time, at this moment, in this place, in the little town of his reconception, his time had come.

After all I have been through, after all the battles I have fought, the pain and punishment I have suffered, I deserve this world. It was promised to me, I have earned it, and now, finally, it will be mine.

5

As Jack searched around for a way to open the cuff, he felt the breeze pick up against his back . . . and continue to increase in force until it wasn't a breeze any more. This was a wind now.

And that hole wasn't any smaller.

Tiny spiders of apprehension ran up and down his spine. He tried to lose them by telling himself that at least the opening wasn't growing. But what was with this wind? Was the gateway going to try to suck him into the Otherness like some giant vacuum cleaner?

Just then Canfield's wheelchair began to roll toward the hole.

As Jack grabbed for it and stopped it with his free hand, he realized, Yeah, that might be just what the Otherness intended.

But no worry. He was attached to a damn near indestructible steel column. He wasn't going anywhere.

So why didn't he feel safe?

Truly, the only place he'd feel safe was out of here and racing for Manhattan. But first he had to get free of these cuffs. Jack gazed longingly at his jacket on the couch against the rear wall . . . but no chance. He'd have to be Plastic Man to reach it.

With the steadily rising wind chugging down the stairs, he looked around for another way.

Canfield's wheelchair . . .

He reached into its rear pouch and found the tool kit. He fumbled it open and searched through the tools. He snatched up the biggest screwdriver and a couple of slim paneling nails, then tossed the kit back into the pouch.

The wooden desk chair began to slide toward the hole. It toppled into the opening and caught on the edges. It hung there, its wood creaking and cracking, then its back snapped and the pieces tumbled out of sight.

Jack stared at the hole. Had it grown in size, or did it just seem that way? He watched the rope ladder twisting and gyrating in the downdraft. He didn't remember that wooden tread sitting on the edge before . . . hadn't it been further back?

Alarmed, he clamped the nails between his lips and jammed the screwdriver through one of the chain links. He twisted the link, using both hands and putting all his weight and strength behind it. He pushed till he thought he might pop a vein in his head, but the weld held fast.

He heard a scraping sound and looked up. The desk was sliding toward the hole. It stopped after moving a foot or so, but the tools and the two remaining crystals atop it kept rolling. The crystals hit the floor and shattered. The amber shards slid and tumbled across the concrete with the tools and disappeared into the hole.

And still the wind increased . . . a full-fledged gale now, blasting down those steps. The wheelchair kept wanting to roll away but Jack had the front of his sneaker hooked through the spokes of one of the wheels.

He shoved the screwdriver into his jeans pocket and began trying to pick the lock with one of the nails. He didn't know if it was possible. Hiatts made serious cuffs. Even if he'd had his pick set, the gale buffeting his arms and body would have made the job a tough go. But with a lousy nail . . .

He looked up to see plastic containers of liquid detergent topple off the shelf above the washer and dryer and slide into the hole.

Jack jumped and dropped the paneling nail as the door at the top of the steps slammed explosively. A piece of molding flew down the steps and wind screamed around the edges of the door.

Jack felt like screaming too as the air pressure plummeted, driving spikes of pain through his eardrums. He lost the other nails as he shouted and worked his jaw to relieve the pressure. Nothing was working. Just when he thought his ears were going to burst, the high, pint-sized cellar windows shattered, hurling bright daggers through the air and into the sucking maw in the floor.

Jack realized he'd be stew meat now if one of those windows had been behind him. But at least the air howling through the small openings relieved the negative pressure and the pain in his ears.

The card table and folding chairs fell away from the wall and slid into the hole. Now the desk was moving again, and this time it didn't stop. It skated across the concrete, straight for the hole, and over the edge. But it didn't go down. It hung up in the opening, canted at an angle with the lip of its top caught on the rim.

"Bit off more that you can chew?" Jack said. Maybe there was some hope yet.

The sucking air shrieked around the desk, bucking it back and forth until the top groaned and popped loose. It angled up and snapped in half with a bang as it and the rest of the desk tumbled from view.

And oh Christ, the hole was definitely bigger now. The more it swallowed, the bigger it seemed to grow. The tread that had been on the edge was out of sight now. Only four more treads remained between Jack and the sucking maw.

He was reaching for Canfield's tool kit again when he heard the whine of the air around the door atop the steps change in pitch. He felt the wind grow against his back again. He looked up and saw the door slowly moving back. Fingers appeared, curled around the edge, white-knuckled with the strain of fighting the gale. Finally with a violent lurch the door swung all the way back on its hinges and a tall, ungainly figure appeared in the opening.

"Lew!" Jack shouted. "Jeez, am I glad to see you!"

"Jack?" Lew said as he clumped down the steps, clinging to the banister and the wall to brace himself against the wind at his back. "What's—?"

He stopped and gaped at the partially denuded cellar, then lurched down to the floor.

"Where's Melanie?"

"She left. Look, Lew—"

"Left?" he said, his face screwing up as he stared at the hole. "You mean she went back ... back down there?"

"Yeah. Look, just get me my jacket over there and I'll explain the whole thing."

"But she said she'd meet me out in the car!" Lew

cried, his voice rising. He stepped toward the hole. "We were going home together."

"She must've changed her mind," Jack said quickly. If he could just get his hands on that jacket, get hold of the Semmerling in its pocket . . . "Lew, my jacket—see it over there?"

But Lew didn't look at Jack . . . he started moving away . . . never taking his eyes off that damn hole.

"I've got to go find her!"

Jack grabbed his arm. "No, Lew! You can't go there! You'll be killed!"

The movement allowed the wheelchair to slip free of his foot. Jack had to choose between Lew and the wheelchair. He chose Lew. The chair rolled away and tumbled into the hole.

But Lew barely noticed, and he sure as hell wasn't listening. He violently wrenched his arm from Jack's grasp and lurched out of reach.

"I've got to be with her!"

"All right!" Jack shouted. "*Be* with her. But give me my damn jacket first so I can get out of here!"

Jack might as well have been talking to a mannequin. He kept shouting Lew's name but Lew gave no sign that he heard.

Lew slipped and almost lost his balance in the gale that was tearing at his clothes. To avoid being swept into the opening, he crouched and kept hold of the rope ladder as he crabbed along the floor. When he reached the rim, he snaked his good foot over the edge, snagged the dangling end of the ladder as it danced in the wind, and started down.

Not until his head had descended to floor level did he look at Jack.

"I haven't got a second to lose," he shouted. "I need her, Jack."

"Aw, Lew," Jack said, sensing it was hopeless to ask

but giving it a shot anyway. "Just get me my jacket first? Please?"

"I've got to find her and bring her back while the gateway's still open. After that I'll help get you free."

"It's not going to close, Lew! It's—"

Before Jack could tell him he was wasting his time and most likely his life, Lew was gone.

Frustration screamed in Jack's brain, almost as loudly as the wind. He was out of options . . . the draw was stronger, and the gateway ever larger—only three rope-ladder treads between Jack and the rim.

The white box of the dryer began a shuddering slide toward the hole. Its electric cord snagged its progress for a heartbeat, then pulled free from the outlet. It wriggled halfway there before its leveling feet hung up on a crack in the floor; it toppled forward and shimmied the rest of the way to the hole on its face, then went down.

Jack wondered if it would clock Lew along the way. He almost wished it would . . . the jerk.

Like a Romeo eager to join its Juliet, the washing machine struggled toward the hole, but its connections to the water pipes held it back.

But nothing was holding back the hole. Its far edge had undermined the sister column to Jack's, leaving it dangling from the house's main beam, its lower end wavering over infinity.

Then one of the overhead bulbs shattered, the pieces darting into the hole like glass buckshot.

Jack found it increasingly difficult to hold his position against the gale blasting down the staircase and into the maw. He put the column between the hole and himself, and braced his back against it—safe for now, but when the edge of the hole reached the base of his column. . . .

He squinted at the couch. It was tucked in a corner with no window, so it had remained unaffected by the draw from the hole. If only he had a stick, a metal rod, anything, he might have a chance to reach his jacket. He wished he'd thought to grab that piece of door molding as it flew down the steps a few minutes ago.

And then, to his horror, he saw the couch move.

Only an inch or two, but that was enough to jostle his jacket, and now one of its sleeves was fluttering in the wind that swirled around it.

"No!" Jack shouted as the lighter side of the jacket flipped over and tugged toward the floor, dragging the heavier, gun-laden pocket after it.

God, he had to get to it. This was his last hope. He dropped to his knees, pulling the loop of chain down to floor level after him.

Another bulb shattered as the jacket hit the floor and began to slip toward the hole. Jack dropped flat, his cheek on the concrete, and stretched his free hand toward it, feeling the edges of the steel cuff dig into the skin of his trapped wrist as he strained every joint and ligament to the max and beyond.

"Damn it to hell!" he gritted as he realized his fingertips would fall at least a foot and a half short. "Not enough!"

Frantic now as he saw the jacket begin to tumble toward the hole, Jack flipped his body around and stretched his legs to the limit—just in time to trap one of the sleeves under the toe of his right sneaker.

"Made it!"

But he began to think he'd spoken too soon as he tried to drag the jacket toward him. With more surface area to work on, the wind was tugging the sleeve from under his sneaker. Jack rolled onto his belly and jammed his other toe onto the sleeve. He trapped a tiny fold of the fabric between them and bent his knees to draw it to his hand.

"Gotcha!" he said as his fingers closed around the fabric, and it sounded like a sob.

The last two bulbs blew, plunging the cellar into darkness as a sudden blaze of pain shot through the small of his back. He hadn't even been aware that the couch was moving until it had slammed into him, and now it was jammed against his spine, crowding him toward the opening that was closer than ever.

The jacket tore from his grasp and flew toward the hole.

Jack cried out and made a desperate blind lunge for it. Searing pain from the torn skin on his left wrist against the cuff registered only vaguely as he caught hold of the zipper. The rest of the jacket went over the edge, pulling and twisting in his grasp like a hooked fish, but Jack held on, even as he found himself sliding toward the hungry maw.

His head and right shoulder slipped over the rim. Pink-orange light flashed impossibly far below. And nearer, he saw a figure clinging desperately to the whipping end of the ladder, looking as if he was trying to climb back up.

Lew . . .

The couch against Jack's back lifted then and rolled over, knocking the wind out him as its full weight slammed onto his body. It slid forward and slipped over the edge, an armrest banging against the side of his head as it tumbled past.

Jack's vision blurred as he fought to breath. He saw the couch go into a spin as it fell, narrowly missing Lew, who seemed to be making progress up the ladder.

Couldn't worry about Lew now.

Jack wrestled the jacket out of the pit and clamped the sleeve between his teeth. He grabbed hold of the first tread on the rope ladder and fought the hurricane-force wind back to the column.

Gasping, dizzy, nauseated, he wrapped himself around the column and fumbled the Semmerling out of the pocket. The tiny pistol felt wonderful in his palm. Now he had a chance—he just hoped it would work. He'd wished for fully jacketed rounds on Friday night, but after emptying the pistol, he'd reloaded with the same frangible hollowpoints. Once again he could have used solid rounds. He promised himself that if he got out of this he would always load the Semmerling with at least one 230-grain hardball.

The steadily brightening flashes from deep within the hole were the only illumination as Jack pulled the chain tight with his knees and held his cuffed hand on the far side of the column; the links slipped in the blood seeping from his wrist. He reached around with his left and pressed the Semmerling's muzzle against the link between the cuffs. The pistol kicked and the cuff bucked as he fired, but the report was barely audible in the howling gale.

Jack tugged on the cuff—no give. The damn stupid soft hollowpoint slug hadn't broken the link.

Stay calm, he told himself. You've still got three rounds left.

But not much floor to go before the Jack's column went the way of its sister, taking Jack with it.

The sound of shattering glass from above and behind him—instinctively Jack leaned away from the stairs as a glittering cloud of jagged fragments whizzed by, spinning through the air like transparent shuriken.

There go the kitchen windows.

He fired again, hoping he was hitting the same spot—the recoil on the Semmerling was such that he couldn't be sure. Still the cuff held. He fired the last two rounds one right after the other, praying he'd feel the cuff fall away. But the chain remained wrapped around the column.

Panicky now, Jack pocketed the gun and tugged on the chain with everything he had—and shouted with relief when he felt the cuffs part. As the chain clinked to the floor, he struggled to his feet.

Free!

Movement at the rim of the hole caught his eye. A hand, its skin glistening redly, clawed over the edge, clinging to the rope ladder. Seconds later, a bloody head struggled into view.

"Lew!" Jack shouted.

In the flickering light, it looked as if the skin had been stripped away from Lew's face, leaving the blood-ied muscles exposed. Jack could see his mouth working but couldn't hear a word.

And then the upstairs door slammed again, even more explosively than before. But this time it shattered and tore off its hinges, sending jagged wooden spears hurtling down the steps.

Jack ducked to the side, but the missiles caught Lew full in the face. One instant he was there, the next he was gone.

And now the edge of the hole was nibbling at the foot of the column.

Jack swung his body onto the steps and started up. Standing was out of the question, so he crawled, squint-ing into the gale as he pulled himself upward one tread at a time.

He heard a faint clatter from somewhere above. He ducked and pressed himself against the wall to his right as a barrage of cups, bowls, and dinner plates hurtled down from the kitchen cabinets. A few of them pelted his head and shoulders on their way by.

If only Zaleski were here, he thought insanely. Real flying saucers.

As he resumed his climb, he prayed that Melanie's folks hadn't been into collecting carving knives.

As if on cue, another clatter from above and then the household flatware—spoons, forks and knives, even the drawer itself—were flying toward him. He ducked again and cursed as the sharper utensils tore his shirt and cut his skin.

And then the whole staircase moved under Jack.

He glanced back and saw the column hanging free over the hole, wagging back and forth. The staircase was attached to its base, and the entire unit was being ripped from the wall.

With the stairs jerking and twisting under him like a rodeo bronco, Jack redoubled his efforts to reach the kitchen, clawing his way to the top. He'd just snaked his right hand around the foot of the jamb when the staircase tore free of the wall and tumbled away, leaving Jack hanging from the doorway.

A quick glance back showed the stairs and the column whirling into the hungry vortex. He heard a loud *crack* as the house's center beam began to sag.

The whole place was coming down.

He had a few minutes, tops.

Through desperation-fueled kicking and scrabbling against the wall, Jack managed to force his head and chest up onto the kitchen floor, now beginning to tilt toward him as the center beam sagged further. He'd just raised a knee over the edge when he saw a dark square sliding along the kitchen counter. It hit the floor with a weighty bang and began tumbling end over directly toward him. It was almost upon him before he recognized it as a microwave oven.

Jack lunged to the side, squeezing himself against the jamb, but the oven caught his knee and knocked him off the threshold. He fell back and was left literally twisting in the wind as he clung to the jamb with one hand.

Sobbing with the effort, doing his best to ignore the agony in his knee, Jack struggled again to lever himself up to the ever-more-tilted kitchen floor. This time he got both knees up on the threshold—those regular workouts were paying a dividend—just as the refrigerator started sliding toward him.

Not again!

An inarticulate cry burst from him as he half lunged, half rolled to the side.

The refrigerator brushed against his back and it slammed into the doorway, blocking it.

Missed me, you bastard!

Wind shrieked around the fridge's edges but no way was it getting through.

Jack lay on the floor, gasping. No gale to fight . . . how wonderful.

Then he felt the floor jolt under him.

Oh, Christ! The increased negative pressure in the basement was putting more stress on the already weakened support beam. The whole place was going to implode.

He struggled to his feet and hobbled to the back door. He turned the knob and pulled but it wouldn't budge. How could it? He'd relocked the deadbolt when he left the other day.

"Jerk!" he shouted.

He turned away and limped hurriedly through the sagging house. At least the lights were still on so he didn't have to stumble around in the dark. The open front door was in sight when a booming *crack* beneath his feet shook the house—the center beam had finally surrendered.

The lights went out and the living room floor dropped three feet as Jack leaped for the swinging front door. He caught the inner and outer knobs and hung there as the carpet was ripped free. It swirled and shredded through the sudden hole in the floor, to be swallowed by the insatiable maw in the cellar.

The outer walls began to crack and lean inward. Jack

felt the door hinges start to give way. He kicked off the wall, swung himself toward the doorway, and leaped through the opening onto the front steps. Without a pause, without a look back, he hopped off the steps and tumbled onto the grass.

6

"Is that—?" Mauricio said as a figure leaped from the shuddering house and crumbled onto the lawn.

The One stared through the dimness. "Yes, I am afraid it is."

"Who *is* this man?"

The One nodded. A very good question. Last year this stranger apparently had wiped out the rakoshi singlehandedly, and now he somehow had escaped the cellar and the gateway.

"Whatever his name," the One said, "he is a nuisance and a menace."

"I've had enough of this. If the Otherness can't finish him, I will."

Movement caught The One's eye as Mauricio crouched to leap from his shoulder. He raised a hand to prevent that.

"Wait. Someone else is here."

"The Twins!" Mauricio hissed. "They could ruin everything!"

"No. It is too late—even for them."

"It's *not* too late. The hole is not large enough yet. They might be able to shut it down. And you—you haven't assumed your final form yet. Until you do, they can still destroy you. And I can't protect you against their strength. Hide!"

He watched the Twins scan the yard, saw them fix on the stranger and start toward him.

This should be interesting. . . .

7

Still puffing, Jack slumped on the dew-damp grass. The night air was cool against his face, Canfield's van was a shadow to his right. Starlight faintly outlined the sagging roof of the house, while pink-orange flashes strobed through the imploding windows.

He closed his eyes and rubbed his knee. Had to get away from here. Soon as he caught his breath. . . .

A thunderous *boom* shook the ground and jerked him forward.

The house—its walls were folding in, the roof buckling in the middle. As Jack watched, the entire structure fell apart and tumbled into its foundation. The pieces—lumber, bricks, siding, wallboard, furniture—whirlpooled down into the Otherness hole, feeding it, expanding it, until nothing, not even the foundation footings, remained.

And the hungry rim expanded farther, flashing its weird-colored light against the trees and vehicles in the yard, still coming for him.

"Aw, cut me a break!" Jack muttered as he fought to his feet.

What was it going to do—chase him all the way back

to the city? And then he realized with a shock that was exactly what it was going to do. Just like in his dream—a giant hole swallowing everything in its path.

He turned and started a quick hobble toward his car. He had to get to Gia and Vicky, warn Abe, head for the hills—

But as he neared the big oak he spotted a black sedan parked at the curb . . . and two dark figures in suits and hats approaching him. Jack didn't have to see their faces to know who they were.

And here he was, unarmed and in no shape to deal with them.

He broke into his best approximation of a run.

They caught him easily—strong, long-fingered hands gripped each of his upper arms and fairly lifted him off the ground. Jack writhed and twisted but couldn't pull free; he lashed out with his feet, aiming for knees and groins, but he couldn't find the leverage he needed to do any damage—at least not to this pair. He remembered how he'd broken one's finger the other night without fazing him.

They wheeled around and began dragging him back across the lawn toward the flashing pit where the house had been.

Panic spiked through him. He tried to dig his feet in, but his sneakers slipped on the wet grass, barely slowing the two golems who held him. He was utterly helpless.

"Wait!" he shouted. He had no hope that talk would help, but he was desperate enough to try anything. "Let's think about this!"

"It wants you," said Number One on his left.

"No! That's not true! I'm just icing on the cake!"

"You are the only way to close the gateway," said Number Two.

"You want to *close* it? I thought you were working for them! Hey, look, we're on the same side!"

They didn't seem to care.

Ahead, the growing hole had undermined the lawn. Jack saw Lew's Lexus tilt sideways and do a slow slide into the pit. The backyard swing set followed close behind.

With Jack fighting them every inch of the way, and cursing himself for using all four rounds in the Semmerling, they dragged him ever closer to the edge.

"This thing isn't here for me!" Jack shouted. "It's for Roma—the guy they call The One."

That got them. They glanced at each other and slowed their march.

The entire front yard was sloping toward the pit now, and out of the corner of his eye Jack saw Frayne's van begin to slide their way.

"The One?" said Number One. "He is here?"

"He was a moment ago."

The van was closer now, picking up speed. Gathering his strength, Jack threw all his weight to the right in a desperate lunge, veering the three of them into the van's path. It caught Number Two behind the knees, knocking him down. He released his hold on Jack as his right arm caught on the bumper and he was dragged away.

Jack turned and immediately began pounding on Number One with his free hand, punching at his face, chopping at his neck and shoulder. He might as well have been beating him with a Nerf bat for all the notice he took. He was far more interested in his buddy who was riding the fast track to the Otherness.

Number Two struggled futilely to free his trapped arm as the sliding van pulled him along. He reached out for help.

As Number One dragged Jack toward his partner, Jack searched his pockets for the Semmerling. It wouldn't fire but maybe he could use it as a club. His fingers found Canfield's screwdriver instead.

Yes!

He yanked it out, hauled back, and rammed the shaft into the side of Number One's neck with everything he had. It didn't go in easily, like stabbing into a hunk of pure gristle, but he left three quarters of the shaft buried in the tough flesh.

That got some attention. Number One's knees wobbled and he staggered a step, relaxing his grip enough to allow Jack to tear free. He gave Jack a quick expressionless look as dark fluid flowed from the wound, but made no attempt to remove the screwdriver. He straightened and continued toward his buddy.

Jack backed away, watching in disbelief. The guy shouldn't even be standing, yet there he was, grabbing Number Two's hand as the van began tipping over the edge. Number One gave a hard, two-handed pull, and Jack heard the trapped one's arm give a sickening crack as it came free of the bumper.

But a louder, deeper *crunch* beneath and behind him seized Jack's attention. He looked around and saw the giant oak leaning his way, tipping toward him like a falling skyscraper. He dove to his right and rolled out of its path as the ground caved in beneath him. The trunk barely missed him as it fell. With a deafening crash that bounced Jack off the ground, it landed across the hole, straddling it like a bridge.

When Jack regained his feet, the van was gone, as were his two nemeses.

8

The One watched the hole in rapt fascination, only vaguely barely aware of the struggle between the stranger and the Twins. This was it. The first of many. This gateway would spawn others, hundreds of them around the globe, all portals for the Otherness, allowing it to flow into this plane, change it, claim it. He would have preferred this first one to have opened in the heart of Manhattan, but this was close enough.

He stepped back with Mauricio when the big oak started to go, and laughed when he saw the Twins tumble over the edge.

Gone! The last vestige of the opposition had been eliminated from this plane! Now nothing stood in his way.

But a howl of dismay from Mauricio meant he thought otherwise.

"Noooo!"

"What is wrong?"

Mauricio leaped from his shoulder and scampered toward the gateway crying, "They mustn't! They mustn't!"

9

Jack crept toward the edge of the hole. He was almost sure the two guys in black were gone but almost wasn't good enough. He had to be positive. Bracing himself against the downdraft, he peeked again into the swirling, flashing depths.

Gone.

No—movement along the near wall, just below him . . .

There they hung, clinging to the oak's ropy roots. Or rather, one of them was. Number One—with the screwdriver still jutting from his neck—had a one-handed grip on a thick root while his other hand clutched Number Two's, whose right arm hung use-lessly at his side. Number One had lost his glasses in the fall. He stared up at Jack with large black expres-sionless eyes.

"Gotcha," Jack said.

With only one good arm, Number Two was helpless; and Number One couldn't climb back up without letting go of his buddy. Strangely, he seemed to have no inten-tion of doing that.

Jack sensed a deep loyalty there, all the more striking for its almost casual nature. Despite all that had hap-pened, Jack responded to that.

Time was running out. With the rim of the hole still expanding, the tree and all its roots would be hopping on the Otherness Express in a minute or so. Every cell in his body was urging him to get the hell out of here, but he needed answers, damn it.

"I'll make you a deal," Jack shouted over the roar. "We call a truce, and you tell me who sent you and why you've been following me. That happens, I'll pull you up and—"

A screech startled him as Roma's monkey leaped onto the tree-trunk and began jumping about.

And then it shouted at him—in English.

"Save them! Don't let them fall!"

Stunned, Jack stared at the monkey, then glanced over his shoulder. Roma stood back on the sidewalk, watching.

"Quickly!" the monkey screeched as it danced back and forth on the straddling trunk. "Help them up! Don't let the Twins fall! The gateway isn't big enough yet! They'll ruin everything!"

Jack glanced at it—yeah, right—then peered back into the hole.

"Damn you!" said another voice, lower and coarser.

Jack looked up in time to see Roma's organ grinder monkey swell into the red-eyed dog-monkey that had attacked him in the basement.

"Holy—"

He rolled away as the thing hurled itself at him with a bellowing roar.

But it wasn't after him. It crouched in the spot Jack had vacated and leaned over the edge of the hole, reaching for the men in black.

"Hang on," it shouted. "I'll pull you up."

Jack peeked over the edge and saw that the monster had grabbed the upper end of the root and was hauling it up.

He watched Number One stare up at the creature a moment, then look down at Number Two. Number Two shook his head. Number One looked back up, this time at Jack, as if trying to speak to him with his eyes. He shook his head.

Then let go of the root.

"Jeez!" Jack said as the two of them plummeted into the depths.

The creature let out a howl—Jack couldn't tell if it was rage or frustration or both, but it was loud—then leaped back onto the fallen trunk.

Together they watched the maelstrom catch the pair and spin them downward until they vanished.

Now what? He thought, gazing into the swirling, flashing abyss.

Suddenly he sensed a change in the gateway. The flashing stopped as a bright speck of fire appeared in its suddenly darkened depths. The spot grew and swelled, rushing upward.

Jack knew—just *knew* he shouldn't be here. The dog-monkey was still raging and howling as Jack turned and ran as fast as his injured knee would let him. He was maybe a dozen feet away when a blast hurled him face-first to the ground. He rolled over and saw a column of fiery white light shoot into the sky, engulfing the tree trunk and the monkey thing. He watched it rip the flesh from the creature, then vaporize its bones along with the center of the trunk. The light shot toward the stars, poised for a heartbeat, then faded.

And now . . . silence. Real silence. The sucking downdraft had stopped, and the flashes along with it.

Jack staggered once more to the rim . . . just a cavity in the earth now, maybe fifteen feet deep. An excavation for a foundation . . . with the charred ends of a fallen oak on either side. The men in black, the dog-monkey thing—all gone. Only one loose end remained. . . .

Roma.

He looked toward the sidewalk, but Roma was gone.

Jack made a quick turn but he was nowhere to be seen. Where the—?

Sirens began to wail in the distance. House lights were on up and down the street and people were beginning to wander out into their yards to find out what all the ruckus was about. He limped to his car—time to get out of here.

Jack kept his headlights off as he eased away.

10

Off to his left, the night sky began to pale as Jack drove toward the expressway. As much as he ached to floor the gas pedal, he kept to the limit. Last thing he needed now was to run across a cop and be stopped for speeding.

He had the windows closed and the heater cranked to maximum, not so much against the cold outside as the marrow-deep chill within as Frayne Canfield's words— he'd spoken them only hours ago, but it seemed like eons—pursued him down Glen Cove Road.

You are involved . . . more deeply than you can possibly imagine. . . .

No . . . he wanted no involvement with anything even remotely like what he'd just encountered. But the worst of it was he still wasn't sure just *what* he'd encountered. His life already was complicated enough. He didn't need to be involved as some sort of pawn in a cosmic conflict.

Cosmic conflict . . . jeez. Got to stop talking like that.

Already the events of the last hour were beginning to

take on an unreal feel. Maybe none of it had really happened. Maybe he'd been drugged or something. . . .

And maybe I shouldn't try to kid myself.

It *had* happened. Something was going on, something *big* . . . an eternal war behind the scenery.

Suddenly dizzy and a little sick, Jack stopped the car and got out to gasp some cool fresh air. He looked around at the trees, the towns flanking the highway, the fading stars . . . and shivered.

Scenery? Was that all that this was? Nothing more than scenery?

He couldn't live like that. It made his day-to-day life so . . . insignificant. He had to believe that what he did mattered, at least to him. Otherwise . . . why bother?

Jack shook his head. He'd hired on to this gig to answer one simple question: Where's Melanie Ehler? He'd answered that one, but now he was carrying around dozens more. With no way to answer even one of them.

All right—what did he know for sure?

He forced a smile. Okay, first off, he was still owed the second half of his fee for finding Melanie Ehler, and he knew for damn sure he wasn't ever going to collect it.

And betting on Roma's murderous monkey monster being dead seemed a sure thing.

Beyond those two, though, everything else was pretty much up for grabs.

He could assume that Zaleski and Kenway and Lew were dead on the far side of that hole, but did "dead" mean the same thing over there?

Melanie and Canfield were in that same Other place as well—but without their "ticket." Jack hoped they were slow roasting over what passed for a fire in the Otherness.

And what about Olive? What had happened to her

corpse? Sent into the Otherness too? Or would it turn up in some alley next week?

Those two black-eyed goons . . . Jack had assumed they were working for the Otherness, and that they'd killed and mutilated Olive. But now he wasn't so sure. At the end they seemed to be working against the Otherness.

Does that mean they were on *my* side?

But they'd wanted to chuck him into the hole—came damn close to succeeding. Hadn't seemed to care one way or the other about him, they simply wanted to close the gateway, by any means necessary. They thought he would do it, so he'd immediately become expendable.

With allies like that, who needed enemies?

But as it worked out—*they'd* closed the gateway. When they hit bottom or reached the Otherness or wherever they ended up, they caused some sort of titanic explosion, a blast of light that must have been visible for miles.

Visible for miles . . . like the Tunguska explosion Kenway and Zaleski talked about tonight. Hadn't Kenway said one theory held that it was caused by an anti-matter meteor striking the earth?

Maybe that was what those two guys had been—antimatter meteors of a sort, striking the Otherness's matter. Or more likely, matter meteors striking the Otherness's antimatter. Because the Otherness seemed anti-everything.

And finally, what about Sal Roma—"The One," as Melanie had called him? Had he been for real—some sort of ageless Otherness superhybrid born in Monroe and waiting to take over? And where was he now? Had he been so closely linked to the monkey thing that when it went up in smoke, so did he?

Jack doubted that. Some primitive part of him sensed The One still out there, prowling around, looking for a new way to create a world-changing cataclysm that would usher in the age of Otherness.

And he knew beyond all reason and all doubt that someday they would meet again.

But even more disturbing was the final look Number One had given him before he'd let go of that root. Jack kept seeing those black eyes, so cold and expressionless, and yet . . . a nebulous feeling that some sort of torch was being passed.

Not to me, thank you.

But like it or not, want it or not, had he come too close and seen too much, and because of that been drafted into some sort of shadow army?

The idea gave him the cold shakes.

He started as he sensed something dark moving above, blotting out the stars. He ducked into a crouch and looked up.

Nothing . . . an empty sky.

He straightened and slid back into the car. No, he couldn't live like this. Had to shake it off. He'd be a paranoid basket case if he didn't.

He'd handle it . . . give him a few days and he'd be back to normal. He'd go on living his life as before, taking on fix-it jobs, kibitzing with Abe, hanging at Julio's, playing with Vicky, loving Gia. Not your normal everyday life, but one firmly grounded in reality—the only reality he knew or wanted to know. He'd put the episode in Monroe behind him and never look back. This page was turned, this chapter closed.

But as he shifted into gear and drove on, Canfield's words seemed to whisper through the heater vents.

You are *involved . . . more deeply than you can possibly imagine. . . .*